ELIJAH

THE NIGHTWALKERS

Also by Jacquelyn Frank

JACOB: The Nightwalkers

GIDEON: The Nightwalkers

And coming soon:

DAMIEN: The Nightwalkers

Published by Zebra Books

ELIJAH

THE NIGHTWALKERS

JACQUELYN FRANK

ZEBRA BOOKS
KENSINGTON PUBLISHING CORP.

ZEBRA BOOKS are published by

Kensington Publishing Corp.
850 Third Avenue
New York, NY 10022

ISBN-13: 978-0-7394-9191-1

Printed in the United States of America

For my rabid fangirls:

Ange, Alaska
Denise, Dragoneen
Jabberwookie, Jennifer
Lasair, Lila
Magic, Nephilim
Serena, Shoshana
Stacy, Stella
Thatch, Treca
Vickie and
Renee (who is also my bestest childhood friend)
As well as everyone else who has helped me through all my
ups, downs, ins and outs this year.
Eye candy, anyone?!?
Also,
For my very own stalker, Amy,
This one's for you guys!!!

PROLOGUE

Whosoever wishes to know the fate of Demonkind must consult these prophecies . . .

. . . as magic once more threatens the time, as the peace of the Demon yaws toward insanity . . .

. . . it will come to pass that in this great age things will return to the focus of purity that Demonkind must always strive for. Here will come the meaning and purpose of our strictest laws, that no uncorrupted human shall be harmed, that peaceful coexistence between races shall become paramount . . .
—Excerpts from *The Lost Demon Prophecy*

. . . it is therefore forbidden for any of Demonkind to mate with creatures who are not their equals, not of their nature, not of their strength and power. Those lesser creatures are ours to protect from ourselves, not to be violated in impure sexual abomination. This is the law and the will of nature. The dog does not lie with the cat; the cat does not lie with the mouse. Whosoever breaks this sacred trust must suffer under the hand of the law . . .
—Excerpts from *The Original Scroll of Destruction*

Elijah fell to his knees, clutching at his chest as warmth spread between his fingers, staining them and his white shirt a bright crimson. He looked down at the blossoming picture of his life's essence spreading over the material, almost with the fascination given to the sprawling, artistic circlets of a tie-dyed shirt.

The warrior Demon was astounded.

He had been injured repeatedly over his centuries-long lifetime. He was certainly no stranger to it. Everything from mystical electricity to wicked blades made of the brutal, burning iron that was so toxic to his kind had cut into him in one way or another over the ages. Some wounds had been serious enough to leave scars in spite of his remarkable innate healing powers, some had not. But never had he been injured in a way he would consider a truly mortal wound. Mortal to others was not mortal to him. Mortal to the average Demon was also not mortal to him, if only because of his stubborn refusal to succumb to something so passé as death.

However, in this case it was not simply because a hole was torn through his chest and very near the vital workings of his heart that his life was threatened, but because he was in the middle of nowhere, too weak to call for help, and surrounded back and front by enemies. Even if he could somehow find the stamina to survive this rending intrusion into his body, these enemies would not let him live any longer than they wanted him to.

Elijah was immediately furious with himself for ending up in this predicament. He was Captain of the Demon warriors, the elite army at the beck and call of the great Demon King. He was the most skilled fighter of all Demonkind, a Nightwalker race renowned for its awesome abilities in battle. He had lived all the centuries of his life honing his craft, learning everything there was to know about battle, war, and the weapons and strategy required for success in those situations. Jacob, the Demon Enforcer, and his liege lord, Noah, the Demon King, were the only ones he would have considered his equals in battle prowess. He was not supposed to be so stupid as to fall into even the best laid traps, nor capable of being bested once caught by said trap.

Even without training, at their hearts all Demons were essentially battle-ready beasts. He believed that—it was a personal philosophy—and he strongly felt that no matter how heavy the veneer of civilization within their race, or within the individual, there were instincts that could not ever be denied. Sure, Demons looked human, although taller and tanner than average, but they were considered extraordinarily attractive when in human circles. Elijah knew this was because the elemental and animal genetics within them allowed for heightened pheromones that called out to the opposite sex, a predatory sense of awareness that exuded attractive danger, and the extraordinary eyes behind which settled extraordinary cunning and intelligence. All the qualities of natural-born hunters, always seething just beneath the surface, waiting for someone to make themselves prey. Demons were capable of behaviors as untamed as the elements they claimed their great powers from, behaviors they had embraced and integrated into every skill they cultivated in their long lifetimes, making them formidable opponents to those who managed to get on their distant bad sides.

Thus, even the most juvenile of fledglings could have avoided his current predicament, the warrior thought crossly to himself. So to be caught like this, like a weakling mouse in a trap, was shameful and enraging. How had the act of doing his duty suddenly turned on him? He was the Warrior Captain, the stalker of all Nightwalkers with a price on their head, those who were not of the Demon race who had committed egregious acts and sins against the Demon people, a direct challenge and insult to the Demon King. He was the specialist in all those species, an anthropological strategist. If anyone wanted to know the true ways of how to destroy Vampires, Lycanthropes, and most every other Nightwalker species, Elijah would be the best source of information. War and peace were, unfortunately, transient things, and it was his duty to be prepared for all possibilities, in case friends became enemies or enemies threatened friends.

Elijah fought off a passing cloak of dimming consciousness and the spinning of his immediate surroundings. It was he alone who belonged at the head of his monarch's armies when needed, and he who must train the spies and assassins who would slink through the cloaking shadows in the face of threatening intrigue. Therefore, he knew everything anyone could currently discover about the humans who dabbled in the perverse arts of black magic. The same kind who stood around him that very moment, circling him like vultures awaiting the end to a victim's final death throes.

The use of this corrupt power turned these foolish human men and women into necromancers, staining their souls with the inky dye of evil and embedding a stench so foul into their flesh that no Nightwalker with a clean soul could bear to breathe the odor of it. They were powerful, capable of growing even more so the more they studied and practiced their vile arts, but they were not powerful enough to capture him, never mind kill him. No, only his stupidity could have provided that opportunity to them.

He must have looked like a holiday turkey, breaking through the tree line and stepping into their trap, necromancers all around, as well as the human hunters who spent time chasing down myths so they could torture and kill them. Mortals who took it upon themselves to not only uncover the existence and locations of the hidden Nightwalker races, but made it their personal quest to eradicate them from the planet armed with little more than myth, legend, and ignorance.

Demons were one of the least exposed Nightwalkers in human mythos, but species like the Vampires and the Lycanthropes were not so lucky. Stories of them abounded, whether accurate or not, titillating the avid hunter into stalking them, looking for proof and personal vindication, occasionally getting lucky in their bloodthirsty quests. For the hunter, it was a victory, a mental trophy. Mental only. The body of a dead Nightwalker would often look very little different from that of a murdered human being, so it was not exactly one of those treasures a hunter could mount on his wall and tell stories about. At least, not to anyone outside of his own secret society of deranged heroes.

It was becoming far too common an occurrence lately, finding the ashes of Vampires left staked in the sun, Lycanthropes shot and stabbed with the silver weapons that poisoned them, and even Demons impaled by weapons made of scorching, disfiguring iron. That was, of course, when the Demons were not instead being Summoned into the mutilating destruction of the necromancers' tainted pentagram traps. Murder upon senseless murder, and between these two groups of humans, the list of victims would go on.

It was a painful betrayal. Demons had always held human mortals in such precious esteem, much in the way a parent protects its young, developing child. They and the other civilized Nightwalkers fiercely protected these humans, perhaps instinctively knowing that though they were not empowered themselves, left to grow and develop, they might someday become so. It would be a beautiful evolution to watch in the centuries to come. Though Demonkind knew it was only a comparative handful of mortals who sought to harm them, it still stung bitterly. And now, with hunters and necromancers joining forces, the danger had doubled for them all.

Tripled, the warrior thought dryly.

Elijah knew he was close to death in that moment, with that thought. The warrior within him would never indulge in reflection during a battle that required all of his attention. But this battle was all but over, so it left him a few precious seconds to reconcile the thoughts in his head. It seemed ironic that these badly informed humans, who sought to destroy the empowered races they so thoroughly feared, would not feel threatened by the black magic they now consorted with. What, Elijah wondered, in their minds, was the distinction? What made a Demon, born and gifted of the clean and beauteous elements of the Earth, so reprehensible to these humans? And yet, the embalming of evil magic that bled through necromancers was suddenly being lauded and accepted by the very same self-righteous groups?

Was it as simple as the fact that the average human mortal was too outbred, in evolutionary sixth sense particularly, to feel or smell that innate evil? Were they really such a child race that they did not have the instinct to determine good from evil, right from wrong, on a purely intuitive level? Certainly, the moment they stepped on the path, there would be no recognition of the error as they were pervaded and overrun, but was there no forewarning at all within them?

These were answers Elijah did not have and, it seemed, would not find in what was left of his lifetime. After over five centuries, thousands of battles, and thousands of victories, it seemed Elijah's so-called immortality was about to come to a decided end. He had finally caught the wrong tiger by the tail.

Or should he say *tigress*?

Elijah lifted dark, forest green eyes, full of malice and contempt, to his attackers, who were all standing so proudly in their defeat of him. The hunters and necromancers surrounding him were all women, part of an all-female sect the Demons had recently become aware of. What burned his emotions with the intensity of a wildfire, however, was the presence of the two female *Demons* standing at the forefront of these murderous feminine forces.

Traitors.

The Demon on the right, the one known to him as Ruth, was a very powerful Mind Demon. In fact, she had been the firstborn female to that youthful element, which had existed in the Demon culture for only a little over five hundred years. She was an Elder, formerly a Great Council member, who had helped form the very roots of Demon society and law over many, many years. The magnitude of her defection was immeasurable. Elijah could barely wrap his mind around the concept.

Though she was the older of the two, her youthful appearance matched that of her daughter, the one called Mary, who stood close to her. Since Demons did not visually age beyond a certain point, the duo looked more like sisters. However, Ruth had an arm around her offspring's waist and was stroking the young woman's hair with a maternal fondness that belied the fact that Mary was nearly a century old herself. It was eerily unnatural and must, even to these human eyes all around them, seem more than a little creepy. Perhaps it would have, had those eyes not been blinded by hatred and fear.

It was the inconceivable idea that both women were of Elijah's very own race, turncoats openly joining up with these malevolent magic-users and self-righteous human hunters, that burned him with such unholy rage. Of course, with even more irony, Elijah understood that none of the mortals realized that these two women were members of the very same race they were now declaring war on with this attack upon him. None of them knew Ruth's motivations were driven by her personal need for warped and misdirected vengeance and that they were merely tools, a weapon she could wield against her former people.

To the mortals, she was nothing more than a beautiful, knowledgeable human woman. A gifted sorceress, perhaps, if she had shown them her masterful ability to command certain aspects of the element of the Mind. It was this Demon deceiver and her daughter who were goading the humans into battles against victims the mortals never would have found with such awful ease and so little effort. Every day Ruth stood on the opposite of that line drawn in the sand by these paranoid and misguided people, she would reveal more and more to them about the Demon race. It would not be long before she carefully gave them the means to destroy those she had once called friends. Beyond that lay every other Nightwalker race, innocent or not, who would be threatened by Ruth's centuries of knowledge.

All that mattered to the humans was their fear of the unknown, terror of creatures whose power so outstripped even their wildest imaginations, making them quake with the conviction that it was only a matter of time before these night-living races fell upon the human race as myth and legend had predicted over and over again. It did not matter that, if they had wanted to, any Nightwalker race could have done so thousands of times over the last millennium alone.

Bitterly, Elijah felt that even if someone gave them the truth, they would still only expect the worst of all Nightwalkers because they were under the sway of stubborn prejudice and fear. The only thought that comforted Elijah in that moment was that his death would rouse a retaliation from the oldest and most powerful of his kind, and it would very likely be the end of this insurrection of evil.

"Spawn!" Ruth hissed the epithet with wicked delight, fueling the bloodlust of the women around him. "Devil in the guise of a human!" She smiled and said softly, "Elijah, the mighty Warrior Captain." Ruth laughed, the sound deceptively beautiful as she leaned forward to peer at him, her voice low so others could not hear her familiarity with him. "Noah's little pet pit bull, felled by mere women. I know your thoughts, Wind Demon. There will be no vengeance in your name. They will never find anything of you by the time we are through."

Ruth straightened, tossing back a length of luxurious blond hair, smiling serenely. She kissed her precious child's cheek, if one could call a fledgling Demon of almost ninety years of age a child, making Mary smile with a fawning affection that turned Elijah's stomach. But a child she was, compared to the adults and Elders of her kind, and even compared to other fledglings her age. Though she had the beauty and the body of a full-grown woman, she was a little girl at heart and in mind, completely under the sway of her overprotective, smothering parent.

Why had none of them noticed Ruth's detachment from her senses? As a Mind Demon, Ruth had no doubt blocked that awareness from other skilled Demons of the Mind. Why had no one ever insisted on separating the child from the unhealthy and domineering behavior of the mother? Because it wasn't their way to gainsay a parent's right to raise her child as she saw fit? Now their entire society would live with these errors and their consequences, just as Elijah would die because of them.

Too little, too late, he thought, with genuine sadness for the path the Demon females were choosing. Both were now spoiled, rotting beneath the breathless guise of their outer beauty. He didn't need his genetically enhanced sense of smell to catch the vile odor of corruption eddying off their tanned flesh.

Elijah fell forward, putting out a hand to try and brace himself and keep his face out of the dirt. Hopeless situation or not, he would not be remembered as being too easy a kill. His pride would not let him make that kind of an end. There were slain opponents sprawled in the dirt behind the considerably lessened circle that attested to his ferocity as he had tried to save his own life. Women or no, anyone who sought to murder him deserved what they got.

He was aware of the others closing in around him. The stench of the dark magic that clung to the human sorceresses was overwhelming and unbearable. Energy crackled all around him as they played with their power. Blue arcs of electricity wriggled between them, almost like a macabre game of monkey in the middle. Elijah's mouth pressed into a grim line as he understood what it meant to be the monkey in this particular case.

The first bolt that leapt from the ring of women struck him in his spine, jolting him into a hard backward arch, his arms jerking to his sides, stretching the muscles of his broad chest and forcing blood to pour out of his wound. The flow came so heavy, so fast, that he felt the gushing heat of it drenching him right down the front of his clothing, the denim of his jeans saturating completely in all of an instant.

He felt light-headed, dizzy, and strangely distant as the next bolt forced him to contort in another direction. He could smell the burning of his own flesh, amazed that it overpowered the reek of the magic-users. He tried to change, to find solace in the form of the wind he was so much a part of. If only he had the strength to metamorphose into even the littlest of breezes, they would no longer be able to harm him. But the time had passed for that. He had misjudged his situation and was now too wounded and too weak to concentrate on even the simplest of transformations.

He cursed himself for being such a fool, for walking into this feminine trap. He had been the one warning all others that no one was safe so long as the defectors, Ruth and Mary, were at large and stirring up unrest in the underbelly of the human populace. Had he not been telling them for the past half year, since they had first realized the traitors' betrayal, that anyone could be a victim of the duo's intimate knowledge of the Demons, their individual importance, their power? Ruth, her dementia disguised as maternal love for a wounded daughter, knew so many names, so many facts. Indeed, she could lead these murderesses to each and every member of the Great Council.

He would be but the first, Elijah realized, frustrated rage burning a second hole in his chest. Next would come the Enforcers, Gideon the Ancient medic, or perhaps Noah, the Demon King himself. And he would not be there to do his duty and protect them. Elijah thought about Jacob and Isabella, the Enforcers, who were the brand-new parents of a beautiful daughter who had her mother's silky black hair and her father's serious dark eyes.

The Warrior Captain had been chosen to be one of the

two who, besides her parents, would attend her naming ceremony. To be one of only two Demons in all this world to be given the honor of standing up as the angelic babe's *Siddah*. It was the most precious distinction one friend could give to another. Near her sixteenth year, he would have begun the Fostering of the child, taking her into his home as if she were his own. He would have taught her the ways and morals of their people, guiding her as she learned how to use and control whatever great power she would be gifted with. This responsibility would be shared with only one other person, the child's female *Siddah*. In this case, Magdelegna, the King's own sister.

Thinking of Legna brought him an even deeper pain. She was with child herself, about five months into term, and safe under the watchful eyes of her mate, Gideon. But what future would there be for both these innocents? Being hunted down? Destroyed? Treated like nothing more significant than the stray fly that needs a good, hard killing swat? Elijah grieved for the babes, blaming himself for not doing a better job of keeping himself safe and strong so that he could be their protector.

The warrior felt blackness creeping across him, but it was as much from understanding that he had failed his people and his monarch as it was from the deadly loss of blood. He heard feminine laughter, contorted into an ugliness of killer joy, a sound no woman should ever make in her natural state, be she Nightwalker or human.

Elijah finally collapsed, rolling onto his back in the grass until he was trying to focus on the stars above him. He was distantly aware of the wicked women toying with him, sending sadistically playful bolts of power through him. The black sky blurred into streaks of light and dark. The warmth of his blood seeped into the dried leaves and grasses beneath him. He had been calling the weather to him since he had been but thirteen years old. What he would not give in that moment for the simplicity of a rain shower. A final act of defiance, soaking the ground so any electricity sent into him would lash back onto his murderers.

But he would not be able to have that last act of retribution. He had known infants stronger than he was in that moment. All he had left were his thoughts. He did not care if Ruth could read his emotions, possibly even his thoughts at her Elder age, though that was usually a talent found only in the males of her type. She was corrupted by her fractured mind and all the evil magic poisoning those she had decided to associate with. Usually, unexpected power came with such malignant associations.

No. All Elijah cared about was the nature of the world he was going to leave behind him. To never again blow over miles and miles of untouched mountains and virgin beaches as the wind. To never wash himself and the world anew as the rain. To never drift slowly from heaven to earth with the random meanderings of snowflakes. To forever be deprived of the joy of these things made his heart rebel with despair and outrage. He opened his mouth to roar with the rage striking through him, but was beyond creating any sound. He forced himself to be satisfied with the screaming of his soul.

To his wonder, Elijah heard the scream echo in the distance.

It was a wild, savage thing. Unbelievably beautiful, and making him shiver as it vibrated across his nerves. He was succumbing to his own internal night, but the scream was repeated and he found himself fighting to hear it, to understand what it meant. The cold of his body was replaced with an inexplicable flush of heat and he felt his senses trying to return to him, to work for him, trying with every last available cell to hold on to that primal and stunning sound.

But he was too close to his death. With frustration clawing through him, he succumbed.

CHAPTER 1

The catamount screamed across the expanse of the forest meadow, making the circle of women forget their dying prey as inexplicable fear coursed through them. Humans were born with instincts like any other species, and they knew as surely as they knew their names that it was not wise for them to remain in the path of the beast that made such a sound. It did not matter that they were a power unto themselves. Nothing could circumvent that inbred terror of prey fearing a predator.

The necromancers backed away, eyes wide and magic blossoming forth as they began to levitate from the ground, hoping height would provide a sense of safety they simply could not feel with both feet on the ground. When it was still not enough, they could only ease their panicking hearts with a full retreat, flying away and above the trees, fleeing for home or any place they associated as being one of true safety.

Some of the female hunters were lucky enough to be re-membered by the fleeing necromancers and were levitated into retreat with them. Those who were not so lucky took to heel and bolted wildly into the tree line, taking only a minute before they were nothing but an amusing, distancing sound of crashing underbrush.

The Demon females were not so easily affected. The younger one was a Demon of the Earth. The creatures of nature were hers to empathize with and control. Though she was just a fledgling, weak compared to the great Elders of her kind, charming animals was a rudimentary skill. She reached out with her mind, trying to touch the thoughts of the approaching predator. Her fair brow furrowed in confusion, though, when the puma proved unusually unreceptive to her coaxing thoughts. The great golden cat broke through the tree line, stalking through the deep grasses in a hunting circle, the rotation of her shoulder blades as she walked both mesmerizing and frightening, her golden eyes fixed on the two females who yet remained in the clearing.

The cat could scent the massive amounts of blood spilled upon the ground. The scent called deeply to the animal's basest instincts. It attracted the catamount with an almost singular lure. Usually she would have avoided approaching other predators, but that blood scent was too powerful to resist. She stalked closer and closer, making the young blond Demon break a sweat as she struggled to touch the animal mind so thoroughly hazed over with the delights of blood scent.

"Mama, I cannot reach it. It will not listen to me."

"Never mind. We are done here."

Ruth tightened her hold on her child, and with a snap of displaced air, the two Demon females teleported to safety.

The great golden cat raised her head, stopping mid-step, testing the air as the stench of the invading women faded. The bloodied body lying in the center of the clearing was the only remaining scent of any strength, and the cat began to advance on the hapless victim.

She was so close to the unconscious creature, she could touch her muzzle to him. She did so, testing his scent. Under the blood was the unmistakable musk of maleness. It was a rich, heady thing, eliciting a speculative purr from the beautiful cat. She lowered her head to the largest of wounds, her tongue lapping roughly over the sweet tang of his blood. Her purr deepened, and the lioness opened her powerful jaws, closing them over the male's throat. All it would take was a single snap and she would finish him.

Suddenly the cat retreated, shaking her golden head as if coming out of a spell. She shook again, like a dog trying to shed water. As she shook, her fur began to peel away, stripping off in long coils until, with a final shudder, the beast became a woman, dressed only in a gold and moonstone collar and foot upon foot of long, golden hair.

Siena, marked by that richly appointed collar as the Queen of the Lycanthropes, took in a deep, calming breath, trying to ignore the urgent craving that tasting the male's blood had inspired in her. She knew this Demon, knew his name and his import to the Demon King. But she also knew that Demon blood was like nothing else in the world. It was rich and full of the power they possessed. However, though she was sometimes more beast than woman, she did not need blood to survive as the Vampires did. She was the most powerful of all her people, and this was a craving she could overcome.

If only there were not so much of it invading her senses.

But she needed to think more clearly, needed to act. As she knelt in the deep grasses trying to control her baser nature, the Demon warrior known to her as Elijah lay dying— nearly dead, in fact. It was a startling sight. She had battled beside this warrior a mere six months ago, knew his skill and power and undeniable strength. How had one such as he come to this?

Siena reached out with a tentative hand, her fingers threading through long golden locks not too unlike her own, though his were a whiter blond than her more purely filigree-colored hair, and only shoulder length where hers covered her entire torso. It was her hair that she reached for next, pulling one long tress between her teeth, her canines rending through the inch-thick coil of silken gold. The lock curled around her wrist and forearm, as if unwilling to leave the body it had been cleaved from. She tossed back her head, ignoring the droplets of blood that sprinkled from the torn ends of the severed strands that yet remained attached to her scalp. She leaned over the Demon, pushing open the once-fine silk shirt he wore, licking her full lips slowly as she took the coil of golden hair and let it curl like a braided carpet, around and around, until it covered the wound in its entirety.

Blood immediately seeped into the gold filaments, blending with the droplets already welling out of their severed ends. The wound instantly began to coagulate, the hair turning into a red and gold bandage that stayed fast to the gaping hole, plugging it quite effectively.

She could do nothing about his blood loss at the moment and could not leave him where he was lest his attackers decide to return and finish him off. His breathing was so shallow, so weak, that if not for her keen hearing she would not have been able to mark it. Luckily, she knew these woods well and could find some excellent shelter. Then she would see what she could do to aid him.

What the Demon was doing in Lycanthrope territory would be something to discover at a later date. Right now, she had to get him away from the approaching dawn. Though sunlight did not char either of their species with the agonizing pain and the promise of death in the way it did Vampires, it was no friend to any Nightwalker race. For Demons, its effect was like that on the nocturnal cat, making them feel fat, lazy, and lethargic. Many Demons actually loved the invading warmth of the sun, finding the daylight to be the best time to succumb to comfort and sleep. Unfortunately, this reaction was often an involuntary one, making them desire nothing but sleep to the point of distinct vulnerability. In this case, any further weakness caused by the light could depress the warrior's autonomic systems completely, finishing the task his attackers had begun.

For the Lycanthrope, it was a little bit more hostile. A changeling became ill in the bright light of day, a literal version of sun poisoning. Since they were a species inherently guided by moon phases, it seemed to make sense that the sun would feel unnatural to them. Being part cat herself, Siena was doubly inclined to remain active in the dark of night when she was most powerful, and to find rest and shelter out of the reach of daylight when she was susceptible to its effects. She did enjoy a higher resistance to the sun than most if she kept mostly to the shade, but it was not something she enjoyed doing.

Siena needed to decide the best and shortest route to reach where she would be able to care for him, and the best way to get them both to that place of concealment. Her people were too far to travel to, and she sensed none but herself in the area. It would be a good choice to find aid, a place where she would find a little assistance in his care, but it was not a logical option given the clear urgency of the situation. The ideal alternative of taking him to his own people, well, that was an even farther-fetched possibility considering they were even farther away than her people were. Besides, the most renowned Demon healer in all of the world was at her court at the moment.

The warrior was not a slim man. He was built in every way a warrior needed to be built to maintain his strength and prowess. The Captain of such warriors . . . well, he was of a most impressive stature, to say the least. Though Siena was tall and quite strong in her own right, his biceps could very well be larger than her muscular thighs.

The distance from help worried her most because the warrior needed medical aid and she doubted she would be able to give him anything near what he would require. He was an entirely different species and probably not as receptive to Lycanthropic ways of healing. It could very well be the equivalent of giving a human patient to the care of a veterinarian. The veterinarian medic could be at the height of his expertise, but even his best care could do more harm than good.

Her people had been at war with the warrior's race far longer than they had been at peace with them. Their knowledge of Demon anatomy was fairly limited, and even that information was restricted to which vital organ would make for the quickest death. With peace only fourteen years old between their races, who would have thought to trade medical knowledge? As it was, they had only recently traded ambassadors.

The Queen rose to her feet, her form lengthening into a proud and Amazonian stature. Nude, as she was at present, or fully clothed, there would never be a doubt as to her sex. She was golden skinned and lushly curved in spite of the obvious cut of her muscular, fit body. She was a huntress and warrior in her own right, a proud and pure Diana, and it radiated from every inch of her. However, the contradiction of a head full of thick, golden, spiraling curls that tumbled down to the middle of her thigh, and the bold curves of her sex made her appear no less feminine than Aphrodite herself. Her enigmatic way of smiling and the natural flirtation in her stride only added to the imagery.

The Lycanthrope goddess seemed to make a decisive choice on her next course of action as her sharp, golden gaze took in all of her surroundings one last time. Soon after, she shook her head again, the long coils of her hair coming to life as she did so. They began to slip silkily over her skin, wrapping her almost lovingly in their soft length. The spreading coat of hair became fur once more, only this time the form she became was half cat, half woman.

This was the shape of the Werecat, Siena's third and final form. Tall and beautifully shaped as the woman she was, but with the fur and claws, ears and face, and whiskers and tail of the mountain lion. Half woman, half cat, with the best of both worlds at her disposal. And that included the strength that would be required for her to lift the warrior into her arms.

The warrior, she noted to herself as she began to gather up his dead weight into her cradling grasp, was brawny and well muscled, weighing in significantly for his height of over six feet, even if he had not been completely unconscious. He had remarkably broad shoulders, almost too wide for her to encompass with her arm. There wasn't an ounce of lighter fat marring his trim waist and thighs. It was all the heavy thickness of a finely honed physique, muscled from head to toe, no part wasted, nothing of his structure resembling softness.

In spite of this impressive mass, she lifted him in her arms almost easily, drawing him close to herself as she began to stride across the field. Her sight was made for darkness, everything lighting up in sharp contrasting shades of black and white. It was bright as day for her as she carried her burden into the trees.

They might have presented quite a sight had anyone been close enough to see them, but a quick scent of the air assured the Queen that all enemies had retreated to places unknown, and all other living creatures had pretty much followed suit. They wouldn't even know that the mountain lion's scream came with a fear compulsion that was so powerful, it would force almost anything within its range to run in terror—even some of the more powerful Nightwalkers.

As the Werecat moved through the forest, picking her way with purpose of direction and leaving as little a trail as possible, she recalled that there had been more than humans in the party that had ambushed this warrior. She was aware of the renegade Demon females, mother and daughter, who had chosen to align themselves with their race's enemies out of a disproportioned sense of revenge, all for a tragic mistake no one could have prevented, not even the powerful Demons.

It had been nearly half a year ago, the eve of last Beltane, that the Demons' usually festive holiday had been shadowed by the aftermath of the war these traitorous females had begun. Siena was part of the Demon forces the day they had been forced into a massive battle in order to protect their own from a slaughter directed by the warped will of those females. It was this battle that had given her a glimpse into the capabilities of the great Warrior Captain. He had impressed her. So much so that finding him in this predicament was somewhat baffling.

Besides his fighting prowess, she had noted the Demon had been particularly affected by the fact that the female Druid who had been targeted had been pregnant at the time. The child she had carried was just as much the focus of retribution as she and her Demon mate were, and the warrior had been incensed to a personal level, though the child was not his, nor did he have any of his own.

Lycanthrope males did not usually feel this sort of empathy with children until they were fathers themselves, and even then it was just as common as not for males to go about their business and leave the rearing of children to the women. It was an instinct that was often determined by the natural behaviors of the animal the male transformed into. Changelings were a female-dominant society in any event. The females outnumbered the males almost eight to one. They had always been the dominant populating sex, but war had made them even more so. The male ambition for battle had driven their numbers down.

There were powerful matriarchal morals in a society of such proportions, and they were quite proud of that. As a whole, they rarely had motivation to seek out a battle other than the hunt for food or in self-defense. But even in the senselessness of war, the idea of setting out to hurt a defenseless and innocent child was completely abhorrent to her people. The vengeful behavior of the renegade females from the Demon warrior's race was a perverted form of a mother's protectiveness when her offspring was threatened.

Siena stopped abruptly, her ears twitching as she took in short whiffs of breath, scenting the area for danger. She felt animals scurrying beneath the remnants of deciduous vegetation on the forest floor, but other than that, there was nothing out of the ordinary. The silence was understandable, considering she was crossing the territory in this form, but the blood spoor trail the Demon was leaving behind could attract another predator.

They were over a mile away from the original battle site and there was a stream nearby. She could take the time to bathe and dress the rest of the wounds and cover their trail more efficiently, as was her instinct, to prevent them from being tracked. But the sun was already breaking through the trees, and once it began to touch her, she would become too sick and too weak to get them to shelter. Though a day lying in the shaded forest under the sun would not kill her, it would take her some time to recover from the resulting illness. It would certainly mean the death of the man who needed her to be in top shape in order to save his life.

Siena decided to risk being tracked. There would be water where they were headed and she was quickly running out of time. As she moved with remarkable speed for one so burdened, she continued to consider the Demon women who had perpetrated this crime against their former comrade. She knew about Ruth and her unhealthy relationship with her child. Siena had been part of those who had initially discovered the betrayal.

There was no animal on earth that stagnated its child's growth by denying it the liberty of leaving the den or nest to discover how to fend for itself. Somewhere in evolution there had been a mutation in bipedal humanoid societies that had allowed this to become possible and, sometimes, even the norm. Though evolution was a natural process, Siena had always felt this to be an unnatural mutation. But who could be completely sure? Humanoids were capable of a great deal of aberrant behavior that conflicted with the natural order of living in harmony with one's surroundings.

To be honest, this included her own species as well.

Though Lycanthropes were often considered by themselves and others to be more animal than human, they were still a society with flaws, laws, and free will. These ingredients, while bold and productive in many ways, could be a volatile combination as well.

For example, the race war between her changelings and his elementals. Had this been but two decades earlier, the idea of her helping to aid a Demon, especially *this* particular Demon, would have been not only inconceivable, but traitorous. Truthfully, there were some who still felt that way, even though their Queen clearly did not.

The previous war between Demonkind and the changeling race had been her father's doing. It had been an aggressive display of manhood that had begun over a small matter of principle and quickly escalated from there to an almost genocidal hatred toward Demonkind. A feeling that, over decades of provocation, the Demons began to reciprocate wholeheartedly. Unfortunately, Lycanthropes were as long lived as Demons, so her father's warring ways had plagued her people for centuries, giving birth to generations who did not understand that there actually had been a time when changelings had not actively despised Demonkind.

This had begun to change the moment she had been elevated to the throne.

Siena had publicly rescinded the declaration of war against the Demon race the moment the collar of her office had been latched around her throat. It had not been a popular decision at first, old and hostile feelings held to heart for so long proving a difficult barrier to overcome. It very well could have caused a massive rebellion.

Perhaps this was where being the female leader of a matriarchal society had its advantages. Her voice had the power to appeal to the large number of females who had never truly wanted to be a part of living and dying in battles that made so little sense. Their Queen had only needed to remind them of that, slowly, surely, day by day. And as peacetime went on, Siena's people began to remember what it was like to live life for something other than preparing for the next battle.

Siena could not, in good conscience, have done anything less. Even though she herself had been raised to mistrust Demons, lectured by a prejudiced parent and the tutors he had chosen for her, teaching her to hate them for the "evil, lawless creatures" they were, fate had intervened, sending her a very powerful lesson that had dramatically changed her perspective on Demons. Her morals and her feminine sense of right and wrong would not allow anything else but a full armistice once she had the power to demand it.

She could not truthfully blame her father's masculinity for all their troubles and poor behavior as a species, but his aggressive nature had done them no justice and she was now the one left to manage the results. Fourteen years of truce was a pittance of time when compared to almost three centuries of altercations.

Peace was an arduous task that could only be done in piecemeal, mincing steps of advancement. Any action done without the proper wisdom of contemplation could lead to an upheaval of the fragile harmony that was just beginning to bud in earnest betwixt them. And frankly, with all the Nightwalker races currently being besieged by these misguided, tenacious mortals seeking their extinction, they could not afford to waste resources fighting each other.

Saving the Captain of the Demons' warrior forces wasn't exactly a delicate step to take. But she would not allow petty politics to dictate whether this champion lived or died. Siena expected no gain and hoped for no ramifications. All she wanted was a cool, dark place to tend his wounds.

She found the cave she was looking for about an hour

later, her speed greatly reduced by then because of not only her cargo, but the morning sunlight streaming through the bared limbs of the trees.

Almost immediately after the entrance, the cave sloped dramatically downward, the rock smooth, cold, and damp beneath her bare feet. It took all of her balance, strength, and even her claws to keep from skiing down that slippery surface and landing in the chilled underground lake of mineral water that began at its end. She quickly navigated the thin ledge that rimmed the water. The minute she left a wet footprint on a dry surface, she relieved herself of her burden by gingerly laying him down on the clean stone.

She sat down beside him, more than a little out of breath, drawing her knees up so she could rest her aching arms on them. She needed to help him, the urgency of that was beating at her, but she also needed to give herself a minute to shake off the blinding headache the sun had given her. She was nauseated from it, her eyes and her fur itching from their solar photosensitivity. She was lucky. She could bear it better than most because her strength and power were unparalleled among her people. By all rights, she ought to have been violently ill at that point. Now, if she ventured out too soon after this, she would be even more susceptible.

The Werecat padded on all fours to the lake, sniffing around herself cautiously for life forms before finally using padded fingers and palms to splash water onto her fur. Feline or not, Siena loved to be clean and perfectly groomed, and that meant water and lots of it. She fussed long enough to lick clean a stain of Demon blood from her fur, but left the rest of her grooming until later. She stood up to her full height this time as she lightly leapt over the Demon and headed into the depths of the cavern.

The soft click of her claws on stone heralded her return. She dropped a sack on the floor and then filled a bottle with water from the lake before turning at last to kneel beside him and tend him.

She ripped his shirt off, what was left of it, even being forced to carefully pull out shredded bits of it from scorched skin. The worst wound, the one over his heart, was already cared for and healing. Clotting and anesthetizing agents were naturally present in Lycanthrope hair. The blood that leaked from the shorn ends of the warm, living tendrils had acted like a disinfectant and a healing balm. However, she could not use her hair for all of his wounds. It would damage her too much. Siena glanced at the raw patch of missing fur on her scalp that had occurred as a result of using what she already had.

Instead, she satisfied herself with cleansing his cuts and burns with water and dressing them with bandages from a first aid kit she withdrew from the sack. Demons healed very quickly and most of his wounds ought to be gone by evening. But the chest wound would take more time, as would a series of others that pierced his shoulder, hip, and thigh down his right side.

He had been lanced through with bolts made out of iron in these three wounds, no doubt missiles from crossbows or some other propellant-type weapon. One had gone clear through the muscle of his thigh, but there were metal rods protruding from the other two injuries. Iron burned Demons just by its touch, often scarring and disfiguring them quickly. These invading weapons must be excruciating for him, although, unconscious and in shock as he was, he was hopefully feeling no pain.

Siena took a small bit of cloth from what was left of the warrior's shirt and used it to get a better grip on the end of the iron dart protruding from his shoulder. She yanked hard and fast, feeling the tear of his flesh as the barbed tip did more destruction on its way out. The wound was black— amazingly enough, the burn of the iron had pretty much cauterized it—but she had begun fresh bleeding by removing it and now pressed balled pieces of his shirt to it, tying them tightly around for pressure.

She bathed his entire torso, inspecting every wound and treating them with the herbs and bandages she had brought with her in the sack as she did so. She found herself impressed by his physical fitness. This was naturally true for many of the Nightwalker races. Born with high metabolisms and the innate sense to regulate caloric intake with activity, overweight members of their various species were rare.

But this, she thought to herself as she traced one golden claw over the defined cut of his right pectoral muscle, this was the body of a being who had trained and honed himself into an artful weapon. He was brawny, yes, but he had the wisdom not to overbuild his stature in a way that would hinder his flexibility and streamlined body movements. She had seen this male move in battle, so quick and lethal, and she remembered it had left her quite breathless with fascination then as well.

Siena caught herself in the realization and immediately withdrew from the unproductive touch and the sensations that went with it. She turned her attention back to his urgent need of healing. She gently probed the bolt that pierced his hip and found it difficult to determine its placement through the denim he wore. Strangely, the denim amused her.

This warrior was a strange one. Most of his people wore clothing that reflected the eras they had passed through rather than the era they were in. It was rare to see such a modern fashion gracing one of their bodies. Then again, denim had been around for well over a century, so if the designer label had been removed, it could have easily been excused as being as much of an anachronism as any other Demon clothing.

Siena reached to unbutton the fly of the pants, tugging a little at the loosened denim in an attempt to see the damage better. Finally, she simply gave in to the inevitable and tore through the tough cloth with razor-sharp claws, stripping him completely. Free to work now, she extracted the second missile and bathed all injuries on his thickly muscled legs.

She washed blood out of the hairs that curled over them in a light dusting of gold, using medicaments on the wound burned so deeply into his hip from the poisonous iron.

These were the wounds that would not heal so quickly. She suspected the wound over his heart had been made by an iron weapon as well. Some sort of archaic mace or morning star, perhaps. Whatever it had been, it had crushed and torn the area, leaving telltale burns, but nothing black enough to indicate a missile that might still be festering and smoldering within the now-closed injury.

Once she had bathed him completely in the soothing mineral water, anointed and wrapped every wound she could find, and assessed him for ones she perhaps could not see, she took the time to wash his blood from his hair. She felt more relaxed as she did this. The scent that had been so mind-numbingly appealing was thankfully washed into the lake as the water rolled down the stone and back to where it had come from. Beast she may be, but she was one that struggled for her civilization with a singular conscience. If she had not earned that distinction, this weakened and wounded member of his herd would have received something other than help from her.

When his hair was clean, streaked with a thousand different shades of gold and white and tan now that it was wet, she quickly brushed and licked her own fur clean. When she had finished her ablutions, she once more lifted the Demon into her tired arms and carried him farther back into the cave structure.

It might have surprised the Demon to find furnishings in this place, but the Lycanthrope Queen had fully expected it. This cavern was the Lycanthrope version of a summer cabin. Actually, a winter retreat was possibly a better term. Lycanthropes were not above hibernation, and so these distant caves deep in the bellies of mountains and earth were often supplied for such things. The furniture was an enigma, perhaps, but one of the effects of civilization was the unabashed preference for living in a great deal of comfort. Even if it meant comfort in the incongruous setting of a cave.

This cavern belonged to one of the Queen's advisors, a woman of impeccable taste and the means to see them suited. Siena had been disappointed upon entering the living area to realize Jinaeri had not yet begun to prepare for the coming winter and there were no signs that she had been coming and going recently in order to do so. When the Queen had last held court, Jinaeri had been present and had mentioned she would soon begin those preparations. Siena had hoped to leave the warrior under her care while she fetched help.

Now she would have to stay and tend to him herself as best she could. She simply could not leave a Demon alone in a Lycanthrope lodging with no protection, no aid. She had no idea how long it took for wounds caused by iron to heal on a Demon. She also knew he had lost so much blood that the healing would be further hindered, if he even yet survived. He was hardly out of danger just because she had dressed his wounds.

A series of steps carved into the cavern led downward far more safely than the original slope had at the entrance to the cave itself. Plus, this far back everything was cool and dry. She stepped down into the living area, a parlor of soft couches and shelved books. There was a fireplace, the chimney of which probably exited out of the mountainside some distance above them. Siena passed rows of bookshelves draped with fabric to keep the must off them, and headed into the second room. This was the bedroom. On the far wall there was a dark, naturally formed alcove with a large hand-made bedstead set within it.

Siena moved to it and carefully laid her burden down onto the mattress that appeared to be handmade as well, and very likely filled with the softest tick the owner could find. The giant male sank deeply into the soft comfort of it, and she immediately covered him with a quilt from the bottom of the bed to keep the constant chill of these underground caverns off him as he healed. The parlor fireplace backed up to a fireplace in this room, so one could see through into the next room if one was not easily blinded by a blaze.

She considered building one to warm the place, but with enemies who were perfectly capable of running around in sunlight and itching to kill this Demon, a smoke trail would not be worth the risk. So long as he was this ill, she was very much alone. Powerful or not, all Siena had to do was look at the felled warrior to know she would have odds no better than his if pitted against those diabolical women.

Exhausted herself, Siena moved back into the parlor and immediately curled up into the deeply plush cushions of the couch. She didn't even bother to do her usual rituals, which often included kneading the bedding for added softness and a bit of moving and turning to find exactly the right spot. She simply flopped down, curled up into a snug ball, and fell fast asleep.

As she drifted off, the golden fur on her body peeled away, slipping off smooth, human skin to dangle in large golden coils, hanging willy-nilly off the edges of arms, hips, and the cushions of the couch. Claws turned into neat little nails, whiskers disappeared. The pads on her hands and feet became nothing thicker than the usual calluses, and her ears had only the tiniest little point to them after changing back to the shape and position of any normal woman's ears.

CHAPTER 2

Siena woke feeling much better many hours later. For one, she could smell the distinct ionized odor of rain. There was a good-sized storm just beyond the cave entrance. The pressure was unmistakable, even if she couldn't hear it with her keen hearing. This bathing of the Earth would hide what remained of their trail to the cave. She suspected that in their usual overblown sense of arrogance, the human magic-users were not likely to think they had failed in killing the Demon, and as a result would see no need to double-check. However, with the female Demons amongst them, she could not assume typical behaviors in this situation.

Siena sat up on the couch, stretching out one long limb after the other, soft, contented vocalizations accompanying each one. Jinaeri certainly knew a thing or two about comfort, she thought as she rose to her feet, shaking back her hair as it immediately curled into its proper places. The Queen moved to a pretty antique chest up against one wall and opened it. Inside she discovered neatly folded slips, dresses, and T-shirts.

The brevity of the clothing, most of it short, simple sheaths, was common for the women of her culture. Those who enjoyed the ability to transform into the form of an animal also enjoyed the type of clothing that would fall easily to the wayside and not impede their movement in the event of such a change.

The Queen plucked a soft, flowing minidress from the chest and donned it with a quick drop of fabric over her head. The cute little garment slid instantly into place, held on her by the thinnest of straps at her shoulders and the fact that she was quite a bit bustier than Jinaeri. She looked even more so as the low, scooped neckline left her in abundant display. The floating skirt's hem fluttered over the tops of her thighs, a soft whisper of sensation that made her rub her fingertips with pleasure over the crushed pile of the fabric. Siena glanced into the mirror near the trunk and smiled as she admired the blue velvet and the way it shone as the garment drifted airily with even a twitch of motion. She might have to exercise the privileges of royalty on a subject and permanently borrow the delightful creation.

Siena then padded across the chilly stone to the fireplace, where she arranged wood and kindling, starting a comfortable blaze without worrying that smoke could be trailed in either rain or darkness. Evening was definitely on them. Siena felt guilty that she had not roused to check on her patient in all of this time, but it was senseless to reprimand herself. There was not much she could have done for him in any event.

She checked on him immediately after the fire took hold, however, crossing into the next room and letting only firelight illuminate her way. She gingerly rested one knee onto the mattress, sitting back on that heel, half on, half off the bed. She slowly began to inspect his injuries. As she had suspected, most were healing nicely, some even to the point of pink, new skin. She removed the bandages from those places.

The iron wounds were not doing quite so well, also as expected. The worst part about iron, as opposed to the silver used against her people, was that it tended to rust and flake too easily, often leaving behind specks of itself even after being extracted. These flecks of metal would continue to insidiously poison the wound as it tried to heal. The only way to remove them completely would be for a Demon medic of great skill to use his powers over the Body to do so.

She knew just the person she needed.

In fact, his wife was the ambassador the Demon King had appointed to her court, the Demon King's own sister Magdelegna. Legna was a bright, beautiful woman, a Mind Demon of substantial power, one whose bravery Siena admired a great deal. It took a woman of great courage to maintain diplomacy in what was often a hostile court of former enemies, as well as expose herself to such a situation while carrying her first child.

However, Legna's husband, the great Body Demon and medic called Gideon, was the oldest of all the Demons, as well as the most powerful. He was the one who could have tended such diabolical wounds, extracting the iron with magical ease. Though his skills as a medic were wasted in the Lycanthrope court, changelings being mostly unaffected by the powers of Demons of the Mind and the Body, Gideon was a valuable addition to it.

He had been the first Demon she had ever met, a prisoner of her father's kept at court for the King's amusement and bragging rights many, many years earlier. However, this had backfired on the monarch, because it was Gideon's teachings that had enlightened the young princess about the true nature and goodness of the Demons.

Now he was back in her court and was quietly assisting his mate in doing the same thing, but on a much larger scale. He also served as his wife's protector in the sometimes hostile task of winning over a prejudiced people. No creature with any sense would dare harm the mate of such a powerful being as Gideon, but in every race there was always someone lacking in good sense. The warrior's injuries attested to that quite clearly.

It was useless to think about the medic. He was too far away and Siena would not leave the Demon warrior vulnerable and alone. It would have to wait until he became stronger. She would, however, need to hunt for food if there was none in the cave. It did not seem likely. As one who took the form of a lemur, Jinaeri was a vegetarian. Siena was mostly a carnivore and preferred the freshest game she could manage. It wasn't likely she would find such in the house of an herbivore, never mind one that was not yet stocked for the winter. The nutrition of meat was something that could only be obtained fresh. It made no sense to leave anything behind from the season before that would attract animals or decay.

Siena gently rewashed the wounds on the warrior and dressed them with clean bandages. The only one she did not touch was the one bandaged with her hair. That would care for itself and was best left alone. She pulled the covers back over the Demon's chilled skin. It was a good sign. Demons ran much lower temperatures than Lycanthropes or humans did. If he were to grow hot, it would mean he was fighting a fever, and that was the last thing the warrior needed. He was still terribly pale, perhaps even a little too cold to the touch, but he did look as if he were breathing easier. She could hear his steady heartbeat, stronger than it had been.

The Queen reached to push back the now-dry tendrils of his hair, the surprisingly soft silk of it slipping through her fingers. He wore it long, a common thing for Nightwalkers. Whatever he had used to bind it back from his face was long gone, and she thought she would make a point of searching for a replacement once she returned with food for them. His hair was quite thick, more like the density of a Lycanthrope's, than what was the norm for a Demon. But Lycanthropes didn't own a monopoly on thick, healthy hair. Still, it was a pleasant tactile sensation.

Siena found her hand drifting down his forehead, fingertips touching each thick, gold brow with a curious tracing of their arches. Even his lashes were blond, like her own. It was a dark, rich gilt color, offsetting the lighter shades of his hair just as hers did.

He had such a good face, she marveled as she traced a thumb over well-defined cheekbones, a strong masculine nose, and a firm chin with the faint imprint of a cleft in its middle. It was so rugged, and yet somehow boyishly beautiful. Perhaps, she mused, it was the fullness of his mouth, almost feminine in its way, that foiled the attempt at being wholly toughened.

Siena laughed at herself as she realized what she was doing. She stood up, shaking out her hand as if in punishment to make it behave itself next time. She pressed back a smile at her silliness and moved to the front of the cave. She stood in the opening for a long moment, listening to the rain and smelling the sleeping forest as best she could. Rain masked even her formidable abilities of sniffing out prey or predator.

Then, stepping out of her dress with a simple shrug of her shoulders, she shook herself into the furred form of the Werecat and ran into the cold autumn wet of the forest.

Elijah had not moved so much as an inch in the hour she was gone. She checked him for fever, careful not to drip on him. She was soaked head to toe, her hair streaming as she padded closer to the fire. She settled onto a small, cushioned stool near the dry warmth of the blaze, using a cloth and the heat to try and dry her hair.

She ought to have remained in Werecat form, fur being so much easier and faster to dry, but she considered it would be unwise to do so. Elijah had made it quite clear during their brief meetings that he would not trust her or any of her kind any further than he could spit. It would not be wise to be in the form of a Lycanthrope when he awoke. He might not take the time to notice the ornamental collar of her office that she never took off. A Demon, even in a weakened state, was nothing to fool with. If her people had learned one thing over the centuries, it was not to underestimate the powers of a Demon who felt threatened. Truce or no, Elijah was bound to feel endangered by her presence alone, never mind the fact that he was already wounded.

The Queen turned closer to the fire, her back to the sleeping Demon as she continued to fuss with her hair. She had spitted one of the rabbits she had caught earlier and it was now rotating quite nicely in the fire, the rotisserie operated by a battery-powered motor. It clanked and screeched, not appreciating the nearness of the elemental male whose body chemistry was causing it to function at less than peak. Unlike Demons, Lycanthropes were not averse to the use of machines and technology, and those things did not react adversely to them. Since this was a simple hibernation hostel, it was not equipped with electricity or any superfluous needs that would go unused as the occupant slept more than she remained awake, and Siena supposed that was a very lucky thing. There was a natural source of water, plenty of wood for a fire, and a forest full of food just beyond the entrance. Truly, there was no need for more.

When her hair was mostly dry, settled once more into happy, tubular coils, she rose to dress herself and set about preparing a stew and a soup from the remaining rabbits and the wild turkey she had caught. She saved the feathers of the bird, a payment for Jinaeri for the use of her home. She shredded herbs and roots into both pots and then allowed them to cook slowly in the fire, suspended in swing-armed cauldrons.

It was true her diet consisted mostly of food that was more alive than dead, but she was humanoid too and very much appreciated a wide variety of culinary tastes. One of her favorite things was wild salad, all the greens and buds of the forest fair game, or in autumn, nuts, herbs, tuber roots, and berries, so long as they were not poisonous. All carnivores were actually omnivorous. What many did not realize was that carnivores preyed mainly on herbivores, not only because they were less able to defend themselves, but because the innards of the animals were usually bursting with the necessary vitamins and beneficent qualities of vegetation. That was why the belly was often the first thing a lion went for after taking down a gazelle or deer.

However, innards were a diet she left for the catamount, and upon occasion, the Werecat. In her human form, she preferred salad and meat, both cooked and raw. This meal was not so much for herself, in any event. It was designed for her patient. The herbs used to flavor the dishes were not merely delicious, they were also quite medicinal. Everything that went into the soup and the stew would serve its purpose toward helping him heal and regain his strength.

As she cooked, Siena filled her time by cleaning and stretching the furs of the rabbits on the frames that had been hanging near the fireplace. Nothing hunted was wasted. If a fellow animal must give up its life for her sustenance, she would see to it that every part of it was put to good use. And again, they would make a nice payment to Jinaeri, who did not even know she was playing hostess to her Queen and the Warrior Captain.

After another hour passed, the Queen ladled some of the piping hot soup into a wooden bowl, dropped in a spoon, and made her way to her patient's side. Once more she knelt on the bedside, settling back on her heel as she held the bowl in one hand and stimulated him with a rubbing motion on his arm with the other. She didn't expect he would wake right away, but she would at least try every fifteen minutes until he did and she could get some nutrition into him.

When the warrior suddenly burst into life, Siena was caught completely off guard. He exploded into movement, seizing her by both arms and hauling her violently over his body. Her back slammed into the mattress, her breath leaving her in a rush. He pinned her beneath himself painfully, his massive strength formidable even in his weakened state, his weight an overwhelming force. Siena did not make a single sound, not even as the boiling hot soup cascaded down her legs. She made no noise or movement that would be mistaken as an act of provocation. The only thing she did do was to encircle the thick wrist of the hand clenching around her throat with the firm, staying fingers of both hands. She would not provoke him, but neither would she let him throttle her to death.

The warrior's green eyes were wild with confusion and pain, his movements highly detrimental to his carefully dressed wounds. Siena was immediately aware of the scent of fresh blood, and her eyes flicked down to the wound on his chest. She saw a fresh stream of blood slipping over his skin, dripping from the ridges of his abdomen onto her dress. His immense body was crushing hers, his hips and legs nailing her to the soft mattress as he braced half the weight of his torso on one hand and supported the rest on the hand attempting to cut off her air supply.

Elijah blinked, trying to take in everything he was seeing through a hazy wall of pain. He was aware that he was trapping one of the females, that he could break her neck in a breath if he wanted to, but there was something not quite right about what he was seeing and feeling and he needed a precious moment to figure it out. He looked down into wide, golden eyes, feeling a familiarity in them that was disturbing. There was also something about the thick piece of jewelry beneath his hand. It prevented him from having a perfect grasp on her slender neck, but somehow he knew that was not the most important thing about it.

The next thing he was aware of was that he was completely nude and that she was not much better off in a short, damp skirt that was gathered up around her bared hips. This made her decided lack of fear impress itself on him. Not that he would take advantage of such a situation even if had she been his worst enemy, but how would she know that he meant her no harm? Considering the fact that he was the one in the dominant, aggressive position, her bravery seemed either very impressive or very foolish.

He looked away from her, his eyes darting around the room, more pieces to a puzzle that still seemed to have too many gaps. He could smell food, was aware of his hunger and unusual weakness. He noticed he was bandaged and healing, and not lying dead on the forest floor. It seemed an inane thought, but it was an important ingredient in his ability to understand what was going on.

His hand loosened slightly as he looked back to the female beneath his body. There was hair everywhere, hers, tangled between them both. She had an intriguing body, quite strong for a female and impressively fit. She was also full of soft, abundant curves just where a male would appreciate such things most. He could feel all of this more than he could see it, just as he felt her appealing warmth, the satin smoothness of the skin brushing his thighs and calves, and the rapid rise and fall of the breasts crushed beneath the weight of his body as she drew for breath.

He became aware of her scent, this aspect also somehow familiar, even though it was layered beneath the aroma of food. It was attractive enough to distract him from his pain, the fight-or-flight reaction he had woken up with twisting with intriguing ease into the powerful stirring of male interest. Powered by adrenaline, he was far deeper into the reactions of his instincts than the civilization of his intelligence. Demons were as much the heirs of their animal sides as the Lycanthropes were, though they never manifested into the forms of that side of their nature. It was this instinctive side, which they embraced in conjunction with their moral side, that made them the impressive hunters and warriors that they were.

When the warrior took a long breath in through his nose, Siena became aware of the fact that he was taking in her scent. She was not concerned at first, because it would have been her first reaction had she woken in a strange place. But something changed the color of his eyes from a troubled jade to a very vivid emerald, and she found herself completely fascinated by the transformation. A powerful sort of speculation rippled through them just before he lowered his head to her ear and drew another slow breath. His lips faintly brushed her jaw, his soft hair falling against her forehead.

That was when she became aware of the change in his scent, a sharp spike of the rich musk that was always present on him. She felt her stomach tighten with instinctive anticipation, even as her mind rebelled against the feeling, understanding that she was in a fair amount of danger and that all of this behavior was primitive and unjustifiable. For her. For him, waking into a world of confusion, it was not. She was the one with her senses about her, she lectured herself sternly, her fingernails digging into the wrist that still pinned her head to the pillow.

The warrior touched his nose to her temple and inhaled deeply once more. His lips touched her; she felt them part just enough to imprint a wisp of moisture, like the barest of kisses, against her cheek. Siena felt a wash of chills flowing down the front of her body in inexplicable and wild response. Her breasts grew taut beneath the heavy velvet fabric of her dress, the pointed crests of her nipples rubbing his chest in an inadvertent flirtation of response.

Elijah made a low, appreciative sound in his throat before raising his head from her again, his jeweled eyes bright but smoldering as they drifted down to her breasts. The vocalization called to Siena, very deeply, sending a rapid rush of heat and awareness bursting across her skin. She felt her mind turning away from logic and reason as the primitive reply to that call bubbled up from her own throat.

Her answering song had a dynamic effect on him, and she could feel the evidence of it solidifying between their bodies. Her golden eyes grew wide as she felt that male weight and hardening heat against her inner thigh. Just like that, an instantaneous metamorphosis, and for some reason just the understanding that she was responsible for it melted her body from the inside out. She inhaled a quick, full breath of emotion. She was suddenly overwhelmed by this feeling, this rush of adrenalized sexual response that she had always tried to tell herself she was not in the least curious about. And she hadn't been . . . until this very moment.

It was raw and base, like the driving hunger that followed a long hibernation. She felt sensations darting around inside her, hot and intrigued, crying out a call that she couldn't hope to understand. She was poorly prepared and felt it keenly. Siena was a creature of instinct, but she was also one of complete bodily control. Until that moment, she would have sworn there was no part of her that was a stranger to her. That was the only way it could be for any being that altered the shape and nature of who it was with the will of its mind alone. Yet, there was no control in and of that moment, and her entire being was now very much a stranger. She was first flushed, and then chilled. She was terrified, but craving. She was seeping liquid heat, and locking up in solid awareness. The contradictions battered her from the inside out and she felt wildly, deliciously out of control of it all.

The warrior felt the female's heart pounding madly beneath him, the sensation causing a curl to one side of his lips as he looked down at her. She was aroused, he could smell it, feel it, and hear it. He was aware of how he was reacting to this delicacy entwined with his body. He was fully aroused against her; her hot skin, so soft and smooth like a thick satin, cradled him. He felt a tremor shimmer through her and he was pressed with the urge to rub himself up against her supple body. It made no impression on him that he was still weak and wounded. His mind was little more than an endorphin-pushed rush at that point. He was blind to everything but the sensations and the desires of his instinctive thoughts.

Elijah was no stranger to women—he enjoyed them immensely, in fact—but this was something quite remarkable. Never had he reacted so strongly, so quickly, to a female before. Except, perhaps, one other time. But he had refused to acknowledge it then for what it was, excusing it as part of the heat of battle. It had been the attraction of creatures who, though they were completely differing species, were joined by the common thread of one warrior appreciating the dynamic skills and flush of battle upon another. Other than that, the very idea of it had been utterly appalling because the woman in question had been—

That was when recognition finally set in.

Elijah's eyes went pale, just as the rest of him did, as he finally realized exactly who it was he held pinned beneath his body. Who it was he was feeling this outrageous craving for. And who it was that was responding with an inconceivable reciprocation of heat and interest.

"Siena," he hissed, his hand finally leaving her throat to reveal the gold and moonstone collar she wore.

Elijah rolled off her and out of the bed in such a swift movement that he ended up staggering as he gained his feet. As he moved, he jerked a sheet off the bed to wrap around his body. He was not doing so out of shyness, but he would be damned if he would stand naked, *aroused,* and vulnerable in front of any Lycanthrope woman.

Especially the Queen.

The warrior ran a violent hand through his hair as everything settled at last into the proper place in his awareness. He watched warily as the Queen slid into a sitting position, smoothing her short skirt down to a somewhat more proper placement. She then, quite casually, looked up at him with those eerie gold eyes that always made him feel like she was dissecting him. No doubt because her people had done plenty of Demon dissecting over the centuries as they had relentlessly pressed a genocidal war upon his society.

"What in hell is going on here?" he demanded, unable to help himself as he reached out to steady himself against the bedpost.

She didn't immediately answer, instead getting to her feet

in one supple motion as his eyes followed her every movement. She moved very carefully as she reached to take fresh sheets from a stack sitting on a nearby chest. Amazingly, she turned her back on him and, of all things, began to make the bed. It was a harmless, domestic thing, and, to say the least, it was an incongruous act for a woman who was not only royalty, but one of the most ruthless fighters Elijah had ever had the pleasure of seeing in battle.

She had finally set the bed to rights, tossing the sheets that had been covered in strange debris, including what he assumed was his own blood, into a corner. It was after that when she finally turned to face him. She folded her arms beneath her breasts, as if she were a stern parent about to give him a decisive lecture on manners and behavior.

"I will explain once you return to bed," she offered generously.

"I'll do no such damned thing!" Elijah barked, his eyes flashing with a bottle-green fire quite indicative of his anger. "Answer me, woman. Queen or no, I'm not above—"

Elijah cut himself off as he was struck by a wave of nausea frighteningly resistant to his efforts at mental and physical repression. She was by his side before he knew she was moving, inserting herself under his arm to give him support.

"I swear, warrior, if you make me carry you one more inch I will be quite annoyed," she warned, using her considerable leg strength to propel him toward the bed.

Elijah had no choice but to follow her lead. She guided him down with surprising gentleness and an impressive show of physical power. He was quite aware that he was no lightweight, and, in spite of the fact that she was a good five inches shorter than he was, she managed just fine. She had him lying in the bed, covered and pillowed comfortably in a heartbeat. He immediately began to feel better. Well enough to flush at the realization of having shown his weakness to her.

"Don't worry," she said with a smirk he could have done without, "I won't tell."

That, of course, upset him even more. Damn her, she was baiting him on purpose. He responded with coarse anger instead of the gratitude that he would have given to anyone else who had assisted him in such a manner.

"Just answer my question," he snapped.

"Well, if you must know, I am in the process of saving your life." She said this matter-of-factly as she bent to retrieve a bowl from the floor.

She disappeared into the next room before he could respond to that particularly inconceivable idea, but returned moments later with a clean bowl. She reached into the fire and the scent of food thickened in the air. He sat up, unwilling to lie there like some sort of invalid, using a pillow behind his shoulder to help prop himself up while softening the press of his wounded shoulder against the stone wall at his back.

Siena carried the bowl over to him and, placing a careful knee on the bed, she settled beside him, facing him and extending the offering of food to him. He looked her over suspiciously for a moment and then reached to take the presented food. She held on to it even after his hands encircled it, as if she were afraid he might spill it.

"It wouldn't be the first time," she noted dryly when he gave her a scathing look.

The remark put together a series of disconnected clues floating around in his head with a click. Quickly he realized he had scalded the skin on one of his arms, exactly the kind of burn that would result from hot soup being spilled over it. What was even more disturbing was he finally understood she had been holding exactly such a bowl when he had suddenly grabbed her.

Immediately he scanned her for burns, and for the first time he noticed both of her thighs were scalded a bright red.

This, he realized, was why her dress was wet. He had caused her to burn not only him, but herself. An answer, he was understanding, undeserved of someone who he was realizing was intent on nursing him.

Elijah took the bowl from her and set it aside. He took hold of her arm before she could move away, holding her tightly when she would have pulled back. His free hand brushed aside a couple of inches of her dress's material, exposing rapidly forming blisters. She tried to push his hand away, to retreat, but he would not let her. He was aware that he was holding her with his injured arm and she might have made a clean escape if she would only apply a little force, but she was clearly unwilling to do any more damage than he had already done to himself these past few minutes.

Suddenly, Elijah felt like an enormous jerk. Nothing was so shameful as the clarity of a moment like that, and it reflected in his eyes quite clearly.

"Never mind," she insisted, trying to push his hand away once more.

"Siena . . ."

"Don't," she commanded sharply. "Don't get all remorseful, warrior. I am aware you did not mean it. You need nourishment. If you wish to make me feel better you will brave my culinary skills and take some soup. I need to cool the burns and bathe. The mineral pool in the next room will help them heal quickly. We both of us heal rapidly, as you know, so this is a waste of your energy."

"It is a terrible way to thank you for saving my life. I remember now what was happening. That scream . . . that was you."

"I thought it would be counterproductive to my hard work offering peaceful overtures to your King if you were found suddenly dead in one of my territories. Believe me, my motivations were highly selfish. As you probably expected."

She finally freed herself, turning away from him and exiting the room quickly. He saw her walk past the fireplace on the other side a couple of times before she retreated to a place some distance away.

Feeling like a complete barbarian, he settled his mind to accomplishing what she had requested of him. He finished the entire bowl of soup by the time he heard her returning to the room just outside the doorway. The only sound she really made was the patter of bare soles on stone. Even so, she walked very lightly for a woman of what could be considered Amazonian proportions. It was quite some time before she entered the room to retrieve the bowl and take a willow broom to the remaining debris of the spilled food that was on the floor. She remained well out of his reach this time, unusually silent as she worked.

As he watched her in similar silence, Elijah was forced to recall the first time he had seen her. It had been in Kane's home immediately after Kane's mate, Corrine, had been abducted. It had been there that they had first come to understand that Ruth could be a potential traitor to Demonkind.

It had been Siena's sources that had led them to the truth of that particular matter. But as seemed to be his sudden habit around her, he had been hostile to her instead of being grateful. Again, it had been an affliction of pride that had instigated the behavior. He had been very irritated that she had been able to unearth the betrayal where he had not. Irritated and embarrassed. It did not matter that she was better equipped to get such information from the start, it just mattered that she had been the one to tell his King how poorly he had done his job, however unintentional it may have been.

On top of that, he had not been able to take his eyes off her. She was a breathtaking creature, a beauty one could not help but admit to being unparalleled, even if she was a Lycanthrope. That was saying a great deal, in Elijah's mind. He knew very well what three centuries of war had done to his perspective concerning her species. He was prejudiced, angry, and unrelentingly unforgiving. So for him to show any appreciation to any of them for any reason was nothing short of a miracle. A miracle, and a total truth. Demon women were very beautiful creatures, inside and out, and there were some that were blindingly attractive, but none he had seen could outshine the Lycanthrope Queen. She was golden, luminescent, and she held herself with all the pride and stubbornness of dignity of her race. He had absolutely no right to be attracted to her on any level, never mind with the ferocity he had experienced. She had turned those enormous eyes on him, meeting his appraisals with an unconcerned air, and Elijah had felt as though she had stolen the very breath from his body with just that single, unblinking look.

It had worsened the day she had joined their forces in battle against the onslaught of human killers at the Battle of Beltane. He had seen Lycanthropes in battle countless times, but he had never once seen anything like her. She was a full-blooded huntress, a warrior of remarkable speed and lethal beauty. She was as merciless as he was, efficient once her mind was set to her purpose. She did not hesitate or shy from the kill. In fact, she reveled in it. And so she should. The necromancers had deserved their fate. They had harmed and destroyed innocents, some of them her own people, and retribution was the only acceptable punishment.

Elijah remembered smelling the scent of the hunt on her, the blood of her prey, and the adrenaline of her victory. He remembered that moment vividly because he had never known such a fast and hard reaction of arousal as he had in that singular, unbelievable instant. His blood had been high and hot, the lust and delight of justice riding him like a wicked mistress, and then those golden eyes of a woman warrior fresh from her victims' throats had skimmed over his body like a siren's touch. It was as if her hands had run over his naked flesh, determined and skilled and just as bold as she was when she hunted anything else.

Then she had spoken to him, completely oblivious of how she had affected him, and made a statement that had haunted him almost day and night for the months since she had uttered it.

He had spoken briefly of his mistrust of her, a knee-jerk reaction to the confusion pounding through his mind, and she had responded.

"I would think you an utter fool if you did not doubt me, warrior. Instead, I am forced to respect your uncommon intelligence. Now what, do you suppose, should I do from there?"

With those words she had proven herself to be the better person. While he clutched his prejudices and hostilities close to heart, she had once more laid down her ideas of peace and a desire to respect him for exactly what he was. She had humbled him by humbling herself, and he could not forget it.

She had shamed him, angered him, aroused him, and confused him, a deluge of emotions so powerful he didn't even recognize them as his own at first. It had been exactly the same less than an hour ago. She had done it to him all over again, but this time he had been at a disadvantage. In his confusion and weakness in that moment when she had been beneath him, oh so beautiful and so incredibly lush, Elijah had allowed her to see what he had spent these many months hiding from everyone, including himself.

Siena was an audacious creature, self-assured to a fault and almost cocky in her attitude toward things that would have given anyone else a healthy dose of fear. She never had to second-guess herself, and certainly would not show it if she did. So her silence after his callous treatment of her disturbed him on very deep levels. He did not imagine her sulking in some simpering, feminine way, the ways that had made it easy for him to discard some of his past female acquaintances.

No.

This was the silence of a female predator who was nur-

turing a pride of her own, trying for all she was worth to remind herself of the greater purpose she served so she would-
n't give in to an urge to break his fool neck. He was forced to
remember the self-control she had used as he'd had his hand
wrapped around her soft, vulnerable throat. She had not
even made a sound when he had inadvertently burned her.

Elijah knew he was notorious to her people as a legendary slaughterer of men, women, and children. Of course,
the worst of the stories were quite exaggerated, as happened
in the case of the differing perspectives of a war. But for her
to be so still, so quiet, when he'd had the upper hand? Resisting every instinct he realized must have been screaming
at her, trying to force her to protect herself, to strike back,
had to have been an act of remarkable inner strength. And
one of utter devotion to the cause of peace that she seemed
to serve so adamantly.

Elijah rubbed at the ache in his healing chest as he mulled
over that piece of information. He was no stranger to powerful women, but this one was exceptional. Unnervingly so.
He was not supposed to think in these ways about her. To respect her in any other way than as a worthy opponent was a
dangerous pastime. She could be his enemy by this time tomorrow. Lycanthropes chose their friends and enemies just
that quickly, and as randomly. One day war, the next peace,
then vacillation back to brutal war.

The warrior felt the edges of the coarse bandage that was
sealing the wound on his chest and he looked down. Immediately his heartbeat quickened when he saw the telltale coil
of hair that was helping him heal. When he shot his gaze
back to her, she was looking at him with a resigned ex-
pectancy.

"What have you done?" he asked hoarsely, his body trembling with the outrage surging through him so violently, so
suddenly.

"I had no choice, warrior. I am sorry for that, but not
sorry for saving your life. At least, not yet." She gave him

another one of those saucy smirks, her golden eyes flashing with challenging amusement.

"I do not find any humor in this," he said darkly. "You have tainted me with your blood!"

"I have healed you with it," she countered sharply, her hands curling into offended fists. "You and your narrow ideas! Thank the Goddess Noah had the sense to send Gideon to teach me your ways, warrior, because if he had sent you I would have had you executed by the second morning! My blood is no more or less tainted than yours is, Demon. Though I'm sure I can produce just as many pigheaded, prejudiced people from my own species that would say yours is utterly diseased. I had hoped you were slightly smarter than those superstitious simpletons." She seemed to be laughing at him even in her resignation over his character. "Are you poisoned? Rotting away? Are parts of you that weren't furred before suddenly becoming so?" Again, that twisting of her lips, reminding him that she had taken quite a detailed accounting of his entire body during his unconscious state. "Trust me, Demon, you are no more or less an animal than you were when this began."

With that veiled insult, she marched out of the room with her broom. He heard her swearing softly in a Russian dialect as she went, being dubiously polite enough to make sure she added some from his own ancient language so he would be quite certain to understand her meaning. It made his ears burn with renewed embarrassment at himself. Hadn't he just told himself to quit being an ungrateful ass? Yet, somehow he had managed to do the exact same thing all over again. And this time she had not let it slide, her careful patience suddenly finding an end.

And why the hell did that bother him so much?

CHAPTER 3

Night turned to day again and Elijah's grumbling nurse disappeared, no doubt to get some sleep. Meanwhile, he had been doing little else but sleeping. Now, set so far back from even the slightest touch of sunlight, he found himself fairly wide-awake. He was feeling stronger with every passing hour and every bowl of the aromatic soup she pushed on him. She had even begun to feed him the thicker rabbit stew.

He was amazed to realize the Queen was no slouch at the fire. One would think such skills were below a member of royalty, but apparently not. It reminded him of Noah. The King stood on very little ceremony and was quite willing to serve his guests himself.

Elijah pushed the comparison aside stubbornly. He didn't want to find any more similarities between her and anyone else he respected. He was having enough trouble as it was from everything else he had been mulling over.

It had been much easier just to blindly hate and distrust all of her kind.

Still, at one point when she had returned to fetch his empty bowl, Elijah had reached out to take hold of her arm. She had turned a dark stare on him, lifting a filigreed brow in mock curiosity. Wordlessly, he had reached for the short hem of the black silk minidress she now wore, sliding the loose fabric up slightly to examine her damaged legs. As she had assured him, she had healed as remarkably fast as he did. The skin had become a soft pink color, the color of newly emerged, healthy flesh.

Satisfied, he'd let go of her. When he looked up at her again, she had seemed perplexed, the sardonic lift of her brow gone. But she did not say a word as she turned to enter the other room.

Elijah had his fill of lying in bed several hours later. He had no company because she was keeping her distance, and he was thoroughly bored. By all accounts he should have been sleeping soundly during sunlight hours, but he'd had enough of sleeping as well. The warrior found a towel under the stack of sheets nearby and wrapped it around his hips since he was unable to find his clothing. He walked out of the room on bare feet, out of habit making as little sound as she did.

He found himself in the middle of a Spartan but tasteful parlor. It had everything it needed, nothing more, nothing less, and everything was very well suited to the environment. He noted the comfortable couch nearby that had a distinct impression in it. No doubt this was where she had been sleeping, but she was not there at the moment. He had always thought Lycanthropes as severely affected by daylight hours as any other Nightwalker, so it surprised him she was not dead asleep. Then again, he was not exactly acting par for the course of his species either.

A breeze blew gently into the room and his head immediately picked up so he could take it in with a deep breath.

All Demons had an innate connection to the base element their powerful abilities came from. He was of the Wind, all of Her properties, temperatures, and volatile ways his to command and enjoy. The Wind filled him down to every last cell of his being, called to him with a lure that was almost unparalleled. And with the crisp, clean scent of Her whisper blowing around him, Elijah realized he had been indoors for far too long.

With a single-minded thinking, Elijah followed the breeze to its source. He strode up the cavern steps, then up the slope of the floor with eager expectation. He was so focused on his goal that it took him a full minute to realize he was approaching a lake of water within the cave, and that standing in the center of it, covered only to her hips with the liquid, was his wayward Lycanthrope nurse.

Elijah stopped dead in his tracks, his entire body tensing from head to toe with a mixture of utter shock and that sharp, brutal sexual awareness she inspired so effortlessly within him. The Queen had her back to him, the long, beautiful line of her spine gracefully exposed as she bent forward to swing her hair through the water she was using to wash it. The water lapped flirtatiously at the site of her tailbone, drawing his immediately riveted attention to that beckoning female curve of sleek waist blending into voluptuous backside. Her skin glittered with water, both real and reflected, hundreds of beads of the liquid sliding down to rejoin the surface of the lake. With her hair swept forward for washing, her long, arching spine was exposed, a palette of perfect, golden skin. She was shaped like a sculpture depicting the epitome of womanhood, strong, curved, and lush with the impression of fertility.

Elijah completely forgot about where he had been headed, his fingers curling into fists in reflection of the inexplicable desire instantly coiling throughout his body. He should have looked away, turned away, run away. He should have done any one of a thousand things except stand there gawking at her like some pubescent boy who had never seen a naked woman before. Though the initial breeze he had been following had picked up, he felt as if there wasn't an ounce of oxygen in the room. He could not explain or control the effect she had on him. All he could do was struggle to breathe, and continue to watch every alluring movement the siren in the water made as her flawless body sang its riveting, seductive song.

Even the wind betrayed him, he realized a heartbeat later. It skimmed over her wet body, full of October cold, and he saw it ripple over her unblemished skin in an ever-expanding carpet of goose bumps. It worked down from her shoulders, along that length of feminine spine, until it was sprawling over her bottom and meeting the waterline.

Siena turned slightly, throwing back her heavy head of hair, releasing an arc of sparkling water from it all the way up into the air where it almost touched the stalactites reaching down from the cavern ceiling above her. She turned a little farther, her hand trailing in a playful pattern over the surface of the water, her breasts swaying gently with the motion of her reaching arm. Elijah's smallest remaining breath escaped him as his darkened eyes burned over her bare form. Siena's muscular fitness might have made some females look too masculine, but the smoothness of the curve from hip into waist, from waist back out to rib cage, and continuing on up into full, perfectly lush breasts, spoke of a creature who was made to be the most pristine of feminine lures to any male with a pair of eyes in his head.

Elijah's gaze became riveted to the dark definition of her nipples, a blended rose and tan color that was boldly offset by the golden color of her skin. They were crested into an attractive thrust from the chilled temperature of the water and air, the effect eddying out into gooseflesh that crept over both breasts. Outside of those little puckered pores, her skin was immaculate and looking every inch as satin soft as he knew it was. She was unbelievably perfect, so well formed, and so beautiful she had the power to literally stop his heart. His chest hurt with the sensation, but not as much as the sudden, blinding urge to go to her did. He could smell her, feel her as every hair on his body became erect, making him feel as though his very skin was reaching toward her. Every sense and natural device for sensing demanded more input.

In the water, the Lycanthrope Queen went still very suddenly. Her head cocked to one side in awareness, her nose twitching as she scented the air in order to identify what exactly it was that she had already begun to intuit on other levels as being amiss. Siena had just identified the familiar scent of masculine musk when she heard the abrupt sound of water splashing behind her.

She whirled around just in time to spin into the warrior's arms.

Siena gasped as Elijah hauled her up against his body with one powerful arm, seizing her by her hair with his opposite hand. His mouth was on hers in an instant, giving her no time to even anticipate or react. Having lived a life of protected privilege and marked reserve when it came to any kind of physical contact, Siena had never been seized in such a manner. No one with an ounce of sense would have dared to do such a thing. She would have thought her initial reaction to such an action would be something in the nature of a definitive, violent slapdown.

Instead, it was great shock that caused her to inadvertently accept his kiss. The warrior was demanding, just shy of being brutal, and reflecting to her every feeling he had been inundated with during his unnoticed moments of observing her. Siena came to life an instant later, finally trying to push away, her hands going to the enormous wall of his chest. But she felt the bulk of the bandage that yet remained over the most serious of his wounds and instinctively resisted any pressure that would potentially reopen the healing flesh. Even to save herself, for some reason, Siena could not bear the thought of causing him harm. She was not that noble a creature in general, and certainly not when she was feeling threatened, so the impulse to protect him left her baffled and disoriented.

By the time she had finished curbing her escape impulse and contending with her feelings of confusion, she was being swamped by a thousand other sensations and emotions.

All of them were centered around heat.

So much amazing, delicious heat. Heat from his body burning its strength and form into hers as if she were a soft putty meant to take the impression of his fit into the memory of her own shape. They were like a puzzle. Two pieces cut apart but always meant to be perfectly reunited at some future point. They locked together like the flow of nature, thigh to thigh, belly to belly, and breast to breast. Even the water running down her steaming skin could not come between that perfect seal. There was heat from her body burning into his, blazing in places she had never felt such intensity before. The sensation was so baffling as it ran along her entire body, even the incongruous places like the small of her back, under her arms, and the soles of her feet, that it was just shy of being ticklish.

She could not laugh at it, though. She was far too engaged by his kiss to even consider it. His mouth was like a demanding and wet fire, his velvet tongue thrusting past her teeth to demand reciprocation from hers, leaving more licking flames in his wake as he went. Had she ever thought his lips to be almost feminine? He was nothing but male, the fit of his lips skilled and aggressive and very, very masculine in their flavor and force. He was drinking from her mouth in long, satisfying drafts, until Siena could hardly catch her breath. She felt her body bowing backward. She was being held so tightly that her body was forced to fit into the aggressive lean of his embrace. Her hair skimmed through the water, the ends recoiling in shock at the contrast of the cold in the face of all that heat. The very same cold she had been enjoying only seconds ago.

Elijah did not know what was propelling him to do what he was doing, and for that blissful moment he didn't much care. Her sweet mouth, her feminine body, her increasing warmth—all suited him with inexplicable precision. She was passive with her shock at first, but it faded rapidly as her senses and sensuality were held in rapt attention by his actions. It was only a matter of a minute before her long, deft fingers were weaving deeply into his hair, sending chills of erotic awareness down his spine as she held him to her mouth and commenced an aggressive seeking of her own.

Siena's tongue slipped over his, slinking across his taste buds and into his mouth with astounding womanly demand. She was just as curious, just as dominant in her nature as he was. The warrior groaned as her sweet, erotic flavor filled his senses, her bold, sweeping tongue forcing every nerve in his body into a clutching clarity of sensation. She tasted like cinnamon and honey, spice and sweetness. It was a confection of flavor and feeling he could not remember ever knowing before, or imagine ever feeling again. She made a small sound, then an aggressive one that sounded like a growl as it radiated past his lips. What that simple sound did to his body was purely indescribable. Like molten *iron* it burned through him, scorching him, an agony, a heat of pain and pleasure that hardened every muscle, every plane of his body.

Elijah's hands were suddenly surrounding her face, cupping it between his palms as he pulled her away from his mouth. It took an entire minute to accomplish the separation, the delight of her mouth impossible to part from as much, it seemed, as it was for her to part from his. Their mouths glistened with the passionate exchange of flavor, each now residing on the other's sense of taste for what seemed to be all time. When he finally could look at her face, the sound of her rapid breath and the sight of her flushed skin were damning. But they were nothing compared to the liquid, golden desire in her dilated eyes. Had she not looked at him as she was doing in that moment, he might have convinced himself that he was prepared to back off from her. It was a self-deception no matter which way it was viewed, however, because his entire body was gripped by opposing desires, none of which intended on going in any direction other than toward her.

They remained separated for all of a few heartbeats, and then he dragged her back to his mouth and into the dominant planes of his hard body, seemingly just as she lunged back into him to imprison him with her own needs. She made one of those primitive sounds that made his blood boil in his veins, urging his hands to her supple back in order to seal her to himself as tightly as the lick of a tongue sealed an envelope.

Elijah felt her on so many levels. Her body, so lush and aroused, locked tightly against his so that he felt every curve, every beat of her heart, and every swell of her breasts as she drew for air. Her eyes were wide open, bold and brave and mesmerizing as they locked with his. He had never realized how arousing, how enthralling such a simple thing could be. She was the purest art of courage, clearly blanketed with awe and delight as she absorbed his taste, his scent, and the press of his urgent, hardened body. Her fingertips slid with silky elegance down the length of his back, all the way from his shoulders to the edge of the towel slung low around his hips. The return trip up his spine bludgeoned him with sensation and a shaft of heat that clutched brutally down his belly and into his groin.

Elijah jerked his mouth from hers, gasping as hard as she was for that broken moment, but then she was being dragged up high against his body by his hands, her knee hooking over his hip in sensual aggression, her bruised and beautiful mouth already opening for him as he understood she was not in any frame of mind to tolerate his doubts, if indeed he had any, any longer.

It was beyond the fact that she tasted so fine, so sweet. It was how she boldly stroked and played with him. It was the way her essence seemed to become branded upon him. It was also the clarity with which he came to understand that it was exactly the same for her. Somehow, he was as perfect for

Siena as she was perfect for him. In all those ways, and so
many, many more.

Elijah ravaged her full mouth like a man starved for
breath after nearly drowning. He took everything about her
kiss deeply into himself, feeling it scorch through his body
like wildfire.

It was utter insanity.

Siena should have been the last woman on earth he would
have touched. She should have throttled the bloody hell out
of him like he was very aware she could. Instead, she had
burst into willing flame, her heat licking over and through
him until he thought he would become only ashes in her
hands. Ashes she could blow away with the softest puff of
cinnamon-sweet breath. Elijah learned how to feel an entirely
new level of arousal. He was hard and heavy with it, the sensation a raging demand that would brook no denials, no refusals. He felt the message urgently. There was only one way
to be satisfied, only one woman who could accomplish it,
only one refuge that would be home to the throbbing hunger
clawing through him. Elijah knew she was aware of his state
of appetite. She moved like liquid need herself, her body
rubbing against his with blatant suggestion. She reminded
him of her nudity, of her heated nearness, of how easy she
was making it for him to simply shed any remaining barriers
between them and find his heaven deep, oh so deep inside
her.

Elijah could feel her hair coiling around his wrist and
forearm, the erotic, living strands caressing him like thousands of tiny hands. Her actual hands were sprawling over
the expanse of his chest, his shoulders . . . down his back and
over the muscles of his backside. The touch made him shudder against her and he felt her sound of satisfaction vibrating
into his mouth. She slid those seeking fingers down to his
thighs, then reversed course back over his buttocks, this time
beneath the heavy weight of the saturated towel slug so carelessly around his hips.

This time he was the one uttering a primal growl, accompanying it with an abrupt burst of movement. The warrior broke his kiss and hauled her up out of the water with one arm around her waist. He heard her release a short, delighted laugh that was pure sexual invitation. She wrapped her hands around the back of his head as his actions brought her breasts to the level of his mouth.

"Yes," she said, the word a hiss of demand and urgency.

He smiled wickedly with his own dominant satisfaction before touching his tongue to one rigid nipple. She threw her head back, sounding out with more encouragement, almost begging him between her needful sounds and twisting body. At last, Elijah drew the crested peak of her nipple into the warmth of his mouth. Fire burned over his tongue, against her skin, flashing into both their bodies with a rage of demands. Siena arched wildly in response as he laved and suckled her, her cries echoing through the cavern in a way that fiercely contented the male animal within him. He was Demon. He was elemental to the earth within which they now sheltered. He was the very breath of life, every gasp of passion, every moan of pleasure. Wind. Breath. Tempest. All of it. And he made her feel it, the thoughts pushing out of him with an almost violent intent, like the fury of nature's storm.

Her fingers gripped convulsively at his hair, pulling it in a way that might have been painful under other circumstances, but only served to deepen the rage of need that flowed so violently between them. He tasted and caressed her without mercy or moderation, holding her to himself with a single arm so he could feel her opposite breast fitting into his palm. Wind poured into the cavern, as if in attempt to cool down the fire that had burst to life within the lake. Siena's hair whipped about them both, blending with his own as the long, loose waves flowed into the demanding breeze.

Siena was blinded by the pleasure his touches and tongue sent streaming through her brain. The entire cavern felt as if it were spinning madly around her. Could a touch truly evoke this much sensation? How could anyone bear so much of a thing without going completely insane? If she were not experiencing it firsthand, she would never have believed it. Even so, she wondered if she had not completely lost her mind, if this was not, perhaps, all a wondrous, riveting hallucination.

She felt herself sliding over his skin, the perspiration that sheeted them making it a slinky, damp slide of flesh and moisture. He somehow managed to hold her to himself with the ease of his impressive strength and yet make her feel as if she was being inundated with his touch. His skillful hands and determined mouth were surrounding her so that every moment was a new experience of fiery arousal and irrepressible sounds of pleasure.

Siena's legs had linked around his waist, and Elijah could feel the ready moisture and urgent heat of her body pressed low to his belly. He caught the heady, precious scent of her as he pulled her up even farther, his mouth trailing kisses and licks of his tongue down her breastbone to her quivering stomach. He was overwhelmed with pounding desires. His head was full of his need and hers. It was almost as though he could hear her begging for a certain touch from him, more pressure from his sucking mouth, the urge to feel him intimately between her grasping thighs.

It was too much to be borne, and Elijah was urgently in need of responding to it all. He swung her full around and surged through the water to put her on her back at the edge of the pool. She gasped at the coldness of the stone, then at the fire in the touch of his hands as he stroked them up the insides of her thighs, over her hips, waist, and breasts, and then just as boldly reversed his path.

Siena felt him grip her hip, sliding her toward him over the slick floor. Her heart beat violently with a combination of arousal and natural fear. She had never known such intimacies as she was experiencing in that moment. Indeed, she

had spent a lifetime avoiding anything that would even re-
motely bring her thoughts to such a point, never mind her
body. She had never expected to know this. She had never
suspected it could be like this. His touch was wicked, purposeful, stroking over her flat stomach, her hips, through the
soft, golden curls that had never, ever known the touch of a
man.

He bent over her, a hand pressed to the stone to bear his
weight slightly as his divine mouth drifted over her belly,
licking a soft trail that echoed the one he'd left with his hand.
Siena felt the silky invasion of skilled fingers, stroking, parting wet, feminine flesh that barely understood why it craved
such a touch so very much. She heard him exhale harshly
against her skin as he sought gently for . . . what, she could
not guess in that numbing moment. Strangely, she imagined
she knew his thoughts in that instant. He was astounded by
her heat, wild about how easily his touch slid over her pliant,
welcoming flesh. Siena released a throaty cry as his contact
evoked yet another sensation unlike anything she had ever
known before. It was strange and strong, deep and light, all
these sensations at once. But above all else, it was pure pleasure.

For that single, astounding moment of nothing but completely overwhelming awareness, Siena understood that she
wanted this powerful man with every fiber of her being. She
wanted to feel the rock-hard press of his muscled body over
hers, wanted to sculpt with her hands the stony sinew he had
built on centuries of battlefields. Every instinct in her
screamed for her to grasp for his hips, to guide him up to
where she burned so badly for him. Her thighs ached to cradle him; her empty body ached for it even more. Though her
body was far ahead of her, her mind at last comprehended
what was happening. She was moments away from a mating
that promised to be beyond anything she had ever imagined,
and she knew she had never wanted anything more in all of
her life.

That was the very same realization that, only a moment later, made her cry out with a sound of pure, unadulterated fear. Panic suddenly overwhelmed her, breaking through the haze she had been entangled in since Elijah had first seized her. The terror was virginal and primal, triggering every defensive instinct within her. Before Siena could comprehend it for herself, she was suddenly shape-shifting into the catamount. She screamed out with her misery and her pain, starting out with the sound of a tormented woman, ending with the wail of a frightened cougar.

The warrior Demon suddenly found himself touching smooth fur and leaning into the center of wicked, flailing claws. Elijah leapt away from the sudden feel of feline sinew, his shock erupting in a vocalized announcement just as loud as hers as he suddenly realized what had happened. He fell back into the frigid water as he lost his balance, but reemerged quickly, shaking water back from his hair with a single, sharp motion of his head and hands.

The gold cat scrabbled to gain its feet, claws skittering madly over the smooth stone surface as it bolted into a dark corner of the cavern, leaving white scrape marks in her wake. Elijah could see her cowering, hunched over, clearly terrified out of her senses. The magnificent creature shook with such violence of fear that he could not even distinguish the blur of her whiskers.

He braced his hands on the stone floor, bowing his head as he drew in deep breaths to try and cleanse himself of the sexual high he had been running on so blindly, a high that even his rude dunking into frigid water had not swayed. He was trying to force himself to make sense of her and of himself. After a painful moment in the chill water, he hauled himself out of the shallow pool, gaining his feet slowly as he kept his eyes on the great feline whose fur was spiked out in all directions from ruff to tail tip. He could see now that her whiskers were full forward, ears laid back as flat as she could get them, her enormous eyes wide and alert, oval pupils expanded in the darkness of her corner.

Elijah ran a thoughtful hand over his slicked-back hair, going over everything he knew about her and her kind as well as what it was he thought must have frightened her. He wasn't at all sure about the latter, guessing only that she had come to her senses where he had not. But the former told him she was likely to be more animal than woman at this moment, and he had best choose the right course of action, or there would be quite a brutal hell to pay for it.

There was nothing more deadly than a cornered cat, and he would be the first to admit that he did not have it in him to survive an attack in his present state. If the beast even so much as pinned him in a fit of rage, it would go right for the gaping wound in his chest, happily finishing the job of ripping his heart out.

Elijah slowly dropped to one knee, everything forgotten except the desire to rectify the situation of the moment. He began by looking down at her paws and not directly into her large eyes. The crouch was giving her an open invitation to attack him, but he hoped his next actions would belay that recourse.

The warrior blinked very slowly and lowered his head in a motion of broadcast submission. He realized in that painful instant that his pride meant very little in the face of seeing a creature so brave suddenly scared out of its courage, its grace, and its beautiful spirit. He would not have seen her thus for all the victories in the world, and he felt it keenly. It was an empathy he had not realized himself capable of until that very instant.

Elijah was not looking directly at her, so he had to use his other senses to their utmost in order to understand her reactions. He could scent her high level of fear, feel on his skin the wary, adrenalized prickles of it. He could hear her move ever so slightly and it made his heart skip a beat in anticipation. Her claws scraped over stone as she settled low onto her belly, the first movement in the dance that would follow.

The catamount spent a minute in the position, pretending to be relaxed when instead she was quite alert. The next step in the ritual was when she rose onto all fours and walked slowly away. The more she pretended he was unimportant, the bolder she became. It was a dangerous dance, for all the posturing involved. The most deadly moment would be when she was in striking distance. She would make the choice to bat his head from his shoulders with the swipe of one powerful paw or choose a different form of aggression to put him in his place. By the time she got that close to him, Elijah was beaded with perspiration and fighting a serious bout of fatigue. The ritual had taken a great deal out of a man too soon from his sickbed. But he still did not budge, wanting with every fiber of his being to make up for whatever part of this was caused by his unthinking behavior.

The mountain lioness was so close now he could feel the warmth of her breath and see the gleam of her collar out of the corner of one eye. She extended one paw in a long, tentative reach. Her claws were sheathed, which was an awfully calming piece of information. Still, he could not move. She had not judged him completely.

She sprang so suddenly that Elijah tensed involuntarily. It took every ounce of control he had not to protect himself, instead rolling with her as her powerful jaws clamped onto his neck. His chest heaved with his heightened breath, but he let her continue. All she needed to do was tighten her grip a fraction of an inch and she would puncture his carotid artery or break his neck.

But the hold was meant only to send a message. This was her territory and she was in charge. He would never frighten her again, the grip communicated to him, and if he did, the grasp she had on his neck would not be so harmless next time.

Siena let go after a very long minute, settling back on her

haunches as the pupils of her eyes began to round out. The huge cat shook her head and began to change into the woman once more. Elijah sat up slowly once she had re-formed completely. Siena remained sitting crouched before him on all fours, eyeing him cautiously. Her hair was wound around her protectively, concealing her bare body in a defensive gesture. It disturbed him because he knew Lycanthropes were rarely shy of parading around in a nude state. The idea that he had terrified her into second-guessing the habit did not sit easily on his stomach. He did not blame her at all, though.

Siena looked at the Demon with wide, cautious eyes, trying to make sense of everything she was feeling. He finally met her gaze, but remained as silent as the grave. His eyes were a swirl of numerous shades of green, the chaos of color reflective of how she was feeling.

How had she let this happen? Why had it happened? Demons and Lycanthropes were as different as cats and dogs. At least, that was the common view in both their societies. If that was true, then how had this been able to occur? They should not have been chemically compatible, never mind the fact that mentally they were in some ways still at war with one another. There was no denying, however, that they had been more than compatible, chemically and otherwise. Her body still, after all this passed time, burned with the memory of his touch and the depth of his passion. What was more, it boiled with her reciprocation of it, of the very clear message that it was perturbed with its unsatisfied yearnings for him. She felt hollow and unfulfilled, felt as though he had vacated her very soul when he had been forced to pull away in defense of himself.

The Queen rose to her feet, turning her back on him and padding quickly into the next room. She felt better once she had dropped another of the loose baby-doll dresses over her head, this one as green as his eyes had been when he had kissed her. She brushed the backs of her fingers over her mouth, feeling the bruises and memory-provoking soreness of her lips. She felt him approaching, her thoughts swirling with a confusion of what she was feeling and what she imagined he was feeling. She was grateful when he did not stop to talk to her, instead retreating into the bedroom. When he was gone, she sank down into the nearest seat and exhaled silently.

Siena could not believe what she had almost done. If things had gone much further, her entire life would have changed dramatically, provided there was such a thing as a life after a mistake of such incomprehensible proportions. She was the sole ruler of her people, no mate, no children, and had never wished for either. The ruling class of her people had one distinctive trait, and that was the fact that when they mated, it would be for life. There were several species that carried this trait, such as wolves and swans, just as there were the polygamous animals, like horses and deer, who changed partners not only year to year, but sometimes moment to moment.

But no matter what the form the ruling monarch took, he or she was driven to mate once and for always. One mate for all time. It was historically believed that this was in order to assure the fidelity and purity of the royal line. The royal's mate would also succumb to this loyalty to monogamy. How this was accomplished, no one knew for certain. They suspected it was a genetic virus of some kind, rather like the one that caused a Demon to trigger the birth of power in a specific Druid. Perhaps one day they would know for certain.

This was why Siena had chosen to remain absolutely celibate, letting no male anywhere near her in a way that would tempt her. She did not want a mate, and she absolutely refused to share her reign with a man who would become her equal in her monarchy just because she had taken him to her bed. In fact, she actively despised the notion of mating with a male who, in the event of her death, could potentially gain her throne.

If Elijah had taken her body in that one wild moment, he could very well have written out both their executions. Fourteen years of peace was not enough of a base on which to lay making a Lycanthrope King out of a Demon. As adored and lauded as she was, the chances of rebellion and overthrow of her reign would have been an unfathomable and inexcusable risk.

The next thing of importance after that would be the very concept of being forced to spend the rest of her life as part of a pair. Part of a pair that included a male who didn't trust a single thing about her. Bad enough to be forced to bear the lifelong company of any male, but this Demon warrior? He had sent so many of her people to their deaths during her father's war, and, even though she had learned to be wiser than her male parent, the families of those the warrior had slain would have disemboweled her as a traitor to her kind, seeing to it her carcass was dragged from here to the original Russian province they had hailed from for daring such an abomination.

How had she ended up in his arms? Why had he even pursued her? True, they had never personally battled each other, but they were the harshest representatives of their people, who had done so for centuries. The idea of kissing, of wanting such a man in any way?

What in the nine hells had gotten into her? Into him?

And why couldn't she erase the feel of him from not only the front of her mind, but the entirety of her body, both inside and out? Her skin was humming even now. Also, she could feel something else, a depth in her body and in her thoughts she had never known existed. She now could name this hollow, clawing sensation for the hunger of desire that it was. Had she not been paying attention to her own thoughts? It was utter insanity to go on feeling such a thing for even one second more! She should be shamed that she had allowed him such intimacies with her body, not continue to crave them.

The Queen rose to her feet, no longer able to sit still. She absently rubbed a palm over her flat stomach as she began to pace the width of the room. She felt as if he had somehow embedded his presence into her, staining her permanently. They had not mated, so why then did she feel as if his very essence was already swimming inside her womb? She was confused, taunted by his scent on her body, struggling with both the human and feline memories of the past days in his presence.

In spite of herself, she was impressed by the way he had handled the cat in its frightened state. She was aware of it now, now that she had changed back, but in those minutes she had been nothing but the puma, more likely to snap his neck in two than anything else. By all rights, she should have been so threatened by him as to gut him on the spot. But instead, the cat had run away. Hidden. Just as the lions in the wilds would do when threatened by anything they deemed more powerful than themselves.

But then to approach him once more and use such a low-aggression mode of punishment for frightening her into the change?

Siena loped up the stairs as her emotions threatened to overwhelm her, hurrying as far from him as she could without exiting the cave. However, it was no better for her in that place near the pool. The room reeked of pheromones and the scent of sexual arousal. Hers and his. It seemed no matter where she turned, she could not escape him. And the sunlight streaming through the trees outside prevented her from bolting into the comfort of the forest.

The Queen bit back a sob, twisting her hands together violently and biting down hard on her bottom lip. She would not do this weak, feminine thing called tears. She had never once cried in all of her life and she would be thrice damned before she would do so over a Demon male. Still, she could not escape the feelings of confinement that rushed through her, the rampant emotions, the confusion of thoughts that seemed permanently tainted with impressions of his.

Siena suddenly, blindly, leapt for the entrance to the cave. She was barely six yards into the sun before Elijah's arm hooked around her waist and hauled her back against his rigid body. She screamed, kicking and struggling against his hold. She would have made it impossible for him to hold her if not for the quick effect of the sun on her physiology.

The light bored into her with astounding speed. In that moment she was susceptible to it in a way she had never experienced before. Had even this changed about her? she wondered with despair as he swung her up into his arms and strode back into their shelter. By the time she was safely shielded, she was already quite nauseated from her exposure. He took her straight back to the bedroom and laid her in the bed, pressing a cool hand to her burning face.

"Are you insane?" he asked softly, the phrase void of the reproach it should have held. It was the brimming concern that was in the question and in his touch that finally broke her. She sobbed once, hard, and then burst into full-blown tears.

Shamed, she tried to turn her face away, but he cupped her cheek in his palm and prevented her from doing so. Elijah, the ruthless Demon warrior, then proceeded to catch each and every tear with his calloused fingers, hushing her softly under his breath, reaching to take her hand in his.

"Siena, please," he begged softly, his fingers moving faster from one cheek to the other to catch the saltwater misery. "I am so sorry. More sorry than you will ever know. I did not mean to hurt you like this. Please, kitten, you are killing me. Please, stop."

But the gentler he was, the more it seemed to hurt. And she had no idea why. After a moment he gave up on keeping her tears out of her hair and, with a strong tug on her captive hand, he drew her up into a comforting embrace. He pressed his hand to the back of her head, holding her face in the curve of his neck, her cheek pillowed on one broad shoulder. She felt his hand move over her back, rubbing gently, soothingly, in one direction only.

How did he know that it would be the most comforting way to touch her? Like a cat who could only bear its fur being stroked in a single direction, she was filled with a powerful sense of comfort and relaxation. She felt the change flushing through her as he petted her so perfectly.

"Siena, listen to me," he said softly. "You are done here. Your duty to my King is done. Come dark, I will leave this place and return home. You will not see me again. I swear to you . . ."

"No. You are not yet well enough," she protested, pulling back to look directly in his eyes. "I committed myself to your care and I will see it through. I . . . I am just . . ." Siena shook her head, unable to find words as she pushed away the last remnants of her weak tears.

"You have to realize what's behind all of this," he urged her quietly, touching fingers to her chin to lift up her eyes. "Samhain is only a week away. Your species is as afflicted by it as mine is. Demons are cursed by the moon of this month to desire nothing more than to mate, however misdirected it may be, with any beautiful humanoid that catches their eye."

Elijah took a deep breath, looking away from her golden eyes and the liquid lure within them that still tempted him. As much as he was forcing himself to believe his own explanation, he couldn't escape the haunting feeling in the center of his gut that whispered with sinister amusement that there was far more to it than that.

"Yes," Siena agreed, latching on to the explanation with gratitude. "Yes, you are right. I had forgotten about how it affects your kind. The effect is not the same for my people. Not exactly. But our animal sides become very dominant during this time. Instincts such as mating are so overwhelming that . . . that they disrupt normal good judgment."

"Then you understand that, if I don't leave, this will potentially happen again?" he asked.

"Perhaps. Perhaps not now that we are aware of it. Regardless of this . . . this trouble, you cannot leave. I know enough about Demons to know that you cannot shift form while you are this badly injured without risking your life. I will not have you ruining all my hard-won efforts to mend you."

Feeling relieved and exhausted all at once, Siena rested back into the pillows of the bed, ignoring the urge to rub her cheek over the pillow so heavily scented with him.

Elijah could see she was ill, despite the fact that she was still trying to act like his nurse. Her dash into the bright fall sun, none of it blocked by the bared branches of the autumn trees, had done significant damage. The Lycanthropes called it sun poisoning. He had seen it up close before, and the effects were unmistakable. She was pale, her skin faded from its usual golden luster, and her usually springy hair hung limply around her.

"You're bleeding again," she murmured, reaching to touch the bandage over his chest wound. "The water disturbed the bandage's seal."

"It will dry. Don't worry about it." Elijah reached to take her hand from him but found he was unable to release it once he had it in his palm again.

He forced himself to let her go by standing up and walking out of the room. He returned shortly with a cup of water, but she had fallen asleep during the time it had taken. He sat back down on the opposite side of the mattress, exhaling long and slow. He turned the cup around in his hands, an idle occupation as he tried to settle his thoughts.

Siena might not know it, but Elijah had broken several laws the moment he had laid hands on her. Demon law was very specific about such things. Frankly, he was amazed the Enforcer wasn't already descended upon him, determined to see him punished as he ought to be. It would be just his luck that the one time he needed such intervention, Jacob was busy with his wife and newborn.

Elijah's entire body ached. And, he realized, it wasn't all from the pain of his healing wounds. Somehow, she had gotten under his skin, this hauntingly beautiful creature. He would be lying to himself if he tried to convince himself it was all about physicality. There was something in her spirit, in her manner, that beckoned to him. It had been doing so since the day they had met six months back.

He had never believed Gideon's plan to imprison himself in the Lycanthrope court would come to anything but the medic's swift demise. But the results had surprised him, even as he continued to mistrust them. Even after the Queen had declared an end to the war, he had walked around waiting for the other shoe to drop. The shoe that would kick them back into war just when they were beginning to relax. However, since he had met her, he'd known she was unlike any changeling he'd ever encountered before. He had even begun to feel more confident in this peace she had so artfully finagled out of her aggressive people.

Exhausted, Elijah set the cup aside and dropped back onto the pillow beside the one the Queen rested on. He turned his head to look at her. All he saw was the delicate fronds of gold lashes against her paled cheeks. For some reason he fixated on that elegant detail, finding himself curious over how fragile they seemed. As if they could break under the slightest touch. He had never thought to equate her with anything delicate or breakable. She was a woman of formidable strength, and he would be a fool to think of her in any other manner. But there was an underlying innocence within her.

It had nothing to do with the fact that he was aware she had never taken a lover. He knew the condition that came with that, and knew that was why she had been so terrified of what had almost happened between them. But it was something deeper than just the physically virgin state of her body.

Perhaps at some point he would understand what it was he thought he sensed, but it was likely never going to happen. Once they parted from this place, the only time they would ever see each other would be during functions at Noah's court that would include her. If he had anything to say about it, they would not meet even then. He was determined to keep his distance from that moment on. He was a warrior, trained in the utmost forms of discipline, and he could easily do this.

Elijah's eyes drifted closed, making him more aware of the confection of her scent. What was most compelling about it, he thought as he drifted into sleep, was that it blended so well with his own.

CHAPTER 4

Noah pushed away one of the dusty tomes that had come from the great Demon library, an archive of their vast history and prophecies located in the dungeons of his castle home. There were three of the enormous books awaiting his attention, but he ignored them and began to pace the floor of the Great Hall in a sign of agitation he had found himself repeating far too often these past two days.

To say he was worried would have been an understatement. In spite of the fact that the Captain of his armies had gone missing, uncharacteristically without a single word to anyone as to where he would be, he should know Elijah well enough after all these centuries to realize the warrior was quite capable of taking care of himself. But these were volatile times. Enemies and prophecies, Druids being rediscovered and hybrid children born with potentially new and powerful abilities. Men and women suddenly Imprinting on one another with a frequency their race had not enjoyed for over a thousand years, if indeed they had ever enjoyed it at all.

This was why he was researching tomes of knowledge, history, and prophecy that had the dust of the ages on them.

Some of them had not been opened in over a millennium, hiding secrets and thoughts that not even Gideon, a millennium old himself, knew about. He was hoping that within them he would find clarity in all of the chaos of the time. However, the archaic nature of the ancient Demon language made the going slow and difficult.

The best scholar for this task would be Isabella, the female Enforcer. However, despite the fact that Isabella's Druidic powers included the ability to easily translate the Demon language in all its forms through the ages, it simply was not possible for a new mother to devote herself to such an intensive study so soon after giving birth.

Scholars like the King were seeking the answers for problems in the present in the works and prophecies of the past. Destiny meant a great deal to Demonkind, both individually and as a society. It was very much like a religious experience for them, to follow the purest path to their destinies, watching prophecies become truth in the present, forming into wondrous history.

It was this that had made Ruth and Mary's betrayal of their people so hard to grasp early on. It was practically unheard of. Noah realized, however, that the female traitors bent on causing heartache and mayhem thought, in their warped perception, that their paths were just as destined as anyone else's. And, Noah supposed, there was probably truth in that. Not every path was destined to be one of moral good and soulful clarity. If that were the case, there would be no wars, no violence.

In the minds of these traitors, these acts of vengeance against their own brethren were justified, even righteous. The siege last May, just before Beltane, had been a brutal act of retribution aimed at Jacob the Enforcer at first, but then had spread like a virulent poison to include all of Demonkind. Since then, Demons had suffered under the hands of these turncoats repeatedly, victims of damaging guerilla tactics with little or no reason to them. If the past six months gave them anything to be aware of, it was that enemies were all around—some closer than they would have ever expected.

All of this lent a strong hand to a worry for a missing comrade the King would normally never consider worrying about.

There was a cry from near the fireplace across the Great Hall, and Noah immediately left his volatile thoughts behind and hurried to the delicate crib the cry had come from. He reached into it, scooping up the littlest bit of a baby into his big hands, taking a moment to tuck the infant girl into the crook of one arm, a blanket wrapped warmly around her.

"So, sweet," he said conversationally to her, "you have something to say about this?"

The babe, little more than two weeks old, who could barely hold her head in a single position for long, made her face squish up even tighter than it naturally was, making the Demon King laugh in spite of himself.

"You are going to be just like your parents, I think. Will you be my Enforcer one day, sweet? Fetching wayward Demons back to me for the punishment they so very much deserve?"

Noah turned his body to ease himself into his favorite seat before the fire. The Demon lifted up his hand and playfully began to light his fingers on fire, making the flame jump from one fingertip to the next, with a speed that made the baby go wide-eyed. She thrashed arms and legs in her excitement, reaching for him, but he made sure he kept the playful lights far out of her reach. She screeched in infant frustration.

"Shh," he whispered. "If your mother knew, she would have my royal head."

Noah grinned and put out his flames with the same passing thought that had lit them. The Fire Demon then reached to stroke warmed fingers over the silky cap of black curls on her head.

"I am quite put out that your parents chose Elijah to be your *Siddah* over me. However, I understand they anticipate you will be too much of a handful for a man busy running an entire species. And no," he continued, stretching out his long legs and linking them at the ankles, "I most certainly did not appreciate your mother's jest about possibly having a family of my own by then. It seems she is taking a great deal of delight in watching one Demon male after another fall under the wily spells of you females."

The baby blinked newborn blue eyes at him, then reached to grab one of his thick fingers with an amazingly strong grip so she could force it into her mouth.

"I am glad you see this my way," he laughed. "I am beginning to regret ever encouraging your father into your mother's arms. Not that I could have stopped him. But since that woman entered this castle, things have not been the same. If this keeps up, Elijah is going to walk through that door spouting love sonnets and children of his own. Bad enough my sister . . ."

Noah trailed off, his humor fading as his thoughts turned back to the missing warrior. Frankly, it would have suited him fine if Elijah would walk through the door, no matter what circumstances. It was not like him to disappear and not tell anyone where he could be found. Especially not with danger looming all around them.

Elijah had behaved like a madman these past months, working himself into the ground trying to find out everything he could about the cult of human females plotting against the Demons and other Nightwalkers. Running himself literally ragged with exhaustion as he hunted for the Demon betrayers, even though policing their own fell to Jacob's jurisdiction. The warrior did not know that Noah was aware of the fact that he had been requesting a great deal of healing services from the Body Demons in his corps. Several of these soldiers had reluctantly approached the King, full of loyalty to Elijah and not wanting to go over his head but terrified he was pushing himself into serious harm. Every one of them had tried to underplay the seriousness of the situation, but their eyes had said everything they were unwilling to. It was why Noah had instructed Elijah to attend a meeting with him yesterday.

Elijah would never have missed such an appointment. He was correct to a fault when it came to Noah's protocols, and he never ignored a summons, even if he had to drag himself to the chamber while close to death. For all his casual manners, Elijah was fiercely loyal, and it showed.

Noah exhaled, trying to calm his thoughts as he did so, turning his attention back to the baby in his arm.

"It appears you are hungry, little sweet. Your mama needs to come feed you before you nibble off my finger."

The babe ignored him, continuing her nibbling.

"I hardly think a baby without teeth can do much nibbling."

Noah looked up, startled to realize he had been so distracted by his thoughts that he had not been aware of the Enforcers' arrival. His eyes immediately went to Jacob's serious countenance as Isabella leaned over to scoop her child out of his hold. Noah knew the instant he looked into those dark eyes that the male Enforcer's news was not going to be good.

"Nothing at all?" Noah asked, his troubled emotions coming through far too clearly with the question.

As soon as Bella had her infant in her arms and had moved aside, cooing softly to her daughter, Noah was out of his chair and approaching Jacob, who was standing back away from his family. The Enforcers had been out looking for any sign of Elijah. A sure sign that Jacob was as worried about him as Noah was, was that Bella had left her newborn babe to go with him, and Jacob had allowed it without protest. Of course, it could be said that what he did and did not protest meant fairly little to the Druid Jacob was married to. Bella was a rather independent, modern woman with a sassy attitude and a will of her own that, it was safe to say, drove her husband up the wall as much as it delighted the hell out of him.

Noah moved back to the desk he had left only minutes earlier, his Enforcer following close at his side with his arms crossed over his athletic chest and his dark head lowered along with his voice.

"I do not understand this, Noah. I should have been able to track him anywhere. It is what I have been doing for all of my life. Especially during Samhain. You know my skills are at their sharpest now. But I followed him to Washington and then lost him completely."

"It rains so much there, Jacob, and you were a full day behind him when you started. It is understandable."

Jacob made a sound that broadcast to the King that he was not so forgiving of his failure as his monarch was. But that was Jacob's way. He had been, and would always be, extremely hard on himself for his failures. It did not matter that they were few and far between. All that mattered to the highly moral Earth Demon was that one failure would always be one failure too many.

"Isabella cannot escape the feeling that he is in trouble," Jacob said tensely, running a hand through his long, dark hair. "She was having so many premonitions back to back once we got to the end of his trail that I thought she was going to pass out from the overload."

That news made Noah look up at the female Enforcer quickly, for the first time noticing her drawn complexion and the way she was cradling her child as if desperate for her warmth and affection. This had been a harrowing task, and this ambiguous result had clearly taken its toll on Elijah's friends.

"What kind of premonitions?" the King forced himself to ask.

"Of battle. Of pain. She kept saying that she was blinded by blood. Even without that information, she didn't have to tell me she was certain something bad will happen or already has happened. I could feel it myself. The only thing I am glad of is that neither she nor I can be certain if he is alive or dead. She cannot say for sure if he has been Summoned. Did Ruth know Elijah's power name, Noah? Could she have given it to one of the necromancers and had him Summoned and imprisoned?" Jacob's hand clenched into a fist. "I swear on my child's soul, Noah . . . if that bitch forces me into the position of having to kill Elijah, I will not rest until I have her black heart in my hand."

Noah understood the Enforcer's rage and fear. If Elijah had been Summoned, the worst of all fates known to Demonkind, he would probably already be perverted into a dark, soulless monster who would be a powerful danger to every creature within his reach. The magic-users used pentagrams drawn and empowered by their vile magic in order to imprison a Demon whose power name they had obtained. Once the Demon was in this trap, it was almost impossible for it to be saved. It was Jacob and Bella's painful duty to destroy these monsters. But if Elijah had become such a creature, the pain the Enforcers would suffer for being forced to kill the Demon they had chosen to raise their child during the Fostering would be unimaginable.

Elijah meant as much to them as he did to the King and so, so many others. The morale of all of Noah's forces, so driven, guided, and flushed by Elijah's very powerful presence, would have a difficult time rallying after a tragedy of that magnitude. The loss of a Demon of Elijah's power and brilliance would devastate their entire race, and there was no need to mention the open wounds it would leave in dozens of hearts, including the heart of a King.

Noah's head was aching and he rubbed at his pounding temples. The tension since he'd first noticed something was not right was packed tightly into those two points. Here they were, two of the most powerful of their kind, and they were

at a loss? What a sad commentary on the future of their people, Noah thought in a rare, bitter moment of fatalism.

Noah pushed the feelings and the pain in his head aside
as he felt Isabella's approaching energy. She was drained and
worried enough without seeing him and Jacob looking thoroughly defeated. Of course, she could read her husband's
mind and emotions as easily as she could read her own, but
Noah was another matter. He was supposed to be the strength
of his people.

Noah turned with a smile to look at her and her baby.

"Hey, how is my newest subject?" he asked.

"Hungry, as noted," she said with a laugh. "I need to feed
her. I want you two to relax, have a drink, and wait till I get
back before you hash this over any more. I am your Enforcer
too, Noah, and I will not allow you to coddle me like some
fragile bird. Is that understood?"

She gave them both an extremely no-nonsense glare that
made them nod obediently.

"Good. If you are going to find Elijah, it's very likely you
will need me to—"

Bella broke off, her entire complexion turning a frightening
gray color as her eyes glazed over. Jacob reacted an instant
faster than Noah, grabbing her sinking body with one arm
while trying to catch the baby up against her with the other.
He managed quite well, making Noah's helping hands seem
superfluous as he reached to assist. As soon as she was
down, Jacob handed Noah his daughter and bent over his
wife to check her pulse and her clammy skin.

"This is too much. It is too soon after the baby for this to
keep happening to her," Jacob bit out as he watched his
beloved mate succumb to yet another harrowing vision, very
likely about Elijah and the fate he had met. "Noah, I think
we better call Gideon. The pregnancy was hard enough,
what with Ruth's attack on her and everything else. I do not
like her color, and her heart is racing at an insane pace."

"Legna is not here anymore," Noah reminded him. "The only way I can get her attention from here would be to set something near him on fire, and that is not exactly something I feel comfortable doing even with my skill."

"Well, I cannot exactly grow a tree under him either," Jacob barked, not marking the tone in his voice in his worry. "And I am too exhausted to drag him here as dust, even if he were not thousands of miles away. Put the baby in her crib and go find a Mind Demon who can either contact Legna so she can teleport them both here, or who can teleport him themselves."

Jacob and Noah both looked to Isabella when she uttered a hoarse, incomprehensible phrase. However, there was structure to it that Noah thought he recognized. Bella had an affinity for languages that had come with her Druidic powers, so it did not surprise him that a foreign tongue would be part of her visions.

Still, since neither of them recognized it offhand, it meant nothing to them until she came out of her visionary trance and could explain it to them. That was providing she could explain it. Bella's sight was often more cryptic than not.

"They get stronger and stronger and she gets weaker. What good is a hellish power like this?" her fearful husband asked bitterly. "Sometimes," he said hoarsely, "I wish I had never touched her. She would not be suffering like this if—"

"Jacob, stop it," Noah said sharply. "You do not mean that and you know it. You would be lost without her and you would not have this beautiful babe. I swear I am going to pass a law against the guilt you browbeat yourself with constantly. And Isabella will be happy to enforce it for me."

Noah moved across the room to settle the baby back into her crib. He twisted into a column of smoke a moment later, leaving his Enforcers behind as he sailed out of a window in search of help.

* * *

Magdelegna sat up out of a sound sleep with a loud, fearful cry. Instinctively, her hands slid over the little mound of her belly as if protecting the babe within from whatever had disturbed her. She was aware of Gideon coming awake beside her, sitting up and turning protectively toward her. Her husband instantly gathered her to himself, the warmth of his bare skin and fit, male form incredibly comforting as he wrapped his arms around her.

"What is it, *Neliss*?" he asked softly, pressing gentle lips to the curve of her cheek.

"A dream . . . I think," she said.

Gideon pulled back to lock his silvered gaze with hers, his equally silver brows pulling down in a frown of concern.

"You keep having these nightmares. I am beginning to wonder if this is not a form of premonition like Bella's. We have been waiting for some other changes in your abilities, perhaps it has been here all this time." Gideon reached to stroke the backs of his fingers slowly down the copious length of Legna's coffee-colored hair. "Tell me what you dreamed, *Nelissuna*."

"It was about Elijah. Something was very wrong. I cannot recall specifics though. Sweet Destiny, I despise this," she said wearily, rubbing at her temples. "If this is what you suspect, I see now why Bella dislikes this particular type of ability."

Gideon reached to touch gentle fingertips to Legna's forehead, closed his eyes a moment, sending a sensation of calm and healing energy into her. It relieved her tension instantly as she smiled a soft, contented smile.

It lasted for a second, then Legna gasped harshly, almost cracking her head into her husband's as she sat up once more, her eyes wide and her hand slamming into her forehead as she was bludgeoned with a painful cry of distress.

"Noah!"

"Okay, this is not a dream," Gideon said darkly, hurdling

over her to get out of bed and pull her to her feet. "What is occurring?"

"I do not know. We had better go. Right away."

"Agreed. Though I would recommend clothing before teleportation."

The jest was just what she needed, making her laugh softly in relief of tension. They dressed quickly and, minutes later, Legna was teleporting them the long distance to her brother's home.

Elijah was the first to wake well after night had fallen.

He opened his eyes and quickly became aware of his surroundings.

The first thing he noticed was that he was trapped beneath the weight of a heavily sleeping Lycanthrope female. His chest hurt, the healing wound being pulled by how she was sprawled over him, but he barely noticed it. Instead, he was fascinated by the slow creep of the soft tendrils of her hair as they slid over his skin.

He was completely entangled, between her hair and her limbs, but it was the touch of those living fingers of hair that truly held him still. The strands were twisted into satiny sheaves, snaking over his chest, around his biceps, over his hips and thighs with a breathtaking, subconscious sensuality. He had known about the changelings' living hair, unique to their species, for centuries, but only for purposes of defeating them. If the hair was bound up, the Lycanthrope could not change form. It could literally drive them out of their minds if they were left that way for a week or more. Also, if severed it could cause severe blood loss and could even kill them pretty much on the spot. A shearing of that kind would be similarly lethal to them as third-degree burns over a massive percentage of the body would mean almost certain death for a human.

He had never considered *this*, however—this silken caress that could stimulate a man from head to toe with its sensual touch. He was very aware of the agonizing response of his body, and that it seemed to draw the flirtatious touch of the curling locks. Elijah groaned softly as the ghosting caress skimmed erotically over the hardened steel of his aroused body. He felt the painful throb of his own pulse beneath that wicked, engulfing stroke. He could not even think, had no hope of devising a way of stopping this devastatingly perfect torture.

Siena literally purred in her sleep. The rumbling trill of sound vibrated from her entire torso, drumming like a gentle massage along the side of his body she was snuggled up against. Her leg slid restlessly over his, her calf slipping up toward his thigh, bringing her knee up between his legs. Elijah closed his eyes tightly, as if bracing for a dangerous impact, but he was not afraid of her causing him physical harm in the expected sense. He reached out to stay her with a hand on that traveling knee. Bad enough her hair was teasing the hell out of him, he didn't need the feel of her skin against him on top of it.

No matter how much he found himself craving it.

Elijah tried to take a deep, steadying breath, but all he did was fill his lungs with her sweet, tempting scent. He was sweating all along the left side of his body, where hers was so cozy against him. By virtue of her species, she was naturally several degrees hotter than his normal body temperature, but it seemed even more of an extreme in differences as she slept, her damp forehead rubbing restlessly against him. She reeked of their combined scents, just as he did, and he could not escape noticing how erotic and sensual a scent it was. His body throbbed deeply with surges of need, with inexplicable urges to roll over and slide her beneath him. Graphic fantasies played on from that point, involving her taste, her touch, and how hot she felt just along the outside of her body. It was agonizingly easy to understand just how that heat might feel if he were inside her.

His heart began to trip in double time as he realized he had better get as far away from her as he could before he made another Samhain-driven attack on her unsuspecting body. He was soon to realize, however, that disentangling himself from her hair was not going to be at all possible without her cooperation. Not unless he changed form, and, as she had pointed out earlier, it would not be the wisest thing for him to do. Wounds had a way of reopening and even worsening if not given proper healing before attempting such a shift in form. All but the iron wounds and the one in his chest had reached that healing point, but those remaining four would do enough damage.

His only choice was to wake her.

It was, of course, going to be incredibly embarrassing for her. If he could say he knew anything about her, he could definitely assure himself of that.

Elijah had a sudden idea.

He closed his eyes, concentrating carefully on the air in the room. He had to be very cautious, but he slowly lowered the oxygen level in the room. As the breathable air diminished, Siena's body reacted naturally with a cough reflex. She gasped slightly, her subconscious refocusing from whatever it was that compelled her seeking hair, to a more distinct self-preservation instinct.

He had gambled on those instincts, and they paid off.

She turned away from him restlessly, her hair releasing and surging into tight, protective coils around her. She coughed in earnest, surprisingly enough without awakening. Now that he was freed, everyone's pride intact whether it was realized or not, Elijah drew a fresh breeze into the room from the front of the cavern. Siena took several breaths immediately, the perspiration on her forehead evaporating in a minute.

Elijah launched out of the bed the minute he was able and backed away from her as if she were some kind of biological contaminant. But in a way, that was exactly what she was.

The warrior found a fresh towel to wrap himself in, making a mental note to get himself something resembling actual clothing as soon as possible. He moved into the next room quickly, running both hands through his tangled hair. His own movements made him aware of the fact that her scent was all over him. He swore solemnly as he marched to the biting cold of the mineral pool. It would set him straight like nothing else could in that moment. Leaving his "clothing" behind, he dropped into the pool and completely immersed himself in its startling cold. Being of the air, Elijah was an expert at manipulating his need for oxygen. He remained submerged for several minutes, until he was chilled to his core, before surfacing. He stood to check his bandages, shrugging off the fact that he had a trail of blood and water sliding down his belly. It was minute and well worth the removal of the enchanting scent Siena trailed around wherever she went.

He had to get the hell out of there.

This would only get worse the closer they got to Samhain and stayed together under the influence of the full moon. Certainly, when she woke, Siena would agree with him about abandoning this place and going separate ways.

Provided she was well enough.

But if he was asked, he would have said she seemed too damned healthy as it was.

Legna sat down in her husband's lap with a sigh, her head dropping onto his shoulder as she searched for comfort. Gideon's hand went to her back and rubbed it soothingly.

"She looks so pale," she murmured.

Gideon turned his eyes onto the woman who slept fitfully in the bed nearby. Legna was correct. Isabella was far too pale. In fact, she was anemic. It was a common ailment in human females after giving birth, and it had been exacerbated by all the exertion she had taken part in since then. It was something Gideon could not cure her of. Anemia in humans, even human/Druid hybrids, was caused by a lack of iron in the bloodstream. Iron was the one thing Gideon could not manipulate. Not without making himself very ill. He couldn't afford to make himself deathly ill when his wife was expecting and their daily life in the Lycanthrope court was still so potentially dangerous.

He could have performed a transfusion from her sister, Corrine, under normal circumstances, but Corrine and Kane, her husband, were nowhere to be found at the moment. Jacob had tried to contact his brother through their own personal telepathic link, but the young Mind Demon had not responded. The link was not strong to begin with, being mostly supported by Kane's telepathic abilities, and apparently Kane was too distant and too preoccupied to notice the small plea for attention calling into the back of his mind. If he had noticed it, he would have teleported himself to Noah's home instantly. But these things were to be expected from a fledgling. Kane was close to his adult stage, about to reach his hundredth year, but in spite of his strengths also had many weaknesses to yet overcome.

"Jacob is fetching foods dense with iron and protein for her. It will help a great deal," he assured his wife, knowing she felt her friend's sickness keenly.

Legna's empathic abilities had intensified dramatically since their joining, a result of how a Demon Imprinting so deeply stirred together the male and female's power, as well as their hearts and souls. Being an Ancient, Gideon's supremacy of energy was phenomenal, and like nothing Legna could have ever expected. She was still adjusting to the overwhelming source of it six months later.

As a result, she was often besieged by the magnified feelings of those she cared about. She was learning to control the intensity of this growing potential but had not made enough progress as yet to keep herself from being swept up in the pains, as well as the joys, of others.

"I feel like a fledgling all over again," she complained, reading his thoughts straight out of his mind. Though she was not a telepath, by nature of her sex, she and Gideon shared a specially formed link that kept them constantly within one another's thoughts. It was the same for Jacob and Bella and all other Imprinted pairs.

"You are too hard on yourself, *Neliss*," he soothed, pressing a kiss into her forehead. "You are in danger of sounding like Jacob," he teased, knowing that Jacob's constant self-reprisals had a habit of getting under her skin.

"Please, you will make me toss my cookies," she said wryly.

"Toss your cookies?" Gideon laughed at the phrase.

"I know, I know . . . I sound like Bella." Legna giggled in spite of herself. "I cannot help it. She used that term her entire pregnancy. It rubbed off."

"So I see," he murmured, reaching to cover her belly with one broad palm. His fingers looked graceful in that way he had, curving over their hidden baby with tenderness and affection.

That was the moment Noah entered the room.

Gideon was happy to see his wife did not move or react in any way. She had a terrible habit of jumping away from him whenever her brother showed up. But as Noah continued to accept their union, she seemed to be less self-conscious.

"I am simply too tired to move," she whispered defiantly.

"Then for once I am glad of your exhausted state," he whispered back.

"Hello," Noah greeted them quietly, moving closer to his sister and brother-in-law so he wouldn't disturb their patient. "How is she?"

"Weak," Gideon said. "And worsening. I put her into a deep sleep, but she still seems to be having her visions."

Noah turned to look at Bella, watching carefully as she twitched restlessly.

"Has she said anything useful? Do you know why she is

being beat to death by her own power? I have never seen so much harm caused by one's own abilities."

"I believe I may have to resort to calling in a male Mind Demon. Legna's empathy is not enough to soothe her. Perhaps a full telepath will be able to set her apart from these visions."

"That would drive Jacob up a wall. A male Mind Demon would probably have to use hands-on techniques, and you know how Jacob reacts to other men touching Bella."

"I think he has gotten better over these past months," Legna said. "He actually reached a point where he was not at all upset when Gideon came to give her checkups."

"That is because he knew that an Imprinted Demon would never be a threat," Gideon said dryly. "I am yours lock, stock, and proverbial barrel, my sweet, and I could not look elsewhere even if I tried."

"True," Legna giggled, closing her eyes and snuggling even closer to her mate.

Noah watched the tenderness between them with a combination of joy and hurt. He was happy to see his littlest sister so content and well cared for. There was no one as powerful as the Ancient Body Demon who held her so closely, and she would be protected by him to his last breath if it came down to such a choice. This contented the King deeply. He could not have parted with Magdelegna as abruptly as he had if he could not be assured of her safety.

He had gotten over Legna's absence from his home for the most part. She had lived with him for almost three hundred years. He had raised her from a small child after their parents' deaths, so he had missed her terribly when first she had left him. But the adjustment was coming along quite a bit easier than he would have expected of himself.

So why did he feel so empty when he watched her and Gideon together?

He had not enjoyed the choice of mate Destiny had pressed onto his sister for many reasons in the beginning, but now he would have no other for her, after seeing how devoted to her Gideon truly was. So he could not blame the vacancies of his heart on the medic.

Noah shook off the feelings shadowing his soul before his sister became aware of them, and subsequently disturbed by them. She was taxed enough without adding his personal deficiencies to her worry load. He excused himself and went back down to the hall so he could brood over books he probably would not try to read in any sincerity, while waiting for Jacob to return.

"Anya, you worry too much. Siena always does this. Especially in the fall."

Anya turned to look at her companion with the flicker of eyes so dark they were easily labeled black. Syreena was unperturbed by Anya's glare and crossed her slim legs casually to add punctuation to her unconcerned manner.

Anya was a half-breed Lycanthrope who was the result of what happened when a human and Lycanthrope had children. Unlike in Demon society, mating with humans was not forbidden to changelings and not punished when attempted. But it was generally frowned on because it took a very special person to be capable of being brought into their fold, and it had to be a total commitment or none at all, because the risk of exposure to the public was too great. It was bad enough as it was with the hunters and magic-users pursuing their existence. It was a horrifying thought to consider what might happen if the entire human race came to understand that myths and legends were more often true than not.

A half-bred Lycanthrope could not shapechange, but instead maintained a human form with all the, mostly nonvisible, traits of the animal they could have become had they been full-bred. In Anya's case, she was part fox. She had the sleek, pointed grace of a vixen to her features, a beautiful delicacy that made her appear deceptively fragile. She was a redhead, though the color of her hair changed seasonally between bright auburn, brownish red, and various other degrees of the shade. At the moment that meant the myriad browns and reddish browns that came with the fall.

She was slim, petite, and one of Siena's most trusted companions. Anya was to the Queen what Elijah was to Noah. The head of her armies, her lead assassin and infiltrator, and the one person who could vex her and make her laugh all in the same breath. It was a distinction of rank no half-breed had ever had in the Lycanthrope court and royal family before.

The second female was Syreena, Siena's younger sister and heir to the throne in the event Siena did not have children. She had been called home and risen to the position of court advisor upon her sister's ascension to the throne for very clear reasons. Firstly, she was a wise counselor, a fearless advocate for her sister's wishes, and the only one who could gainsay the Queen without worrying about being banished from court. But what made her truly unique, one of the most unique Lycanthropes alive, was the fact that Syreena was the only living Lycanthrope who could transform into five distinct forms.

Every full Lycanthrope had three forms. The human, the Lycanthrope, and the animal, with the Lycanthrope being the Werecreature, half-human half-animal, like Siena's Werecat form.

Syreena had two others.

It was generally believed that the anomaly had been caused by a life-threatening illness she had suffered during her adolescence. It had almost killed her, this mysterious illness, but having survived it she had become mutated in some way that, once she became capable of changing, she realized she was privy to two different genres of form. It had often been jokingly referred to as the Lycanthrope version of a split personality. This description was not too far off from the truth on many, many levels.

To begin with, her two animal shapes could not have been more opposite of one another. The first was of a peregrine falcon, a sharp-eyed hunter in flight. The second was of a bottle-nosed dolphin, a playful water creature with inconceivable intelligence. Though characteristics of both these creatures were quite apparent in her human form, such as her keen judgment and her fearless predatory nature, it was the peculiar nature of owning two so opposite Wereforms that made her somewhat unpredictable.

As a human, Syreena was slim and light, looking very much like a delicate bird but moving with the sleek grace and speed of her dolphin half. Her hair was split down a center part, one half a beautiful multitude of feather-soft browns, the other a sleek iron gray. Her eyes were dual-colored as well, but like the harlequin, the gray eye was on the side where the brown hair was, and the brown eye in its opposite position. Though this seemed extreme, it somehow worked to make her look quite exotic and unique outwardly, a handsome reflection of her nature overall.

Syreena was an anomaly, yes, but she was a precious one. She was in great demand by those who considered her nothing short of perfection. To be one such graceful and wonderful form was enough to put her genetic code in demand, but two? The power her stock could potentially have was something many coveted, provided she could pass the mutation on to her young. But it was clearly a chance many were eager to take.

Syreena herself, however, felt harangued by the covetous attention she received, and as a result had completely buried herself in her work as her sister's advisor. She had made herself just as inapproachable as Siena had, but for very different reasons. Syreena actually craved a mate and family, but she trusted no Lycanthropes' motives or intentions. It was rather like wealthy and famous people who could never be sure what motivated others to become their friends.

"Siena does not disappear without a trace," Anya continued to point out to the counselor. "If she's going to spend time away, she always tells me so. You are only just beginning to become reacquainted with your sister. I have known the Queen all of my life and she does not always do this."

"I have been back to court since the war ended," Syreena said, her tone reflecting how she did not appreciate being reminded that the half-breed across from her could be considered more of a sister to Siena than the Princess and heir apparent could. "I think it is safe to say I have learned enough about my sister in the past fourteen years."

"No insult intended," Anya apologized in solemnity. "Forgive me, I am just worried."

"If you are so concerned, why not send out some of the Elite to search for her?"

"I would," Anya hesitated, "but if it *is* solitude she is seeking and I should happen to disturb it, she will be livid and I will find myself leashed to her throne."

That made Syreena laugh. The Princess tossed back her bicolored hair and grinned at Anya.

"What a pair we are. I do not believe we would know a vacation if it came up and bit us on the flank. What we should be doing is preparing for the Samhain festival."

"What are you going to do at the festival? Cross your legs and be a voyeur?" Anya teased her.

The Samhain festival always ended with hundreds of entwined bodies scattered behind the trees and bushes of the forest just beyond the castle and the village. Syreena had no mate, and due to the same restrictions Siena suffered under, she could take but one lover in her lifetime.

"You know, you are fortunate that our Queen adores you," Syreena threatened with a sparkle in her eye. "Else I would leash you to the throne myself." The Princess sobered quickly. "You have me worrying now. I think I will skim some of the territory."

Syreena stood up and tossed her hair over so that the gray side was buried beneath the brown. The brown hair immediately began to slip over her body. Feathers and wings replaced humanity, and in a breathless flash of speed that Anya could not help but admire, Syreena took wing across the throne room's vaulted ceilings.

She soared out of the underground castle in an instant, leaving Anya alone with her worries. At that moment, however, all Anya could do was marvel over the Princess's abilities. There was no Lycanthrope alive who could change that fast. Perhaps Siena, but she would have to work extremely hard at it or be startled into the change.

Anya both did and did not envy those who were full-blooded changelings. On the one hand, most changelings could change form at will. It was a handy skill that would have been a tremendous asset to the General of the Lycanthrope Queen's armies. And besides that, it seemed like so much fun to be able to experience the world as an animal.

In the con list was the tendency Lycanthropes had toward less controllable animalistic behaviors. Though those with great strength like Siena and Syreena could control most of these urges, the majority of the population tended to be less assertive over their baser natures. Anya enjoyed the instincts she had been born with; they made her a determined fighter and an excellent strategist. But she would hate being under the impulse of her instincts. Control meant everything to her.

In that moment, control meant taking some action of her own. Syreena had given her an idea. She could send out those of her Elite who were aviary. As birds they could skim the land quickly and out of immediate notice. Siena might sense one of them passing by, but so long as they kept going they would not disturb her if indeed it was solitude that had drawn her away.

If it was something else, Anya would not be able to forgive herself for not acting. Siena was indeed her sister, and she was a friend as well. She would be remiss if she did not think of the Queen's protection at all times. These times above others especially.

Siena was a remarkable leader with unequaled skill at her position. Though Syreena could step into her place if needed, the Princess did not have the same affinity with the people Siena did. Syreena had lived a great deal of her lifetime in the monastic enclosure of The Pride. Like those great and wise teachers, she knew more about her studies than she did about relating to others. This often showed during gatherings and it made others just as uncomfortable as it made her. Siena was the leader the Lycanthropes needed in this era. There could be no substitute, especially not the markedly antisocial Princess. Her time would perhaps come one day, but hopefully that would be a long time into the future, long after Siena's influence of peace and wisdom had erased the blood-thirsty legacy their father had left in his wake.

The remark about preparing for Samhain had been a jest. Syreena would not be found anywhere near the festivities and intense crowds of that celebration. Siena had thought to try and draw her out this year as insistently as she could, and this was why her absence sat so unwell with Anya. Siena could not coax her sister into joining the party if she was not here to do it, and it had been practically all she had talked about for weeks now.

No.

Something was not right.

Anya strode out of the throne room to find her Elite and see if she couldn't put that feeling of wrong back to right.

CHAPTER 5

Elijah came out of the rear room dressed more appropriately in a pair of jogging pants that were somewhat small on him, but much better than running around in nothing but a towel. They were flexible enough to be comfortable and served their purpose.

"Close enough," Siena remarked as she took his measure. "I didn't realize Jinaeri had men's clothes here. Something tells me she has a secret she's been keeping from me."

"And do you require your subjects to tell you about their affairs?"

Elijah knew he was baiting her, but she smiled and moved to sit on the couch with her feet curled up under her. She was looking a bit better though, if a little tired around the edges. Elijah joined her by sitting on the couch across from her, hooking an ankle over his knee with casual ease.

"No. But I do require my ladies-in-wait to do so. Jinaeri is one of my closest aides. I only keep unattached aides near me."

"Why?"

"Because my senses are quite powerful and it is too easy for me to detect the scent of a mate on them."

"And why would that be so bad?" Elijah pressed her. He suspected the answer already, but wanted to hear her say it.

"It is a . . . distraction. I keep myself far removed from those distractions. I would not punish her or condemn her for it, I would merely replace her and give her another position."

"You mean a demotion. No wonder she is reluctant to tell you."

"It is not a demotion."

"To go from a valuable aide close to the Queen to . . . whatever? You don't consider that a demotion?" Elijah laughed with a short, disbelieving snort. "I'll bet you anything Jinaeri does."

"Perhaps," Siena relented.

"And for what? For having a lover? That sounds quite discriminatory, Your Majesty. All because you don't want to be made uncomfortable with thoughts about a mate or about sex?"

"I would not expect you to understand," she snapped suddenly, her body becoming rigid with her irritation. "It's well known that you Demons will rut with anything that sits still for you long enough."

"Oh, really? Is that fact as well known as the whole 'Lycanthrope blood is tainted' thing?"

He made his point, that was clear. He could tell by the color flushing her cheeks. But to his surprise, she once more relented.

"Perhaps you are correct. I am afraid some of my prejudices still show themselves from time to time, despite my efforts otherwise. I apologize for the disparagement."

"I wouldn't worry about it," Elijah said quietly, feeling a bit low for taunting her. "I've said enough rude things to you recently to more than compensate."

"This too is true," she noted, her brow lifting teasingly as her eyes sparkled.

"You know," Elijah raised a hand to shake a finger at her, "you have an attitude problem."

"I certainly do. Your attitude is a huge problem for me."

"Oh, very funny," he said, sarcasm dripping from his lips.

But in spite of himself he was enjoying the harmless sparring. She had a quick and ready wit. This did not surprise him. He had seen evidence of that quite a bit already. Still, it was a pleasant attribute. He had been surrounded by strong and brilliant women all of his life. It stood to reason she would be appealing to him because of that fact alone.

"Are you hungry? I need to hunt for us if we are to eat," she said.

"You don't look like you are ready for a hunt yet," he cautioned.

"And I never will be if we start to starve to death. Don't concern yourself, warrior. I haven't had a rabbit take the breath out of me yet."

She stood up, the skirt of another one of those little dresses falling into place only after giving the Demon a glimpse of a temptingly curved bottom. Heading for the cave entrance, Siena was oblivious to the reaction it inspired in him. When he followed several minutes later, he found the empty dress pooled on the floor right near the opening. Unable to help himself, he picked the garment up and, touching it beneath his nose, he took a breath full of her scent.

It was getting harder and harder to resist these lures she so unwittingly left in his path. Whether it was moon madness or just plain old-fashioned overactive hormones, he had to get out of there. He dropped the dress back onto the ground and turned abruptly back to the little parlor.

He was still pacing in front of the fireplace when she suddenly appeared at the top of the short steps. Elijah looked up at her and froze instantaneously in place. She was flushed, breathless, and beautiful. Fresh from the hunt and, he would swear on Noah's life, she smelled a thousand times more provocative than she had when she'd left. Elijah stood still as she stepped down lightly into the room and moved past him to lay several freshly killed rabbits on the hearth. She crossed back over his path to head for the pool, intent on bathing away the remnants of blood that had stained her hands.

Siena was not blind to the warrior's rapt attention. And what she did not see outright, she certainly felt. She had an affinity with all animals, a telepathy of sorts that told her what actions and urges and feelings a specific creature was experiencing. It worked on humanoids as well when their emotions and sensations were born of their more animalistic sides.

And lust was certainly an animalistic aspect.

She washed her hands slowly, dawdling on purpose because she did not want to go back to that part of the cavern and feel the weight of those vivid green eyes and the equally clear desires that burned behind them. She was not immune to her own awareness of him and the things about him that attracted her equally honed senses. Demon or otherwise, he was a remarkable man, both physically and chemically. Siena left it to those narrow prospects. She could not bring herself to admit that there could be anything more personally appealing than just physicality. She didn't want to feel these things, but they were relentless. No matter how hard she tried, she could not push away these thoughts that would only serve to draw her to him. She hoped that by accepting at least that aspect of her attraction to him, it would remove the untouchable lure that he presented.

Siena splashed water over her face and neck, hoping the brisk cold of it would cool her speculative thoughts. She stood up and moved slowly back to the near room. To her relief, he had gone into the back bedroom. It wasn't much of a distance, but it helped. She immediately busied herself with preparing another pot of stew, using the last of her herb supply, wiping the tangy scent of them off her hands by absently brushing them over the skirt of her dress. Her thoughts wandered into the bedroom, wondering what he was doing. She reached to sense his movements in any way she could.

It was a mistake.

She sensed him all too well. She could see him vividly in her mind, seated on the bed, hands draped loosely between his knees and his head bent as he struggled with himself. She felt, in that reaching moment, everything that he felt. He, too, was hoping that putting a room between them would lessen the sharpening pain of the inexplicable attraction he found himself feeling toward her. He was humming with taut nerves and the screaming desire to fling himself into the next strong wind. He had to escape, had to fly, but he could not do so and expect to survive. Not just because of his wounds, she felt him admit to himself, but because when he thought about never seeing her again, about putting any great distance between them, it began to suffocate him.

Siena braced both hands on the countertop, her head bowing as she tried to take in a breath, as she tried to remind herself that he was the one struggling with borderline claustrophobia, not her. She also tried to tell herself that his impassioned feelings were not the reason why her heart began to pound. That the sparkling sensation that tightened her chest had nothing to do with what it meant to her to finally be wanted for herself. Not for being royalty, an heir, or a sister, but the woman as a whole. Wanted as all of these things, as well as for the huntress, the vindicator, the Queen, and the servant to the needs of her deprived body. To the warrior in the next room, she was golden and soft, shaped perfectly for his hands and his body, exuding the perfect scent to call him to her. She had hot blood, noble thoughts, and a wit like a treasure box that when sprung open he could not help but feel rich and prosperous in its presence.

Even as he thought all of this, she was aware of the height of arousal in his scent as it grew with every thought directed toward her. She felt the pounding of his heart straight through to her temples, and she gasped out a soft, astounded laugh when she felt the startling heat that pulsed hard and low in a body that seemed to be permanently solidified with need for her. Siena sucked in a deep breath, trying to sever her connection with him, but she was far too fascinated by the purity of it to truly want to let it go. She had never empathized with a being so perfectly, had never felt within her own body everything that another being felt. She shook, uncontrollably, as she ran a hand across and then down her belly, as if she would suddenly find her sex changed, allowing her to touch the masculine thrust of uncomfortably straining heat low in the vee of her hips. Tears sprang into her eyes, her pain and her struggle as unbearable as his.

Oh, but she could *feel* his honor. His determination never to give in to his impulses no matter how much it killed him. This was what stabbed through and through her. The realization that though she was a remarkable temptation, though she was forbidden to him by all the natural and written laws of his people, though he could condemn himself to punishments beyond her comprehension, it was none of this that stayed him.

There was only a single thing that would anchor him into his honor, and that was the understanding that he could never again do anything to hurt her. That he would rather see himself dead than see her cry or be afraid of him or anything else like that negative pain ever again.

In all her lifetime growing up as royalty, she had been valiantly protected from any number of things, but never once had she been cherished in such a manner. How could it be that so staunch an enemy could display so tender a sense of honor to someone who represented everything he had despised for three centuries?

The Queen absently hooked the stew pot onto the fireplace arm and swung it over the flames. She barely hesitated before moving closer to the bedroom entrance. She listened to the fast, hard fall of her own breathing, watched with clenched fists for a moment as it moved in and out of her chest, as she told herself to turn around and head in the other direction.

Distance. She needed to put distance between them.

But instead she took it away. She did not understand what propelled her into the room, but she went under its power until she was finally able to stop herself just as he looked up at her. She watched with a fascination she couldn't comprehend as his lax hands curled into tense fists. Her breath quickened even further when she realized it meant his control was being sorely tested just by her presence in the room. Why did that give her such a thrill? The rush of heat and excitement made her tremble with anticipation. There was power here, she realized, one she had toyed with all her life once she had discovered the flirtatiousness of her body as she had become a woman. She had learned how to use it to calm and soothe, to charm and win, to beckon and deny. It was always a rush, but here lay a path so dangerous that her entire life could explode from it. To move straight along this path lay certain disaster, certain pleasure, certain wickedness of power over the most potent man she had ever known. She stepped a single step closer and he surged to his feet and faced her, his face a storm of emotion in the flickering firelight between them.

"Siena," he warned, her name breaking over his tense vocal cords.

"Elijah."

It was the first time she had ever said his name, and it had an astounding impact on both sides. For her, it made her laugh with unexpected delight. It made no sense logically, but there it was all the same. For Elijah, the simple word beat at every last defense he had tried to erect to protect himself from her lure. His name on her lips, passed through the rich tone of her seductive voice, stabbed through his libido like a hot knife plunged into butter. He turned his head away from her, swearing under his breath as he forced himself to stand in place and not move toward her.

Siena made it a useless effort. With a speculative gleam in her golden eyes, she began to walk toward him. His head snapped back up, his fierce eyes trained completely on her, the moment she took her first step. He could hear the brush of the soles of her bare feet as she moved, stirring sand and dust against polished stone, the arch of her foot and flex of her legs so tight that her heels never quite touched the floor. Her hands were linked behind her, allowing the flirtatious little skirt of her dress to twitch and swing with the natural slink of her body.

Elijah was forced to remember how that perfect, sensual body had felt against his. Every velvet slide, every eager twist, every wave of sweet, heated musk that had risen from her skin. He was compelled to remember it even more vividly as she came up so close to him he could feel her body heat.

"Siena," he said hoarsely. "Don't. Don't touch me, or I swear . . . I can't . . . I will have to . . ." She looked up into his eyes, looking so speculative as she did that he imagined he could read her boldly sexual thoughts. His speech abandoned him as he looked down into those eloquent eyes of gold. Though she said nothing for a long minute, she spoke molten volumes with those hungry eyes. He watched the sweep of her delicate lashes go lower and lower as she so obviously took his measure, and so clearly did so as a woman interested in taking the measure of a man. But, as requested, she did not touch him. Her hands remained linked behind herself and she stood just close enough to not make contact with his skin.

"Will you answer a question?" she asked softly, her eyes drifting over his face, his chest, and down his clenching abdomen.

"Siena—"

"Yes or no," she interrupted firmly. When he resisted further, she lifted a hand to him, her palm hovering over his right pectoral muscle. The threat was terrible and clear. "Yes or no?"

"Yes," he relented quickly, breaking immediately under a form of threatened torture he had never once anticipated in his career as a warrior.

She lowered her hand back to her side and smiled. She enjoyed every battle she won, Elijah realized, no matter what it might cost her in the process. She was, in essence, exactly like him.

"Tell me what it feels like to have sex."

Elijah stepped back under the impact of the question, but she followed relentlessly until his broad back was touching immoveable stone that would not give him another inch of escape.

"Why would you ask me such a thing?" he demanded, trying for all he was worth not to give in to the thousands of impulses rushing through him like so many pinpricks.

"Because you know," she said simply.

"Siena, you have to leave. You don't want to know this and you don't want to be this close to me. You know that."

"Perhaps. But it has occurred to me that since you are not of my species, perhaps certain rules do not apply."

"A risk I cannot see you wanting to take. Siena, this is not you . . ."

"And how is it you presume to know who I am?" she said with sudden sharpness. "No one knows me. No one knows this part of me and no one ever will! Do you have any idea how much that infuriates me? I am half cat, warrior, and every natural instinct in me that belongs to the cat is one of sensual ease and bitterly acute need. Sometimes I want to scream with the intensity of the pain denying myself such pleasures causes me!" Siena sucked in shallow breaths, and her voice and eyes roared with the passion of her emotions. "It's like an animal in heat who is locked in a cage. No freedom, no release. Nothing eases it. So I ask you this question with the hope that somehow your answer with help bring some of that ease. Do you hate me so much that you will deny me even this? Even after I saved your life?"

"I do not hate you, Siena! Of all of your people, it is you who have given me the least reason to hate, no matter how hard I tried to do so! I am trying to protect—"

"I do not need your protection! I need your response." She leaned even closer to him, her face a breath away from his as her gaze bored into him, her cinnamon-sweet breath cascading over him with heat and breathless need. She shuddered and radiated with need. Deep in her eyes, he saw her pain, saw 150 years' worth of denial and sacrifice.

"Why won't you take a mate, Siena?" he asked, his tone quiet and undeniably tender. This, in spite of the irrational surge of jealousy the very suggestion burned into him like a violent brand. Every cell in his body screamed with possessive, predatory protest. "There's no call for you to hurt like this," he said hoarsely, hardly able to speak under his emotions.

"Because the last time a female ruler mated, it was to a bloodthirsty bastard who nearly destroyed her people after she died and left him to rule alone!" Siena's hand fisted as her rage toward her father flared. "Three hundred years wasted with war and the ramifications of it. Thousands of both our people slaughtered. And for what? Over what? An imagined slight? A male ego slightly bruised? No, I would rather die than subject my people to such a torment again."

"Siena, not every man is like that," Elijah argued.

Siena laughed at that notion. She reached out and touched him suddenly, both hands slipping over his lower ribs, making him draw in a sharp breath.

"Certainly you do not speak of yourself. You are the most seasoned warrior of your race, this muscle built on the battlefield."

"Because it has to be, not because I thrill in it," he said

tightly, biting back the groan building under her curious touch.

"And you took no pleasure in killing my father?" she asked, the accusation whispered hotly.

"I took as much pleasure in the doing of it as you took in the occurrence."

"Oh, yes," she mused absently, her hands drifting up his sides slowly. "You did do me something of a favor, did you not? You freed me to free my people."

"I did what I had to do to stop the killing."

"So noble," she noted, her hands lifting away so just her fingertips skimmed his skin as she drew graceful traces over the definition of his chest, shaping pectorals, ribs, and the bumping ridges of his abdomen.

"Siena, stop," he commanded, grabbing her hands into his, forcing them into stillness so she could not keep him off balance with the temptation of her touch. "If you want to hate me, then do so just as things are. Don't create more reasons to despise me. We have had enough hatred between our people."

"But I don't hate you either, Elijah," she insisted, again battering him with the sound of his own name. He could not understand why that affected him as it did.

Of course, her proximity and her allure did not help much.

"Then why are you acting like this?"

She stilled as she seemed to think on it. Her tongue came out to lick slowly between her lips, that erotic speculation brightening her eyes once again.

"Because I have never in my life felt this . . . this desire that I feel at this moment. I want to understand why that is, Elijah." Elijah was not expecting her to lean into him so suddenly, her nose drifting across his skin as she took in a deep breath. "Why is it your scent appeals to me like no other?"

Elijah couldn't speak to answer. The beast that was his need for her was rearing up violently within him, thrilling over the way she brushed against his body as she took in his scent. Before he could counter the impulse, he lowered his head to her throat where it curved into her shoulder and re- turned the action without hesitation. The smell of her was di- vinity. Ambrosia. She was highly aroused, and it was reflected with a heavy dose of feminine musk that bled through him like an erotic poisoning. It burned through every vessel, every nerve, releasing endorphins and blood all along his body so both would settle heavily in anticipa- tion of her next action.

He did not resist when she pushed her hands out of his hold, the movement sending his slack hands sliding down her forearms as she reached for him. At first, all she did was drift haunting touches of fingertips over his hairline, his forehead, his nose and cheeks and chin. Without truly touch- ing him, she cradled his head between her hands, her finger- tips fluttering like the wings of a butterfly near his ears as her hands shook violently with her pent-up needs. She reached up with her mouth, her lips and breath brushing over him with sensations both there and nonexistent all at once. Elijah made an anticipatory sound of agony, low in his chest, painful conflict exploding over his pupils as she looked up into them with aching clarity of purpose. He dreaded it, longed for it, both with every fiber of his soul.

"Siena, please," he begged one last futile time.

Then her mouth was against his and all protest faded to nothingness. She was perfect. So utterly perfect.

No woman can be so unbearably perfect . . .

Elijah thought this fiercely, even as he convinced himself otherwise just by leaning in to meet the lush caress of her mouth. He drew hard for a breath that might actually provide a measure of oxygen for a change, and it did so on the back of her scent and the cinnamon confection of her taste. Her lips were hot against his, and pliant beyond reason. Elijah encircled her head with his hands, drawing her up tighter into the kiss she had just barely begun, and showed her exactly what it was she was toying with. Part of him still hoped the intensity of it would frighten her as it had the day before.

And part of him did not.

His mouth burned fire into hers, his powerful hands pressing fingerprints into her scalp as he clutched her tightly. His hands shook as hard as hers had, and she felt the vibration from head to toe. He tried for violence, tried to frighten her with the rough, slashing intensity of his kiss, crushing her beneath his mouth, even going so far as to release a predatory growl of warning, of danger. He battered and bruised her, bit at both of her lips as he threatened to devour her like prey, tearing at her soft, vulnerable flesh with hunger and intensity.

Siena refused him any avenue of salvation, slamming her hands against his chest, thrusting her weight into a push that pressed him aggressively to the stone wall behind him, unlocking her mouth from his just long enough for her to tilt her head in the opposite direction and capture him once more. She reached boldly for the caress of his tongue, rushing into his mouth with her urgent seeking in a way that made every nerve in his body sing with pleasure. She was no virginal miss who patiently accepted only what he orchestrated. She would conduct as much as he would, and the idea of it floored him. With that change of aggression and the honesty of reaction it forced from him, she released a sound of delight and encouragement.

Discouragement fell to the wayside as he burned with the press of her body and the appetite of her mouth. She wriggled her body into his, her soft curves spreading over the hard planes of his muscles. She fit him perfectly, so tall and so elegantly shaped. He did not dwarf her, and he found that enticing beyond reason. His hands drifted to her neck and throat, slipping under her heavy hair to encircle the warmth of it. Even the collar she wore was warmed by her body heat.

Before he realized he was even attempting to do so, he had unlatched the intricate collar and it slid down the front of her body.

Siena jerked back suddenly in shock as she felt the collar abandon her throat in order to be replaced by his hands. She grabbed up the collar before it could slide down her chest and then looked from him to it in disbelief.

"That's not possible," she whispered, shivering as he once more closed the distance between them to nuzzle her bare neck with his mouth, his cradling hands holding her to him though she was trying to keep a specific balance to her body. She moaned at the astounding sensitivity of the area. It had not been exposed to the touch of anything but gold and moonstones for her entire lifetime.

"Put it aside," he urged her, his tongue tracing her carotid artery up the entire length of her neck in a way that turned her legs to jelly. She gasped with pleasure, her eyes closing as he repeated the circuit in the opposite direction, adding the teasing scrape of his teeth until she was trembling with chills. Siena felt as though her entire body was moving out of her control, just as her world careened off its axis.

"Elijah, the collar . . ." she tried to explain, her words little more than soft pants of sound.

"Put it aside," he commanded again, enunciating each word firmly.

Siena let it fall from suddenly nerveless fingers and tilted her head so he had increased access to her neck and throat. He made a sound of male approval that sang through her with an operatic note of delight. He was encircling her with the steel bands of his arms a moment later, lifting her up to the tips of her toes. He seized her mouth and kissed her into a state of total breathlessness and numbness of thought. She felt light and utterly feminine. He could make her forget her own strength so easily with his large, powerful hands and demanding masculine body.

Elijah lifted her off the floor, swinging her easily around

until her feet touched the bed. She laughed when she found herself standing on it, looking down into his eyes. Her laughter faded the moment she realized the access their new positions allowed him to her breasts. His lips twisted into a devilish smile as he lifted his knuckles and skimmed over first one nipple, then the other, teasing until she could no longer bear the sensitivity. She was fascinated by the instant response of her body, the reactive thrust seeming erotic even to her as she watched him taunt her with his touch. She could barely catch a full breath as he leaned into her, nuzzling her through the fabric of her dress. The silky material seemed like nothing to him as he drew one of the points into his mouth, sucking until she thought she was going to collapse from the intense pleasure. He lifted his head away only long enough to hook the strap of the dress with his pinkie, peeling down the dampened silk until it was no longer a barrier to his mouth.

Siena cried out soulfully as his mouth, so full of wet fire, surrounded her once more, drawing her deep onto his tongue and then releasing her to pull his teeth across her teasingly. This time her knees did buckle, but he held her in place as if she weighed no more than her dress.

Elijah reveled in the taste of her, the feminine fullness of her breasts, the sensitivity of the gold-and-rose point of her nipple as he flicked his tongue over it until she made another of those sexy little whimpers of unmistakable pleasure. He sucked her deeply into his mouth when she did, and she jerked bodily against him. He felt her hands clutching at his head and shoulders, the mindless grasp of a woman lost in her bliss, and it rushed through him in ripples of tightening need.

As he tormented her with sensation, she slid against his body, feeling every contour of the sinew that was roped like bundles of steel cords over his frame. His feet were braced apart, his entire form as rock hard and rigidly set as a great stone statue. When she grasped his arms with clutching fingers, they hardly made an impression in his skin. He reeked of passion like he reeked of power, unapologetically and dominantly. This was not a man who liked to second-guess himself. He preferred to drill himself with skill and knowledge so that when the moment came, he would react with instantaneous decisiveness. That was what he had done at the mineral pool. He had seen, wanted, and acted. Ever since then he had forced himself to rethink what had come so naturally to him in that chain of minutes.

So now he was back in his element, one hundred percent, and thrusting himself fully into what had originally felt so right. He devoured her with a voracious and passionate mouth, and all the while he was touching her long body with bold, searching strokes of his hands. He was careening down the slope of her back and backside one minute, and then dipping under the hem of the dress to splay searching fingers over the back of her thigh. He stroked upward over her satiny skin, her bottom as bare as ever beneath the dress, her flesh fitting his palm as it moved over her to the arch of her lower back, around to her belly and along her breastbone.

There was so much sensation inundating her from so many places at once that she was light-headed with her pleasure and arousal. She was searching his body with her hands, the tendrils of her hair eagerly joining the exploration. She surrounded her senses with the feel of him, burying her face in his blond curls. Muscles rippled beneath her hands, twitched as she glided over them with her sensual, searching touch.

His burning mouth came back to hers as her stimulating touch sent his body temperature skyrocketing. He released her in increments so that she slid down his body and onto the bed. He followed every inch of the way, his mouth clinging to hers as he drank deeply of that hot cinnamon flavor so unique to her. His hands braced his weight above her as he moved over her body. When she felt him settling against her, she purred with encouragement and delight. The sound struck him exactly as it had before, only this time he was going to act freely on those feelings.

Elijah instantly swept his hands under her dress, stripping it from her in a single motion that included the careless toss into the room beyond. The torrid speed of the exposure caused Siena to arch against him, bringing her hot skin in contact with his with unbelievable sensuality.

Oh, how he remembered the burning feel of her skin, how he had craved little else but a repeat of the sensation since it had originally occurred. Even then, she had been chilled by the lake water, so it paled in comparison to now. She was a sheet of seductive satin beneath him, enveloping him in the rare purity of suppleness and richness that only came from so perfect a source. Her legs slid out from beneath him until her thighs framed his hips wantonly, settling him deeper into the feel of her, fitting them together like lock and key. Elijah gripped at the bedding as he felt himself settle into that heated cradle of her hips, only his clothing providing an obstacle between them, an obstacle that felt like nothing, like so much wind. His fingers gripped with such pleasurable agony that they punctured the ticking of the mattress, even without a reflexive growth of sharp claws. Those lengthened into existence a heartbeat later, when she ran eager hands down the slope of his spine and over the hard muscles of his backside, clutching him to her so she could shift her hips and rub her heat against the hard length of his sex.

"Siena!" Her name was a vicious growl in his throat, but she felt the shaking of his body as he looked for restraint and control, as he fought his vulnerability to her methods of encouraging his excitement.

In return, she moved her mouth to his ear, her lips rubbing breathily over it until he shuddered, and then slowly, softly, she drew out his name. A guttural gasp hitched into the single word as she felt him moving intimately against her.

"Kitten," he groaned from the bottom of his tormented

soul, "Sweet Destiny, kitten, you feel like paradise. *My paradise.*"

Siena responded with a smile against his neck as her hands began searching him with flawless intimacy. She stroked strong, graceful fingers back up to his shoulders in a caress sealed tightly to his damp skin. She moved around to his chest, down his sides once more, where she paused to drink in the feel of his rapid breathing. Her fingers slid down his flank and then beneath the waistband of his pants. She felt the defined muscles of his backside tighten under her enticing touch, but she was not satisfied with only that reaction. She drew her legs up just a little farther, allowing her hands the freedom to slip around his hips and into the heat and hardness resting so close to her.

Elijah had been stroking his tongue against the vital beating of her pulse in her neck when her fingertips brushed over that sensitive part of his body. He lifted away from his tasting of her, his back arching reflexively as he swore vehemently under his breath. Siena was not disturbed in any way by this. She had never touched a man in this fashion before and she was not about to relinquish the experience too soon. She wrapped silky fingers around him, feeling with fascination as he pulsed against her palm. He shuddered from head to toe as she stroked the length of him slowly, learning his shape, his weight, and especially his sensitivity. She had never imagined that flesh could become so incredibly hard. There was heat so intense that it nearly burned the pads of her gliding fingers. Most importantly, every touch, light or firm, had him practically contorting with a pleasure that seemed to border very close to pain. Again she came to understand a single truth. Power. The power to drive him mad with just the skill and intentions of her hands.

The rush of arousal that followed that understanding was hers, not his. Siena panted hard with it as it flooded her with molten gold, a precious liquid burning through her and then spilling slickly out of the very core of her body. She understood, all of a sudden, that there was only one way to her own pleasure, and that was to dive into his. It was one of those revelations that would change everything, even though it seemed so small a detail. She knew it. She knew it from the bottom of her soul. When her fingertips drifted over the wet tip of his arousal, one after another, coasting silkily through moisture and over highly sensitive skin, she learned a whole new description for stimulation.

Elijah exhaled a low, rough sound of ecstasy, his jaw clenching as he blindly thrust his hips toward her wicked little hands. She got the message, his reaction prompting her to repeat the stroke, only this time more slowly. Elijah couldn't think straight from that moment on. Not that he had been engaged in much thought beforehand that didn't center around the luscious feel of her body and skin sliding against him. Siena was relentless in her curiosity of his body and he was utterly mindless under her increasingly bold caresses. Before he knew it, he was on his back and she was stripping him quickly.

Then she slid up his body and sought his mouth. She kissed him and caressed him, trying to outdo herself first with one, then the other. She reveled in the abandon of his reactions, of the sounds that escaped him. She could make every rigid muscle twitch and flex, using the hot velvet touch of her lips and tongue to do so. His hands dove desperately into her hair, crushing the sensitive strands beneath fisted fingers.

Siena had never thought such a stranglehold could actually feel so incredibly good. It was a part of her body as sensitive as any other, and his touch was like wild magic as he grasped her in passion. It was an instantaneous erogenous zone, and she felt him suddenly comprehending that as he began to drag his fingers through the body-length coils.

"Oh!" she cried throatily, her body rising up over his and arching like a sleek python. She was straddling his stomach, her hands braced on his chest, her head thrown back as his calloused fingertips streamed through her grasping, clinging hair.

Elijah freed himself from the golden ivy curling around her body, a smile turning up one corner of his lips. Her position over his body left her vulnerable to an entirely different assault of sensation. His hands dragged rough touches down the center of her torso, over breasts and ribs and belly and hips. Then he went seeking for the heat and the moisture that had called to him relentlessly. His fingers slipped through a tangle of golden curls and touched the flesh beyond. She was slick and swollen with the arousal her manipulations of his pleasure had caused to her own body. Siena squeaked with a thousand impulses, thoughts and feelings crowding for expression, and Elijah plunged a free hand into her hair and dragged her down to his kiss. She gasped into his mouth when the invasion of his touch registered on her nerve endings with violent eroticism. He found the sensitive nub that would respond the most to his stroking fingertips and circled it with a flirting, skilled touch.

She had never suspected how breathless such a seemingly simple caress could leave her. He was touching her in earnest now, forcing her to go weak and wild with the strange, building sensation that flowed outward from that one small spot. She couldn't concentrate on what she was doing anymore, so her hands fell away from his body.

Elijah rolled her over onto her back, taking back control as she moaned with incredible intensity into his hungry mouth. She was a factory of brash sounds of pleasure from that moment on, the auditory stimulus sending urgent need clawing through Elijah's soul. He left her mouth quickly, sending uncaught cries into the room by doing so. But he was busy learning the taste of her throat, her collarbone, and breasts once more. He felt her shuddering, closing in on the release she wanted, needed so desperately.

His fingers stilled against her, making her sob a sound of protest.

"Elijah, please," she cried, her head turning side to side as her mind and body sought for what was missing.

He did not give in to her pleas immediately. He had something better planned. Her exotic scent had taunted him long enough. This was his one and only thought as he reached to replace the touch of his fingers with the caress of his mouth.

Siena's hips surged upward and she cried out so loudly that the cavern echoed with the sound. Elijah caught her bucking hips in eager hands and held her to his tasting tongue. She was pure aphrodisiac. Flavor and scent combined together with the perfection of strawberries and cream. She was shaking so hard in his hold as her pleasure was coiled up tighter and tighter inside her that he could predict the power of her coming release by it.

Siena suddenly was surging up into an oblivion beyond mere bliss. Her body locked even as it released. She heard herself screaming wildly, but hardly recognized herself in the unfettered sound. Pulsations of ultimate pleasure rode through her like shock waves, and still his tongue stroked over her, pushing her further and further into the extraordinary abyss of relief and delight.

She had barely settled back into the mattress before he was sliding up her body and sharing the confection of her sweetness with her in the form of a soul-searing kiss. He was so hard and so heavy with need for her that he was slightly mad. Her orgasm had pushed him to his limits, and he needed to be inside her with a desperation he had never known himself capable of. Her thighs fell open for him easily as he settled between them, and he rested against her saturated flesh with a hot, insidious slide.

Her eyes flew open in shock at how astoundingly stimulating the sensation was. He looked down into those golden pools, looking deep into her soul, past the haze of desire and the endless need to be who she was in this moment.

"Tell me what you choose," he said hotly against her swollen lips. "I have to hear you—" He broke off when she shifted her hips, bringing him right to the threshold that he so badly needed to cross. She swallowed his groan greedily, her mouth ravaging his with unparalleled intensity.

Elijah reached between them for her throat, encircling it to keep her from following after him when he broke away from her kiss. She was heaving for breath, her eyes wide and demanding that he let go. Of her. Of his doubts. Of everything.

"Siena," he gasped as she purposely slid against him once more. "I need to hear it."

"Of course," she whispered seductively, catching him once more in the perfectly poised spot where a single forward thrust would bury him inside her. "Elijah, I want this," she breathed.

"Do you accept me?" Elijah demanded of her, clutching her so hard it was a wonder she did not break. "Do you choose *me*?"

"Yes," she gasped, her body groaning for the completion he kept from her. "I accept you. I want you. You, Elijah . . ."

Elijah released his restraint with a savage growl of intent. He surged forward, pushing into her body with a single, rending thrust. Siena cried out, but not with any kind of pain. He could feel that with every fiber of his being. Her maidenhead gave way with ease, letting him sink deeply into hot, welcoming heaven.

Heat, tightness, slick surrounding honey. She was a burning sheath of immeasurable bliss, and he was deeply surrounded by her at last. In this she was beyond perfect. She fit him as if she had been hand-fashioned for him. Elijah was blind with the beauty and wonder of it. She was so tight around him it felt as if it should be impossible to move, so for the longest minute he did not. Siena was clinging to him, her hands on his shoulders, her body permanently arched into his, it seemed. She gasped and gasped, her eyes wide as she stared up at him with shock and amazement. As he remained deeply embedded in her, he was deeply embedding the memory of the moment into his brain. He would never forget this, and he would make sure she never did either.

But she was silky and slick and incredibly tempting, so he could only bear it for a few more heartbeats. He needed more of her, needed to give her himself. He began to withdraw and she dug her nails into his shoulders.

"Elijah!" she gasped helplessly, her golden eyes wild with the confusion of knowing something instinctively, yet not fully understanding the method to his seeming madness.

"Oh," he teased softly, "I am not going anywhere."

He stroked within her deeply, making her groan until the lusty sound was echoing off the surfaces around them. He loved that sound, loved her raw passion. The thrill of it pulsed through him, hardening him even more until he felt so incredibly thick within her quivering body. He knew she felt the new surge of heat because she purred with a deep, deep rumbling vibration. The sound urged him on, even though he needed no encouragement. It took only a moment for him to find the perfect pace for them both. She met his thrusting hips with natural ease after one awkward second. He guided her with a hand on her slender hip, the other hand trapped in the tangled clutches of her hair. He felt her nails bite into his back and he surged forward with the backlash of the resulting pleasure.

"Siena," he groaned, "kitten, you feel so damn perfect."

"Elijah . . ."

That was all she said. His name. Over and over, with increasing urgency, until she was sobbing it to him like a chant. Elijah could do nothing but bury his face in the curve of her neck and send them both spiraling toward an outrageous release. It was going to be torrid and fast, violent and ecstatic, and he just gave himself over to it. His name bursting from her throat was the most erotic thing he'd ever experienced in his long lifetime. He plunged into the sweet silk of her body again and again, until he felt he would shatter from the pleasure of it. Siena felt the world go up in heat and flames, her body burning and burning until it needed to explode. She was already crying out with her release when he finally broke into his own, adding fuel to an already raging fire. He crushed her into his embrace as he pulsed into her with violent surges of relentless climax.

It was all he could manage, to keep himself from crushing her with the weak collapse of his drained body. He scooped her up to his chest and rolled with her so that she was sprawled over him instead. He felt the separation of their bodies and it left him feeling powerfully bereft. He held her to him with a heavy arm, his fingers wrapping possessively around her shoulder.

"Thank you," she murmured a few minutes after their breathing had normalized.

"For what?" He laughed, tilting his chin to his chest so he could see her face as he pushed back the half ton of hair that obscured it.

"For answering my question."

He recalled the question and turned his gaze up to the ceiling formations.

"I hope it was a good answer," he said softly, not wanting to feel the trepidation that was trying to creep over him.

"Very adequate," she said.

"Adequate?" The term nipped at his ego, making him pull away from any looming worries immediately. "Would you care to rephrase that?"

"Must I?" she asked turning her face toward him as she lifted her head.

Elijah saw the humor glinting in the troublemaker's eyes and thoughts. He gave her a poisonous look and she started to laugh. Siena was not much of a giggler, he noted with pleasure. She had a bold, sexy laugh that dared you to gainsay her humor. It had the knack of ferreting out his libido with unerring ease.

The warrior rolled her off his body so abruptly that she laughed even harder. When he trapped her on her belly beneath him, his hands pinning hers to the bed, she became nearly hysterical.

"Have I happened to mention how that sexy laugh you have tends to affect me?" he asked silkily, showing her exactly what he meant with a strategic shift of his hips.

Siena stopped laughing, raising her head to try and see over her shoulder. Realizing it was a useless effort, she settled her cheek onto the sheet and smiled.

"You actually have not mentioned anything of the kind," she informed him.

"Then allow me to explain," he murmured.

Elijah made love to Siena relentlessly. When she complained about the abuse to his injuries, he lectured her on the healing qualities of her delectable body. The lecture was long and thorough, spoken across her skin and driven home inside her body.

After that, she never complained again.

At least not about that. She did find she liked his lectures, though, and so found other topics they could discuss in depth. Siena had never come close to suspecting what this kind of intimacy would feel like. She had claimed time and again that she wanted no part of it and would not miss it in the least. She had maintained there was no possible avenue for enrichment in such things. She had thought that her life could never be better than it had been before walking into this cavern.

How foolish and wrong she had been. The arrogance of ignorance! She was Queen of her species, but she had not truly begun to know the world until she had ascended, her sheltered, limited life depriving her of so much practical information. This thing, what she had chosen to allow here with the Demon warrior, would change that forever.

Change *her* forever.

Other than that thought, she pushed all other realities between them aside. Whatever tomorrow brought, she desperately wanted today to go on as long as it could. It wasn't just the physical completion that lured her into feeling this way, she admitted to herself. Elijah was a natural wit, making her laugh in a carefree manner she had known so rarely while growing up the offspring of a royal warlord. There was something about him, about his confidence and the surprising intelligence behind all that brawn and battle-hardness. She had never suspected him of being multidimensional in this way. It had so surprised her, when they had first met, his loyalties and obvious sensitivities when it came to the needs of those he loved.

In her childhood home, warriors did not love. Attachments were weaknesses. How could such a man as Elijah have stood toe to toe with the warlord who had reigned before her and come out the victor when he so clearly was susceptible to all the things her father had claimed were drawbacks to a warrior?

Siena knew the answer to that already. She had discovered it on her own as she had become older and wiser. Ironically, her father's coldness and lack of attentiveness had propelled her into becoming the very opposite of what he was. The only reason she was such a powerful fighter in her own right was because it was the only skill he had demanded of her and had supervised himself. She had dared not fail to impress him, and if she satisfied him he would be comfortable leaving her to reign in his stead as he warred.

So she knew what it meant to blend these seemingly incongruous parts of oneself. He was as comfortable with himself as she was, just as arrogant, just as wise when it came to what he should or should not let others see. But they had both lowered their formidable defenses in order to allow for this union of the moment. It was so out of character, so outrageously dangerous, and so incomprehensible in origin.

It was so magnificent and so very revealing.

Siena had never doubted her femininity or her womanhood, always a clear product of her confidence, but her sexuality had been little more than a tool for intrigue and manipulation. Otherwise, it was to be denied. Here, closed off from the world, centering herself on his body and in his hands, she now understood so much more than she had ever suspected.

She now understood what that slink of her spine was made for, what the lowering of lashes over smoky eyes could truly do, and what power there was in the tiniest, softest little sounds her throat could make. She began to truly understand what every shrug, every shift, and each soft, curvaceous slide could truly earn her in return.

She looked down on Elijah through her lashes, her amber eyes smoldering with the reflection of all her need, of all she was wanting and determined to get from him in that moment. She was straddling his hips, knowing that to him, she looked bold and beautiful as she entrapped him within her determined body. He actually had his hands folded beneath his head as if they were having a discussion about the weather, pretending the way she was moving over his rigid body was having little effect, in an attempt to taunt her.

Siena was not fooled. She felt his burning emerald eyes on the sway of her breasts as she moved. She felt the pulse and growth of the hard shaft inside her body every time she closed her muscles around him like a vise. She knew that his jaw ticked at its hinge because his teeth were clenched with the pleasure she made him feel. She had powerful legs, unparalleled flexibility, and she was stubborn as hell. He would lose this contest of wills, though it would make winners of them both in the end.

She braced her hands on the bed beside his shoulders, leaning over him so that her nipples brushed his chest with every exhibition of her spine's reptilian ability. She dipped forward against him, her breasts brushing his lips and nose, allowing for both temptation of taste and the musky scent of her perspiration-coated skin. She knew he was crazy about how sweet and sexy her skin smelled. Crazier still for the taste of her.

Before long his withheld hands were on her body, molding and cupping the full flesh of her breasts, drawing her toward his mouth until she was just as tortured as he was by her seductive libido. He was groaning under the relentless undulation of her hips, yet unable to drown out the sexy grunts and gasps she made as she pleasured herself with his body. He did not touch or guide the work of her pelvis. She had proved a quick study, and an uninhibited one. She had no qualms about finding her way over him herself. She also had very little mercy when she was ready to drag him into her world of climax. She spoke to him, low, soft, and sexy, verbally contemplating how she could make him lose control. Elijah could have told her that control had gone out of the window ages ago, but it would have spoiled her wicked little manipulations, and he would be the last to rain on her parade.

She drove him nearly insane, though. She was so hot, and she was learning how best to burn him very quickly. Her fingertips were always searching his body, looking for those places that were so erotically sensitive to her touch. When that did not work, or work fast enough for her liking, she employed the use of a sizzling tongue. She drew wet maps over his chest, taking paths over both nipples in order to avoid his bandage of her hair, and traveled to his neck and throat. She slid up over his jaw until she was devouring his mouth.

Hips, hands, and lips combined in a blissful barrage of sensation. She felt his building torment, and it echoed back to her. Still she gasped hot whispers of need and feeling into his mouth. The detailed accounting of how she felt as she rode him so relentlessly blinded her with her own pleasure. Siena cried out into his mouth, lifting away a second afterward and arching back, flinging her hair behind her until it fell heavily over his thighs. Now he grasped her hips, holding her to the rhythm as she convulsed violently around him. He pushed her and pushed her until she was screaming and he was obliterated by the vise of hot, velveteen muscles. He joined her release with a roar of agonizing gratification.

When she finally fell across his chest, trying desperately to catch her breath and bask in the afterglow of her amazing level of pleasure, Elijah became aware of the fact that he was in a great deal of trouble. He knew she intended to part ways with him after they left this place. She planned on defying this condition to her crown that she deemed a curse, this sentence that declared she take only a single mate in her lifetime who would reign as her equal on a throne she had suffered and struggled long for. She was giving everything to the now because she refused to devote anything to the future.

But in spite of the fact that he was repeatedly breaking about a thousand natural laws himself, Elijah felt a desperate sensation in his gut that warned him it would not be so easy to extricate himself from her golden embrace. He felt entangled with her in a way that was far more intricate than the grasping tendrils of her determined hair. He also knew that if he made the slightest suggestion about that, she would shut down and all of this would come to a crashing end.

He pushed back the dark cloud that came with his thoughts for just a little while longer. With a single movement he hauled them both off the bed. She complained and laughed all at once, but obediently circled his neck with her arms and his hips with her legs. He walked them to the mineral pool and tried to coax, and then pry, her off him.

"No, it's cold," she argued.

Elijah just grinned and lofted their weight sideways off the edge. Siena was screaming as they hit the frigid water on their sides. She pushed away from him, leaping up with the shock of the water. When he surfaced laughing, she gave him a very hard shove that sent him back under.

"Damn it!" she hissed, rushing through the hip-deep pool

as fast as she could to reach the side. But of course he encircled her with a single arm and dragged her back into his body before she could haul herself out.

"What's the matter, kitten? Don't like water?"

"That was low, even for you, warrior," she said sharply.

Her verbal daggers fell on deaf ears. He was nipping at the sensitive side of her neck in the way he had come to learn melted her completely. Before she knew it, her hands were deep in his hair and their mouths were deeply enmeshed.

It took them almost a full minute to hear the very distinct sound of a throat clearing.

Siena whirled around suddenly, almost knocking Elijah over. To her shock and utter despair, her sister stood in the cave entrance, leaning her back casually against it and raising a very curious eyebrow at the couple in the pool. She sensed Elijah's impulse to lay hands of comfort on her waist, and she let him steady her as the entire world began to spin.

"Your Highnesses," Syreena greeted them politely.

CHAPTER 6

"Hello, little flower. You look better," Jacob greeted his wife as she came down the central spiral staircase, her nightgown trailing lazily behind her.

She smiled at him, moving into his embrace the minute her feet touched the same floor he was on.

Legna and an adult Mind Demon named Amos followed behind her. Amos had provided the buffer Isabella had needed to catch her breath and heal. But it was clear the experience had taken its toll on the Demon. He looked exhausted and excused himself quickly after turning Isabella's care over to her husband and friends. Legna would continue to monitor Bella and would notify them if they needed to fetch further assistance, but at the moment, Jacob's petite mate looked rosy and healthy. More so than she had in months.

"Are you okay?" Jacob asked, framing her face with his hands as he inspected her for the thousandth time since she had become conscious and lucid a day ago.

"I am now," she insisted, reaching for his kiss and letting him feel how much she had missed being close to him.

She had always stirred him so easily. Kiss and body contact, these things would grab his attention on so many levels. However, all she truly had to do was look at him with those beautifully amused eyes of violet and he would be instantly under her spell. Of course, her response to the feel of his graceful touch and the intensity of his emotions for her left her similarly weak in her knees.

They had not been intimate in quite some time because of pregnancy and illnesses. The strain of the waxing Samhain moon was beginning to show in how deeply his fingers pressed into her soft flesh and how tightly hers tangled into his hair.

This was all part of the Imprinting between them. Their souls were forever deeply bound. Because of this, everything would always come with great intensity to them. It would never change and, despite the moments where he regretted having opened her up to the danger and intrigue of his life, Jacob had been thankful for the precious gift of her every day since the moment he had first touched her. She eased his heart. She was the only one who could lighten the weight he often made himself carry on his soul.

For instance, early on, just after the accidental death of the Druid male who would have been the mate of Ruth's daughter, Mary. Jacob was not truly to blame for something no one had understood the nature of until far too late. But he was a man of particular conscience. Taking such joy in his mate, the first Druid hybrid to become known to any of them, he felt Mary's lost potential keenly.

However, he would never be able to convert that incident into a reason for the brutal acts of deception and violence that both women had perpetrated against their very own people. Especially not after Isabella had suffered as a target of one of those attacks, nearly losing her life as well as the life of their daughter.

It had been his wife's love and soft assurances that had helped him come to grips with his conscience in this matter. She was always there to halt him when he tried to backslide into those feelings of responsibility and guilt. Jacob could no longer remember what life had been like without her support and the way she made him feel when she sought his support in return.

Still, he sometimes feared the risks to the safety of his family that came with being an Enforcer. He tended to forget that his mate was gifted with remarkable power, fighting skills, and a unique cunning that had come from her humanity and the life she had led before she had changed into her Druidic form. Jacob knew his disproportionate perception of Bella's abilities was due to all the weakness and injury she had been subjected to over her enceinte term. It had been such a long, harrowing time of worry and he had pretty much forgotten how strong she could truly be.

But the flush of her complexion, the warmth of her body, and the robust energy of her embrace eased him into understanding that she was getting well quickly. She would soon be able to care for the needs of her family and the demands of her duties, just like he knew she wanted, the enthusiasm singing through his thoughts in a way that made him laugh out loud.

Bella slipped out of his embrace, her thoughts turning in the direction of her infant daughter. She moved to the cradle that sat beneath Noah's hand and looked down at her daughter, who was finally sleeping after the proper breast-feeding she had longed for. Bella smiled at the King, leaning to kiss his cheek warmly, ignoring her husband's tensing hand at her waist.

"She adores you, Noah," she told him softly, looking down at how the King's enormous hand blanketed the babe's back securely.

"The feeling is quite mutual, I assure you," he said. "She loves to be close to the fire. A girl after my own heart."

"I see that. Noah, I have news for you."

"Yes," the King sighed. "Jacob said you would. I suppose it concerns Elijah?"

"Yes." Bella moved to sit in the chair nearest the monarch. "I believe he was badly injured in a battle. A trap he was not expecting. But before I explain further, I want to tell you all that I think I am beginning to understand why some visions affect me so strongly and others do not." She looked up at her husband and the others who were gathered around her. Legna had come to stand close to Gideon's side as he stood with his usual firm efficiency near the fireplace. The medic relaxed instantly, however, when his wife leaned into his embrace. "Actually, Amos helped me with this understanding. I believe it depends on how close I have been to the person who is the subject of the vision."

"How close? As in emotions, or proximity?"

"I cannot be one hundred percent sure, of course, but I believe it is proximity. A very specific kind of proximity. My power to dampen and then absorb the powers of other Nightwalkers, to be exact. I have absorbed Elijah's powers repeatedly over the past year, and in a way, because of it I feel connected to him. Almost as if a part of him remains living inside me. The same is true of Legna, and Jacob, and you as well, Noah. Before I learned to control the ability as I do now, I accidentally took that part of you all within myself. I believe the reason the visions overwhelmed me while I was searching for Elijah was because he was equally overwhelmed with injury and pain."

"It's a form of empathy," Legna remarked, her own empathy making her the expert.

"Yes. It is. And though Amos was an enormous help in buffering me from the harsh reality of the exhausting visions, as time has gone on, it has become less necessary. I believe with my entire being that Elijah has been taken to a safe place and has been healing all of this time, allowing me to become calmer and more relaxed with every moment the urgency passed. I also sense he is returning to us very soon."

"Thank Destiny." Noah exhaled suddenly, a weight of oppressing proportions finally lifting off of his shoulders. "Bella, I am so glad to hear that."

"I think in the future," Gideon spoke up, "and until you are stronger and more experienced, you need to limit the instances of absorbing the powers of others. We cannot change what has already occurred, but there is so much we do not know about human/Druid hybrids, Isabella. You are nothing like the Druids I knew a millennia ago. Your sister as well. Corrine's powers—"

"What about them?"

The fireside gathering looked up to see the exact redhead in question standing in the center of the hall, hands on hips, her husband Kane standing behind her. It was at about the same moment that the familiar scent of sulfur and smoke, the usual residue a young Mind Demon left behind when teleporting to and from a location, drifted over the group. Bella reached to fan away the odor from her sleeping baby, wishing Elijah was already there to blow away the fumes with a breeze.

"They are nothing like what they should be," Gideon finished. Kane was getting better at teleporting, he mused. It was rare that one so young could sneak up on such an elder, highly experienced group of Demons.

"Well, well, look what the smoke dragged in," Noah greeted them wryly. "Where have you two been?"

Corrine blushed an immediate bright red, passing the reaction back to her mate, who colored under his natural tan.

"Call it a delayed honeymoon," Kane explained sheepishly. "There's been so much going on since the wedding, what with looking for Ruth and Mary and fighting these sporadic attacks they keep leading against us, I asked Elijah if we could take off for a few days. He said we could."

"That explains why you were too preoccupied to hear my summons," Jacob teased, feeling good-natured about it now that Bella was safe and healthy again.

"So why did you need us? And why are we discussing my powers?" Corrine asked, moving toward them, her husband in tow. She led him to a chair where he obediently sat down and she found her seat in his lap.

"It's a long story. Suffice it to say," Gideon said, "we are learning there are some drawbacks to Druidic powers that are not in my experience."

"Oh, great," Corrine said dryly. "I finally start to get mine, and now you're telling me there are going to be ramifications?"

"Firstly, Corrine, I don't think we have seen all of your abilities yet. I do not believe the ability to seek out Druid mates will be all there is to you." Gideon took a seat as well and crossed his legs casually. "And the two Druids you have recently found are a very good example of the diversity hybrids seem to be gifted with. One can become invisible, walking through walls and all solid objects. The other not only has the gift of flight, but he has an uncanny knack for sensing the presence of other Nightwalkers."

"I think it would be wise for all of the Druids to be careful with how they use their abilities. If Bella has a drawback, we can bet the rest of you will." Noah lifted his hand from Bella's baby at last, rubbing his hands together absently. "Frankly, it makes sense. Nature always provides a measure of balance. She has gifted you all with immortality and rapid healing, as well as a variety of powers. It is her way to balance this with a compensating weakness."

"Just as our powers and immortality are vulnerable to the presence of iron," Jacob added.

"You mean every hero has his or her kryptonite," Bella said.

"Exactly," Legna agreed. "'Thropes have silver. Dwellers have light. For Mistrals it's agoraphobia."

"Vampires have the sun," Kane added.

"Yes. But they all understand and are familiar with these weaknesses, and have learned to adjust to avoid them and the danger they represent. Until we know what it is specifically each Druid needs to be wary of, you are in a reasonable amount of danger." Gideon made sure to level a firm gaze at both of the Druids present. "Stay close to your mates, ladies. They will potentially be the ones who can most immediately protect you."

"Wait a minute," Corrine complained. "I thought our kryptonite was the fact that we need to remain exposed to the energy of our mates regularly. That is how I almost died, isn't it? That's why Mary's mate died. Because we didn't realize he had been exposed to her already, like I had been exposed to Kane. That's why we began to starve to death. Because of lack of that needed energy. You found me barely in time and it took me all this time to recover what I lost. According to you, I'm still recovering."

"She has a point," Kane remarked.

"Yes. But you might recall that Vampires also can be poisoned by the blood of magic-users. Lycanthropes cannot bear the binding of their hair." Legna leaned forward as she explained. "There are no absolutes, Corrine. If we act as if there are, we will damage ourselves in the long run."

"Yes. Of course." Corrine blushed until she nearly matched the color of her long, coiled hair. She waved herself off with one hand. "Don't mind me, I've only been on the planet for thirty years. What do I know?"

"It was a good point, honey," Kane assured her. "You only learn by asking questions."

"I do not believe it." Jacob spoke up in sudden, laughing shock. "My baby brother did not just repeat something I have spent the past century trying to pound into his thick skull, did he?"

"I do believe he did," Noah speculated with a hum of interest.

"I think he ought to 'honeymoon' more often," Bella teased, giggling hysterically when the pair blushed hotly once more.

* * *

Siena instinctively found herself reaching for her throat, suddenly feeling the absence of her insignia of rank. But there was far more to her reign than a piece of jewelry.

"Elijah," she said softly, her eyes never leaving her sister's expression of barely repressed amusement.

She didn't even need to say his name. The warrior already knew what she wanted. He hesitated for a small second, gripped with a reluctance to let go of her he couldn't comprehend. Slowly, he slipped his hands from around her waist, moved away, and with a single, lithe movement, gained the stone ledge of the pool. He immediately left the area of the pool and strode boldly into the back sections of the cave. Syreena watched him go, the lift of her brow both curious and appreciative as she perused his nude body during his retreat.

Then she turned that cocked brow to her sibling.

Siena was already out of the water herself, the liquid streaming off her body as she approached her sister with hostile speed.

"Siena," Syreena warned, instinctively holding up a hand to ward her off.

Siena approached her so that they were almost nose to nose, her hands curled into fists.

"Heed me carefully, Counselor," she whispered with intense warning, her gold eyes flashing with molten temper. "You do not give my title to anyone until I give you leave to do so. I will not brook that insolence, not even from a sister."

"If you did not wish to share the title, Siena, then you should not have slept with him."

"What has happened here is my business, and mine alone. I will dictate the ramifications of my actions, Syreena. Not you, nor anyone else, will force their opinions on me."

"By all means, Your Highness." Syreena inclined her head in a serious bow of acknowledgement. "Your authority is, of course, paramount to anyone else's. Far be it from me to gainsay you."

"You always gainsay me," Siena said, sighing heavily as she ran a hand through her damp hair. "Come. Jinaeri has left clothes in the back room. It is too cold to stand here trading words in the nude."

Syreena nodded and followed her sister into the back of the cavern. The Demon was nowhere to be seen, but Syreena could sense him in the room set just behind the fireplace. Siena was uncharacteristically nervous as she tossed one of Jinaeri's dresses to her sister before slipping one onto herself. Syreena made herself as unobtrusive as she could, finding a seat in the corner of the couch.

To her surprise, the warrior did not continue to hide in the back room. He made a fairly immediate appearance, dressed a little more appropriately in his pants.

Elijah glanced from Siena to the other female with a discerning eye. He had never seen a Lycanthrope quite like this woman who had disturbed their solitude. Her bicolored hair alone was enough to inspire his curiosity. It was as long as Siena's, but heavy and straight as it fell down her body. Having learned a bit more about the significance of a Lycanthrope's hair, Elijah knew there was something a little extraordinary about this intruder.

He turned his attention to Siena. The skirt of her newly donned dress swished sharply as the Queen made herself busy at the fire and the counter. He felt her distress and her internal struggle for composure very keenly. She was preparing dinner for them as if they were attending a casual party instead of . . . instead of what it was.

A moment of reckoning.

The moment she made the mistake of passing into his reach, he seized her by her arm and drew her close.

"Would you give me a moment?" he asked her, his direct gaze daring her to argue. She nodded and allowed him to draw her into the back room.

The minute they were out of sight of her unexpected guest, he turned her back to the wall and trapped her to it lightly with a hand braced on either side of her shoulders.

"I know what you are thinking, kitten," he said softly, his jade eyes penetrating deeply into her soul. "You are thinking we will pretend this has not happened. That you will escape with your little confidante back to your world and I will be nothing but a very intriguing memory."

"How do you presume to know what I am thinking," she asked, her whisper sharp on her rapid breath. But the color flushing up over her skin tattled on her quite effectively. "And what do you propose as an alternative? Sweeping me off my feet and making me your bride?" She laughed softly, breathlessly, the sound derisive and raw. "I have no intention of taking this one step beyond this cavern, and I know you have understood that all along."

"Yes, I have," he agreed, "but I don't recall ever agreeing to it. I asked you what you wanted, Siena, and you made it perfectly clear it was me. And until you stop wanting me, this doesn't come to an end."

"Trust me, warrior, my desire for you ends the moment I cross the threshold of this cavern."

Elijah did not argue with her. Instead, he reached to touch her cheek. She jerked her head away, but it was with panic in her eyes. He followed easily and settled his warm fingers on her flushed cheek. With purposeful intent, his fingertips slid down to below her ear and then made that sensual circuit down the side of her neck that so easily stimulated her. He felt the blush and swell of her reaction to the touch on a purely spiritual level. By the time his touch stroked back up to her face, she was turning into his large palm, her lips nuzzling over the calluses within it as her eyes slid closed.

"Elijah," she whispered, her breath pooling into his caressing palm. "My feelings—my desires," she corrected herself, "are beside the point." She looked up into his eyes with the weight of her responsibilities gleaming in her golden pupils. "You are Demon. I am Queen to a species that still feels the bite of your sword. You will find another to be with soon enough who will be more appropriate. This . . ." Siena suddenly turned from his touch, trying to ignore the bereft feelings that resulted. "This ends here."

She ducked out of his trap, but he was just as fast as she was and whirled her back up against him in a heartbeat. His hand bunched up her hair as he held her head still for his kiss, the other hand locking her forearm to his chest.

Siena felt intense pain slicing through the center of her body as she opened her mouth to his demand, to his purposeful brand that burned her soul deep. His message was violently clear. This was not over between them, and he was going to prove it to her by any means necessary. No matter what the cost to either of them.

He let her go slowly, hands first, lips last. His eyes were dark and serious as he stepped back from her, raised his arms, and with a simple thought twisted into the brisk chill of an autumn breeze. He rushed past her, through her, making her inhale with sudden surprise as his essence streamed through her hair and over her skin.

The only things resting in his stead were the borrowed trousers and the circlet of hair that had sealed the wound on his chest all of this time.

Elijah lived in the States, so he was forced to end his trip at a location closer to the Russian forest he had just left. Noah's home in England was the closest place he could think of, and so he streamed into one of the upstairs bedrooms, where upon solidifying into his biological form, he stumbled and fell to his knees, clutching the freshly bleeding wound on his chest.

He barely noted the bite of the stone floor against his knees. Noah would sense his energy momentarily and would come to find him. Before that happened, he needed to get to some soap and water and rid himself of the Lycanthrope Queen's scent.

He was loath to do so. Even as he got up and made his way into an adjoining bathroom he could feel the resistant cry of that place deep inside himself that Siena had managed to touch. The place that needed her scent clinging to him until he could find a way to convince her to come back into his embrace.

He was barely under the water for five minutes before he heard the outer room door open. By then he was so weak from fresh loss of blood, he had been forced to sit down in the corner of the shower stall. With water streaming through his hair, he tried to focus on the opening door.

To his momentary surprise, it was not Noah who had felt his presence and come to him.

It was Isabella.

She gasped with shock when she saw him and all the blood washing down over the shower tiles. She hurried toward him but suddenly jerked to a halt, a hand slamming into her forehead as if she were under a mental assault.

"Well then, get up here!" she growled viciously to an unseen conversant. "And bring Gideon with you."

Then she promptly ignored what had clearly been a voluble complaint from her notoriously possessive husband and moved to Elijah's side. She shut off the taps and, ignoring the fate of her pretty white gown, knelt beside him in the pool of water and blood that remained yet undrained.

"Hey," he greeted her, giving her a wan smile. "Jacob's going to murder you."

"Yes, well, he'll have to come up here to do it, and that's all that matters to me at the moment." She snatched a towel off the other side of the shower door and bunched it up against his wound, pressing with all her weight. She was a little thing, top to bottom, so Elijah could barely feel it. "We've been so worried about you," she whispered, leaning to kiss his forehead, her free hand pushing his soaked hair out of his eyes.

"Can't a man take a little vacation?" he quipped, wincing when the bathroom door burst open hard, recoiling off its backstop and almost cracking Jacob in the head.

"Damn it, Bella!"

"Oh, would you please give it a rest, Jacob!" she snapped back at him. "When are you going to get it through your thick head that I am just as Imprinted into this marriage as you are? I am really getting sick of this!"

Jacob had never been on the receiving end of his wife's temper in the entire year they had known each other. It left him so shocked that Gideon had to physically move him aside in order to get past him to his patient.

Bella ducked so the medic could step over her and squat down across from Elijah.

"Well, you look like something the cat dragged in," he remarked, immediately laying a hand on the warrior's forehead and closing his eyes in order to assess the damage done to the warrior's abused body.

Gideon did not understand why Elijah found his remark so terribly funny, but the warrior was laughing so hard that his nurse pinched him in the arm to stop him.

"I can't keep pressure with your chest bobbing up and down. Besides, Gideon will never be that funny," she said, giving him a cockeyed look.

"What possessed you to take a shower, Elijah? It could have waited." Gideon shook his head in bafflement, reaching to move Bella aside so he could inspect the worst wound. "Playing with iron again, I see."

"Yeah, well, the other kids weren't playing fair," the warrior murmured.

Gideon looked up at Jacob, who was standing awkwardly in the center of the room.

"So, are you going to challenge him to a duel, or would you mind donating some blood?" Gideon asked.

Bella stood up and moved out of her husband's path, giving him a look that should have cut him to shreds. Jacob moved to his friends' sides and bent down on one knee. He extended his wrist to the medic, who grabbed hold of it in one hand and Elijah's in the other.

"I'm sorry," Jacob murmured to the Captain. And it was clear he meant it sincerely.

"Save it for your wife, friend. She's more upset by it than I am. You've been pigheaded all my life. I'm used to it. She isn't."

Color flared into Elijah's skin even as his donor paled. Despite her pique, Bella was there to help her weakened mate to a seat in the bedroom. Having gotten his patient out of the immediate danger of bleeding to death, Gideon began to heal the wound itself. He had his hands pressed to the rent flesh and was completely focused on his task. Elijah felt the peculiar stretching that came with the knitting of tissue, deep inside his chest.

"You are going to have to tell me exactly how you managed to survive this long with this kind of wound. It is half healed. One would think you would have the sense to stay put until—"

Gideon stopped abruptly, his silver brows furrowing into a frown as he tilted his head and tried to analyze what he was experiencing. When those sharp mercury-colored eyes bore into Elijah's, the warrior knew without a doubt that the Ancient had somehow gained a clue to what had transpired the past few days. But to his relief, the medic did nothing more then lift a single brow of curiosity.

That was all.

Gideon returned to his task, not saying another word.

CHAPTER 7

Siena walked the length of her throne room slowly, her arms folded across her middle as she paced, her bottom lip between her teeth as she continued to mull over all that had happened to her recently. Any hopes she might have had about maintaining an air of normalcy had flown out the window the moment she had begun to approach the crowded receiving rooms laid out before her throne room. She knew she could never survive under such scrutiny, that she would go mad trying to maintain this sudden secret if forced to face a melee of her subjects. So she had made use of a lesser known and far lesser traveled route to her bedchamber. Since her return was not announced as it always was, no one awaited her there. She was able to dress discreetly and take other steps toward discretion.

The throne room and outer receiving rooms had been emptied at her command, a command that was reinforced with a low growl of annoyance when it was questioned as being unusual. Siena also knew that the garb she wore, a caftan of aquamarine silk, was also met with questioning eyes, the shining garment somewhat conservative for her as it reached her ankles and hooded her head.

But she was Queen, and it was very clear she would brook no questions and no hesitation to any of her orders. She had sent away all of her ladies and companions, all pages and advisors, leaving no one in her sphere save the two females that stood in the darker shadows of the room watching her movements. She was highly aware of their curiosity, and she could feel their stares upon her. Siena indulged in her court and her station quite richly. It was not at all like her to request such utter solitude. Even her guard remained outside of all the doors, rather than inside.

Siena tried to push it all away, even tried to push her thoughts outside of the sealed doors of the throne room she paced so rapidly and fiercely.

Syreena watched her sister pace, her bicolored features plagued with the same puzzled and bemused expression that had beset her since the moment she had caught the Queen in a most compromising embrace with, of all the beings in the world, the Demon Butcher himself. The man who had murdered their father. True, Syreena was more apt to see what the warrior had done as a favor, just as her sister and quite a few others did, but that one good deed of death would never make up for thousands of others over the centuries. There was not a breed amongst them that had not lost someone close beneath the Demon Butcher's sword. Siena had to be completely out of her mind to choose such a man as her mate.

That she had chosen to mate at all was astounding enough on its own. Though there was much Syreena did not know about her sister after living a hundred and thirty years in the Monastery of The Pride, she knew Siena was a woman who prided herself not just on her control of all things, but especially of her control over her monarchy. She had heard Siena preach on the ills and evils of hostile, aggressive males, and her loathing toward her own mother for choosing such a man and allowing him to take them into those three dark centuries of war. She had sworn she would maintain her virgin state until her death, passing the throne to a female heir, rather than mate with a male who would greedily claw at half her monarchy.

There was no mistake in Syreena's mind, however, that Siena had broken all of her own vows, and she had done it with a sweeping glory of irony. Syreena had seen them naked in each other's arms, the stubborn and passion-cold Queen and the merciless, destructive warrior, kissing with remarkable fervor and clearly mutually marked and bruised from what had no doubt been some very passionate love-making. Syreena still couldn't reconcile the image with what she knew her sister to be, with what her sister had drilled into her these fourteen years concerning the certain evils of men and monarchies mixing.

Perhaps Anya would have had a better insight into the entire occurrence, but Syreena had been sworn from sharing her knowledge with even the half-breed who knew every secret corner of the Queen's mind and heart. So the Princess was left to her baffled thoughts, trying to reconcile how such things could come to pass, and in such insignificant amounts of time. Of course, Syreena had always ignored her sister's prejudices toward men, being the one sister who actually craved husband, hearth, and heirs. She knew where all this anger came from and that Siena might be forced to reevaluate her opinions as she grew wiser . . . or more lonely, but the Princess would never have suspected such a tinderbox as this to light Siena's fuses and blow all her theories to hell. Syreena's pity warred with amusement, and she slipped farther back into the shadows so her sister would not sense her thoughts and feelings and grow incensed.

Anya heard Syreena's movement but kept her eyes fixated on the image of the royal female who paced around the room slowly, her arms wrapped around herself as if she were in need of comfort, her unusual silence worrying her and making her edgy and watchful.

"It is not like her to be so . . ." Anya tried to put what she was seeing into words, glancing at Syreena for assistance.

"Withdrawn," Syreena supplied. "We are used to her coming directly to us when something confuses or disturbs her."

"What do you suppose happened?" Anya whispered.

"I cannot begin to guess," Syreena lied easily. "She looks pale. If I am not mistaken, she is sunsick."

"Siena?" Anya made a soft sound of disbelief. "Siena does not feel the sun like the rest of us."

"Nor do I, but that does not make me immune. Even those of us highly resistant to the normal speed of sun sickness will show the signs of it if exposed long enough," the Princess said quietly.

Syreena crossed her arms beneath her breasts, seemingly studying the hand-carved pattern of the stone floor beneath her feet.

"It is strange that she should spend all this time in solitude only to come back looking so disturbed," Anya remarked. "Something has happened to make her thus."

"I would not begin to speculate. She will tell us in her own time, I imagine."

Anya looked at the other woman, her foxy eyes narrowing keenly.

"Did you not see anything when you found her?"

Syreena turned her dual-colored eyes on the half-breed. "Such as?"

"I don't know," the half-vixen murmured. "I just have this feeling like something is off. She doesn't . . . smell right."

"If you say that too loud, you're going to find yourself on the opposite end of that leash after all," the Princess whispered. It made the other woman laugh. "We can only wait and trust she will come to one of us eventually to discuss whatever the matter is," Syreena added. "For the time being I will not take part in your penchant for gossiping."

"My gossiping has been quite useful to this court on

many occasions," Anya rejoined. She then chuckled softly. "But I will tell you this, as far as the Queen seeking confidences goes, I find myself glad I am not the court advisor and the Queen's Counselor. Judging by the way she dismissed the court, whatever is pulling her tail is very likely political, and it clearly has her quite put out. Political aggravation falls into your advice-giving milieu. Mine is limited to her personal problems and her fighting forces. And for once I am quite grateful that she has no personal life outside of bitching about you."

"I will keep that in mind," Syreena said dryly.

Sienna was aware that her two closest attachés were whispering with their heads together, no doubt mulling over her behavior. She knew Syreena would not break the vow of silence she had sworn her to, so she was not worried about that. She was not prepared to discuss the matter with anyone yet. She was hardly prepared to even face it within her own thoughts.

The Queen continued to pace around the enormous room, occasionally rubbing her hands together, trying to warm them from the chill that seemed to go soul deep.

She was in trouble. That much was all too clear.

For beginners, there was the issue of her detached collar.

The collar was a work of legend and magic, stories of which everyone in the entire Lycanthrope society was raised on from infancy. Every member of the royal family wore the mystifying collars, each differing in shape and style by virtue of the wearer's rank and importance, from birth to ascension to death. They were a series of complex puzzles, these intricate pieces of jewelry, designed that way for very specific reasons. They expanded and decreased in size when the wearer altered form, never slipping free, always broadcasting the rank of their owner.

The legendary mysteries went deeper still. Firstly, only a member of The Pride could attach the collars. Only members of The Pride knew the secret to joining the complex

links. This was so that the royal insignias could not be repli-
cated or forged, or worn by anyone other than the rightful
heirs to the throne. Though made of gold, they were enchanted, making them indestructible, so they could not be
cut off by enemies or thieves or the monarchs themselves,
for whatever reason. To add to the trick, the collars could not
be removed by anyone in The Pride, the puzzles never working
in reverse and their secrets impossible to unravel.

Siena had heard all of her life how her collar could only
come off one of two ways. Either by the wearer being be-
headed . . .

. . . or under the destined touch of the ruler's one true
mate.

The mysticism claimed that only the touch of a perfect
mate for a royal soul could free the collar. The male or female who performed such a task was destined to be wed to
the collar's owner, and there was no arguing the point. Who
else could unravel the impossible puzzle that wise men had
toyed with unsuccessfully for thousands of years? Only one.
A perfect one. A soul as royal and complementary as the collar's owner.

The very idea made Siena's stomach churn with nausea
and a fear she had never known. Now that it had been removed, the collar could only be returned to the Queen's
throat by the hands of a member of The Pride, or, if the legends were true, by the hand of the lover who had originally
removed it. The puzzle was out of Siena's scope of knowledge and was purposely kept that way to keep the ruler who
wore it from doing exactly what she was trying to do . . .
hide the fact that she had taken a mate.

Her true mate, if legend had its truth.

"This is insane," Siena hissed under her breath as she
turned to make yet another circuit around the room.

A Demon the destined mate of a Lycanthrope? What did
it matter that they were so . . . so compatible? Chemistry and

sexuality aside, there was more to ruling thousands of people then the ability to have good sex. She slid her hand into the pocket of her caftan, closing it tightly around the links of the collar. She marched up the steps of her throne and sat down, staring really hard at the whispering women across from her for a long minute.

Syreena might know how to return the necklace to its rightful place. She had lived amongst The Pride for over a century. Perhaps she had picked up the secret during her time there. But Siena knew she could not ask Syreena to betray her mentors. It would be like someone asking her to reinitiate the war. And now, more than ever, she had reason to despise the idea of such an abomination.

No! she cried out in her thoughts. *There are no more reasons than there were before! That would intimate I have some sort of feelings for . . . and I do not!*

The Queen was back on her feet and pacing a heartbeat later.

She needed a solution to this awful conundrum, and she needed one fast. There was no way she was going to introduce a Demon male of such infamous renown to her court, name him King, and sit him by her side! Such a warrior? The idea revolted against every good intention she had forged for her people in order to lead them into a brighter, more peaceful future. She had intended on ruling by herself until the day she died, and somehow she was going to find a way to continue that plan. She would hang herself before taking part in such an abomination against everything she stood for, and she would be damned before she would take that man back into to her bed!

Siena stopped in her tracks as searing agony clawed through her at the very thought. She could hardly breathe for the pain of it, and she clutched at the place over her womb that ached with the most intensity. She felt so hollow, so bereft of life and reason when she thought about abandoning

Elijah for all time. He had promised it would not be the end, and, Goddess help her, she screamed with every molecule of her body for him to keep his promise.

Siena dropped to the floor with a sob, doubling over with the pain and nausea of self-betrayal. She knew she craved him, knew that her cells screamed for the nourishment of his hard, aggressive body around and inside hers. She had been taken to remarkable heights, unimaginable places of pleasure, and, like a fast-addicting drug, the idea of never returning to it was almost impossible to bear.

But she must find a way to bear it. She must break this spell, defy this magic of legend that claimed he was perfect for her. She had far more to consider than just her body. She had thousands of people who were counting on her to make the wisest and most considerate choices for their well-being that she could manage.

She had not been doing that when she had fallen into Elijah's arms. Unfortunately, a few days ago she had made the choice to save a man's life, and, it seemed, she hadn't made a single proper decision since then.

Siena was determined to change that.

It had been almost two days since she and the Demon had parted company. Yet she knew his presence still clung to her. She knew Anya must suspect something, even though she had yet to let her half-breed General close enough to get a good whiff of her. But it was more than that as well. It was as if the Demon warrior still followed her everywhere. Sometimes she imagined she could still feel his touch. In her mind. On her body. It haunted her, half memories and half fantasies, always leaving rivers of heat bleeding throughout her system in its wake. If this obsession was the nature of a mating, then she truly, more than ever, wanted no part of it. It made her mad to think of it, in terms of both sanity and temper.

As soon as she was through healing from her sun sickness, she was going to go to the Demon court and demand that Noah resolve these issues by making his Captain keep his distance from her.

Siena discarded that thought a moment after thinking it. The last thing she needed to do was go anywhere near where Elijah might be. Samhain was mere days away and she knew enough about Demons, thanks to Gideon, to know she would be tying the cat up in the doghouse if she went anywhere near their territory during that volatile time. The last thing she needed was to come up against the power of the Demon warrior's passion and irresistible seduction, magnified by the Hallowed moon to an intensity far beyond anything she had experienced so far.

She did not trust herself to resist him if she did.

Siena gained her feet once more, her hands sliding over her stomach as she paced, rubbing back and forth in a soothing motion that was habitual for her when she was uptight. But something had changed about the sensation, making it more sensual rather than comforting, as it had always been. It was because, she realized suddenly, she could feel his touch on her torso as keenly as if he was still administering it. Her breasts, belly, and hips seemed to burn with the imprint of his hands, to the point where she wondered why they did not glow brightly, the damning fingerprints showing themselves for all to see. She could still smell the masculine musk of his scent on her skin, and wondered if others were aware of it as well. Or was it just the madness of this untenable situation that made her believe in an illusion? She had bathed more than once since they had parted ways, and yet it would not leave her senses.

Truly, she must be going mad.

Siena crossed the room toward her throne once more, but could not sit in it. It was too symbolic of all the things at stake in the moment. She could not have sat still in any event. The Lycanthrope Queen resumed her pacing under the watchful eyes of her companions.

*   *   *

Isabella leaned over Elijah, brushing his damp hair off his forehead, biting her lip with concern. The warrior had been dreaming fitfully on and off since he had finally fallen into a restless sleep. It was an unusual occurrence for someone under Gideon's powerful sleep inducements. Usually the healing sleep was a still one, quiet and calm and allowing for the most healing in the shortest time.

The warrior had not answered any questions from those who were so perplexed by his state of injury and the clues from Bella's visionary trances of his activities during his disappearance. The healing of Elijah's wounds had been simple enough for the Ancient medic. Gideon had spent meticulous time extracting iron, bacteria, and a slew of other detriments to the healing process from the warrior's body. However, he was equally tight-lipped when others questioned him about the nature of the warrior's injuries and any suspicions he might have as to where the Demon had been all this time. All he would say was that they would have to ask Elijah themselves. It was cryptic enough to have more than one male pacing the marble floors down in the Great Hall.

Isabella should not have been there, what with Jacob still raw from the scolding he had received from her. She was perhaps meanly pushing his patience by spending all this time at the warrior's bedside. She had not meant to lose her temper, but was glad she had after all. Jacob was a brilliant man, sophisticated and wise with over six hundred years of life experience behind him. One would think such a man would be above something so petty as jealousy.

She tried to understand that having never known love before, Jacob had also never known jealousy. He had no experience with it and needed to learn just as anyone else would. But with his possessiveness fueled by a nature imbued with the temperaments and skills of all the animals of the earth, it would probably be quite some time before he came to grips with the volatile emotion. In the meantime, it was driving her up the bloody wall.

Since it had been a millennium since the last Druids had lived amongst the Demons, there was no one other than the long-lived Gideon who knew anything about them. Even he had been a fledgling at the time, a youth with only minimum knowledge about the Druids his people had been intent on destroying in the war at the time. A great deal of history had been rewritten since then. The truth was buried deep in the Demon library, and they had not yet begun to unravel the history of the Druids to be found there.

Along with the eradication of the Druids had come the reduction in instances of Imprinting. Demons Imprinting on one another, as Legna and Gideon had just done, was a one-in-a-million occurrence. It was now believed that all along, Destiny had intended the Demons would find their purest mates in the Druids, the very creatures they had systematically destroyed a millennium ago. It was written in a prophecy that had been lost to them for a thousand years.

No Druids, no Imprintings.

So, there was no standard in the current Demon generation for the behaviors and emotions a Demon would have to contend with during Imprinting. That meant, unfortunately, that they were walking around blindly, finding the answers as they went. Bella tried very hard to understand that. Jacob was a strong man, for all his sensitivity when it came to her well-being. He would learn to cope with it just as she would. She had no doubts that he would accept her help and eventually overcome. She should not have lost patience so easily.

Isabella heard the door open behind her and she looked over her shoulder to see a red head peeking into the room. Bella put a finger to her lips and gestured for the visitor to enter.

Corrine, Bella's sister and, amusingly enough, also her sister-in-law, entered the room and silently pulled up a chair beside her. She leaned forward so that they were almost touching foreheads, just as they had done all through their childhood when sharing secrets.

"I knew you'd be here," Corr said, picking out a single coil of her long red hair so she could nibble on it in an old nervous habit. "Jacob is going to throttle you."

"You worry about your husband, I'll worry about mine," Bella responded, her voice extremely hushed but clearly amused. Her violet eyes danced with irreverence. "Besides, my day is not complete without the daily Jacob lecture. I do hope his brother has better tolerance."

"Well, Kane was born over five hundred years after Jacob and wasn't brought up in the Stone Age." Corrine laughed softly. "So my husband tends to be a little more forward thinking than his brother."

Isabella grinned and impulsively reached out to grasp her sister's hand warmly. They had always been close, but after coming so near to losing Corrine a year ago, she had forged an even more powerful bond with her sister.

As mentioned earlier upon Corrine's arrival at the castle, Corrine had transformed from a regular human to a Druid/human hybrid just as her sister had after a brief encounter with her destined Demon mate, Kane. It was contact with a specific genetically appropriate Demon that triggered the birth of power in a Druid. Even a hybrid Druid. However, no one had even known hybrids existed until Isabella began to enter the process shortly after being exposed to Jacob. But Druids needed constant exposure to the triggering Demon from that first moment on, or they would become ill and "starve" to death.

Corrine had been deep into the starvation before they had realized what had happened. It had taken months of exposure to Kane for her to recover. Much in the way the victum of a serious accident had to go through extensive physical therapy, Corrine had been forced to develop far more gradually than the norm, recovering her power slowly over the past year.

This brush with death had been the glue that had reforged their already tight sisterly bond. Plus, they had often turned to each other as both had adapted to the lifestyle of a Nightwalker race as complex in culture as the Demons. They had also helped each other discover new ways to control and use their budding abilities.

"Does Kane know you are here?"

"No." Corrine gave her a conspiratorial wink. "Looks like both of our big, strong men are sleeping. One of the blessings of being half human is that we aren't driven to sleep in daylight as strongly as they are. What an awful feeling that must be, to be so lethargic that you have to sleep whether you want to or not."

"The same thing happens to humans. It's just not limited to daylight hours and we can sometimes push off the inevitable. I hear Gideon is at a point where he can remain awake all day without even a yawn."

"He is extremely powerful," Corr agreed, her awe clear in her voice. "So are you trying to get a premonition, or just playing nursemaid?"

"A little of both." Bella turned her head to frown at Elijah's sleeping form. "I have never seen him so weak. We can't get him to tell us anything. Gideon told Jacob that the wounds were not fresh, that the wound in his chest had obviously been healing for a couple of days before reopening. It looked as though it had been bandaged and that, when Elijah had transformed, he had left the bandage behind without taking it into account, reopening the injury."

"He's lucky he made it here alive. But that's a mistake I wouldn't expect an Elder Demon to make," Corrine remarked.

"I was thinking the same thing," Bella agreed, once more putting her head together with Corrine's. "Something happened to him."

"Yeah, well, that's obvious. I don't need a premonition to tell me someone kicked the shit out of him."

"No," Bella chided quietly. "I mean something else. Something that made him . . . act rashly. Make mistakes. And I have no idea what it was. I just keep seeing this image of cat's eyes. It's the only thing I get when I try to focus on this."

"I wish I could help, but my powers are limited to seeking Druids out. Maybe I could find his mate for him, but that's about it," her sister chuckled.

"Lord, don't say that out loud or you'll really send him into a coma. Elijah has been hiding from you ever since we figured out what your powers were."

"And Noah," Corrine added, making Bella giggle. "I swear, I have heard of gun-shy single men in my time, but these two take the cake. Then again, since I found the Druids Miranda, for Councillor Simon, and Yuri, for Yoshabel the medic, I have had only two other Demons seek me out for a search. Two out of thousands who know about my abilities by now."

"Some remember their history lessons about the Druidic Wars too well. It will take time, but they will come around." Bella rubbed her hands together as if they were chilled. "I wish I could control when these premonitions come. Right now it's like playing Russian roulette with a half-loaded gun. I've been here for half an hour clicking on empty."

"When you want them, they are nowhere to be found. When you don't, they are all over you. Reminds me of dating," Corrine quipped, making them both laugh.

"Well, something better happen soon. Jacob will wake shortly, and if I am here there will be hell to pay."

"Bell?"

Bella and Corrine both gasped softly and turned to look at the man lying in the bed. They both flushed, realizing they had pretty much forgotten he was there.

But Bella got over it instantly and moved to sit on the edge of Elijah's bed, taking up his hand eagerly as she leaned over him.

"Hey you, what the hell are you doing scaring the crap out of everyone like that?" she demanded.

"Good to see you too," Elijah said dryly, glancing up to see his second guest. "Whoa, two gorgeous women. I've had this fantasy before."

"Ha! And probably not just in your imagination, if I know you," Bella teased, making the warrior smile in that roguish, cocky way of his that eased both women's worried hearts. Bella reached out to push back an errant blond curl once more, noting he was still pale in spite of a second blood transfusion. "How are you feeling?"

"Depends. Did you stop the jetliner that ran me over, or let it keep going?"

"Are you kidding? Who would want to upset three hundred underpaid, underappreciated business men on the way to a long, boring conference?"

Elijah laughed, reaching to take her hand from his hair. He briefly kissed her fingers, his fondness and gratitude clearly reflected in his emerald eyes.

"Thank you, by the way."

"Humph. I was just worried my daughter would be out a perfectly good *Siddah* if I didn't save your sorry ass."

"Then you haven't had the naming ceremony without me?"

"Elijah," Bella scolded. "Really! What do you take me for? We would never do such a thing. Not while you were missing." She reached with her free hand to push back his hair again, but he took that one in hand as well.

"Stop touching me," he said. "The last thing I need is your insanely jealous husband pounding the stuffing out of me."

Elijah pushed her hands into her lap.

Bella fisted her hands and stuck them onto her hips in a familiar gesture of exasperation.

"You know, I used to be a nurturing, affectionate person. My unreasonable, domineering husband has to learn to get a grip, Elijah. When are you all going to learn I will do what I want, when I want, and you all can bite me if you don't like it!"

"I believe biting would also be an unwise action considering your husband's unreasonable, domineering, and jealous behavior."

"Oops," Corrine whispered from behind her sister as all three of them turned to look at the husband in question.

Jacob was leaning in the doorjamb, arms folded over his chest, his dark, serious eyes lit with enough amusement to make Bella sigh in relief.

"Now, since when can you sneak up on me like that?" she demanded, getting up and hopping over to him so she could jump up into his embrace.

Thank you for not being a beast, she murmured into his mind.

Thank you for forgiving me for being such an idiot, he returned softly.

Jacob cuddled his little wife, scooping her up and burying his face in her silky hair and laughing. His dark eyes flicked up to look over her shoulder at Elijah, speaking volumes about how relieved he was to see his old friend awake.

Jacob released his wife and moved to Elijah's bedside, pulling up her abandoned chair to sit in and crossing an ankle over his knee once he was settled. Bella stood behind him, resting loose arms around his shoulders.

"Hello, old friend," Jacob greeted. "It's good to see you awake and alert."

"You have no idea," Elijah sighed, moving to sit up. He rested a hand briefly on his chest, noting the fresh pink skin that had replaced the wound.

"Are you able to tell us what happened to you?" Jacob asked.

Elijah nodded, his momentary hesitation going unnoticed by the trio of guests.

"I was ambushed by Ruth and Mary and about thirty

necromancers and hunters. Talk about 'Hell hath no fury . . .'"
Despite the joke, Elijah's eyes were far too serious for his
nature. "They nearly killed me."

"Jacob, ladies . . ."

They all turned their attention back to the door at the
summons just in time to see Gideon stepping over the
threshold.

"I do not believe I gave leave for visitors," he remarked.

One thing they all knew not to do was gainsay Gideon
about the well-being of a patient. They all stood up and immediately took their leave of Elijah. Jacob clasped his
friend's hand briefly, and both women leaned to kiss him and
tell him how happy they were he was back. They hustled out
of the room past Gideon, Jacob shutting the door behind
himself.

Gideon remained leaning against the wall opposite Elijah's bed, his silvery head bent slightly as he watched the
warrior move to sit up. Elijah was not an idiot. He knew the
Ancient Demon was on to something. But he wasn't going to
help him out in any fashion. He would let Gideon put down
his cards first.

And Gideon was nothing if not direct.

"You were tended for at least two days," Gideon said.
"Why did you go into a metamorphosis, risking your life just
to get here? You should have stayed where you were until
you were much stronger."

"I couldn't," Elijah looked away from the medic just long
enough to catch Gideon's sharp attention. It helped confirm
something he had already begun to guess at.

Elijah's hand curled into a fist as he felt the Ancient's
gaze resting on him with calm patience. Still coming awake
after such a long sleep, Elijah might not have been aware of
many details about the past few days, but he sure as hell remembered his encounter with Siena. And he realized he carried evidence of that even to this moment in spite of his
efforts to conceal it.

"I realize it is not my business, but I am aware of the change in your scent and will not pretend otherwise," Gideon mentioned quietly. "I am also familiar with that scent. As much as I am familiar with the make-up of Lycanthrope blood when I see it in a body it does not belong in."

"Has anyone else . . . ?"

"If they took note, they did not mention it. It is possible they overlooked it, but I would not bet large sums of money on it." Gideon paused long enough to brush a thoughtful hand at some invisible piece of lint on his trouser leg. "The female's scent is Siena's, is it not?"

"Don't play games with me, medic," Elijah said bitterly. "You know exactly who it is and don't need to ask me useless questions."

"I do," Gideon admitted. "As improbable as it seems."

"Believe me, I am as shocked as you are," Elijah admitted with a sigh. "It gets worse, Gideon." Elijah laughed humorlessly. "The beautiful Lycanthrope Queen wants nothing further to do with me. So if you planned on setting the Enforcers on me for breaking the law or giving me some sort of purity lecture, I might take that fact into consideration if I were you."

The silver-haired Ancient did not respond immediately, instead studying the warrior's expression and noting the strain around his attempts to brush off how much he was affected by the situation he found himself in.

"Siena may not have much choice in the matter, Elijah," he informed him quietly.

"I am sorry?" Elijah wasn't sure he'd heard that correctly. He sat forward slightly, meeting the medic's unwavering gaze. "Explain that."

"There are very distinct rules governing Siena's fate."

"Yeah. I know. One mate only. A rule she feels doesn't apply to a lowly Demon male such as myself." Elijah's sarcasm was sharp, but not directed anywhere other than his own bruised ego.

"I do not believe that is her decision to make. Destiny—"
Elijah's sharp laugh cut the Ancient off.

The warrior moved out of bed, shedding the bedding and reaching into the closet for pants and a shirt. At least these would fit him because they were his, left behind for the frequent times he was a guest in Noah's house and in this room. He was shrugging into a white moiré satin shirt when he finally turned back to Gideon.

"Don't talk to me about Destiny, Gideon. If you ask me, it sucks pretty royally at the moment." Elijah jammed the tails of the shirt into his trousers.

"You truly do not know what has happened?" Gideon asked, looking puzzled.

The remark gave Elijah pause. He halted in the middle of buttoning a shirt cuff to look at the other man.

"Do you think you could do me the favor of keeping the cryptic statements to a minimum?" Elijah asked, ignoring the sudden, anticipatory thrum of his heart.

"Elijah, you have to be the first Demon male I have encountered who does not recognize the effects of an Imprinting for what they are."

Now that definitely got the Warrior Captain's attention.

"Imprinting? Are you out of your silver head?" Again, that embittered laugh. "Between a Demon and a Lycanthrope?"

"As improbable as an Imprinting between a Druid and a Demon was a year ago," Gideon mused, "but here we are nonetheless."

Elijah forced himself to fight back the surge of excitement and hope that inexplicably rushed through him.

"Explain why you think . . . just explain," he demanded.

"You mean other than telling you that I can see it plain as day in your body chemistry? That had Jacob sat there a few minutes more, he would have noticed you carry the scent of a woman all over you despite your attempts to cleanse yourself of it? Or perhaps I might mention the fact that your hair has changed color."

Elijah's eyes widened and he turned back to the closet to look into the mirror hanging on the door.

Sure enough, his hair had changed to a uniformly gold color, identical to that of the Lycanthrope woman he had recently made love to. It shocked him that no one had noticed outside of Gideon. It shocked him, period.

"Your hair was wet when they first saw you. And frankly, they were far more concerned with your health than the color of your hair," Gideon informed him.

"Damn," Elijah whispered, running fingers through the waved strands of gold. Bella had even touched it and hadn't noticed. "But I thought Imprinting changed a woman's eyes. Siena's eyes are as gold as ever, I assure you."

"The Imprinting is marked by three very distinct traits, Elijah. The first is an uncontrollable desire between the male and the female. One that cannot be resisted for long, and absolutely not at all on the Hallowed moons of Beltane and Samhain, sometimes even the Solstices." The Demon raised a silvery brow. "I believe it is safe to say you and Siena have met that criterion?"

"Yes," Elijah admitted quietly.

"For your second sign, though it is true the female of an Imprinting often takes on the eye color of her intended mate, sometimes it is hair color or even their mate's powers. And the change can come to either the male or the female. It is exactly this kind of alteration, I assure you," he said, indicating the warrior's hair. "In my case, Legna gained my eye color. As for the Enforcers, and Kane and Corrine, in their cases, with a Demon/Druid Imprinting, it is the awakening of the Druid's powers that takes place."

"And the third is the telepathy between the couple," Elijah finished for him. "The ability to be in constant mental contact with the other person." Elijah made a sound of frustration, smacking an abusive palm into his forehead. "Now I understand why I feel like I can still hear her voice. Why we always seemed to know what the other was thinking or feeling without saying anything. I don't know why I didn't notice it myself."

"It takes time for it to become strong between Druids and Demons. Perhaps it is the same for any Imprinting across species."

Elijah laughed at that, but the sound was terribly painful and Gideon felt a reflexive response in the back of his mind from his wife. Hard as she tried, she could not cut herself off from him completely, and he felt that she had wanted to leave them in privacy. It was one of her foibles, this notion of privacy, that he would not understand any time soon. Privacy was not a Demon concept. It was a human one. Where she had picked it up was beyond him.

Do not worry, sweet, he assured her softly. *He will recover from this shock just as you did when you discovered I was to be your mate.*

Who said I recovered? she teased him. But he felt the sadness beneath her humor. *It will be so hard for them, for so many reasons.*

It always is, he agreed gently.

Gideon turned his full attention back to the warrior. He had moved to a window and was staring down at the manicured grounds outside of it.

"Correct me if I am wrong, but isn't this whole thing against the law?" he asked, a corner of his mouth lifting in a wry smile.

"That did not stop you from taking her to your bed," Gideon remarked.

Elijah swore softly, the sharp term aimed at Gideon's cold attitude. "Is there anything you don't have an answer for?" he bit out.

"Elijah, I am being direct for a reason," Gideon said.

"The Hallowed moon of Samhain is not five nights away. You will not be able to keep from her on this night. You do realize this, do you not?"

Elijah's answer was another bluish string of words. His temper got the better of him and he grabbed the nearest object and threw it across the room, where it shattered against the stone wall.

"Damn! Damn it!" Elijah whirled to face the medic, his fists clenched so tightly they were turning white. "She's going to hate me. Do you understand that? You know her better than any of us and you know she is going to hate me for this."

"Only in the beginning," Gideon assured the other man with surprising gentleness. "And it will be resistance and fear, not hatred. Trust me on this."

Elijah understood what the Ancient was telling him. He had been through this very situation himself. He'd had to win his mate over on many levels himself.

Her. Her friends. Her family.

But the difference was, all of Legna's friends and family knew about the permanence of the Imprinting and the futility of fighting it. Siena might know something about it from what she had heard and seen from Gideon and Legna living in her court, but experiencing it firsthand was going to be difficult, and explaining it to a society who didn't believe in such things was going to be nearly impossible.

"I will do what I can to help, Elijah," Gideon offered magnanimously. He had known Siena the longest of them all, a fact Elijah tried not to feel slighted by. But if anyone could make her see light, it would be Gideon.

"I appreciate that. And do it soon, Gideon. I need to see her, to talk to her. *Before* I end up tearing into her bedroom with nothing but animal lust on my mind. She has to understand this. If she doesn't . . ." Elijah turned back to his window, sighing as he rested his forehead against the glass. "If she doesn't, to her mind I will be taking her against her will."

Gideon understood that better than Elijah thought he did. Siena was made of proud and stubborn stuff. As long as she resisted the inevitable, any move Elijah made toward her would be seen as hostile. The more that happened, the harder it would be to regain the lost ground and connect them. The worst shortcoming of an Imprinting was that it usually occurred close to those urgent holy days. It was as if nature was giving them a few days to get a grip, but would have her way in the end. And that end would come quickly.

"She found me in the forest, frightened away my attackers before they could finish me off. She carried me to shelter, tended my wounds, fed and cared for me . . ." Elijah paused to flick a startling emerald gaze up to the medic. "And then she turned my entire existence inside out. What a hell of a way to thank her for her hospitality." He paused, rubbing a finger at a smudge on the window. "And what about Jacob? Noah? The law? Remember? *The dog does not lie with the cat. The cat does not lie with the mouse.*' And that's only one out of about a dozen purity laws this is breaking.*"

"The Imprinting is not something you can resist or avoid, so if it has happened, you can hardly be held to blame," Gideon remarked. "If you recall, there are a great many laws we have needed to rethink over this past year. If we have learned one thing this annum, it is that our ancestors tended to interpret prophecy the way they wanted it to be interpreted. We may not be the dogs to her cats, Elijah. She is a powerful Nightwalker female. She is intelligent and just as prone to her animal instincts as we are. She may have different traditions, but her people celebrate the exact same holy days we do. It may turn out that we were never any more different from one another than we allowed ourselves to be."

"But Jacob . . ."

"As I recall, there was a night about a year ago where you

stopped Jacob from making what, by law, was an enormous mistake. That law has since changed. Elijah, our world as we know it is in flux. None of us who are your friends will beat you with criticism. This is a time of temperament and change. A time of special destinies. You would do well to remember that."

Gideon lowered his head and lifted a corner of his mouth in a smile as his wife's praise for his uncommon tolerance whispered through his thoughts.

"I would, however, make a point of speaking to Noah relatively soon," he added. "It would be better coming from you as soon as possible . . . before someone else figures it out."

Elijah turned to look at the Ancient. After a moment, he simply nodded.

CHAPTER 8

Gideon approached the locked doors of the Queen's inner sanctum, giving the guards a smile that dared them to gainsay him. The Minotaurs had fought Gideon once before, though not truly in earnest, but it was enough to make them understand that the Demon was not only not to be messed with, but also allowed privileges to the Queen that no one else would have dared to assume. Not only that, but the medic could astral project into the chamber if he wanted to. It would be like trying to capture a ghost.

Gideon rapped his knuckles against the door and waited for a response. He ignored his wife's voice in his head as she cooed to him about how pleasing it was to see he had at last learned the concept of knocking.

One does not do otherwise when royalty is involved, he remarked dryly.

Oh, and no one else but royalty deserves the courtesy? she argued.

Foreign royalty, he added.

Ah, yes. A sense of privacy is not the Demon way, she mocked him with another of her light, pretty laughs.

"Come," came the resigned call from inside, the locks tumbling as someone inside freed them.

Gideon put aside his playful mental argument with his mate and focused on the task at hand.

Siena was seated at her loom, her hands deftly shooting the shuttle back and forth at a speed and degree of precision that only someone with supernatural reflexes could manage. She did not look up, and Gideon suspected he knew why. There were two waiting women in the room, but it was clear they had been ordered to a fair distance from the moody Queen and were more than happy to obey.

"Leave us," the Queen said without looking up, sending the servants scurrying out into the hall as Gideon closed the door. "Do you think it wise to attend the Queen in her bedchamber in the plain sight of all her subjects, medic?"

"Better to do so openly than in astral form. Tongues would wag then for sure, and I am not certain my wife would hold her significant patience for very long should she overhear such gossip. Ambassador or not, an insult to you of this inference would also be an insult to me, and she would not likely stand for it."

"Yes," Siena agreed. "I have come to know Legna quite well. She is not one to bear an unjust incident in silence. It makes her a good ambassador for your people, and her patience makes her a good one for mine. She and thee have changed many stubborn minds these past months of your residence among us." The Queen's shuttle continued to fly between her threads. "But I do not imagine you came here to discuss your wife or court gossip trends."

"No. I did not."

"Then speak, medic."

"I should first like to ask at what point it was that I changed from 'Gideon' to 'medic,' " Gideon queried archly.

The shuttle stopped, held in the Queen's hand for a long, thought-filled moment.

"My apologies," she said softly, setting her work aside

and turning to look at him. When he stepped closer, however, she turned her gaze to the floor and to the right, her hand gathering together the material of her collared gown around her throat.

"Siena, my powers may have very little effect on you, but I have eyes in my head and a sense of smell as good as most of your kind. I know the scent of the man you now carry as well as I know my own, and when I went to heal him three days ago, I recognized your mark on him. It does not take a genius to notice how you are concealing yourself beneath these clothes, surrounding yourself with half-bred Lycanthrope handmaidens whose senses do not include a heightened sense of smell."

"You are too shrewd, med—Gideon," she said, her voice distinctly hoarse. "Hopefully shrewd enough to tell me how to get out of this predicament."

Siena looked up, releasing her hold on her clothing, and Gideon drew in a soft breath of shock. He had been not been expecting to see Siena's bared throat. He had never seen her without her collar of office and had lived at the court long enough to know the significance of the legend and mysticism that accompanied the thick piece of jewelry.

He had been correct from the moment he had entertained the idea of this unusual Imprinting, but it was still quite something else to see the evidence of it growing in such leaps and bounds right before his eyes. A Demon Imprinting on a Lycanthrope? It should have been impossible, and yet, here it was, plain as could be, flickering with emotion between both sets of the Queen's golden lashes.

Gideon advanced on her, looking into her with his power as best he could, sorting through her alien physiology. He could not affect her much as far as the ability to heal was concerned, but he had lived in the court of the Lycanthropes for five years once before, and during that time had learned how to read enough to distinguish the normal from the abnormal.

Elijah's stamp was all over her. Being apart from each

other these three days was clearly taking its toll on the beautiful Queen, just as it was taking its toll on the warrior back home. She was paler than usual, clearly out of spirits, and though she fought it, clearly yearning for her inconceivable intended.

"Gideon, if you owe me anything for the kind treatment I gave you when my father imprisoned you all those years ago, you will repay me by stopping this."

The request was as desperate as the uncontrollable tone of her voice.

"I am powerful, Siena," he said softly, "but no one is powerful enough to overthrow Destiny. From what I have seen of Elijah, and now of you, she has made her choice and it will simply have to be accepted."

"Simply?" The Queen surged to her feet, beginning to pace in a way that set her long, silky gown into a float around her calves and bare feet. "There is nothing simple about this and you know it as well as I. A Demon ambassador is one thing, and that alone hard enough to get my people to accept, but a Demon King for the Lycanthrope throne? Elijah and I would be slaughtered on the spot if I ever dared force such an abominable union upon my species. Not to mention the fact that I am aware it breaks about half a dozen of your people's laws as well. And I cannot even begin to tell you my personal outrage over the entire mess or I will drop dead from a stroke!"

"What you fail to understand, Siena, is that every law has its exceptions. For my people, the Imprinting supersedes all else because it is a demand of nature in its purest form, and unlike law, not open to interpretation."

"Imprinting?" The Queen stopped pacing, a numb laugh jumping out of her as her hand went to her bare throat. "A Lycanthrope? Imprinting is a Demon condition. A Demon hell, if you ask my opinion about it. No offense to you and yours, Gideon, but I would rather spend the rest of my life as a fungus than be so much a part of another being!"

"What you are neglecting to realize, Siena, is that you do not have a choice in the matter."

"Oh, as long as there is breath in my body there is a choice!" the Queen snapped, marching up to Gideon with fire in her glowing eyes. "It may be irresistible to you Demons, but I am a Lycanthrope of incredible power and I will use all of that power to fight this thing! Imprinting? Ha! Try *imprisoning*. I have seen you and your mate, Gideon. How can you bear it, this constant need you have to be in each other's presence?"

Siena paused, color flaring into her cheeks as she rubbed an absent palm over her stomach. The sky blue material of her dress tangled around her legs as she turned to continue pacing once more, but she strode through the confinement.

"I have been on my own since the day I was born," she hissed, not even aiming the comments at Gideon anymore. She was looking up to the ceiling, and it was more like she was crying out in rage to her Goddess. "My father wanted nothing to do with children. War was his legacy. My sister was ill so often as a child that I was never allowed near her. After the genetic virus that altered her, she was sent to The Pride to be trained. My life was this court. After Mother died, I was left to tend the court while Father traipsed around the world trying to hunt down your people and pick fights with them. No rhyme, no reason that I ever knew of. Just hatred and prejudice.

"So my life has seen thousands of people constantly moving in and out of it, but none coming too close. Every moment of every day since I was a child has been this way. This court and every single soul that passed through it. I was a Queen, even when I was only a Princess. So I have, in a sense, ruled my people all on my own for one hundred fifty years. I will never take a mate, no matter what you and your Imprinting think to force on me! I will never force my people to accept such a blasphemous insult to our throne.

"Even if they could accept a Demon for their King, do

you think that they would ever accept the man they refer to as the Demon Butcher? The peace we have worked so hard for will be destroyed instantly. Frankly, my people did not truly enjoy the idea of their Queen getting into bed with Demons figuratively—they most certainly will not accept it literally!"

"And you are so positive about this? Are you certain it is your people's reaction that is frightening you?"

"Frightening?" Siena stopped to whirl around and glare at him. "You come into my home, my private chambers, and now you insult me?"

"If you wish to see it that way. However, your efforts to push me away are unnecessary. You need only ask and I will accept your dismissal."

Gideon watched the seething Queen closely, aware of Legna's ready attention in his mind. Siena's fingers were curling into fists and she was literally shaking with her emotions. Able to see and hear everything through her mate's eyes, Legna was aware of how volatile the situation was.

"Your condescension serves no purpose but to anger me, medic. You wish dismissal? Consider it accomplished. You and your nosey mate can consider yourselves banned from this court until I say otherwise!"

"Siena," Gideon warned quietly, "you will feel foolish for doing this in a few days' time."

"Out!" Siena's wild shout brought guards in through the door. "Get out! I will not tolerate this!"

The guards, seeing their Queen upset and so out of character, didn't care if Gideon was a frightfully skillful fighter who had already bested them once. They would still defend her honor and her wishes to their last breath. It was clearly in their stances as their fur bristled and bullish nostrils flared.

Gideon listened to the soft feminine voice in his head, her skill in diplomacy quite unique and effective. His direct manner often upset people, and perhaps he had misjudged by not bringing Legna's softer touch along. But he had never seen the Queen act irrationally, so it had simply not occurred to him that she might. He heeded Legna's pleas and sketched a slow, respectful bow to the Queen.

"As you wish," he said softly, a moment before his wife snatched him up into the soft pop of a teleport, preventing him from any residual temper or action that would come to be regretted later as well.

Siena turned to her guards.

"In an hour you will take a contingent to their dwelling and ascertain that they are no longer there. If they are, you will hurry them along, but they are not to be harmed. Not one hair, do you understand me? This is not to be construed as a hostile separation, merely a temporary distancing so I can concentrate on state matters without the presence of any Demons interfering with me."

"Majesty," the guards echoed in assent, bowing precisely before leaving her and returning to their posts outside.

They were barely finished closing the doors before she yanked them open so hard they ricocheted off their stops and shut on their own shortly after she had passed through them.

"Syreena! Anya! Attend me this instant!" the Queen bellowed down the echoing stone corridor, making many a servant start with unaccustomed shock.

The Princess and the Elite General were shrewdly within immediate reach, popping up behind Siena as they headed for the cold and quiet inner throne room that Siena had continued to keep empty. As soon as the doors were closed, she turned to them. Her only family. For the first time in days, she met their curious eyes, making them both react with expected surprise.

"No comments," Siena said sharply, shedding her overdress and stepping out of it, breathing a sigh of relief as she shook out her hair and adjusted the simple dress she had worn beneath it.

Syreena had been expecting the revelation, but upon seeing Siena's bared throat, Anya's eyes grew wide. She looked as if she were fighting the urge to drop her jaw open, but to her credit succeeded in resisting the impulse.

Siena rapidly filled them in on what had occurred, all the while pacing with the sharp, marching energy of someone itching for a fight. It was, of course, for Anya's benefit alone she did this. Syreena kept a neutral countenance, even when the half-breed's black eyes narrowed on her with suspicion.

"I have decided to fight this so-called inevitability. Syreena, you will go to meet with The Pride. Surely those great scholars can find a way to reverse these effects. Legends and Imprintings aside, it all cannot be in the hands of storytellers and this Destiny the Demons are so proud of. Tell them they have only four days. Make it clear to them that I would very much prefer a cure to this disastrous turn of events. I imagine they will be quite compelled to agree when they realize exactly who it is that will become their King if they fail. Do not return until you have exhausted all of their intellect.

"Anya, your duty is to fetch the female Mistral named Windsong and bring her to me. She lives in a Parisian suburb called Brise Lumineuse, and you should find her there. She is something of a xenophobe and will not want to travel away from her homeland, but you must beg her attendance in my name. She will come for me."

The Queen hesitated long enough to rub her temples. It was clear the turmoil she was wrestling with was causing her a painful amount of stress, a condition she was not familiar with in the least. Siena had always handled her reign with the ease of confident surety and instinctive clarity. Stress and doubt were never a part of her decisions.

Not until now.

"I don't understand," Anya said, confusion etched across her features. "What would you possibly want with a foreigner? What could a Mistral do about any of this?"

Siena turned cold gold eyes on her Elite General.

"Yours is not to ask why, Elite. Yours is to obey me un-questioningly. Go and go now, or I will choose another more capable of executing my commands!"

Anya had never heard such harsh temper from the Queen in all of her life. Had she not been seasoned in reacting to or-ders automatically, she might have hesitated in a way that would have been damaging to her career. Instead, she moved immediately to do the Queen's bidding, no further question on her mind. She would leave the handling of Siena to Syreena, the only one who could not be banished from the court at a temperamental whim.

Syreena turned to her sister as soon as the other woman had left.

"Siena, I do not need to go to The Pride and you know it as well as I do. No matter what the circumstances, they will not break a trust that is thousands of years in their keeping."

"That may be, but you will go and you will try."

"And when I do, that makes them aware of what you have done. After they refuse me, they will demand you take your mate to ascension, Siena, no matter who he is. You will run out of time."

"If I don't solve this before Samhain, I will run out of time anyway."

Siena suddenly seemed to deflate, covering her face with both hands as she tried to blink back the sting of emotion in her eyes. She tried to take deep, steadying breaths, suddenly moving to her throne and sitting in it because she couldn't stand a minute longer.

"Sweet Goddess, what have I done?" she said hoarsely, clasping both shaking hands between her knees. "Syreena, I can't do this. I can't be ruled by a man. And such a man! He is warrior from blood to bones! His entire world is nothing but battle and intrigue."

"As is Anya's," Syreena pointed out. "And yet she holds a special place in your life, your trust, and your heart."

Siena laughed humorlessly, nodding in agreement as a single tear slid down her face.

"And do you think for a second I could find such things in the arms of a Demon? It is my treatment of Anya that has helped remove the stigma attached to half-breeds, will it be the same if I take the warrior into my bed, possibly my heart? Will this," she pulled the necklace from her pocket, "make the choice of who I should love for me? Will gold and moonstones and cursed magic dictate who will rule this land should I die? I want it to be you, Syreena. A woman. A woman's heart must lead this society into the future. It was always meant to be that way. This is why the throne is passed to eldest daughter, not eldest son."

"No woman can truly know everything she needs to in order to rule a country if she has never known what it means to love. To care for a child. To honor a mate as her equal."

"I am doing just fine so far," Siena snapped.

"Have you? You have a singular way about you when you deal with the law and the court. You curse Father for his bigotry, condemn our people for the same behaviors, but do you not see your own?"

Syreena moved to seat herself at her sister's feet, taking her cold hands from between her knees and holding them between her warm ones.

"I have seen your bias in the courts, siding more often for the woman's side of an argument over a man's. When it is two males involved, you are not so patient and attentive. You try. I know you try," she soothed when Siena looked away from her, unable to meet her truth in her sister's eyes. "Your need for fairness is so powerful. But you are a product of your life as much as any of us are. You are, for want of a better term, only human."

For some reason, that made Siena laugh.

"Sometimes I think I wish that were true. I tell you,

Syreena, I envy Anya at times. She is the true meaning of the blend between the animal and the woman. She does not struggle so with her two halves . . . three halves . . ." She laughed again when her sister did.

"Five halves?" Syreena offered.

"Yes," Siena agreed, leaning down toward her sibling and bringing their joined hands to her lips. "Yes, that is true. I complain so much in this moment, but it is true when they say there is always a problem worse that your own that afflicts someone else. You have endured all of your life, spilt between multifaceted sides of yourself."

"I endured them in a glass house, Siena. The monastery is not the world. You lived in this world, dodging our father and all the things about him you grew to abhor, including assassination attempts after he learned your feelings about the Demons, and how they so differed from his. We cannot say who has had the harder life. It is like comparing apples and oranges."

"Cats and dogs," Siena agreed.

"Demons and Lycanthropes," Syreena pressed. "Though I suspect from all I have heard from your own lips that we are not all so different as we might hope to be. And if there is one person who can close that gap, it will be you. You are adored, sister mine. Remember that. You have never made a secret of your open mind and attitude toward the warrior's people. They may perhaps surprise you, our people, with the level of acceptance they are willing to take from you."

"I may believe that, if only I were capable of acceptance myself. If it is this difficult for me . . ."

"There is more to this for you than the race of your potential mate, Siena. Much more."

Siena nodded, too honest to lie to anyone other than herself.

"You are right, of course. Do me a favor, Syreena?"

"Fetch Anya back and tender her your effusive apologies?"

Siena laughed, nodding.

"And the Demon ambassadors?"

"Oh . . . damn . . ."

"Do not fear, My Queen. I will see to that as well. And your guards will not gossip. They are not the sort to do so."

"Have they even followed my orders, do you suppose?"

"It would not surprise me to find them dragging their hooves, waiting for their unusually temperamental sovereign to come to her senses. But I will see to it first. My suspicions are that Anya is dawdling over her packing in any event."

Syreena stood up, bending to kiss her considerably calmer sister on the cheek before releasing her hands.

"We will find a solution to all of this, Siena," she promised. "The three of us together. Just like the Goddess's trinity. Wisdom, Strength, and Nature, blended together in harmony."

The Princess turned away and moved to see to her duties, leaving Siena in the solitude of her throne to try to further reconcile all she had to consider from that moment on.

"Okay, Elijah, if this is one of your jokes, you had better come forward immediately."

Elijah raised dark, brooding green eyes to his King, making certain Noah knew this was no joke with a simple look.

"I was afraid you weren't going to say that," Noah sighed, sitting down and rubbing his once again pounding temples. "Siena. Of all the women in this wide world, it has to be Siena!"

"Funny, that's what I thought too," the warrior remarked, setting the glass of exotic tiger's milk on the table, turning to look into the fire he had watched Noah stare into for hours when in search of clarity.

"You will break about a half dozen laws if you do this."

"Are you planning on setting Jacob on me?"

"No. But I will have to tell him," the King noted. "And then I will have to tell the Council."

"How did I know you were going to say that," Elijah asked with a sigh. "I love the idea of my personal life becoming fodder for Council discussion."

"Be thankful you have many friends on that Council. And with Jacob, Gideon, and myself in your corner, it will not become an issue. However, it would be considered favoritism if I were to make the choice on my own, and I will not have griping Councillors harassing you over this matter any more than you are yourself." Noah gave the warrior half a smile. "And if I have learned anything about Siena in our short acquaintance, it is that she can be quite stubborn in the face of great odds. You, my friend, have something of a battle on your hands."

"Then I suppose it is a good thing I am your most skilled warrior, is it not?" Elijah returned, a wolfish smile of his own twisting at his mouth.

"You know, I have a feeling part of you is going to enjoy this," Noah said suspiciously.

"You know, I do believe you are correct," Elijah returned. "And in more ways than you will ever know, Noah."

"Mmm, somehow I do not doubt that. She is . . . a remarkable female."

Noah did not say anything more than that. If he did, he would potentially risk his neck for making too bold a supposition about another man's mate. If he had learned anything this past year, it was the powerful nature of the possessiveness that sometimes came with the Imprinting. And friend or not, Elijah was not a man whose bad side he wanted to get anywhere near.

"Now," he added quickly, "let us discuss the matter of these rogue females and what exactly you intend to do about it."

"I? It is Jacob who polices our own. Jacob and Bella."

Noah was not fooled by the warrior's casual dismissal of the question.

"And I suppose it never occurred to you to get back at them just a little for what they did to you?" the King asked knowingly.

"Now that you mention it . . ."

CHAPTER 9

Siena paced the halls of her castle slowly, stone walls and subterranean ceilings all around her carved with stonecutters' artwork that had been there for ages. Every new monarch took a new wing and had it immortalized with artwork they felt was representative of themselves and their reign. The process took a lifetime to accomplish, but it was fascinating to watch the carvings advance as the years passed.

It was a gratifying tradition. It meant she did not have to sleep in the same chambers that had seen her mother's death and her father's twisted dreams. Not that he had spent much time there.

Now it was her own dreams she was trying to escape.

Dreams of the blond warrior who had somehow branded her body, mind, and soul with his touch.

It had been two days since she had blown up so uncharacteristically in the faces of her friends, family, and confidantes. She had yet to visit Gideon and Legna and apologize for her behavior. Frankly, she couldn't even focus on that for the minute it would take to formulate a proper apology.

No. She was too sick for that.

Sick was the only term she could content herself with

when describing the way she was feeling. She was run down, lethargic. Sensations so alien to her that she was made dizzy by them. And those were the symptoms she was willing to acknowledge.

What she refused to acknowledge was the burn beneath her skin, the sporadic rushes of adrenaline that surged through her, followed by maddening impulses to run. To run and run until she was wrapped up in arms of steel and cradled in calloused hands. And it grew worse with every passing minute. Syreena said it was because she was not meant to be segregated from her Demon mate for so long, but Siena refused to believe herself capable of such needy behaviors.

And somehow, she felt as if he was constantly whispering into her thoughts.

She remembered that Gideon and Magdelegna shared a mental bond with each other, and that Gideon had once told her that it was common for all Imprinted pairs to be intimate in that fashion. But the idea of someone being privy to her every thought was appalling to her.

Appalling *and* irritating.

She had found herself angrily warning him from her thoughts, just in case he truly was there. And sometimes she thought she could hear the lilt of damnable confident male laughter echoing in her mind in response.

Samhain was two nights away.

And she felt it down to her last molecule.

She touched her throat, the comfort of the collar being returned to its rightful place the only thing that soothed her soul. It had, of course, cost her the sacrifice of facing The Pride and airing her rather soiled sexual laundry. They had agreed to rejoin the puzzling links of her collar, and had also agreed that they all should take time to consider the ramifications of what was occurring before opening it up for debate by the general public.

But Siena already knew their take on the matter.

The collar had proved in their minds that, as unlikely as it seemed, the Demon warrior was indeed Siena's one true mate. She would not have been sexually attracted to him otherwise. She would not have surrendered her maiden status to him. And he most certainly could not have unlinked the enchanted collar if he were not this mate she was destined to be saddled with.

Siena moved to lean her weight against one of the subterranean "windows" carved into the hallway she was currently navigating. The castle was rumored to be miles wide and to have more rooms and cubbies and passageways then one being could possibly walk in a single lifetime. That was saying a lot, considering how long lived her kind generally were. She couldn't count how many times she'd been lost in these halls as a child.

These glassless windows, more like carved archways than anything else, looked stories down onto the outer houses of the castle. Those houses were also covered by the cavern ceiling, whose echoes reached down to the inhabitants below. It had been her only way of calling for help then. But once she had learned how to change and use her sense of smell to backtrack her own trail, she had never been lost again.

Not literally, anyway. Figuratively speaking, she couldn't have been more lost.

A subterranean breeze blew over her, chilling her skin. She shivered, rubbing her arms and starting to move once more in order to warm herself.

She was very far back in the halls and hadn't seen another soul for hours. She had waved off her guard and her ever-vigilant companions, who had remained available to her at any hour should she feel the need to confide her feelings of the moment. Anya and Syreena were truly special creatures, and she would reward them for that as soon as she had sorted out this predicament she was in.

So she was indeed quite alone and surprisingly comforted by that knowledge.

The cold of another breeze rushed up from behind her, blowing at the brief skirt of her dress and whipping through her hair. It surrounded her, engulfed her, forcing her to come to a halt just as muscled arms appeared around her waist.

Siena sucked in a startled breath as the cold vanished, replaced by the warmth, the heat, of a familiar male body. She was drawn back against his chest, his hands splaying out over her flat belly and pushing her deeper into the planes of his hard body.

"Elijah," she whispered, her eyes closing as a sensation of remarkable relief flooded through her entire body. Every nerve and hormone in her body surged to life just to be held in his embrace, and she was light-headed with the power of it all.

He put hands on her hips, using them to spin her full around to face him. The warrior dragged her back to his body, seizing her mouth with savage hunger just as she was reaching for his kiss. She could not have helped herself. Not after the deprivation of all these days. But still, the weakness stung her painfully, leaving frustrated tears in her eyes.

It was all just as she remembered it. The vividness of the memories of their touches and kisses had never once faded to less than what it truly was. It was all heat and musk and the delicious flavor of his bold, demanding mouth. His hands were on her backside, drawing her up into his body with movement she could only label as desperation.

Elijah had not meant to attack her in this manner, but the moment he had sensed her nearness, smelled the perfume of her skin and hair, he could not do anything else. He devoured the cinnamon taste of her mouth relentlessly, groaning with relief and pleasure as her hands curled around the fabric of his shirt and her incredible body molded to his with perfection. He pulled her hips directly to his own, leaving no question about how hard and fast her effect on him was. He felt her swinging perfectly with the onslaught of his pressing body and adamant kisses.

Everything was perfection. Top to bottom, beginning to end, and he had been starving without her. He also knew she had been just as famished without him.

She was the first to put any distance between them, by breaking away from his mouth, letting her head fall back as far as it could as she drew for breath hard and quick.

"Oh no," she groaned huskily, shaking her head so her hair brushed over the arms around her waist.

Even those strands betrayed her, reaching eagerly to coil around his wrists and forearms, trapping him around her effectively, just in case of the outrageous scenario that he might want to move away from her. She lifted her head and opened her eyes, their golden depths full of her desire, and her anguish.

"I did not want this," she whispered to him, her forehead dropping onto his chest when the heat in his eyes proved too intense for her to bear. "Why will you not let me go?"

"Because I can't," he said, disentangling one hand from her hair so he could take her chin in hand and force her to look at him. "No more than you can."

"I hate this," she said painfully, her eyes blinking rapidly as they smarted with tears of frustration. "I hate not being able to control my own body. My own will. If this is what it means to be Imprinted, it is a weakness I will abhor with my last breath."

Then she pushed away, defying every nerve in her body that screamed at her to step back into his embrace. She could only backtrack a couple of steps, however, because her hair remained locked tight around his upraised wrist, pulling him along with her . . . as if he wouldn't have followed her anyway.

When she realized her back was to a window, she felt a

moment of panic. However, she realized no one was likely to see them, because they were over three stories up from the houses and people below.

"You call it weakness, and yet as affected as I am by it myself, I choose to call it strength."

His rich baritone voice echoed around her, making her heart leap in alarm. She grabbed his wrist and pulled him farther down the hallway, the dark shadows enclosing them as they reduced the potential for echoes.

"Why are you here? And do not blame it on a holy day that will not arrive for two days."

"I do not intend to 'blame' anything. I don't believe I need an excuse to see you, Siena." He reached for her face, but she jerked back and dodged him. "And it is because of that holy day two nights from now that I am here. We need a little bit of resolution between us before that night comes, Siena."

"I am not in need of resolution. If you are, you must come to it on your own."

She turned to walk away from him, but she forgot he was just as quick as she was. No one could outrun the wind. His hand closed easily around her forearm, pulling her back . . . and snapping the temper and pain she had been holding in tenuous control for days.

She released the cry of a wounded animal and flew at him. He saw the flash of claws and felt the sharp sting of their cut as they scored his face. Shocked by the attack for all of a second, Elijah reacted on instinct. He had her by her hair in a heartbeat, wrapping it around his fist in a single motion, turning her around so her back was to him and her claws pointed in a safer direction. She grunted softly and then screamed in frustration as she found herself trapped face first against the stonecutter's art.

His enormous body was immediately flush against her back, securing her to the unforgiving stone as he caught one hand and pushed it against the stone as well.

"Let go of me!" She struggled in vain, unable to move a micron in any direction. "You'll have hands full of a spitting-mad cougar if you do not release me this instant!"

"I highly doubt that," he purred easily into her ear, his mouth brushing over the lobe of it in a way that made her shiver involuntarily. "Your hair is bound around my wrist, and if I am not mistaken, that is more than adequate enough to keep you from being anything than what you are in this moment. Which is nothing more dangerous than a spoiled child, I think." Her response was to call him a name he was not familiar with, but had a good idea as to its meaning all the same. "Then stop throwing tantrums because you cannot have your way, kitten," he instructed her smoothly, his mouth drifting down the side of her neck slowly. "I have come here before Samhain because I did not want to hurt you, Siena. If you do not reconcile yourself to the inevitable by then, I will end up doing just that. And you may not believe it, but it truly is the last thing I want to do."

Siena closed her eyes, trying not to listen to his words and the patient, soothing tone they were delivered on. She clenched her teeth against the rivers of fire bleeding into her body from the touch of his artful mouth. She did not want to be swayed so easily by him. He could call it a tantrum or anything else he wished—it was her independence that was at stake, and she would not give it up without a fight.

"I am not here to rob you of your independence, kitten," he said softly, making her exhale in frustration at how easily he was beginning to know her thoughts. "In fact, I would rather cut off my own hands than do equal damage to you. It is your spirit, your independence, your fight, and all those instincts you cradle so close to your heart that make you so perfect for me. And make me perfect for you."

"How are you perfect for me?" she asked bitingly. "Because you can make my body respond to yours? Is this your idea of perfection?"

"It is a start," he mocked her, chuckling against her pulse.

"But there is much more to it than that, and I don't think you need me to point that out." He moved close to her ear once more, whispering his next words on the softest of breaths. "What better mate for an accomplished huntress then a warrior who brings the scent of her prey on the breezes? Who better to be the companion of the sensual cat then the male who will never get enough of her scent, her movements, her taste, and her touch? And who would you prefer over the one who can bow his head beneath the power of your hold around his throat? Have you forgotten that, kitten? Have you put away the memory of how easily I accepted your assertions in that moment, and all the moments when we were in bed together?"

"I am amazed your ego survived such wounds," she said, her bitter sadness heavy in her voice as she struggled to ignore the truths she did not want to hear.

"My ego is satisfied just to hold you. To feel your body against mine and know it will be there always. I would be happy simply to watch you as you hunt, hold court, sleep . . ." Elijah touched his mouth to her temple. "And I wish you would look into me to know what it means for a man such as myself to say such things."

Elijah released his grip on her hair, stepping back from her.

She took a long moment before she pushed away from the wall and turned to face him. It took her a moment more to lift her golden eyes to his.

"Why would you allow anyone to do such a thing? To invade your thoughts." She shivered in such a way that he felt it along the fine hairs of his body.

"Because I grew up in a society where such things are commonplace. We are very forward and up front with our thoughts and feelings. We share easily with one another. Something you may find liberating one day."

"I already do. I speak freely with Syreena and Anya, my thoughts as available to them as they would be to the probes of your Mind Demons. The difference is, I choose to do this. The choice is not taken from me without my permission."

Elijah leaned his back against the opposite wall from her and folded his arms across his broad chest. The movement made her suddenly aware of the fact that this was the first time she had seen him in perfect health since last Beltane. He emanated it. He was a tide of power, a current of lethal strength, and an elemental sexiness that made her shudder within her own skin. What would it be like, to make love with him now that he was strong once again?

He smiled, a cocky, amused grin that made her remember he was attuned to the things she thought. She made a sound of vicious frustration and purposefully looked in his eyes, refusing to act girlish.

"My people believe that the moment a female accepts the Imprinting," the warrior said with deceptive neutrality, "she has given her permission to be a part of all that it means. The telepathy is included in that."

"I did not give my permission for this! You know that!"

"Untrue. The permission was given the moment you moved into my arms of your own free will. The moment you told me you wanted me and accepted me."

"I wish I had never said those cursed words!" she bit out vehemently. "You have been throwing them back at me ever since, to the point where I wish you would choke on them!"

Siena realized she had gone too far about a heartbeat before she actually finished saying the harsh words. Elijah's eyes flared with green fire, causing her breath to freeze in her lungs as he sprang away from the wall and seized her arms with incredible strength. She had never felt anything like the power of those gripping hands. She suddenly realized exactly how much restraint he had constantly been using with her. By feeling this power, she now understood the vastness of his gentleness.

She found herself so close to him that she could see the striations her claws had dotted across his cheek. It had been only a glancing blow, the marks only releasing tiny drops of blood that looked like someone had stamped Morse code over his skin.

"You can't undo what has been done by your own actions no matter how hard you wish it away," he ground out, giving her a single, harsh shake. "Don't say things you will come to regret, kitten. We can make this easy between this, or we can make it hard. The choice is yours and you have two days to make it in."

"You will have to find me first!" she hissed back at him before she thought better of it.

"Very well," he said coldly, releasing her so suddenly she stumbled backward. "If this is the way you wish it to be, you will only have yourself to blame for it."

Elijah lifted his arms and with a blink twisted into the nothingness of the wind.

Once again he took his path right over her, whipping through her dress and hair violently, stamping her with his emotions of the moment in a dozen ways at once.

When she was sure he was gone, Siena finally let her rubbery knees give way.

She slowly sank to the floor, her back sliding over intricate carvings of a pair of swans, their necks entwined in such a way that it was impossible to tell which head belonged to which bird.

Isabella lifted her head from its position over the baby's crib when she heard the windows shudder in their casings. It was not a windy day, so she suspected it was not a naturally occurring phenomenon. She hurriedly kissed her fingertips and touched them to the sleeping infant's head before moving to close the nursery door and taking quickly to the stairs.

She paused halfway down when she saw Elijah pacing back and forth, his hands running repeatedly through his hair. Now that she was looking for it, Isabella noticed the change in the color that had previously escaped her notice. She rolled her eyes at herself.

Some Enforcer you are, she remarked to herself mentally.

Elijah looked up at that second and looked relieved to see her. He hurried over to her, leaping up the stairs and practically dragging her down them and into the living room. He gave her a little push that sent her bouncing into a seat on the couch.

"I need to talk to you," he said restlessly, immediately resuming his agitated circuit across the carpeting.

"So I gathered," she responded dryly.

"I do not know what to do about this insanely stubborn *female!*" He said "female" the way some would say "nuclear weapons." "She is determined to drag her paws, kicking and scratching every inch of the way. She will force me into doing something rash and painful, and the very idea of it is burning a hole right through the middle of my chest!" He barely paused for breath. "Iron weaponry is nothing compared to this, I promise you that, Bella. This is exactly why I never sought a mate—you know that, don't you? I knew it would be nothing but trouble."

"Yes, I can see how you'd feel that way."

Her sarcasm went completely over his head.

"All I had to do was watch how Jacob gets turned into knots over you and I just knew it was not for me." He stopped short and looked at her with sudden sheepishness. "Not to imply it is your fault, of course."

"Of course," she agreed wryly.

"But all you have to do is look at the way you had to tell him to back off when you were trying to help me. There's no sanity, no reason behind thinking and acting like that. I think I even understand what Siena is so afraid of. It is taking me over like some kind of . . . of . . ."

"Disease?" Isabella supplied helpfully.

"Exactly! It is like a sickness, and she is the only cure. Her! The most pigheaded, stubborn, irrational, pigheaded—"

"You said that already—"

"—woman in the world!" he finished, a sharp gesture of his hand punctuating his declarations. "Do I have time for this? I mean, really have time? There are two psychotic female Demons running loose out there and I need every last ounce of my attention focused on that if I am to be any use to Noah and Jacob. Any one of us could fall into another of Ruth's traps at any time, or be Summoned because she knows so many power names. It sickens me to think of her running around with such deadly knowledge. Her next victim is not likely to be as lucky as I was."

"Yes, there isn't a Lycanthrope Queen running around in every forest, after all," Bella added.

"Exactly!" Elijah looked relieved that she seemed to understand. He was completely oblivious of the giggle she smothered behind quick fingers. "And then there is your daughter, poor thing, running around without her names because of all that has happened. At this rate you will be calling her 'Hey you!' for the rest of her life."

Isabella bit her bottom lip, resisting the urge to give in to the smart remark that surfaced.

"And don't get me started about necromancers and hunters."

"Wouldn't dream of it," she assured him.

"There now, see? How hard was that? You understand, right? You use simple logic. One plus one equals two. There is no other answer, no changing it no matter how hard you try. So the only other choice is to accept the inevitable and move on. In spite of all the trouble this is causing me, I am willing to do that." He gestured to make an invisible path in front of himself. "Just accept what is what and move into the future. But she refuses to see that."

At last, Elijah ran out of steam. He plopped down onto the couch next to Isabella so hard she bounced in her seat.

He sighed with heavy frustration and defeat, closing his eyes and leaning his head back.

"I have a headache," he complained. "What kind of Demon gets a headache?"

"A tense one?" Bella offered.

"Exactly!" He sighed again. "I am so glad we could talk about this. There aren't many people I would confide in, but I trust you, Bella. You are more like me than the others. Your attitude, sense of humor . . . your total disrespect for all this bull we all take too damn seriously."

Elijah stood up again, bending to give her a brief kiss on her cheek.

"I will stop back later. I am going to go hunt down some necromancers and blow off a little steam."

In an instant he was nothing but a breeze blowing out of the open windows he had entered the house through not five minutes earlier.

What in hell was that all about? Isabella's exasperated husband asked in the forefront of her mind.

Well, my guess would be woman troubles.

Well, little flower, I would say I know exactly how he feels . . .

Except you'd get killed when you got home.

Exactly.

CHAPTER 10

Jacob drifted gently down from the sky, manipulating gravity with a perfection of Earth Demon skills unparalleled amongst their kind. In fact, it was widely believed that Jacob would be the first of his element in over a thousand years to reach the level of Ancient.

It was not comforting, however, when one understood that was because all the rest of them had simply not lived long enough to reach the age of 700 years, the time where such distinction took place.

Jacob's feet rested lightly on a thick tree branch and he lowered himself into a crouch until his hands also touched the bark of the old oak tree.

The Enforcer could very well be considered the closest thing to a Lycanthrope their people had. He could hunt, scent, camouflage, and behave in dozens of ways that all the beasts of the Earth could behave. Not many of his people knew this, but he could not only charm the animals, he could mimic them by taking their form.

It was not like the Lycanthropes, however. It was all just a Xeroxing . . . an adoption of physical make-up and skills. Changelings were as much the animals as the animals themselves. Jacob would need several more centuries with his relatively new ability before he could enjoy a perfection of emulation that could be considered on par with the Lycanthropes' natural metamorphosis.

At the moment he was in his normal form and seeking through the night and the trees with his uncannily sharp vision. He had been tracking the Demon for quite some time, finding it easy to mask himself from his target in spite of the other's skill. It only proved how distracted and intent the Demon was on its course of action.

The wind blew harshly through the creaking limbs of the forest trees, tugging last, stubborn leaves down into spiraling deaths where they would join the others at rest on the forest floor. Jacob glanced up at the nearly full moon, rechecking his position by it, then watched as a whirlwind of leaves burst apart to coalesce into Elijah's natural form.

The Wind Demon crouched on the forest floor, mimicking the very position Jacob was in as he let his hand drift through bloodstained leaves and short forest scrub. He then moved toward the bodies of his victims from that day not so distant and touched each briefly, scattering the remains into the winds with little more than a thought.

Knowing how brutally distracting the time of the Imprinting could be, Jacob was more than a little impressed that Elijah had remembered to come and see to this sort of cleanup. It was, of course, important to remove all evidence of such battles and the beings who were not supposed to exist. Clearly the necromancers and hunters who had lost their compatriots in the battle did not feel the same need to cover their tracks.

But there was a need for secrecy even for the mortals who thought to live as Nightwalkers. Human society was too skeptical of magic and far too entrenched in its religious prejudices for magic-users to risk exposing themselves. And as voluble as hunters might want to be, even they had to conceal themselves for fear of being labeled insane . . . or even homicidal. Amusingly enough, their own kind—mortals, that is—could be more dangerous to these misled humans than the true Nightwalkers were.

Jacob had decided to follow Elijah because the warrior's temper was clearly off its mark, and after his parting comment to Bella, the Enforcer worried that the other Demon was not yet well enough to face the kind of trouble he was looking for. He had not been strong enough to face it alone the first time. What made Elijah think he could have any better luck this time was completely beyond the Earth Demon.

Elijah straightened from his task of disposing of the mortals' remains and braced his feet hard apart, balancing his significant weight firmly between them, an ages-old habit that was recognizable as distinctive of the warrior.

Both Demons suddenly turned their heads as they heard something their instincts told them was out of the normal for the forest. It occurred to Jacob that he had never found out what it was that had lured Elijah to this particular territory, Lycanthrope territory, in search of trouble in the first place.

Jacob burst into dust, riding the currents of the natural wind until a second later he was coalescing beside the warrior. The Captain did not seem surprised to see him.

"I figured Bella was going to send you after me," he whispered in greeting to the Earth Demon. Together they both returned to low positions near the ground. Jacob closed his eyes, extending a cloak of camouflage over them both.

Jacob did not affirm or deny his friend's speculation. He was concentrating on the movements of the forest that were both natural and unnatural.

"It has occurred to me that perhaps I was not ambushed after all. That perhaps I walked into something I wasn't supposed to, as hard as that is for me to admit."

"I would agree," Jacob confirmed. "I find it odd that you would be lured into Lycanthrope territory on purpose. Too many variables."

"So this begs the question, why are these women hiding out in Lycanthrope territory?"

"And my answer would be that Demons are not the only ones on their hit list. We already know that."

"Yes, but why would Ruth and Mary lead resources this way? Frankly, it's you and Bella and the rest of us they hold a grudge against."

"Perhaps," Jacob agreed in a whisper. "But since the Vampires and the Lycanthropes helped us defeat their troops during the Battle of Beltane, they may have made themselves part of that revenge."

Elijah was quiet for a moment and then remembered something Siena had said to him when he had first awoken in her care.

"Wait a minute. She said it . . . and it never even clicked!"

"What?"

"Siena. Siena said to me, and of course she was just being a smart-ass at the time, but she said she had to save my neck because she wasn't about to ruin years of peaceful overtures by letting our people find me dead in Lycanthrope territory."

Jacob's eye widened slightly in understanding.

"I see. What better way to dissolve any helpful relationship between the 'Thropes and the Demons than to lay suspicion at their door for the death of a Demon! And not just any Demon . . ."

"Me? Then that means I *was* ambushed."

"And may yet be so." Jacob's eyes narrowed as he peered into the trees. "It is your job to track them, Ruth knows that. So they leave an obvious trail. And when you go missing . . ."

"They lie in wait for you to come and investigate. You and Bella . . . and even Noah. They are still here." Elijah paused to listen to the wind a moment, marking where it blew around this object and that, and which of those objects were warm-blooded.

"Siena scared them away so they did not realize you were

rescued. They have guards posted, waiting to report on anyone that enters the forest looking for your body."

"Which means we're in trouble."

"I would say so," Jacob agreed, feeling the sudden life
swarming toward them through the trees. "Damn her, how
did she mask so many of them?"

"Beats the hell out of me. We better get out of here."

Jacob nodded in agreement and moved to change his
form to the dust that could not be harmed, as Elijah's form of
the wind could not. But Elijah suddenly stiffened and
grabbed the Enforcer's arm. Jacob went still and directed his
attention to where the warrior's gaze was focused.

The gleam of gold in the moonlight winked in the tree
line across from them. A falcon burst from the trees and
swung into a lazy circle over the clearing, unaware of the
camouflaged Demons sitting in the brush below it.

The warrior was still fixated on the tree line, knowing exactly what he was going to see even before the golden cat
leapt into the clearing. It was not a coincidence that Siena
was there, Elijah realized suddenly. She didn't realize it, but
she had mistaken his intentions to investigate the scene of
his near death as her own.

He had led her here.

Jacob felt Elijah's body tensing next to him and he
reached to hold the warrior still.

"Do not move," he hissed.

"Why can't she smell them?" Elijah demanded under his
breath.

"I cannot smell them either," Jacob informed. "It is a
powerful glamour."

Elijah watched with despair as the falcon swung over the
ground and metamorphosed in midair so that the Lycanthrope with bicolored hair he had met in the cavern touched
down at a light run. She stopped and turned, looking for her
sister.

Her sister.

Syreena.

Elijah suddenly knew exactly who she was and what her significance was to Siena. As Siena shapechanged herself, half a meadow away from the other woman, Elijah closed his eyes and tried to exert his connection with her more strongly than he had ever tried before.

Jacob saw the Queen go still, crouching down instinctively.

Siena tried to shake off the strange sensation creeping up the back of her scalp. She felt an inexplicable feeling of panic and warning, but it was not her own instincts she was feeling. She frowned and pushed the intrusion aside, assuming it was the busybody warrior in her mind protesting her actions. Well, she would be damned if he was going to tell her what she could and could not do. Investigating the occurrence that had brought them together was her responsibility and must be done to protect the safety of those who wandered this part of their territory. It was her duty to protect her people, and he wasn't going to dictate to her otherwise.

Elijah shook Jacob off and stood up. With a single stride he burst out of Jacob's camouflage influence and ran toward the stubborn Queen. She scented him before she saw him and stood up in shock as he stepped out of nowhere and ran for her. He was so fast that she felt him impact against her between one breath and the next. The next second she felt the molecules of her body literally disintegrating into his.

She suddenly knew what it felt like to be the wind. For a moment she felt as if she couldn't breathe, although everything was air. But his presence surrounded her as they soared into the night together, brushing past naked tree limbs, pine needles, and bats.

The Earth passed beneath them so rapidly that Siena was dizzy and a little queasy from it. She had no voice to protest his highhanded treatment of her, so she had no choice but to just cling to the essence of the air that was him.

It was barely a minute later before the Earth rushed up toward them.

She was solid again so suddenly that, had he not held her so tightly, she would have fallen face first into the ground. After a moment of discombobulation, she realized she recognized where they were. They were standing at the entrance of Jinaeri's cave, the one where all of this had begun.

Siena shoved away from him the minute her balance was settled, glaring at him with outrage and fire.

"Just what do you think you are doing?" she demanded.

"Saving your spoiled backside," he shot back.

That was when she realized he was angry. Not just a little angry, but positively livid. It was flaring in his eyes, the green of which was so dark it was nearly black. She suddenly felt vulnerable and at a distinct disadvantage. Instinctively, her hair circled tightly around her bare body.

Several heartbeats later, two other people coalesced from a shower of dust into the forms of the Demon Enforcer and her sister Syreena. Syreena was used to flying, so she was not as disoriented as Siena was. Still, being suddenly demolecularized was disturbing to anyone who wasn't experienced in the occurrence, so even she was a little paler for the incident.

"It was a trap!" Elijah snapped at Siena, drawing her startled attention back to him. "There were about a hundred necromancers and hunters closing in on us!"

"Impossible!" she shot back at him, her slender hands curling into fists. "I would have smelled them. You know as well as I do that magic-users are the vilest smelling creatures on the planet to us Nightwalkers. There's no way—"

"Apparently there is!" Elijah cut in, leaning over her so closely that she had to step back instinctively. "You aren't dealing with just misaligned humans anymore, Siena. There are Demons out there who have the power to deceive you in ways you can't even conceive of. There is a reason why your father never won a battle against us, no matter how hard he tried. And believe me when I tell you that, for all your people consider me a butcher, I could have done a lot more harm to them than any of them realize!

"A Mind Demon of Ruth's caliber can make you see, smell, and hear anything she wants you to. She can do it to us, her own people who are aware of it, so she can surely do it to you. The only way Jacob and I were able to see through the glamour was because we could use alternate abilities to sense their body heat."

"He's telling the truth, Siena." Jacob spoke up more gently, knowing Elijah was not going to be very diplomatic in the moment. Jacob knew what the terror of watching your mate come close to danger and death could do to your personality and your heart. "You both would have been slaughtered in a matter of minutes if Elijah hadn't seen you. I guarantee you, this time they were prepared for the possibility of a Lycanthrope. I am sensitive to all metals of the Earth, and I promise you they had enough silver on them to kill far more than two unsuspecting changelings."

"I saw nothing," Syreena said in disbelief. "I purposely circled the forest and the clearing several times before signaling to Siena that all was clear."

But it was clear the female with the dual-colored hair was not arguing the point Jacob and Elijah had tried to make. She was just more than a little shocked.

"If you need proof, I would be happy to take you back and dump you into that clearing so you can get your stubborn butt kicked," Elijah threatened.

"How dare you talk to me that way!"

Jacob winced as the second female turned to roll her eyes at him. It was then that he noticed this woman too wore delicate links of gold and moonstones around her neck. This jewelry was only a half-inch thick, as opposed to the over two inches of thickness to the Queen's collar. Jacob suspected that this other woman was also a member of the royal household, although he had never heard of a second Princess in the court from Gideon's reports during his time there.

The collars were remarkable, Jacob mused. There must be some sort of enchantment on them that allowed them to expand and contract when their wearers changed shape. To go from falcon to humanoid made for a significant difference in circumference, even though the Princess was a small, fine-boned little thing. She couldn't have been much over five feet tall, though. Like her sister, her presence was impressive enough to make her seem a little larger than life. And the harlequin-colored hair and eyes were beautiful, but also un-nerving.

Jacob gently took the Princess's arm and led her several steps away from the bickering pair.

"I am Jacob, the Demon King's Enforcer. I apologize for taking you over without warning, but you were both in jeopardy."

"I believe you," she assured him, reaching to take his offered hand. "I am Syreena, the Queen's Counselor and sister."

Jacob watched as she looked back to check on her sister.

"Is it me, or are we about as useful as a holes in an umbrella at the moment?" she asked, the gray eyebrow raising above the brown one slightly.

"Are you suggesting we abandon your Queen and my Captain to their fates?" Jacob smiled slightly. "That would be incredibly bad form."

"I know," she laughed, "but you have not had to live at court with her these past few days."

"Trust me, he has not been much better."

They exchanged one last look before changing into dust and falcon, both flying off unnoticed by their companions.

* * *

"I am not the stubborn one here," Siena insisted, irritation snapping in her golden eyes. "If you would have stayed away from me, none of this would have happened!"

"I would really like to know how you figure that," Elijah demanded.

"If you hadn't bullied me around earlier—"

"Bullied?" he interrupted. "I have done nothing more than try and convince you of how stupid it is to torture yourself by resisting the inevitable. I am trying to protect you from—"

"I never asked for your protection, and I swear by the Goddess this very minute that I never will!"

"Too late!" he reminded her with a mean look of satisfaction. "Better be careful what you swear to or you will pay the price at your reckoning."

"And what, go to hell where all the Demons live? I think I'm already there, thank you very much for your concern."

She turned to move away from him, wanting nothing more than to run into the forest and as far from him as she could get. This time she anticipated his reach for her hair and ducked him smoothly, a cry of triumph on her lips as she jumped back and laughed at him. She changed so fast from human to Werecat that Elijah barely had time to blink.

This was something else completely different, Elijah realized, taking a wise step back as he stared down oval pupils, bared claws, and a tail that twitched with challenge. She had just made herself three times as strong as she already was, enhancing every feline instinct she already had.

This was not a form he wanted to do battle with.

He didn't want to do battle with any of her forms. He was tired of fighting her, of trying to make her understand what she refused to understand. So he ignored her challenge and, with a resigned sigh, turned his back on her and walked away several steps. He changed form about five yards away from her, disappearing into the approaching dawn.

Siena was surprised by his retreat, automatically reverting to her human form in her confusion. She looked around, feeling the lightening of the forest keenly. She put off trying to figure out what the Demon was up to this time, transformed into the cougar, and began to travel quickly toward home.

At top speed, she should make it back to her castle only an hour after daybreak.

She didn't even take notice of the cloud cover that seemed to follow her the entire distance.

"No doubt they now know you are not lying dead on the forest floor," Noah noted. "And that their trap has been discovered."

Noah waited for a response, but when it didn't come he looked up from the scroll he was trying meticulously to decipher. Elijah was leaning against his desk with his back to him, arms folded tightly over his chest, legs crossed at the ankles. But in spite of the relaxed positioning of the warrior's body, it was clear he was wrapped up tightly in tense thoughts and emotions.

"Elijah?"

The Captain looked around at the King with a raised brow of surprise.

"I am sorry, did you say something?"

"I said it is only one more night until Samhain. Have you had any progress with Siena?"

"No. She is just as obstinate as ever." Elijah gave him a grim smile of sarcasm. "However, she has learned a unique use for our developing telepathy. Do you know how many derogatory names there are in the Lycanthrope language?"

"No, but I have a feeling you do."

"Oh, yes," Elijah forced a smile and attitude of sarcastic delight, "and the hits just keep on coming."

"Look at the bright side. You will know their language before long at this rate."

"Yes, but I don't believe it is going to be a vocabulary that will endear me to the biased populace any more than I already am."

"Good point," Noah agreed. "Why will you not ask Gideon to talk to her?"

"After what happened last time? Don't you think the developing war with the lawless mortals is enough?"

"Elijah, I find it hard to believe Siena is that irrational. She has always proven to be a woman of uncommon wisdom and remarkable clarity of purpose."

"She is," the warrior agreed. "And her wisdom and clarity of purpose are directed full bore against me. As she delights in telling me," he reached to tap his forehead in indication, "there is a large variety of farm animals she'd rather make her King."

Noah winced, carefully pushing back the humor of that remark so as not to bruise the warrior any more than he already was. Siena was shrewd indeed. She was going after Elijah's most vulnerable spot—his ego. But there was a decided lack of wisdom in her abuse. It would only make things harder on her the next night. As it was, Noah could see the strain Elijah was under as that time closed in on him. Siena had no idea the remarkable restraint he was forcing on himself. She had no clue about how hard he was trying to protect her from himself, no matter how bratty her behavior.

Tomorrow all of that would be a moot point. If only she would use their connection to search Elijah's true intentions toward her, perhaps she would look on him a little more kindly. To the King who had known the warrior all of his life, Elijah was on his way to being completely in love with the spitfire Queen. In fact, the temper that so vexed him was no doubt a large part of his attraction to her. Elijah was warrior, through and through, and nothing suited him better than a challenge. A battle to be won. A victory hard earned.

However, Elijah would consider the occurrences bound to

happen during Samhain brutally bad form and beneath his sense of honor.

Siena had no idea what that would do to him.

"I thought you were drilling the warriors this evening."

"I am," Elijah agreed, pushing away from the desk. "I wanted to bring you up to speed on what happened last night. You were sleeping by the time I got back."

"Well, keep everyone moving and prepared. Make sure all your warriors understand the importance of no one venturing out on his own." Noah paused a moment, turning to look into the fire across the hall. "And report any more disappearances to me as soon as possible."

Elijah nodded, understanding quite well what he meant. Ruth's knowledge of Demon power names was taking its toll. One by one, they were being Summoned into the black-magic pentagrams. Ruth was an Elder who had fostered many Demons over the centuries. She had been a popular choice for *Siddah*. Now every parent who had trusted her with their child's power name was in mourning and felt the agony of terror for the lives of their children. Ruth was feeding their names to the vile necromancers, and they were being Summoned one by one to do their bidding. There was no stopping it. No protecting them from it.

The only Demon to ever escape the fate of the pentagram had been Legna, and that had been a fluke of pure luck. All these others would already be mindless monsters that, eventually, Bella and Jacob would have to find and destroy before they could cause harm. Over the past months Jacob had been doing little else besides trying to track down the pitiful creatures and their captors. Now that Isabella was almost entirely well, she would finally be able to help him carry that burden. It was her Destiny to do so.

"Pairing up will also lighten Jacob's usual Samhain responsibilities," Elijah said. "Less chance of rogue attempts of seduction of humans and others if we monitor one another."

Noah could tell that Elijah could only wish something so easy would help him resist the mating instinct that would overwhelm him on Samhain. Demons misdirecting their mating instincts to humans on Samhain was one thing, and Jacob's duty was to stop that because it could be stopped. Elijah was Imprinted, and nothing would be able to stop it for him. Nothing outside of death.

The warrior dissolved into the air a few moments later and Noah watched the eddy of the breeze he had become as it drove past the fireplace and out an open window.

A moment later, Gideon's astral form solidified across from Noah.

"Is there anything you can do for him?" the King asked.

"No. Elijah is not the one being unreasonable. The fault lies with Siena."

"I know that. But I cannot blame her either. She does not understand our ways, other than what she learned from you, and this is a lot different than growing up knowing what is expected in a situation like this."

"But she is resisting even the traditions she did grow up with," Gideon informed him seriously. "The lore of the necklace she wears is very clear. The minute Elijah removed it, she became his. I do not think Elijah even knows about this. I have not told him myself because I see no need to cause him further pain. To know she would rather defy her own traditions then take him to mate would be tremendously painful."

"There has to be something we can do."

"There is. We can let the Hallowed moon of Samhain come and let nature take her course with them both. Nature did not make these compulsions come upon us for no reason. It is quite a clever trick, if you think about it."

"To force a rape? That is how Siena will perceive it. Had you not won over Legna in time, would it not be the same?"

"Perhaps. Perhaps not. Legna would have understood that I would have had no choice. She herself would have been thusly compelled. I do not believe it will be any different for Siena. It is no different for Bella or Corrine or any of the other Druids. If it crosses those species, the compulsion will very likely cross this one as well. I have seen Siena lately. She is pale and clearly yearning for what she is trying to resist."

"I am not sure I understand her, Gideon. If anyone would accept a Demon into her society with open arms, it would be her. Just as she welcomed you and Legna."

"We are not a threat to her reign and her sense of independence."

"Elijah couldn't care less about sharing her throne. All he wants is her. And willingly. He wants her to come willingly. Her independence is vital in order for that to happen."

One of Gideon's silver brows lifted in sudden contemplation.

"Perhaps this is an important point," he mused to the King. "Siena values her throne so highly . . . Noah, I think I may be able to help our Captain after all."

Gideon disappeared with a wink of silver light, leaving the King without explanation.

Give me a moment alone before you join us.

Are you certain? It only took a moment for her to lose her temper last time.

You will know when to come. I trust you, sweet.

Legna settled on that remark with pleasure. She drifted lightly in her husband's thoughts as he approached the throne room.

Siena had welcomed her court back to her outer and inner throne rooms little by little, so there were quite a few people there and the guards let him pass easily. They were not the ones to witness Siena's outburst those few days ago, so they had no reason to hesitate in doing so. Legna was in the room herself, in a distant corner well out of sight of the Queen, talking within a group of Lycanthrope gentlemen who found the gorgeous Demon female a delight for their eyes and their intellects. Unlike Jacob, Gideon was not disturbed in the least by this. Her smiles and her laughter were abundant and beautiful to see and hear. It gave him a remarkable sense of pride to watch her wrap the formerly stubborn members of this species around her pretty fingers. Her pregnant state only magnified their eagerness to cater to any desire she might voice. But he knew that at the end of the night, when dawn came, she would seek his bed and no one else's for the rest of eternity.

He could feel her eyes on him even as several of the women of the court approached him with equal warmth and greeting. He was not as social and diplomatic as his wife was, but this somehow managed to make him even more sought after. He had been puzzled by this unsought attention for months before his wife had deigned to explain it to him. Apparently, they considered him "mysterious." And this, for some reason, was attractive to them.

Gideon was his usual cool and direct self as he moved through his admirers. He felt the Queen's attention the minute she noticed him. Company parted as she stood up from her throne, where she had been in a discussion with her aides, Anya and Syreena.

She looked terribly pale and it was clear she was not sleeping properly. In fact, not at all, he thought as he measured her physiology with sharp senses. She descended the steps to the throne platform and continued from the platform to the main floor. She was dressed in a ceremonial outfit of gold cloth. The jacket was an intricately embroidered bolero vest that left her midriff, sides, and back completely bare. The long, light skirt that matched was settled very low on her hips and was made up of about a half dozen panels of fabric that fluttered behind her as she moved toward him.

She reached out to him with both hands, the gold and diamond bands around her upper left arm glinting in the overhead light. He took her offered hands in his and bent his head in an elegant bow to her. She reached to place a rare kiss of public affection on his cheek and whispered to him as the crowd around them murmured with speculation and surprise.

"Can you ever forgive me? I behaved like a child," she said.

"Untrue. You were upset, and I am capable of understanding why."

Her kiss was a distinctive honor in this court. By bestowing it upon him, she had just changed his and, by association, his wife's position in the court. No longer were they to be just a fascination, a curiosity, and foreign ambassadors. They were, from that moment on, to be considered close personal friends to Her Majesty.

"You wish to press your Warrior Captain's suit, I suppose," she said shrewdly, after taking a moment to measure him.

"I believe that you might be interested in what I have come to say. I recommend you hear me out."

"Apparently my advisors agree," she noted, lifting a hand to indicate Syreena and Anya, who had their heads close together in discussion while watching them. Siena linked her arm through Gideon's and he walked with her as her people parted to let them pass. "Did you see Myriad when you were visiting your King?" she asked conversationally, making small talk while still in earshot of others.

"Your ambassador comes to the castle often. I believe she and Noah have formed an antagonistic relationship over the chessboard."

Siena laughed, the sound seeming to brighten her appearance.

"Myriad is a stubborn creature. She will not give up until she defeats him," she informed.

"I beg your pardon," Gideon said smoothly, "but I believe it is Noah who is trying to beat your little half-breed."

"Really?" Siena laughed again, her golden eyes lighting with amusement. "Clever thing. I knew she was the proper choice to send to your court. I can only pray she doesn't get Noah so miffed that he declares war again."

Gideon smiled as she took him away from the populated areas of the throne room and its halls and strolled with him into the more distant reaches of the endless structure. She was the first to break the companionable silence that had formed.

"If you are here to remind me how futile my resistance to this Imprinting is, I can assure you I am already getting the picture. I am not myself, and I know it shows." She paused, and Gideon gave her time to decide what she wished to share with him. "I do not understand how you and your mate enjoy this thing so much. Whenever I see her, she is glowing and beautiful and smiling. Your wit is the first thing I have been able to laugh at since returning to court."

"When Legna and I first Imprinted fully on each other," the medic began, "we were not what one might consider the best of friends. In truth, we had been hostile toward each other for nearly a decade because of an incident that had wounded her pride. One I completely fouled up because of my distorted sense of right and wrong. The moment we Imprinted, however, we always understood it was inevitable that we would become lovers. That we would be mated for the rest of our lives. We understood this because as Demons it is part of our history and physiology, though until recently a very rare occurrence. Fortunately, the one thing we were able to control was the time we took to resolve issues between us, to get to know one another before Beltane forced us to each other. That preparation was vital and precious, Siena. Without it, I am certain that it would have taken much longer for us to find each other's hearts.

"Samhain will force you and Elijah to one another. I will make you this guarantee. I see the compulsion building within you as the time nears. It is mirrored in Elijah as well.

Ramifications in both of our societies aside, I assure you that despite your struggles, you will find yourself waking next to him the morning after Samhain."

"You tell me to put my society aside when that is the one thing I cannot do. Anything that affects me affects my people." Siena bit her lips gently. "I am not a Demon female. You have never seen this particular cross in species before. You say it cannot be fought, but I am no ordinary being."

"Nor am I," the Ancient Demon reminded her with a cool, level tone as his mercury-colored gaze fell on her golden one. "Siena, you have learned after a long and arduous acquaintance to trust the truth of my words. Knowing me these twenty-five years, you choose to doubt me now? After you put the fate of your throne and all of your people on my word and my teachings of what your so-called barbarian enemies were truly about?"

He watched as she pressed a palm to her forehead, her pace beside him never changing. He felt her pain, could see the tension of the ache pounding in her head. It disturbed him that he did not yet know how to manipulate Lycanthrope physiology well enough to be much use to her. He had spent those five years of captivity learning and this past half-year reteaching himself the basics about their physicality. But it would take another few years of study before he began to make progress in healing this complex species. Humans and Demons were one thing, but the intricacies of the chemistry of a changeling, the DNA, the alterability of their entire bodies, made the art of healing them the most difficult challenge the highly skilled medic had encountered in all his long life.

The only thing he could offer her was words. Hopefully the right ones that would help her to understand she was making herself sick over something she simply could not change, even with all the power in the world. This was an act of supremacy too far beyond any of them, no matter how powerful they became.

My love . . .

Yes, sweet? he asked the soft, bright presence in his mind.

You must tell her something she wants to hear, Legna said wisely. *It is not like you to be indirect. She does not respond to dictates. She will respond only to possible solutions. Siena cannot separate the woman from the Queen. She has repressed her womanhood savagely out of fear of being forced to share her throne, out of fear of losing control of her surroundings. This is why she is so terrified now.*

Gideon knew Legna understood the matter far better than anyone could. As a Mind Demon, Legna had an amazing grasp of psychology that had grown exponentially since they had mated, sharing their power with each other.

"Tell your mate to mind her own business," the Queen remarked dryly. "I feel her presence buzzing around you, Gideon."

Siena had telepathy with other animals, including Lycanthropes in their animal forms, but she was not reading Gideon's mind. She did, however, sense Legna's presence in his mind and had something of a sixth sense that allowed her to have a vague idea of what their thoughts and discussions were tending toward. It was rather like the ability of predator to sense the next move a prey would make.

"She tells me to inform you that your well-being is very much her business," Gideon relayed. "And she reminds you that we are your friends, not your enemies."

"Everyone is my enemy," the Queen said bitterly, her pacing finally slowing as the weight of her saddening emotions weighed on her. "Or they soon will be. What will happen to our peace now, old friend?"

Siena felt the telltale pop in the air that heralded Legna's teleport. She had expected it, just as she expected the comforting hands Gideon's mate laid on her shoulders. Siena finally stopped moving, turning to look up into Legna's bright, sterling eyes, perfectly identical to her husband's.

"You must not mind Gideon. You know he is far too direct for good," Legna said soothingly, tossing a wink to her mate out of Siena's sight.

Gideon felt a swell of pride in his chest as he watched his lovely mate work her own brand of magic. He should have known to bring her with him from the start. The Ancient male was still learning to be part of a duo and sometimes made these errors, but it was to be expected after living a mostly solitary existence for over a thousand years. Some habits would take far longer than six months to break.

"I understand your feelings in this moment, Siena," Legna said earnestly. "Can I help you to imagine how I felt when I realized I was going to be saddled with this old man for the rest of my life?" Siena couldn't help but smile as she looked over at Legna's handsome "old man." "Despite what he says, I was not as accepting as he would like to think, and I can also assure you I was quite disturbed over the prospect of telling Noah. But we believe in Destiny and fate, as you know, and it is clear this is destined. It must be even to you."

"That does not make this any easier," Siena argued.

"No. I know that. But hear Gideon out. He may be able to help you."

"I already have heard all of your arguments."

"I do not offer an argument, but a solution." Gideon took a hand of each female and led them to a bench in an alcove where they both sat obediently. Legna instantly picked up the Queen's hand, pressing it between hers in silent support.

"You know you must give yourself and your people time to adjust to this. You have told me that they will not accept a Demon as their King, correct?"

"Yes. I am positive of this."

"Then do not make him King, Siena."

"But you said I cannot resist this Imprinting . . ."

"I said do not make him King. You have no choice but to take him as mate, and you do know that, in your heart and your soul, you want and need Elijah close to you." Gideon lowered himself into a crouch, resting a hand on the Queen's knee as he looked up into her perplexed eyes. "Do you recall the day I asked you to tell me about the history of your monarchy? The traditions and how they have grown and changed over the centuries?"

"Yes." She smiled. "You kept me occupied with the discussion for over twenty hours. I have never enjoyed a discourse more."

"Then think, for a moment, about those traditions. Did you not tell me that before you allowed males equal measure in your society, there was no such thing as a King? That it had changed by example about nine hundred years ago when . . ."

". . . when Queen Colein elevated her Consort to equal level," she supplied when he searched for the names of the people involved.

"Yes. Alexzander. The first King in your history."

"I do not understand your point."

"Siena." Legna spoke up, her voice soft and urgent. "Elijah does not want to be your equal in your monarchy, only in your heart and soul and body. He is content with his life and his duties to Noah. Do you not understand this?"

"You see him as a threat to your throne. So I offer the solution of removing the threat until such time as you decide otherwise," Gideon urged her. "Make him your *Consort,* Siena, not your King. If one day you choose to elevate him as your political equal, then it will be your choice to do so and no one else's. There is no Lycanthrope law that demands you make him your equal in the throne, only that you make him your mate. Invoke an old tradition, keep your power over your people, and stop punishing Elijah and yourself with these fears of yours."

"Do you know what you are asking?" Siena asked hoarsely, her head spinning as hope and relief tried to overwhelm her. "You are asking me to publicly treat him in a way . . . in a way no man of his ego could tolerate."

"We are asking you to do what you have always done. To do the best thing for your people. That comes as natural to you as breathing, Siena."

"You do not know Elijah so well as you think," Legna added. "For you, I believe he would make any sacrifice. He does not need to impress your court. Only you. His position to Noah is more than enough for him. And I will tell you this, even if it did bruise his ego, Elijah would still take you to his heart under any conditions."

"But . . ."

"Siena," Gideon said with a sigh, "nothing is gained without venturing to risk."

CHAPTER 11

Elijah woke the next night with a start.

He sat up in bed suddenly, making his body protest the quick movement. He caught his breath, reaching to rub at the sore muscles of his shoulders. He had pushed himself and his troops to the utter limits the night before, hoping on some level that total exhaustion would do them all some good, considering the coming of Samhain.

Elijah didn't know exactly what it was he had expected, but at the moment he felt fairly normal. Well, as normal as he had felt for the past few days. Which basically meant he was dragging his feet, feeling indescribably blue, and was pretty much completely pissed off at a certain Lycanthrope female.

He had slept at Noah's, also with the hope that remaining close to the King would somehow provide a buffer for this overriding impulse to attack Siena that he was supposed to be feeling. But now, waking to feel nothing out of the ordinary in his thoughts and desires, he was ridiculously relieved.

He pushed back the bedding and walked over to the closet. He made a point of selecting his most comfortable pair of worn jeans and a rather ordinary basic white button-down shirt. It was what he considered workday clothing. Nothing special, not even the silk, a holdover from the time he had been raised in, he often favored in shirt material. He was not about to do anything he could misconstrue on any level as preparing to see or seduce a woman.

He rolled the cuffs halfway up his forearms and actually smiled at his casual reflection in the mirror. The warrior did take a moment to run his hands through his hair, still not quite used to the change in color. He had been fairly tow-headed most of his life. It was still strange to see the strands of gold filament in place of that.

He wondered if it was meant to be a purposeful reminder of who he was supposed to be mated to. Every time he looked at it, he thought of where the color originated. No doubt it was the same for Legna when she saw her changed eye color in the mirror, the distinctive silver color all Gideon.

Elijah left his room and headed to the Great Hall. He hesitated midway down the central stairs when he saw Noah sitting by his fireplace, in pretty much the exact same position Elijah had seen him in when he had gone to bed. He glanced at Noah's desk as he passed it, seeing the stack of notes and translations that had grown during the daytime.

"Did you sleep today?" he asked the King directly.

"Of course," the King lied to him without taking his eyes from the flames he seemed to see so much in lately.

"Is everything all right, Noah?" Elijah persisted.

Noah finally looked up at him, giving him half a smile in reassurance.

"Hadn't I ought to ask you that question?"

"I feel fine. In fact, better than fine. I'm beginning to wonder if Gideon has his facts straight about all of this."

"Do not allow yourself to get overconfident, my friend," Noah warned softly. "Gideon is rarely wrong."

"Thank you for the vote of confidence," Elijah said.

"Noah, forgive me for saying so, but exactly what planet are you on these past few days? You haven't been yourself."

"You know, I notice that people often think that way when they are avoiding talking about themselves. Worry about yourself, warrior. I am as I ever was."

Elijah didn't push the matter any further. Noah never kept his own counsel for long. He would talk when he wanted to and not a moment sooner. For the moment, the King was correct. He had his own troubles to focus on that night.

"I think I'm going to see about giving Jacob a hand tonight," he said, turning away from the King. "With Bella still not able—"

Elijah stopped when he felt Noah's hand encircling his upper arm. He turned to see the King standing behind him and raised a curious brow.

"I do not recommend that. Jacob will manage on his own."

"But—"

"Elijah, do I have to spell this out to you? Jacob and Bella are Imprinted and it is Samhain. I assure you, if you drop in on them unannounced, you will not be welcome."

Elijah raised both brows in understanding as Noah's meaning dawned on him.

Thickheaded male.

Elijah was almost getting used to the name-calling that went on in the back of his mind, but this was the first time he had heard it in response to something going on in *his* life. He was so distracted by hearing that lilting voice and the laugh that echoed after it, he forgot all about Noah and metamorphosed into a swift wind that shot out the nearest window.

Noah was left holding . . . nothing, a perplexed expression on his face.

Elijah's first stop was the training yards.

He stood in the center of the working grounds and heard

nothing but the creak of wooden training dummies and tar-
gets. It was actually eerie how abandoned the place was.
Usually it bustled with activity from dusk to dawn. But it
was a holy holiday, and no one was required to be there. In
the past, however, there had always been someone working
out there, trying to refocus energies that could be dangerous
if otherwise directed. Apparently, Elijah had exercised them
a little too hard while trying to exhaust himself, and no one
was in the mood to come anywhere near their Captain or the
training facilities.

So that was two strikes. He slowly walked across the
training yards as he tried to think of what else he could do to
occupy his time.

Perhaps you ought to make a sacrifice to the Goddess.

Elijah stopped in his tracks.

It is a holy day, after all, the voice continued.

"You know, you sure picked a fine time to get talkative,"
he bit out, his voice echoing across the empty fields.

Elijah took a deep breath and turned his thoughts away
from how that voice of hers, sexy even in her thoughts,
seemed to seek out his spine in a way that stunned every
nerve in his body. Cursing under his breath, he twisted into a
wind devil that kicked up the worn dust of the practice arena
as he left.

An hour later, Elijah finally materialized in his own
home, half the planet away from any Russian territories.

Content at last, he began to light lanterns and dusted off
his favorite chair before sinking into it with a sigh. He
leaned his head back and closed his eyes, trying to release
himself into the quiet of the night. His home was actually one
of the modern log cabins. Though it had every amenity that
came with modern housing, there was no use for it. Electricity and such would not work for him or anyone of his
species, their kinship with the forces of nature making technology and most mechanics react adversely to their Demon
biochemistry.

I know. I have had to resort to using the old gas lighting system in the castle since Legna and Gideon came to court.

Elijah sat upright in a shot.

Why was it that she sounded even closer than she had before?

Damn her, she sure picked a lousy time to taunt him. It was almost like she was asking for him to completely lose his mind and come looking for her. And, if he judged correctly the tension surging through him and the urges that followed, she would have her way soon enough if she kept this up.

I'm not afraid of you, she whispered.

You should be, he warned, trying the connection himself for the very first time.

You'll have to find me first.

Her original threat. She was no doubt taunting him because she believed she could hide herself from him. She believed herself to have superior skills, and therefore she had nothing to fear.

The challenge was a foolish one, and Elijah had thought her smarter than that. He felt frustrated and upset as he stood up and began to pace the floor.

Siena, you are playing with fire. You do not want to do this.

Shouldn't I be the judge of that?

Damn her!

Elijah tried to push her out of his thoughts, running up the dark stairs to search for something, anything, to occupy his mind. To keep himself from thinking about her and his memories of her. The more she spoke in that soft, sexy whisper, the more he remembered the same whisper in his ear as she purred and urged him to move deeper into her sweet body. He remembered it right down to the feel of her fingers in his hair, her nails skimming his back.

Elijah entered his library, quickly striking a match and lighting two of the lanterns on the table. He was not much of a reader this century, tending to concentrate on his fighting skills and strategic abilities. Last century it had been perfecting his skills as a master weapons maker. As the library lit up, proof of that gleamed from every wall. There were about twenty swords, the variety diversified, and each made with his own hands from pommel to scabbard. Even the mounts they were displayed on had been painstakingly crafted by his own touch.

These were not just showpieces. He had practiced with them all and had used more than half of them in actual battle. Now he surveyed them slowly, waiting to see which one would speak to him the loudest.

The katana won his attention.

The blade was tucked tightly into a pure silver scabbard, and the light of the lantern flickered against it in a way that made the etchings on it come to life. He reached for it, then hesitated and lowered his hand. He tried not to remember the last time he had used it, knowing Siena was so close to his thoughts.

The blade that killed my father.

Elijah winced, not even realizing her tone was speculative, not accusatory.

I am sorry, Siena.

Do not be sorry, warrior. You changed both of our worlds for the better with the stroke of that blade.

Overwhelmed, Elijah backed away from the blade and dropped awkwardly into a nearby chair.

"What do you want from me, Siena?" he asked aloud, his voice hoarse as he tried to filter out his emotions.

I want to know what you want from me.

"Nothing," he whispered. "I don't want anything from you." He paused for only two strong heartbeats. "Except you," he said at last.

He stood up and walked to the glass doors leading from the library to a balcony that wrapped halfway around the house. He exited the house and took in the night air with a deep breath as he leaned on the wooden railing.

Your touch, your laugh, your beautiful eyes, Siena. Your temper, your brilliance in both your skin and your mind. I want to wake in the morning wrapped up in your hair and looking into your eyes. I want to learn what it truly means to know you.

Elijah's eyes closed as he felt physical pain singing through every fiber of his body.

I am not such a mystery, Elijah. I am the woman who wants nothing more than to lead her people into an era of peace and comfort.

Nothing more, Siena? Elijah lifted his hand to rub at the pained furrows of his forehead.

There is one other thing I want.

And that is?

I want you to see me, Elijah.

Elijah straightened away from the railing when she said that. His heart jumped erratically with a sudden surge of hope. He narrowed his eyes and peered into the darkness, the night breeze blowing over him as clouds moved across the face of the waxing moon.

He caught a faint, familiar scent and he felt every blood cell in his body suddenly rush to all sorts of locations, leaving him a little dizzy in the aftermath.

And then he saw the gleam of moonlight on gold.

Bracing a hand on the railing, Elijah leapt over it, dropping two stories down to the ground. He broke into a run, but stopped when the soft scent disappeared. He looked around for the source of the golden light and suddenly saw something hanging from the bony fingers of a tree limb. He reached for it, pulling it free and turning it over in his palm. It was an armband, made of gold and moonstones in a fashion as intricate as Siena's collar.

Tell me what this means, Siena, he demanded.

It is the band of the Queen's Consort, Elijah.

She said nothing more, explained no further. She knew she did not have to. Elijah was a man close to the details of a monarchy. He knew full well what it meant to be a Royal Consort.

Elijah's heart was pounding so hard, he barely heard her. In that moment, everything seemed to change. The feelings overwhelming him were irresistible, longing and craving and just shy of maddening.

"Tell me where you are, Siena. Tell me *right now!*"

I am home, Elijah. And I am waiting for your decision.

Siena knelt before the beautiful stone altar, carefully lighting the natural, homemade incense that Anya had given to her as a gift last Beltane. She sat back on her heels, closed her eyes, and tried to focus on her prayer. It was difficult, however, because she felt him coming with more than just her heart and her soul, and definitely more than her body. What that was exactly . . . she could not fathom in the moment. Nevertheless, it was as impossible to ignore as it was to explain.

He was still an ocean away, but she already had goose bumps rippling up her arms, across the back of her shoulders, and swiftly along the back of her neck until the sensation was prickling over her scalp in a way that made her hair rustle to attention.

Her chamber was already full of the scent of incense. It had been burning all day, according to tradition, in preparation for the night to come. Also according to tradition, Siena had spent the entire day doing nothing more then sleeping, bathing, perfuming, shampooing, and smoothing on a variety of oils and lotions meant to make her skin the utmost in soft perfection.

She had been a Princess before she had been a Queen, all of her life spent at the court. So all the fussing and primping and the attention she had been paid was exactly what she was used to, and exactly what she enjoyed. In fact, the familiarity of it alone had helped her to keep calm, relaxed, and focused on most levels. As a result, there wasn't a spot on her body that was not soft and delicately scented, and she was still able to maintain an image of dignity and calm while she was waiting.

Just the same, Siena had been lucky.

Elijah had been asleep until fairly late that night, up until about an hour ago. If he had woken up sooner, she might not have been able to conceal her activities, or excitement, as she prepared for a night he didn't even know about. As controlled as she was, this connection that was growing stronger between them would have had the potential to give her away. She could conceal so much from a great many others, but Elijah was embedded in her very spirit, and soon, she had finally realized, there would be nothing she could keep from him. And as he came for her, she felt the rushing of his heart and his blood, his adrenaline and every other endorphin in his biochemistry flooding into his system. It was like a stunningly potent drug, making her head whirl and rush as if she were swimming in stimulants.

Technically, she should wait for him to give her a proper response about becoming her Consort. But she had felt, in her heart, the minute the warrior had come to understand the meaning of the armband, and any step he made in her direction had been everything a voiced acceptance could have been.

Siena pushed up from the floor, the stone cold beneath her warm, damp palms as she did so, and stood up. Her quarters were filled with women in the form of aides, guards, and ladies-in-wait. And, of course, Anya and Syreena were right by her side.

She was flanked by them, each dressed in a very specific ceremonial robe. Each robe was loose with long angel-wing sleeves. Anya's was made of a sheer green material, a very thin, fine silk that only their oldest and most accomplished artisans could create. Woven into the pattern of the silk in a way that, by touch, could not be discerned from the silk itself was the image of a vixen whose tail wrapped over Anya's hip and down her thigh.

Syreena's robe was made out of the same sheer silk, except hers was cerulean blue. Twisting in one direction around her body was a dolphin, and in the other, a peregrine falcon. Sparkles of diamond-dust sprinkled about doubled for the splash of the ocean and the starlight in the night sky.

Siena extended her arms palms up, and each aide took one side of the white lace and satin robe she was wearing over her own gown. Slowly, their fingertips moved to the ribbons in the front of the gown and they began to weave them intricately together, as if tying shoelaces, except that they each used only one hand, the other's hand acting as their second. It took concentration, coordination, and cooperation to be successful at such a task, and Siena's best friends, sisters of her soul, if not both in her blood, performed it flawlessly.

When they were finished, Siena picked up Anya's hands in her own and squeezed them affectionately.

"You have been my most trusted companion for almost all of my life, and it honors me to have you here by my side during this . . . this event that neither of us thought we would ever be a part of." Siena pulled Anya's hands close until she was pressing the palms of them just above her heart. "But by tradition I can no longer choose you to bear the marriage dagger. That honor must go to my sister, Syreena, despite her protests otherwise." Siena's golden gaze flicked up to quell the supporting protest on Syreena's lips. Syreena had felt that Anya deserved this right, no matter whose blood was whose. "It is her right," Siena continued, her eyes warming, softening as she looked from one to the other. "I have longed to honor her in a way that a sister honors a sister. For though she hardly knew me when this ruling journey began, she has earned every reward for her unquestioning loyalty."

"I know, My Queen," Anya said softly, her expression softly amused because they both knew she was not the one who needed the reassurance of such gestures. Despite her constant countenance of independence and confidence, Syreena's heart was a social one, in need of acceptance and supporting love.

Anya pulled her hands free slowly and then turned to face Syreena. The Princess's eyes were closed, and the half-breed gave her a moment. When her dual-colored eyes flicked open at last, the dampness on her lashes glittered like the diamonds of her dress.

The Princess then held out both hands, palms up, while Anya withdrew the ceremonial dagger from its scabbard, the sharp singing of metal ringing off the high ceilings of the bedroom. The sound was echoed by the abrupt stamp of the guards' feet as they suddenly came to perfect attention. All of the guards drew their swords with the echoing song of finely honed blades, slamming them down hard, point first, into the stone floor. Sparks flew as stone chipped away and metal was bent or pitted.

By tradition, all but two of these guards would now spend the night reforging their blades. Supposedly, the heat of the forge was a blessing on the marriage bed, that it be equally well fired and able to mold the future protection of the throne. But the symbolism went deeper than that. The guards would shape new blades to serve the new shape of the regime. A Consort lacked direct ruling power politically and legally, but he was given all the social respects and courtesies of a King.

An equal in all things . . . except her sovereignty.

Anya placed the dagger on Syreena's fingertips. Syreena bowed in gentle respect.

At about that moment, a chill rushed into the room. The bed curtains and the tapestries that hung around the room began to snap louder and louder as the subterranean breeze grew stronger and stronger. Unable to help herself, Siena breathed a little quicker. Her cheeks flushed, contrasting sharply with her unusually pale complexion. But it only served to flatter her beauty and set up a contrast to the white gown that she wore.

A remarkable sound, like the sound of rolling thunder, reverberated around them. All of the women in the room gasped. There was no such thing as foul weather in a subterranean castle. It seemed to pique everybody's excitement about their soon-to-be-arriving guest. Half of them did not know whether to be afraid, upset, or just plain curious.

The one thing that they did know for sure, however, was that life at court and life in general was never going to be the same again. What that meant exactly was unknown to any and all of them, including the Queen herself. But fate had spoken, and the Queen as well as The Pride had said they must comply. They must welcome yet another Demon into their court.

But such a Demon? The Butcher himself?

Those closest to the Queen would of course accept anything she asked them to, but they feared for her life and for her safety. Growing up on stories of Elijah's infamy had done its damage. Plus, to any Lycanthrope, a Demon was so alien. So different. The women who watched the Queen prepare for this unorthodox wedding were filled with questions that were even now echoing through the court.

Would she be murdered in her sleep? The Queen was a huntress through and through and the warrior Demon would not find her an easy mark, but the Queen was actually excited by this coming prospect, and that was the most confusing part of all. True, the male Demon in the court, the one called Gideon, was a remarkably handsome creature and fascinating for the mind, but he was an educated man of uncommon wit and skill.

One could hardly expect the same from a barbarian who swung a sword and slaughtered enemies for a living. Was he attractive enough to hold the interest of a mate who took the form of the lusty cat? Would he, in fact, be affected by the meshing of the mating and be forced to keep to the Queen's bed only, or would they experience the first royal affair in the history of their race at some point?

Would their chemistry even be compatible enough to provide heirs for the throne? Now this was the most important question. Even with the existence of half-breeds proving that breeding across species was apparently possible, there were no creatures alive in their culture who had been concocted from such a volatile DNA cocktail as Demon and Lycanthrope. What would a blend of the animals and the elements produce, if indeed it could produce anything at all?

That was actually the most fascinating question of all of them. Lycanthropes found mutation interesting and exciting. The more powerful, the better. It was why Syreena was so coveted. This could perhaps be the only aspect of the marriage that would win over the more distant members of their society, who would not be so easy to please or so quick to comply when it came to the topic.

But the Queen had been quite blunt when she had announced her intentions of taking this man to mate. This was a duty, yes, but she had not sobbed and sniffled about it, she had made sure everyone knew it was an arrangement she welcomed quite deeply. She had confessed the doubts she had mulled over these past few days. Then she had told them of her solution. He would only be her Consort and not her King, certainly not *their* King, and he would be neither if he would not accept that condition.

Many thought he would not accept these terms, by which reasoning they thought they were safe from ending up with a Demon anywhere near the throne. The Demon ego, they thought, especially the ego of such a man, would never be able to tolerate such a lesser position of power. Siena had reminded those who voiced further protests of old traditions, customs which included royal marriages as a way to resolve wars, to secure peaceful borders. And though they were no longer at war with the Demons, the Goddess, in her wisdom, had chosen a way to solidify that peace forever. And for those who most stubbornly persisted to protest with prejudice, Sienna reminded them that it had been her father's acts of terrorism that had forced the Demons to pick up the gauntlet and defend themselves in the first place. This was a convenient fact of history that had been rewritten in a lot of minds over time.

There had been only silence after that last slapdown.

So the wedding was coming to pass.

The guards quickly opened the doors to her chambers, leaving them welcoming and wide as she turned to face them, her aides by her sides. The ladies-in-wait were lined up beside the bed. Siena closed her eyes, her hands nervously sliding over her stomach as she held her breath and felt the wind around her continue to grow.

He was so powerful!

She knew he was at a distance still, but projected a great deal of power and energy before him, perhaps without even realizing it. His race to her side was raising the level of frenetic urgency that he was feeling. She could feel it in his mind, in her mind. The electricity of it was all around her, inside her, sparking through her hair with static charges that sent shivers of anticipation to her spine.

All but two of the guards proceeded out of the room and down the hall, heading for their night at the forge. The two remaining guards moved to stand on either side of the door out in the hallway. The only thing they were to protect, however, was the Queen's privacy on her wedding night. To say that they were perfectly calm would be misrepresenting them. Elijah's entrance was becoming increasingly unsettling.

Siena had been very careful, though. She had made certain that the two guards that remained had never stood in battle against Elijah. There was no chance of them acting on any impulses that could become hostile or unwelcoming. Siena wanted nothing to get in the way of that night.

Too much had come between them already.

She had never thought to be as excited about this as she was, but she realized she could not help herself. As much as she had dreaded taking a mate, she found that the benefits and anticipations that would come with this particular mate actually outweighed her doubts, dreads, and fears. At least they did now that Gideon had provided her with a solution that, while not perfect, had allowed her to come more than halfway.

Now all Elijah had to do was come the rest of the way. His words earlier, so powerful and so sincere, made her feel as though she was looking into his heart. But she could not be certain and she would not be certain until he stood before her and told her with his mouth, his eyes, and everything that he was that this commitment was what he wanted and accepted.

The wind that was her mate was whipping around her by then, causing the thin gowns on the triad of women to snap sharply behind them, blown back and clinging to every feminine curve on their bodies. The ladies-in-wait, made nervous by the display of power, reached to take one another's hands. Soon they were closing the distance between their bodies protectively so that they were all almost squashed up together like an accordion.

For some reason, this made Siena smile.

A moment later, she knew what that reason was.

Elijah coalesced into his imposing form with an impressive twist, standing so close to her that they were nearly toe to toe by the time he became solid. He was such a tall and remarkable figure of a man that all the ladies in the room, even those directly before the Demon, let out involuntary murmurs of surprise. These sounds were followed by soft whispers of speculation that had no place in this particular ritual. However, Siena was far too busy looking up into beautiful, startling green eyes. Eyes so full of emotion, the vastness of which she realized she would never be able to touch upon in the span of that mere second. She found herself swallowing hard, although her entire mouth and throat had gone completely dry.

Slowly, she let her eyes roam down the entire length of his body. Her initial foray was quickly diverted when the gleam of gold and moonstones surrounding a flexed, sturdy bicep caught her eye.

"How did you . . . ?"

Siena stopped herself from asking the question. The armband had been linked. It would have taken nothing for him to slip it over his arm so long as he distorted himself into some form of the air. It would be interesting to see if this unconventional choice in mate would be able to escape his enchanted badge of office as easily as he had managed to put it on. But Siena no longer had to envy him that freedom. The touch of his fingers and the clever or inadvertent manipulation that could free the collar from her throat could happen at any time.

Siena looked up into those eyes once more, so vivid, so green, so clearly starved for her.

Elijah flexed the muscle beneath the armband as he turned one shoulder toward her slightly. He lifted one gold brow.

"Is this the answer you were looking for?" he asked, his voice so low, so rough that it made heat sing past every red blood cell in her body.

"Only if you truly know and accept what it represents."

"I am no stranger to what it means to be a Royal Consort, Siena. Say only that it means we will be equals in all things except your rule, and my affirmation is yours." Elijah reached out to touch the curve of her cheek with his fingertips, unable to help himself in spite of all the eyes he felt on him. "I never wanted your monarchy, kitten. Only you. Just you."

His conviction was strident, unmistakable. Siena's heart was pounding so hard she couldn't even hear herself breathe.

"I wish you had said so in the first place," she whispered, a lift to one corner of her mouth matching the light in her golden eyes.

"My apologies," he whispered back, leaning so close their foreheads almost touched. "I had not realized there was more than a single option."

"To be honest, it had slipped my mind as well."

Syreena cleared her throat softly, drawing the Queen's attention.

Siena suddenly understood the draw of the chemistry that came with this kind of bonding. Her people referred to it as "mating for life," his called it the Imprinting. But "a rose by any other name". . . it was clear they were more similar than not after all. In any event, every part of her that lay beneath her skin was yearning toward him. She was the magnet, and he magnetic north.

Siena took a painful step back from him, allowing Syreena the space needed to step up to him and present the dagger to him on the very tips of her fingers. Her hands were steady, her balance flawless. It was notable considering how heavy the weapon was and how long she had been holding it.

"My Lord Elijah, Warrior Captain of the great Demon King, trusted and respected by that great lord who is our ally, do you accept our Queen as your everlasting mate, putting her above all others and below no other importance for the rest of your natural life?"

Elijah was silent for a long moment and Siena could feel the brief flit of hesitation that marked his heart. This did not disturb her. His honesty had always impressed her.

"In return," she said aloud, her tone strong and sincere, "I swear never to put you in a position that will conflict with your loyalty to Noah. There will be no war between our people for as long as I reign and live."

"He is my King, Siena, but you are my mate, my wife, and I am unable to do anything that will harm your heart or your soul. So long as I am at your side, for all that I am a warrior born and bred to conflict, there will never be a need to consider war between our people again. And I will endeavor the rest of my lifetime to help generations far into our future come to understand the best of both our worlds."

Elijah paused only long enough to slip two strong fingers under the blade of the dagger, just beneath the hilt, lifting it perfectly balanced from Syreena's hands. There was a flash of light reflecting off metal, the blade moving nimbly through his fingers as he caused the momentum that would twirl the hilt directly into his palm. The dexterity of the move, the confidence of it, was mesmerizing.

Syreena could barely step away in time as he came closer to his bride once more. Siena tilted her chin up just as he loomed over her and tilted his down. His mouth came close to hers, his free hand reaching out to encircle her slim throat.

"As of this moment, kitten, I am yours. Once I complete one last task for Noah, I will resign my post. If this is to be my home, the land where my heart and soul is occupied, then my body and my skills must come to stay as well. But you must understand that there will be no peace in my conscience if I leave my duty incomplete."

"I would expect nothing less from you," she responded, her tone firm and assuring. The promise was more than she had wanted, but as soon as he made it, she realized his wisdom in the gesture was but one more step toward easing the wary hearts of her people. The magnitude of the sacrifice was not lost on the Queen.

Siena reached for the blade, her palm curling firmly around its honed edges. When she turned her hand over, it was bitten and bloodied in two lines from the double-edged weapon. With a mental prompt from his bride, Elijah did the same. Then, palm to palm, they laced their fingers together.

Anya raised her hands to the ceiling and let out a celebratory cry that was immediately echoed by all the women in the room. It ended almost as soon as it began.

"Behold, the Queen and Consort! We are all the blessed ones to be here on this remarkable day! No one can claim to have seen its measure," Syreena declared.

"And now, for the bedding!" Anya added, her laughter bold and mischievous. The women all cried out again, their fears and doubts swept away by the aides' enthusiasm, the sound rising from them a feminine cheer of encouragement.

Elijah lifted a brow that could only be described as a cross between amused and lecherous. Siena was not a shy woman, but she still could not help the soft flush of color that tinged her cheeks. There was too much excitement and anticipation rushing through her.

"My Lord," Anya whispered softly. "You must sever the ribbons with the dagger."

"Oh?" Again that smile and the lift of a brow. "I like it here already," he mused, forcing his Queen to smother a laugh by pressing her lips firmly together.

Elijah inspected the weaved ribbons down the front of the robe that might as well have not been there at all. It, and the gown beneath it, was so sheer he could see every curve of her body, and every accent from golden curls to dusky nipples.

Elijah flicked bold emerald eyes up to her gaze, the look coming from under his lashes intriguing her. In a quarter of a heartbeat, light winked like a little supernova from the blade he held.

It was the only sign of movement any of them saw, but the ribbons of her robe parted perfectly. The ladies all gasped, and this time Anya and Syreena were impressed enough to join in the surprised murmur. Siena, however, took it completely in stride, smiling as her mate grinned in that cocky way of his.

The Queen moved from his side and approached the bed. The ladies suddenly remembered their duty to her and reached to draw off the neatly separated cloth from her shoulders. As they peeled the second shift of silk and lace down their mistress's shoulders, they were all aware of the Demon's covetous eyes. The ladies were proud of their Queen's perfection and it pleased them immensely to make slow, silky work of her disrobing.

Elijah's smile faded rapidly as he watched this. He had never known the sound of silk and lace on skin could be so distinct. But it was. The light fabric paused to cling teasingly to the thrust of her rigid nipples. Finally she stepped from the tissuelike garment, slowly tossing her hair over her shoulder, giving him a perfect view of a gorgeous, pale golden figure.

And that was the moment he finally understood what it meant to be an Imprinted male on Samhain.

CHAPTER 12

Elijah's attention was riveted as the women around the Queen helped her into bed. Siena was gently laid back in the center of the enormous expanse of plush pillows and white and gold velvet bedding. She smiled at him as he clearly became increasingly tense. She was nearer to his mind now, so knew quite well what he was thinking and feeling in the moment. And all of it was quite primal. More so, she realized, as the ladies-in-wait sprinkled her body with the petals of late-season sunflowers.

Syreena and Anya had a sense of the tension in the room and, as soon as they were done anointing the Queen, guided the giggling young women from the room. Elijah completely ignored their curiosity and speculation. Clearly, they did not realize that the fast whispers they spoke in were easily heard by him and would continue to be so, unless they waited until they were much farther away. He also noted that someone, the sister Syreena with the strange hair and eyes, had taken the marriage dagger from his hand.

And that moment was all the time he spent giving thought to it.

The next moment, the click of the closing doors being latched galvanized him into action.

Siena watched with quick breath and anticipation as he moved to the foot of the bed. He reached out swiftly, grabbing her by both ankles and sliding her completely off the mattress with one very firm pull. She laughed as he scooped her up against his body with one arm around her waist, saffron-colored petals crushing between them.

"You are mine," he said softly through clenched teeth.

He leaned in with an aggressive male sound rumbling from his throat. Siena closed her eyes as he searched for her scent at the curve of her neck, drawing it deeply into his lungs until he sighed with satisfaction.

"I have been parted from you too long," he announced, moving her back just enough so he could devour her body with his eyes even as his bold hand slid over her belly and ribs and cradled her breast with firm intensity. "I am half mad from wanting you, kitten, and I am afraid I will not be very gentle."

She did not speak aloud but instead wound her fingers deep into his hair and drew his head, and his mouth, closer to hers. Her lips parted, rubbing soft and warm over his, teasing him with her spiced taste.

"You are mine," she said, feeling the chilled flash of stimulation her voice and words sent rushing over his skin. "And I never"—she licked his lips teasingly, making him groan— "never once"—her body curled erotically up to his, every inch of her skin a caress that reached deeply into him—"asked you to be gentle," she finished at last.

Elijah captured that wicked, teasing mouth with a fervor that bruised her hungry lips. She had fooled herself into believing all of this had come about by her choices and machinations, a product of her reluctant will, but in that second she understood there had never been a choice. She had always wanted him with this intensity, even when he had already been buried deep in her body. Her flesh flushed with the first true life she had felt since they had parted last, and even that encounter in the innards of the castle had been too brief, too bittersweet.

His hands on her skin were a balm for her paled soul. He had such large, calloused palms, the roughness of them suiting the roughness of his sweeping touch. His fingers pressed into her soft flesh, and she welcomed the idea of him leaving his prints behind this time.

Siena felt the sudden release of her collar of office, the jeweled weight of it dropping carelessly to the floor as he broke from her lips in order to devour the sweet, pulsing skin of her bared neck. She went so limp so suddenly that she was supported solely by his powerful hands and the balanced lean of his body as he bore her weight with careless ease. She was a woman of remarkable stature, and yet he managed to make her feel fairy light, a delicately feminine insignificance she hadn't thought could be born in the heart of an Amazonian huntress such as herself. But it seemed practical it would take a mighty warrior like Elijah to make it so.

"Elijah . . ." she whispered in his ear, needing to speak his name, needing to feel the emotions that came with the knowledge that she was permitted to do so without worry, without guilt. Their journey was far from over, and would be far from easy, but she had made the choice and would now revel in it as much as she might come to suffer for it. She was suddenly allowed to be that someone she had never allowed herself access to, that someone she had glimpsed those other times in his arms.

Elijah's mouth was like magic, casting spells wherever it went, his hunger for her taste coming through in his actions as well as his thoughts. To be in the mind of a man in such a moment was like nothing she could have ever conceived of. To be in the mind of this man, in this moment, was incomprehensible pleasure. His need for her was unfailingly overwhelming, as consistent as it was voracious. She felt the way he drank in her heat through his fingertips and mouth, like passionate straws that thirsted for her unlike anything else in the world.

Then the warrior began to fade beneath her grasping hands, the wind that was his power buoying her as he rushed past and through her, materializing at her back, one hand around her waist, the other on her throat and chin, guiding her head back onto his shoulder.

Siena laughed, a cross between joy and relieved sobbing. The warmth of his suddenly bare flesh was like heaven itself, and she realized her limp fingers were still clinging to the shirt he had abandoned with his maneuver. She let it fall to the ground on top of the other discarded clothing and reached past her hips, behind herself, until she was touching the powerful thighs bracing both of their weight so easily.

Elijah wrapped her up in the embrace of his hungry hands, her supple, soft skin a searing, tactile perfection to him. He would never get enough of touching her. He went from thigh to breast and back again until she was making those soft sounds of lost wit that so enthralled him.

As promised, he was not gentle. He did not want to mark her but could not seem to help himself. And also as promised, she only seemed to respond all the more for it. He found himself resisting the urge he had to lay his teeth on her, marking her for his own. It was part of the animalistic mating ritual the night was visiting on him. Then he remembered she was mostly animal herself and he finally released his restraint, his mouth closing over the soft curve of the back of her neck possessively. Siena writhed sensually in his hands, a bold, rumbling purr vibrating out of her until he was completely inundated with the arousing sensation of it.

He leaned forward slightly in his enthusiasm, and Siena's foot finally touched the floor. She reacted instantly, using the purchase to shove her weight back against him. Caught off guard, he was forced to step back to recover. She used the opportunity to spin around in his hold, leaping back into his embrace in a way that propelled him back a few steps more.

He recovered quickly, however, in spite of what her subsequent attack on his mouth did to his already shattered equilibrium. Still, as one arm wrapped around her wild body, the other reached out blindly for support. He touched the smoothness of cool stone and leaned back into it as he reached to meet her onslaught.

Siena dodged his mouth, seeking the strong column of his throat with eager lips and tongue, doing to him what he so easily did to her. She wriggled so she slid down his dampening body with her own, her mouth following suit. Her tongue licked silkily over his collarbone, her fingers splaying over his sides and belly, the precursor to her oral exploration as she continued to slide down the length of him. Elijah was drawing for breath, his head falling back against stone as his eyes slid closed. She had left him with nothing to occupy his thoughts outside of the feel of her traveling mouth and his hand clinging deeply into her hair.

Her industrious tongue slid over a dark nipple, her lips skimming through fine golden hairs as she sought to give equal attention to the other. Then her voracious mouth licked down the ridges of his abdomen. Her hands encircled his hips, her strong fingers massaging the clenching muscles of his backside and thighs as she continued to torture him, her progress becoming slower and slower until he was gritting his teeth with the sweet agony of anticipation.

She touched him first, the ever-so-light brush of teasing fingertips, curiously experiencing the hard heat of his aroused body. She slid those soft, searching fingers over the length of him, experiencing the tactile sensation of smooth skin stretched over hot, steely engorged flesh. But it was when he felt the brush of warm lips and breath that he gripped her hair with renewed intensity and swore with vehemence, both curses and prayers, for strength, control, or even the smallest flash of civility.

Then the moist heat of her lips diligently surrounded him, the flick of her tongue so sure, so heated, and far too eager for his sanity. He tried to push, to pull away . . . to escape her before he completely lost his mind. She was too bold, too curious, and she was going to destroy what little control he might have had by then. His urges and emotions were too primal as it was—the night, the deprivation, and the approaching fullness of the moon.

But she would not give him quarter. She had tasted him as he had tasted her, and it was as much a drug to her senses as she had been to his. He knew it, felt it, and heard it in the eager focus of her thoughts. She taunted him with the fit of her mouth, taking delight in the groan the movement elicited, feeling the clench and the tremor of straining muscles with that feline satisfaction that always rushed over her when she experienced an exceptional victory.

"Siena."

He was begging her hoarsely, trying to warn her with his thoughts, but she courted his volatile reactions with the heaven of her heated exploration. It left him victimized, helpless, and lost with the pure ecstasy of it.

Finally, she released him from her talented trap, retracing her path up his body. But she had barely begun her journey when his hands clamped around her shoulders and jerked her up to his mouth. He launched himself off the wall as he ravaged those sinful lips of hers with brutal passion. As soon as the backs of her legs touched the mattress, he turned her back to his chest once more and shoved her onto the bed. She burst into laughter as she bounced hard on her face, knowing every thought in his mind with delightful clarity, hearing every wicked name he hurled at her for her wanton disregard of his sanity.

She barely had her palms under her before he enclosed her hips in his hands and jerked her back toward him, pulling her up onto her knees as he settled her back into the cradle of his pelvis. One hand came up to clamp the back of her neck as he thrust forward into her with absolutely no warning, not even an anticipatory thought to prepare her for the divine invasion. Siena gasped on her laughter, overwhelmed by the way he seemed to fill her beyond her capacity. She shuddered top to bottom, involuntarily clenching around him so that they were chorusing sounds of lost bliss an instant later.

"Siena," he groaned.

He moved forward within and above her, his hand reaching to cover hers, his fingers lacing tightly through hers as his forehead briefly touched her spine between her shoulder blades. He kissed her gently in that spot, the tenderness out of place with the ferocity of his passions. So much so that she felt it all the more for the loving gesture that it was.

That was when she realized the truth of his feelings. He hid it under animal passion and the barely leashed savagery of a dominant male, but she was seeing deeper into his heart even as she saw deeper into his mind.

Siena closed her eyes as her body accepted his surging invasion, feeling acutely alive and aware, even as she felt numb with what she was beginning to understand.

Elijah suddenly vacated her body, making her gasp with bereft shock between that moment and the moment his hands flipped her over as if she were light as air.

"I need to see you," he ground out roughly. "I want your eyes on me while you are thinking your thoughts, kitten."

Siena felt her chest swelling with indescribable emotion and more than a little fear as he covered her with his warm strength and bored into her gaze with unrelenting sight that speared into her soul. He moved into her more slowly this time, purposeful. Watching the pleasure that blanketed her entire expression as she accepted him so readily with her body, and so reluctantly with her endangered heart.

"You know. I see it," he said heavily, whispering against her lips. "I feel it, Siena."

Siena mutely shook her head, closing her eyes so she

could hide from him. But there was no hiding from someone so connected to her. Bodily, mentally, and whatever it was spiritually that had refused to let them remain apart.

"Elijah, just . . . just be with me," she begged him. "Just for now."

And because of the day, because of how desperately he needed her, he had no choice but to comply. This once he would allow her to retreat behind the last walls she was using to separate them.

He knew she had read his soul a moment ago, that she now understood that he was in love with her, and that this was what she could not face. Elijah's pain went deeply through him in that moment of understanding, but he pushed it aside severely. He would wait for her. If it took every moment of every day for the rest of his life, he would wait for her heart. And that was the only thing that kept him from shattering emotionally in front of her.

He shook back the feelings robbing him of breath and voice, and refocused on her sweet body. If this was the only way she would allow herself to accept him, then so be it. He was going to take every advantage of the intimacy. Not that he could have chosen otherwise.

The warrior allowed himself to be lost in the physicality of their rhythmic embrace within and around each other. He altered his thoughts to pure sexual need, eliminating her access to his yearning heart, allowing her to burrow her head beneath the sand for just a little while longer.

Her distracting fear evaporated quickly as he manipulated her body as skillfully as he manipulated his hidden thoughts. Soon he was lost in the sheer sensation of her as she embraced him more and more powerfully, the tension of her rising need strangling him blissfully. The fulfillment that came was bittersweet. She ignited with a sound of utter gratification, the clutch of her convulsing body dragging him under her bewitching spell moments later.

*   *   *

Elijah's eyes roamed over the etched stone on the ceiling above him, the pattern peeking through the streamers of sheer white silk woven in a loose X shape across the canopy.

Beside him, trapping his arm beneath the weight of her body, Siena lay deeply, peacefully asleep. He had used her to the utmost, exorcising his emotions with a physical passion that had exhausted her. But he was not even close to such a restful repose. While she lay in the only state where his thoughts would be safely guarded from her, he took them out to examine them.

He freed himself from her easily, at least in the physical sense, and sat up on the edge of the bed, letting the cold of the floor seep into his bare feet as he ran his fingers through his tousled hair and the rough growth of his seven-hours-old beard.

Seven hours. And in that time his entire world had been tumbled head over heels.

Elijah stood up carefully, moving slowly so the removal of his weight did not catch her subconscious attention. He scooped up his clothes and dressed quickly. He should not leave her. He should not allow her to wake without him beside her. But he needed this time to himself. He would possibly be back at her side before she even noticed, but he could not remain still a moment longer, watching her look so damned beautiful and content when he was in such turmoil.

He needed a wise ear because he knew he did not have the wisdom to hash this out on his own. He was too engaged, too close. And he was in far too much pain to see straight.

And for once, it was a pain he realized would not be as easy to survive as a physical wound might be.

No.

Dying was far less painful than a hurting heart.

CHAPTER 13

Gideon opened his eyes barely twenty minutes after he had drifted to sleep. The stained glass windows of the bedroom blocked a great deal of the dawn light, making it a shower of warm colors rather than intrusive white, and he adjusted to it in seconds.

He and Legna had decided to spend the day in his former residence. As opposed to their dwelling at Siena's court where people came and went constantly during times of holiday, here they were assured absolutely uninterrupted privacy during their Samhain night. They had not stayed long at the usual castle festivities with Noah and their other friends, the urgency of the night chasing them quickly to bed just as it had Jacob, Bella, and the others who were Imprinted and even those who were not.

Gideon had planned on sleeping as lengthily and as thoroughly as he had just made love to his wife, who lay in a deep sleep herself. Legna was sprawled over him, exactly as she always was, exactly in the way that made his heart pound with his deep-seated emotions for her.

But something had stirred him awake, and as he absently

stroked her soft hair, he searched for some clarity about the disturbance that had done so.

The moment he realized who it was that approached his house, Gideon rolled Legna off his body quickly and ungently. He ignored her sleepy protest, jerking the coverlet up over her as he grabbed for his robe.

The Ancient medic paused for a moment of uncharacteristic indecision. Then he reached down to Legna and closed his hand over her forehead. He sank into her body mentally, expending quick energy into her as he manipulated her in a way that no other could match. Once she was completely submerged from the world, her spirit, thoughts, and biosigns repressed into nonexistence perceptually, he scooped her up into his arms and hauled her over to a swing-away bookshelf that concealed the room that had served as his meditation place for centuries. Placing her gently on the floor within the secret room, he didn't even spend time kissing her before parting from her, although he wanted to more than anything in that moment.

He exited the room and hurried out of the bedroom. He grabbed the banister, vaulting over it and dropping all three floors down the center of the spiral stairwell.

Gideon landed on his feet, remaining in a crouch as he tilted his head and altered his senses until they were at his most acute. He was out of time and he had not even had the chance to astral project to Noah and tell him where Legna was in case . . .

. . . just in case.

"I feel you waiting for me, medic."

The voice was artificially enhanced in volume within his thoughts, causing him remarkable pain. He realized then exactly how powerful his enemy had grown. A Demon had never dabbled in black arts outside of a pentagram before. Gideon would never have expected it to have this kind of effect, this extraordinary enhancement of power. But it was corruptive all the same, he could feel it, smell it, the dark stain of it spread deeply over Ruth's soul as she winked into existence with a flash of strange, dark light.

Gideon gained his full height, narrowing his eyes on the bold bitch who dared to threaten his home and his family. But he kept his temper, as always. He had not lived over a millennium without learning that losing your head in your emotions when confronted with a battle was a sure way of signing your own death certificate.

"Ruth," he greeted coldly. "Even you cannot be this mad."

Ruth did not seem to pay attention to him. She was tilting her head, looking up toward the ceiling with curiosity.

"Sleeping without your wife on Samhain?" She made a tsking sound. "Am I supposed to believe she is not here? You are right, I am not that mad."

The cool blond's eyes roamed thoughtfully over the Ancient, her gaze clearly avaricious. Her lush body curved, beckoning in a way that had once been quite alluring, and still might be had she not chosen the path she was now clinging to so greedily. But now she was as sinuous as a poisonous reptile, and clearly just as deadly as she was beautiful.

"I once had the most terrible crush on you," she confessed, her countenance amused. "You were so powerful. And handsome. Quite handsome." Ruth slid a hand over one smooth hip, her movement obvious and practiced. "Does your hidden wife know we were once together on Beltane?"

"That was three hundred years ago," Gideon said, his tone as neutral as ever. "And if I recall, women were somewhat scarce in our population at the time."

Ruth looked as if she had been slapped, and in effect she had been. But a second later her face flared with outraged color.

"How dare you!" she hissed. "You enjoyed it well enough at the time! Even you cannot deny that!"

Gideon let her indulge in her rage. He was intent on remaining focused on the power that was outside the walls of his home, gathering far too quickly even for his comfort and abilities. He had been right to conceal Legna from them. Ruth would never be able to figure out what he had done with his wife; she was not quite that powerful. But his mate was vulnerable, left upstairs in a state that simulated death in order to mask her presence. If the condition was not reversed within an hour, she and the baby would be in terrible danger. But in order to revive her from the stasis, he had to remain alive and must protect her by being victorious in this encounter.

The odds of this diminished with each new presence that he sensed. Gideon was strong, but not against the odds that were becoming all too probable with every passing minute. He should have known better. He should have never brought Legna into territory Ruth could discover with a little creative ease. But there would be time for self-recrimination later.

"Ruth, is there a purpose behind your visit besides a walk down memory lane over a quick tumble behind a random bush most of your lifetime ago?" He narrowed frigid silver eyes on her. "It must be, because you could not possibly be so stupid as to try and take on me."

"It is exactly what I intend to do. I am more powerful than even you can imagine, Gideon. And I am not alone."

"Forgive me for saying so, but it is not as if I could not smell your stench from a mile away. You are corrupted, Ruth. You must be aware that the stench of the others no longer affects you because of that."

Gideon was already mentally reaching toward the female Demon's body, her physiology, preparing to manipulate her into death the moment he could. But her chemistry was troubling, confusing. She was transforming on levels even she was unaware of. It made her unreadable, a puzzle that would take too much time for him to sort through.

Ruth gave him that faint smile again, the one that reached

too far into her mad eyes. She was a powerful Mind Demon and no doubt was aware of his attempt, and his stalling out.

"You know, Gideon," she said softly, stepping so close to him he had to fight off the urge to back up from the corrupt smell of her. "I may have been a quick encounter for you, but I know *she* is not. She and your unborn baby. And I will find her, even if we have to burn the house to the ground to do it."

"You will have to go through me first, traitor."

"Exactly my plan," she mused.

"Then you better call in your little minions."

Gideon moved so quickly, he had his hand around her throat before she could even anticipate it in his thoughts. She was slammed back into the nearest wall a second later, Gideon using the pain and the surprise to keep her from concentrating on her abilities. But she was an Elder and far too empowered to be held at bay with disruptive tricks for long. So the medic did not waste time; he immediately cut off her air and the blood supply to her brain. She gagged, her eyes wide as she looked into the deadly threat in his eyes.

"Your problem," he murmured to her, almost in a lover's voice, "is that you waste time boasting and building yourself up with empty talk. You should have struck while you could."

While he throttled the Demon defector, he reached out to the perimeter of his home, grabbing unsuspecting necromancers one by one with sheer force of power and will, stopping their black hearts dead in their chests. For all their power of magic, the necromancers were still as fragile as any human, making it a ridiculously simple task in many respects.

The others, watching their comrades fall inexplicably, began to panic and rushed toward the house to find the source of the damage to their ranks before he could cause any further harm. They were clearly shocked at how easily he had done this attack. Once again, Ruth had not prepared them for what she was leading them into. It would perhaps be his one true advantage.

Ruth regrouped even as he throttled her consciousness out of her. Her eyes rolled back as she accessed her power, and he felt her pushing into his mind. The force was stunning and impressive. Gideon was blinded by pain, his free hand reflexively going to his head as she sought to turn his brain to a pulp with her telekinetic power. He had never met a female telekinetic before, but Mind Demons were relatively new to their species and, poisoned as she was, it could be an unnatural mutation. It took all of his mental fortitude to fight her off, and even so he felt blood drip from his nose as it filled his pressured sinuses.

When he was forced to take his attention from the others, they invaded the house within minutes. The evil flock of women hovered like wingless harpies over the floor, speaking the tainted words that would bring forth the electrical bolts of power they wielded during attack.

Gideon spilt his attention. He struck Ruth in the face, dazing her with the sharp thrust of his palm to her delicate nose. He could have killed her with the blow had he been more focused, but he was also reaching for magic-users, muting several of them in a sweep of thought, cutting them off from the verbal means necessary for access to their power, sending them crashing to the floor.

Others he panicked with blindness, others still with deafness.

It bought him time only.

Gideon felt something strike him, the unmistakable puncture of teeth sinking into his calf. That was when he dropped a barely conscious Ruth to the floor and spun around to face her daughter. The spoiled automaton that was Ruth's offspring, Mary, was more powerful as well. Gideon felt it. He breathed it in as the wicked stench eddied toward him. She was drawing swarms of wild dogs, wolves, and even poisonous snakes in through every smashed window and doorway she could, coiled serpents even dropping down the chimney and into the cold ashes of the fireplace.

The animals were not responsible for the compulsion Mary had them under, so Gideon was pained when he had to reach to break the neck of the wolf that had buried its canines deeply into his flesh. By the time he turned, there were a dozen others on him.

Razorlike teeth sliced into his flesh from every direction. All he could do was cut off the pain and the blood as they tried to drag him down, seeking access to his throat.

Gideon considered that he might have made a mistake by not waking Legna and allowing her the freedom of thought to escape. But then again, he knew his beloved wife all too well. She would have insisted on being at his back, fighting where she had been born to fight. And that was exactly why he had done what he had done. He would rather die than see her hurt or worse.

But by leaving her helpless, that might be just what he had sentenced her to.

Gideon could only do one thing to possibly save her.

Though it would take several highly talented medics to reverse the stasis he had put her in, and even though they might not succeed, he had to try.

Gideon gave up his fight and projected his astral self into the dawn, reaching for Noah as the attacking forces began to drag him down.

He was not even aware of the sudden, violent wind that made the house shudder from foundation to rafters.

Siena woke with a start, her heart racing as her head rang with warnings and filled with bloodred rage.

She turned over swiftly, reaching for Elijah in panic and feeling an awful, clawing sensation of dread and despair as her hand came up with empty sheets and blankets.

He had left her, and as sure as she knew that, she knew he was in trouble. Oh, he was trying to keep it from her on some sort of automatic, protective level, but he could not hide the rage and horror flooding through him because of whatever it was he was seeing.

She closed her eyes, trying to concentrate, wishing suddenly she had never let him out of her sight in the first place. From what Gideon had told her, if they had spent the days since Jinaeri's cavern together, they would have had a stronger bond mentally, to the point where she would have seen through his eyes perfectly.

The minute she thought of Gideon, his image flashed into her mind, but it was washed away by silver and red.

Blood red.

Siena flew from her bed, transforming into the Werecat on the run as she flew out of her quarters. The guards were startled to see her exit in such a wild manner, and in her Wereform to boot.

"I want Anya this moment! Tell her to meet me at the Demon ambassador's home with troops immediately!"

"But Majesty—"

"Do not question me! Do as I say this instant!"

"Majesty, it is daylight," the guard pressed on, though clearly loath to countermand her again.

She did not blame him. She hadn't appeared to make a rational movement or decision in over a week. But this . . . this was something even she could not fight.

She had a sudden wash of terror, and tears of frustration, burning behind her eyes. Her hand went to her heart as it threatened to beat right out of her chest. Elijah needed her. Needed her help. Gideon as well. She was sure of it. They both were closer to her heart than she had been willing to admit, and now when they needed her, she was utterly helpless to aid them.

The sun.

A thrice-damned star hundreds of thousands of miles away, and yet it prevented her from going to Elijah's side.

"Your Majesty remembers it is Samhain," he prompted gently. "The ambassador and her mate were attending the functions of their own court for the holiday and said they would not return until tonight."

Even worse! It meant they were in England. Thousands of miles away from the remote Russian province the Lycanthropes dwelled in. As fast as she was, she would never be that fast. She would be forced to use the modern human conveniences that would take hours despite their jetting speed.

Siena suddenly wished her court was full of Demons. Any one of them, especially Mind Demons who could teleport, would have her where she needed to be in a heartbeat.

For the first time in her life, Siena truly felt the limitations of her race and her personal abilities. Oh, she had felt somewhat helpless during her father's regime, but at least then she had managed to maintain a fair rule while he was off trying to conquer unconquerable foes. This was something utterly different.

But Siena refused to give up.

"Find a half-breed runner and send them to Anya. Tell her to assemble only half-breed troops. They, at least, are not affected by the sunlight. And for once I would give up all my forms if I could but say the same. Time is of the essence, so you will go this instant! Move!"

This time there was no argument. The Minotaur female ran off, leaving her perplexed male counterpart behind. He was trying to glance into the bedroom behind him as unobtrusively as he could.

"What is amiss, my lady?"

"My mate is in danger. Dreadful danger," she explained, her hands coasting over her furred stomach anxiously, clearly uncaring of what the guard thought about the fact that her mate ought to have been in bed with her on their wedding day. "And he is so far away. I need to help him, Synnoro. I cannot lose him like this! Not because I cannot reach him because of the damned sun!" The Queen paced a couple of short steps. "Goddess, please," she prayed softly, closing her eyes as she tried to think, "please help me!"

"My lady, what of Myriad?"

Siena stopped suddenly, her eyes widening.

Myriad. The half-breed in Noah's court who was acting the part of her ambassador to the Demon King. There were no technologies in a Demon household, but, unwilling to give up such luxuries of humanity because Demon chemistry made such things go completely awry—sometimes dangerously so—Myriad had chosen to live in the village a few miles away from Noah's castle and the discombobulating influences of the Demons that constantly came and went there.

"She has a phone," Siena whispered, sudden hope flaring in her breast. "Synnoro! She has a phone!"

Siena forgot etiquette and rank and leapt up to throw her arms around the furry guard, bussing him loudly on the cheek before hitting feet to the floor at a run. The castle had been stripped of technology when Gideon and Legna had arrived; everything from lighting to communications had been restored to the state the castle had been in during the five years of Gideon's captivity among them. But Anya would have a phone in her residence, and Siena hadn't thought she would ever be so grateful for so simple a convenience.

All she needed to do was reach it fast enough.

Noah woke with a disoriented jolt, the sudden rush of nearby and alien energy seeping into his senses. He opened his eyes to see the Lycanthrope half-breed standing over him, reaching for him as if she were going to touch him. Instinctively, his hand shot out and grabbed the reaching wrist, jerking the raven-haired woman to her knees beside the bed.

"You had better have an explanation for being in my bedroom uninvited, ambassador," he threatened her, sitting up as he twisted her captive hand further.

The room was dimmed by drawn shades and drapes, and her eyes were yellow in the dark, more blatantly so than in gas or torchlight. It was eerie seeing them staring at him so unblinkingly. She had told him that, had she been full-bred, she would have been some sort of wild dog or wolf. It clearly showed in her eyes in that moment.

"Your Warrior Captain and your medic are in trouble. My Queen thought you might like to know."

Noah was on his feet in an instant, releasing Myriad as he reached for clothing.

"Explain!" he commanded, not bothering to waste time with apologies.

"She says that Elijah is wherever Gideon is, and that both are in terrible danger."

"I thought Elijah was with Siena tonight. Gideon said—"

"Apparently he left her bed while she was sleeping. I did not think it wise to question *that* fact of my Queen."

Noah looked at the enigmatic brunette, lifting a corner of his mouth as he tucked his shirt into his jeans.

"A wise decision."

"No doubt," she agreed in the easy humor that had helped her win over many thickheaded Demons these past months. Siena had proven herself beyond wise by sending this sturdy, half-bred woman to him on her behalf. She had the perfect temperament for making friends, and, clearly, never held a grudge for more than a heartbeat.

"Can you join me?"

"The sun does not affect me. I am at your service."

"Good. We have to find someone who can notify Jacob and others. I have the terrible feeling we are going to need help."

"And Siena. She will have both our heads if we do not fetch her as well," Myriad insisted.

"Agreed!"

CHAPTER 14

If there was a nature of things that Noah knew with perfect clarity and instinct, it was smoke and fire.

As they neared the home of his family, he could smell and feel both.

Terror flooded Noah as he came over the crest of the mountain, dragging himself and the half-breed out of smoky form and into solid shape. The only thing he could see of the house was smoke and the tumble of flames roaring from gaps left by shattered glass. Everything not made of stone was conflagrating easily and wildly because of its age and richness in fuel.

"Legna!"

Noah released his power and seized the flames burning the structure. The heated backlash that followed as he violently sucked the fire's energy into himself literally blew Myriad off her feet. She landed about ten feet away on the charred grass, shaking her head as she tried to resettle her jostled brainpan. Again, she took it in stride, not even bothering to dust herself off as she scrambled after the Demon King.

As they ran, Demons began popping up around them. No

matter how much she saw it, Myriad swore she would never get used to the suddenness of Demon teleportation. Clearly the Mind Demons Noah had contacted were working overtime to bring reinforcements to them. The Enforcers blazed into form, assorted warriors coming quickly in their wake.

Noah had to crash bodily through the charred front door, skidding across the floor as he shot through, barely in balance. He fell in a rare moment of awkwardness, soot and melted debris sliding beneath his feet. His fall brought him face-to-face with a body, and he suddenly found himself looking into the open, vacant silver eyes of his brother-in-law.

"Gideon . . ."

His shock was written all over his voice and face. He slid to his knees and leaned over his sister's husband, feeling for a pulse. Noah had never known such fear as he did in that horrible moment. Not even when he had seen his mother's violated body upon her death had he allowed himself to feel such a debilitating, paralyzing emotion. He had been forced to be strong then, for Legna's sake, because she had been but a babe when she had seen her mother in that state. But this he felt and felt deeply. Just as Legna would—

"Legna!"

Noah's head snapped around as he reached out, mentally screaming for her, demanding she answer and searching with all his power for her energy signature.

"Legna!"

Jacob and Isabella came rushing into the half-destroyed house. Isabella cried out in despair when she saw Gideon's lifeless form. But she was rudely pushed aside when Siena burst into the house and moved to see what had so horrified everyone into standing so stock-still.

"Gideon!" the Queen gasped, dropping swiftly to her old friend's side.

He could not be dead. He was too old, too powerful! If he was dead, that meant that Elijah . . .

Siena pushed the thought aside violently, reaching for Gideon's throat as Noah gained his feet and ran up the stairs three and four at a time.

"Is he . . . ?" Bella dared to begin to ask.

"We need a medic in here!" Siena screamed, her voice echoing in the desolate house. "Where is Elijah?"

"Elijah?" Jacob demanded. "Elijah is here?"

"Yes, he is here somewhere. I felt him when I woke earlier. It is what led us here. I know he is here. Where is he?" Siena asked urgently, standing up and looking all around herself for signs of her new husband. She was breathing hard enough to hyperventilate, coughing on the residual smoke seeping through the room. She searched her thoughts and her soul for any sign of Elijah's consciousness, his powerful presence suddenly vacant from her awareness, clouded by her panic.

Jacob and Isabella took her vacated position over Gideon, and Isabella gasped when she realized she had just knelt in a pool of the Ancient's blood. Closer now, under the charred clothing and soot from smoke, she saw he was severely wounded, burned and also bitten, his flesh torn as if he had been brutally attacked by a pack of wild animals.

"It *was* animals. Dogs, wolves, and snakes. Venomous snakes!" Jacob hissed.

Jacob, the tracker to the end, turned over Gideon's limp hand, pulling several long blond strands of hair from between his fingers.

An Elder Body Demon, a medic in the warrior corps, hurried into the house, followed by about a half dozen other warriors, who immediately took to searching the house. The medic joined Bella and Jacob, laying hands on the Ancient Demon.

"He's dead," he murmured. "But only just. Move back."

The Enforcers did as commanded, leaving the medic to do what he could in peace, their sense of duty firing through their joined minds.

"Ruth," Jacob said needlessly, snapping the fine blond hairs between clenched fingers.

The name drew Siena's full attention.

"Ruth?" There was nothing but rage and pain in the Queen's eyes as she repeated the cursed name. "That bitch did this?"

Furious, the Lycanthrope Queen made a low, dangerous sound. All she could remember all of a sudden was how she had first found Elijah, bleeding, in agony, and close to the end of his mortality because of his last encounter with the Demon female who had betrayed her kind. Driven to a near emotional madness, she barely recognized the weak whisper of scent that drifted into range of her senses.

Then suddenly her head perked up, her ears and whiskers twitching forward. She was quite a sight, few of the Demons present having seen her Wereform before now, finding the sleekly furred and formed female cat as powerful and intimidating as she truly was, her wild fear and racing bio-signs apparent to even those who did not naturally sense such things. Jacob knew, as he would know with any wild creature of nature, that she had caught the scent of what she had been looking for.

"Elijah," Jacob whispered.

Siena growled, the half-cry of the puma making warriors step back out of age-old habit. Lycanthropes were a tough breed and nothing to mess with, not even in peacetime, and they knew to give her a wide berth. But the Enforcers followed her as she raced out of the door with her remarkable speed.

"She's going to kill herself," Jacob bit out, rushing after the heedless woman.

"How . . . ?"

"The sun," Jacob explained to his less experienced mate. "It makes her kind sick. It poisons them. She's strong, but not that strong. There isn't even a cloud in the sky or a tree to shade her."

But Bella knew what was propelling the Queen. She had once knelt in Jacob's blood, just as she had Gideon's a moment ago, terrified he was about to die. In that moment, nothing could have stopped her from doing everything she could think of to defy fate in order to save his life. It had been Gideon who had saved him then, but now it was Gideon who was in need of being saved by his own miraculous skills. But who could work that miracle? She had only ever seen Gideon perform such feats.

The physician, in this case, could not heal himself.

Jacob and Bella ran after the Queen, but she was powered by the speed of the cat that she was. Only Jacob would have been able to match her, but he refused to leave Bella behind in this dangerous situation.

Siena tore over the lawn at full speed, but that speed downgraded visibly to her pursuers the longer the sprint became. She was heading for a distant tree line as her gait shortened, began to become awkward, dragged as if she was running through a sea of water instead of air.

"I have to catch up with her. She is never going to make it in this sunlight," Jacob shouted to his wife.

"Catch her! I'm fine," she insisted, pushing at his shoulder to urge him to the speed he was capable of.

Siena was blinded by tears, heedless of the nausea and weakness dragging at her struggling body like thousands of claws bent on rending her to shreds, working to slow her down and freeze her in position just short of the goal she needed to reach so desperately. The Queen fell over her own feet, crashing clumsily to the ground with a painful jarring. The strike on the ground seemed to burst her apart, her frantic sobs, held trapped within herself until that frustrating moment of impact, blinding her as she tried to stagger to her feet.

An outraged cry of wild terror echoed into the morning air as she struggled halfway to her feet, forcing herself forward with hands and feet and any other part of herself that would gain the purchase to propel her toward her goal.

Siena reached the tree line just as Elijah's form solidified suddenly before her, reaching for the frantic crash of her propelled body. He was overwhelmed by the emotions of his mate that had drawn him there, her feelings of distress having lured him like a clamoring beacon. She was so hysterical with paralyzing panic that she hadn't heard a single thing, felt a single feeling he had tried to communicate to soothe her.

They crashed into each other as she finally reached him, his opened arms scooping her up as she threw herself awkwardly against his body. She pushed herself into him, and into him again, forcing him to hold her tighter to keep her from harming them both in her desperation. She was so violent as she grabbed at his body that her feet came up off the ground, her arms nearly throttling him. She held on to him as if the world was ending and she needed to meet doomsday with him from the inside of his body, or his soul, whichever she could reach with all her efforts.

Her claws retracted to safety as she reached for his face, cupping it with desperation as tears fell over her furred face and dripped onto him, her soft lips trembling with sobs as she kissed him. She could not even breathe she was so upset, her padded fingers inspecting his scorched and wounded body frantically. It was merely battle scarring, nothing lethal, since this time his surprise at running into a pack of magic-users at Gideon's had been buffered by the fact that the open area had given him visual warning. In fact, he had been the one to surprise them. He had been fighting them, chasing them into the woodlands even as he picked them off one at a time with hailstones, lightning, and hurricane-force winds that blew right past any defenses they tried to throw at him.

He had only broken off when he had felt Siena's arrival and her highly panicked distress. He hadn't even realized she had come awake until she had entered the closer proximity. He had mistakenly thought that between his efforts and her sleeping state, she would remain blissfully unaware of the danger he was facing.

"Get a medic," she sobbed, gasping the words out as her terror and pain continued to overwhelm her body and soul. "Get a medic. Please. Goddess, please! Don't just stand there!" she screamed at Jacob who had finally, breathlessly, caught up to her and Elijah. "Get him a medic!"

Siena fell apart, not even seeing that Bella had also caught up to them, leaning hard into a stitch in her side. The Queen was lost in her pounding emotions, her body reverting to its human shape as she lost all strength and buried her face and fingers into Elijah's scorched shirt and burned chest.

"Siena!" Elijah grabbed her arms and gave her a shake. "Calm down, kitten. I am not hurt!"

But as he tried to get her to see sense, he felt her wobbling limply in his grasp. Her head bobbled weakly as her strength seemed to bleed out of her with the suddenness of a mortal wound. He heard Bella gasp, and, out of the corner of his eye, was aware of her hand covering the appalled opening of her mouth. The Enforcer was near to tears herself as she watched the Queen collapse so hard and fast. Elijah had to move with the reflexes of the wind, changing his grasp on her in order to hold on to her, keeping her from dropping like a stone. The hands that were grasping at Elijah's shirt went lax, her gold eyes closing halfway as they rolled back into her head.

"Siena!" Elijah bent to lift her into his arms, but she was dead weight now, her body suddenly locked into the rigidity of a seizure that made it impossible to do anything but follow her down to the ground.

The worst part of it was when his mind went completely blank of her presence. Elijah had never known such fear as he felt when she seemed to vacate his soul so suddenly. Not even when he had faced his own death a week ago had he known this kind of terror. The sudden silence after so much pain and panic tore at him, leaving him with open wounds in his spirit that outstripped the pain of those on his body by massive proportions.

Then he was forced to watch her body lock and release in wave after wave of rigid muscular contortions, her skin fading from gold to gray to a splotchy red, her clenching teeth tearing at her own tongue so her mouth filled with blood that spilled over her face and into her slackening hair.

"No! Siena, don't do this!" Elijah shouted as he bent over her, holding her thrashing head between his hands in an effort to keep her from further injuring herself on the rocks and forest debris scattered underneath her.

"We have to get her out of the sun, Elijah. She's killing herself," Jacob commanded, a strong hand on the warrior's shoulder to try and draw his attention.

"Wait," Bella said, gently urging her husband aside as she reached for Siena. "I can absorb her power. If it works like it did on Legna when she was Summoned, her weakness to the sun will disappear as Legna's vulnerability to the pentagram did. It could keep her just as safe as Legna was. It will give you the time you need to get to safety without allowing the poisoning to advance any further from continued exposure."

"Bella, don't!" Jacob warned, trying to grab her to stop her. But his mate pushed his hand aside, turning glaring violet eyes up to him. "Damn it, Bella, you have no clue what you will do to her or yourself if you do this! Stop fighting me every time I try to protect you!"

"Would you rather I let her die?" she demanded. "Should I let someone I love as a brother, who has treated me like family since the day I arrived among you in spite of everyone else's condemnations, be deprived of his soul mate? Should I protect myself and allow an entire people to be deprived of their Queen?"

"Not at the cost of *my* soul mate, Bella!" He was breathing harder, edging toward a volatile alarm, a condition he was not prone to unless her safety was at stake. "You do not know what will occur if you do this. You could end up killing her," Jacob argued, his hands fisting at his sides as he forced himself not to reach for her again, "or yourself."

"The possibility of death is a risk all of us take the minute we wake up in the evening. My safety is in jeopardy every time I accompany you to destroy the Transformed or track those who need enforcing. You don't make a stink about it then, so stop doing it now." Bella turned her attention back to the Lycanthrope female, feeling Elijah's frantic gaze on her. "Everyone step back. I don't know how to narrow my abilities yet. I don't need to draw all of you in."

"All the more reason you should not do this," Jacob snapped, losing all sense of awareness for anything but the danger to her safety that was clawing at him relentlessly.

"Fine, then stay where you are. I'm doing this with or without your cooperation, Jacob," she said hotly, the determination in her voice and the set of her stubborn jaw putting an end to her side of the argument. "Without is only taking longer."

Elijah suddenly decided for all of them. He stood up and physically reached to haul Jacob back away from both women. The Enforcer struck the warrior's hand aside, his dark eyes flaring with outrage that the Captain would try to strong-arm him from protecting his mate.

"Move back, or I will move you, Jacob," the warrior hissed, understanding that Bella's suggestion was the quickest, most plausible action to take to stop Siena's agony. Had he simply tried to carry her to shelter, she would probably have died from the continuous exposure to the sunlight before he reached his goal. Even he was feeling the drag of lethargy that affected his kind in the sun, in spite of his own strength at resisting that very condition.

Jacob could have held his ground, but it would have clearly invited an altercation. Outvoted, he finally backed away and gave Bella the room she had requested. The only other solution would have been for each man to assert his need to

protect his mate above the other's through violence. In spite
of the volatile emotions involved, it was not worth the price
they would pay should it come to that.

Feeling her husband watching her with mental as well as
visible anxiety, the Druid took a deep breath and closed her
eyes. She reached out to touch Siena's bare skin with tentative fingers, more to focus herself than for any other reason,
and sought within herself to unlock the power that had lain
tamped down deep in her body for so long now. Bella had
not released this power from her repressive control since she
had been attacked six months ago by Ruth and her brethren.

So when it flared to life, it was with a visible eddy that
pushed at the everything like an artificial wind, making the
trees bend with loud creaks of stressed branches, the leaves
and grasses blowing and scattering in a circular tide outward
from the Druid. Jacob felt his heart leap into his throat. He
had never seen this exude from her before. Usually hers was
an invisible, imperceptible ability that insidiously bled
Nightwalkers of their innate gifts. It terrified him to see
everything around her blow back with sudden violence.

A minute later, the surge hit both males, even at their distance of several yards back. It propelled them both off their
feet, slamming them to the ground in startled unison as all
the capability of their elemental bodies was sucked out of
them in a heartbeat.

At the same time, Bella robbed Siena of all her innate nature, from shape-shifting to the sensitivity to the sun that
came with it. Unfortunately, Jacob also remembered a moment later that Bella not only dampened the innate abilities
of Nightwalkers, she took on all of their characteristics.

Bella fell back onto her backside as all the power she had
just invited into herself hit her hard. Suddenly the wind
picked up and began to whip at them all. Then the grass
began to grow at a frantic rate, becoming a tangled mass of
blades in a heartbeat. Too much, too enormously powerful,
the abilities she had stolen from them were out of her con-

trol. And as Siena finally fell into a relaxed loss of consciousness, Bella's hair began to spread, forming into black, silky fur all over Bella's body.

"Damn it!" Jacob bit out, staggering to his feet under the press of remarkable weakness, the power of which he had never felt before. He lurched over to his wife just as her form began to mutate painfully, her half-human body never intended to alter in such ways. One minute she was looking at him in wide-eyed shock, the next she was a violet-eyed jaguar, struggling to wriggle out of the confines of her jeans, T-shirt, and underclothes.

"Bella! Calm down!" Jacob said as he reached for her mind on both the level of an Imprinted mate and a creature of the Earth who could charm any animal he set his mind to. He worked quickly to free the huge cat of the clothing it was caught in, watching with actual awe as those eyes so eerily familiar to him seemed not to know him all of a sudden.

He had known that she could absorb and utilize Demon powers, but he would never have thought the same would apply to Lycanthrope powers. He had thought, until a moment ago, that the ability to shapechange had been as natural as a heartbeat for Siena, something Bella could not borrow or steal or use for herself in any way.

But he was clearly wrong. And even though this was Gideon's area of expertise, even the medic had never seen anything like Bella's abilities before she had arrived a year ago. This was new to all of them, and none of them should underestimate these hybrid powers. So it was with caution that he tried to soothe her. But he realized quickly that his power to charm had been stolen along with everything else, and all he was left with was the connection of soul mate to soul mate.

Elijah moved to Siena's now totally lax body, hastily scooping her off the ground and out of reach of the unpredictable danger the situation might provide. Bella had achieved her goal, however, and Elijah knew it on some inner level of his spirit. Siena was horribly ill, but the little Druid's brave act had effectively halted her vulnerability to any further damage.

The Warrior Captain met Jacob's eyes briefly, apologetically, and then he turned and hurried back toward Gideon's home with his limp burden, leaving Jacob to handle his altered mate. Without his powers, there was nothing Elijah could do in any event. It was best to leave them alone. Powers or no, Jacob knew more about dealing with animals than anyone else among them.

Noah was perhaps the only one who could have found Legna in her present state, and the only reason he did was because of her residual body heat. But she was already mostly cold to the touch as he scooped her off the floor. He knew immediately that this was Gideon's doing. He could sense the tracks of the Ancient's residual energy in her. And he also understood he had done it in order to try and protect her, to keep her from sticking her neck out into the situation that had clearly been desperate and dangerous to the degree that it had killed even the Ancient as a result.

Noah also knew his sister was dying. He felt what remained of her life force fading as he rushed out of the room and down the stairs to find medics. Unfortunately, there was only one at present, and he had his hands full working on Gideon.

Noah commanded a Mind Demon to fetch more help, then laid his sister on the ground outside of the charred house. He tried to focus, pushing aside the fear clawing at his soul. He covered her heart and her solar plexus with his hands, seeking her fading source of life and energy. He began to feed the depleted supply, slowly, careful of the also-fading spark of life within her child. Perhaps it was because he was of her own blood, or merely by force of their stubborn wills, but she began to warm, to flush with energy, if not true signs of life. His momentary relief was profound. At least he could maintain the stasis. Though he could not reverse the effect, it was enough until he could find others skilled enough to do so.

Elijah shouted for help, earning the attention of several warriors who rushed to his side, eager to be of any assistance.

"I need a medic!"

Elijah pushed into the house and for the first time he saw the destruction that had been wreaked upon it and its inhabitants. He had given chase to the assailants who had fled the scene, never once considering that Gideon couldn't handle his end by himself. Seeing a medic leaning over the Ancient took the Captain's breath away.

The younger medic looked up at his superior, then stood up and rubbed his hands nervously as he approached the Wind Demon.

"Sir, there is nothing we can do for her," he informed cautiously. "Not even Gideon knows how to heal a Lycanthrope."

"Don't tell me that," he commanded with a bark, gently laying his mate down in a dark corner before turning to confront the other man harshly. "You have basic skills, something that can cross species, and you will do what you can."

"Elijah . . ."

His name, spoken hoarsely through a rasping, gurgling sound, brought him around with a sharp turn. He dropped to his knees, scooping up her hand automatically as her throat worked to help her speak.

"What can I do, Siena?" he asked, his golden brows rippled with worry and distress.

"Do not let me die."

"No. You won't. We will help you." His tone was angry and frantic, outraged at the very idea of the suggestion.

"Do not . . ."

"Shh . . ." Elijah soothed.

". . . let me die . . . until I have killed that Demon bitch."

"You and I both," he promised fiercely as Siena slipped away from consciousness once more. "You and I both, kitten love."

Once Elijah and Siena left the immediate area, Bella was deprived of her continuous source of their power, her ability to absorb them no doubt having been left on as she was ruled by little more than animal instinct. It was practice and concentration that allowed her to shut it off, and as a wild cat, she was not likely to have that focus.

So it was over several gradual minutes that her husband felt her senses returning to her, and several more before her body began to realter itself into its natural formation. Silky black hair pulled away from skin as the power she had absorbed from Siena bled away. The act had cost Bella, Jacob could feel that as she reverted to her natural form and dropped into the thickly grown cushion of grass, panting for breath. But it had allowed Elijah the time needed to get Siena out of the sun, and Jacob knew that was all that would immediately matter to Bella.

So when she opened her eyes and saw him leaning over her with clear concern and barely repressed anger, she knew she had succeeded, in spite of not remembering any of it.

"It worked," she sighed.

"Yeah, you could say that, if you really stretch it," Jacob said, his tone clipped because he was unable to help himself. His heart was still pounding violently from his fright of seeing her so brutally altered and affected.

Jacob reached to pull her clothes closer, drawing her up into a sitting position so he could slip her T-shirt back over her body. Her head rested on his shoulder as he did so.

"You have a daughter, Bella," he said, his voice hoarse with pent-up emotion. "You cannot do these reckless things, risking yourself like that without taking her into consideration. She needs you, even more than I do, and you know how much that is all on its own." He exhaled, his breath shuddering as he did so, his dark eyes sliding closed with tight pain. "I ought to wring your neck."

"And would you have wanted Siena to do less if it could save my life?"

The question stung, sobering his anger with its brutal truth. His frantic motions to clothe her stopped, and with heat burning behind his eyes, he turned his face into the black silk of her thick hair, inhaling her fragrance deeply, gratefully, as he covered the back of her head with a warm, possessive hand.

He did not answer verbally, but the language of his gestures and thoughts were all the answer she needed. She wrapped her arms around his waist, hugging him tightly.

"Now," she whispered, "we have some tracking to do, my beloved. We can't let these people continue to hurt us."

"We will. Soon. Right now, we need to get back to the house so I can help Noah and Elijah, and so you can recoup some strength."

She didn't argue. She knew they could pick up the trail later on, and she also knew he was right about how tired she had made herself. The downside about such a rush of power was the letdown that followed immediately after.

But as she had noted a few days ago, she felt as if a part of the Lycanthrope Queen was now stamped onto her mind. She pushed the understanding aside, however, not wishing to upset Jacob any more than she already had.

Upstairs in the castle the Demon King called home, Noah was leaning against the window frame of Legna's bedroom, the one she had occupied for the three hundred years spanning from her childhood to the day she had married Gideon six months past. The King was staring blankly out at the gardens stretching on and on just below him, his memories of those years of her graceful influence tumbling through him like an undertow, dragging at his heart with painful repetition.

His sister was surrounded by medics, but he could tell from their whispering voices that they were still as befuddled over her condition as they had been for an hour now. If not for his ability to maintain her stasis, Legna would have been dead by now. What in hell had possessed Gideon to choose such a dangerous masking method? Surely there were other ways—ways that would not have left her in such danger!

Noah closed his eyes and exhaled.

He knew that was unfair. The moment Gideon became unconscious or died, any other glamour to mask her would have died with him and would have left her just as vulnerable. In fact, she would very likely be directly dead if not for the fact that he had forced their enemies into resorting to the randomness of a fire, hoping that it would eventually get to her wherever she was secreted so effectively from them.

Noah pushed away from the window and moved one of the medics aside with an almost ungentle push of one hand on the man's shoulder. He glanced up briefly at the midwife across from him who was monitoring Legna's baby closely, and she instantly backed away. All it took was that frighteningly authoritative look on their usually casual King to make them respond quickly. They all knew that there was no one more precious to Noah than his youngest sister.

Noah leaned over Legna, wrapping one elegant hand around her pulseless neck as he pressed his lips to her forehead and began to whisper to her.

"I forgave you for leaving me six months ago," he murmured, reaching with his mind and his heart for her, using all the focus and strength of his long lifetime and the mental fa-

miliarity with her that he had achieved under her patient tute-
lage over the centuries of her own. "I will not allow you to do
so again. Not this way. Come, little sister, and wake for me.
You have his power inside you. You have his child inside
you. I cannot believe that means nothing to your safety."

Noah's eyes slid closed and he lowered his forehead to
rest beside her head on the pillow, speaking softly into her
ear.

"When Mama died, I swore you would live to be an Ancient, little girl, and I will not tolerate breaking that promise.
Come back to me. I . . ."

He had to stop as emotion overwhelmed his voice. He
tried to breathe, but no matter how deeply he drew, it was not
enough. He was starving for oxygen in that moment, and
like any flame, felt as if it would extinguish him.

"I need you," he said at last, his voice hoarse and breaking. "If Gideon survives, he will need you. The babe . . . all
of us. You are now the eldest female Mind Demon among us.
Who but you will teach the young?" He again tried to inhale
a deep, painful breath. "Who else," he said, softer than ever,
"will continue to teach me what it is I am missing by not
knowing the love you share with Gideon? The day I live
without you to teach me as you always have is the day I will
forget how to truly live."

Do not leave us, he begged from all the resources of his
mind, pouring his emotion into her. *Gideon will die without
you. He will never be able to bear knowing that while trying
to save you both, he became the instrument of your death.
Do not leave him with that legacy.*

Noah had no fact to base his attempts to reach her on, so
had no proof they would be successful in aiding Legna in
any way. But he continued on, tirelessly, feeding her energy
and emotion and every compelling reason he could think of
to draw her back.

* * *

Syreena and Anya stood at firm attention on both sides of the door to the room Siena was being tended in. Elijah stood back far from the bed, hidden in the dark shadows the pulled shades provided while keeping out the sun. The female attachés were flicking eerily aware eyes from Queen to Consort to the two members of The Pride, their most accomplished healers, trying to treat the Queen for her sun poisoning.

"She is beginning to blister," one informed them softly.

It was not a good sign. It meant she had received the equivalent of a lethal dose of radiation. The Monks of The Pride would be hard-pressed to help her recover without long-term effects of the damage.

"You will do your utmost," Syreena reminded them, her voice that of a monarch for the first time in her life.

The command was stolen right out of Elijah's mouth, so he speculatively narrowed pale eyes on Siena's sister. His voice would no doubt have little influence in this room. He had not earned any authority or loyalty from them as yet. He'd not even had the chance to do so. It made him relax a little to see Syreena advocating so powerfully where he could not. That was when he understood these women loved Siena as deeply as he loved Noah, and for all the same reasons.

"What a waste . . . over a Demon."

Anya went stock still, her eyes widening when the words passed the second Monk's lips. Remarkably, it was not Elijah who reacted to the offensive remark. Instead, it was that moment that Anya truly learned how fast the Princess was.

And how volatile she could be.

Before anyone could twitch, Syreena had leapt for the Monk, doing the unthinkable by grabbing his entire weight and body off the bed with a single hand around his throat. He squawked in shock as she slammed him brutally into the nearest stone wall. The resounding smack of his head making Anya wince and gasp with shock.

Syreena's harlequin eyes bored into those of the dazed man who had once been one of her mentors.

"Speak thusly ever again in your lifetime and you will find yourself taking an involuntary vow of silence for the rest of your existence." She tightened her grip on his throat to make certain she had his unwavering attention. "I swear it, Monk. I will have your tongue should you ever do so again. Siena has sacrificed everything for peace, and I will never tolerate anyone belittling her efforts in such a disrespectful manner. Am I being understood?"

"Child, you will release your brother," the second Monk commanded her, pulling that tone of authority that parents used with disobedient young.

All Anya could do was watch with queer fascination. She would never in her life have even considered laying hands on a member of The Pride. In fact, by law, it was pretty much a capital offense. She had not thought Syreena capable of such a thing until she saw it happen right before her eyes.

The Pride was so old, and so powerful, that they were considered even by other races to be the ultimate scholars and the most learned fighters. They knew techniques for fighting that were ancient and deadly, handed down amongst them as well-guarded secrets for generation upon generation. To challenge one was akin to suicide, or so she had always been told.

And apparently Syreena had paid close attention to her lessons in the more deadly categories.

Until then, Anya would have labeled the Princess a pacifist, more interested in her studies, her meditations, and her position as Counselor than in fighting or joining in the training programs the Elite held in a rigorous manner on a daily basis. Now it was quite clear it was because she did not need the practice. And clearer still, by the look in the eyes of the Monk trapped beneath her grasp, was the fact that even this learned man of The Pride was not willing to fight her, not even to protect himself.

That gave Anya a chill down her spine.

Everyone fears the lion, but what does one feel toward something that frightens even the mighty cat that tops the food chain?

Anya's glance flicked once more to the glimmer of light green eyes watching the actions of the Princess with a remarkable, dispassionate calm. Anya's respect for the warrior hiked up a few notches as he let Syreena deal with their own without interfering. She had assumed he would be pushier, more volatile, and begging for altercation opportunities. It was frighteningly enlightening to realize you were in a room with two creatures of power you clearly knew too little about.

"He is no more my brother than you are, Konini."

Syreena turned to look at the other Monk with frigid eyes, and Anya was once more shocked by what she saw in the expression of the Princess. It was the unmistakable temper that the royal family had been tragically famous for during all these generations. Siena controlled hers remarkably well. Apparently Syreena did as well.

Until now, at least.

"Heal her, or answer to me," the Princess hissed.

"I do not perform to threats," the Monk said serenely, clearly not understanding that his pious ways were only getting him deeper into trouble. "You will cease this foolish violence, sister."

Before Anya could blink, one Monk was released to crumple to the floor and the other was between Syreena's fingers in a peculiar grip the Elite General had never seen used before. Syreena used the leverage of the hold to force Konini's face close to his patient's blistering countenance.

"What you see before you, Monk, is a true sister. My only sister. My only brother. At my heart, *my mother*. You had best save her, because if I become Queen, you will know not only my wrath, but I suspect the wrath of her husband's people as well." Syreena glanced up even as the Monk did, his eyes widening with fear as he looked at the only feature of the still Demon male he could see.

Those pale eyes glowing in the darkness.

"Remember, Monk, that even without his fury there are ways I can destroy your precious Pride." She leaned closer to whisper more harshly to him. "I beg you to recall just how good and thorough a student I really was, Konini. And I know you know what I mean, *brother.*"

She let go of him after that cryptic remark, and he fell onto the bed awkwardly, gasping for breath until his purple face began to change back to normal. To Anya's further amazement, he argued no further, threatened no punishment. Konini dragged his compatriot healer to his feet, slapping away his hands when they went to touch the cut the wall had left on the back of his head. He glanced worriedly from harlequin eyes to jade with clear trepidation and disquiet.

Anya watched Syreena march back into her guarding position with two steps and an about-face that would have put most of the General's fighting corps to shame.

"I noticed you left the room for a few minutes just now, half-breed," she remarked coolly, not even looking at the other woman.

"I . . ." Anya cleared her throat. "I was thirsty," she agreed, knowing full well she'd rather dehydrate than ever leave the Queen unprotected. Just as much as Syreena knew it. "Anything . . . uh . . . unusual happen while I was . . . um . . ."

"Out of the room?" Syreena prompted. "Not a thing."

"Good." Anya smiled an amused smile. "Good."

In the darkness, Anya could swear she heard the stoic warrior her people had feared for centuries chuckling under his breath.

*   *   *

The medics left Gideon's room, letting nature do what it could do best. They had done all they could, and the rest was up to Destiny and the Ancient's own resiliency.

Bringing his life signs back had been easy enough. So long as it was soon enough, an Elder Body Demon could time his own vital signs to take over those of the victim's, rather like a person-to-person bypass mechanism. The Elder took over the damaged autonomic systems, bringing the victim instantly back to life. However, healing the body fast enough and far enough to take over on its own had been the trick. Gideon had suffered enormous damage to vital organs and a blood loss that few could recover from.

The medics believed it was only Gideon's age that had saved him. Everything else aside, his was the fastest-healing immune system in the world. The only thing he was not capable of doing was replenishing his own blood supply rapidly enough. Nor was Gideon able to do the deep, complex healings that, while in reach of some of the Elders, lacked his artistic finesse for perfection. It had been difficult to sort out venom and rabies, bacteria and bone marrow, the clots and the residual scarring that had polluted his systems.

He should have died. Might still die. It was only his natural healing that could save him from whatever they had missed or had deemed out of their range of skill.

Hours passed and darkness swept over the castle that doubled as a hospital. There were guards outside all of the doors, a mixture of Demon warriors and Lycanthrope Elite that was eerily unprecedented. More so, the Lycanthropes brooked no argument to their demands to guard the door of the Warrior Captain and his bride themselves.

Baffled by Noah's command to comply, the warriors did so despite the loyalty that tempted them to disobey even the King's command. The castle was swarming with other forces, most of them out of doors, protecting the perimeter. Noah had left his sister long enough to spell Corrine, who had been given the care of her sibling's baby. Sitting by the comfort of his fire, holding the snug bundle of warmth over his heart, Noah could allow himself to release his pain. He was not an emotionally demonstrative man in public, but in his solitude of the moment, with only the nameless child to witness it, he allowed himself to be so in utter silence.

The weight of the little babe upon it was the only thing keeping his heart from splitting apart.

CHAPTER 15

In the darkness of the recently fallen night, a figure of perfect stealth moved with imperceptible speed toward the guarded perimeter of the Demon King's home. He would pass the guards completely undetected, his skills so far beyond anything they could perceive that he would be able to do so with an almost laughable ease.

He could sense the occupants around and within the stronghold with just a sweep of his eyes, the body heat they all exuded flaring infrared within his remarkable sight. He knew the cooler, more pinkish blobs of heat indicated Demons, whose body temperatures ran colder than the others by a few degrees. There was a human signature in a distant room, and then about a dozen beings who bore the bright red heat of the Lycanthropes. It was the one he determined to be in a horizontal position that attracted his attention most. He stepped past the perimeter of guards with silent speed, springing up with silent ease from the ground to the second-floor balcony that led into the room.

The Vampire Prince hesitated before using the door, sensing that someone was in the room besides the Lycanthrope Queen. Whoever she was, and he could sense that she was in-

deed a female, she was alert to her duty. If her heart was anything to judge by, she had noted his intrusion. Her fierce
heartbeat was unbelievably compelling, so strong and so fast
that it was circulating her blood almost too fast for her to
oxygenate her cells.

"Come."

It was a whisper, spoken on such a soft, feminine breath
that at first Damien thought he had mistaken the challenge.
Intrigued, the Prince actually smiled in anticipation as he
drifted in through the sliding glass door that stood already
open, hovering a moment before resting softly on the floor-
ing.

The Vampire's eyesight was excellent in the darkness
even when he didn't use his infrared capabilities. He made
out the silhouette of a distinctly feminine figure. She was
standing at a perfect placement near a window, no doubt on
purpose, letting the moonlight backlight her so even with his
keen vision he would only see shadows.

But it was not just the smooth curve of a cocked hip and
strong bracing of well-shaped female legs that stood in relief
against the incoming light. One arm hung straight down the
length of her body, pushed out by that jutting hip, the gun in
her hand winking its nickel-plated gleam as if she held a star
instead.

"Bullets?" he queried, his deep voice rich and compelling
even in his obvious humor. "An anomaly in a Demon household."

"I am not a Demon," she pointed out, her tone still soft,
still quite sultry in its mysteriousness.

"True. But if you shoot me you will only be wasting bullets. Surely you realize this?"

"I know," she assured him.

That was when her other hand parted from the rest of the
shadow that was her body, the swift, nimble twirl of a
wooden instrument rotating like a propeller between her fingertips for a breathtaking second.

Damien laughed, noting the object had once been the fourth leg of a now three-legged chair that sat behind her shadowy figure.

"You know that is a myth, do you not?" he asked, folding his arms over his chest.

"Of course," she confirmed again. "However, a stake through the heart has a way of causing traumatic bleeding that will weaken you considerably and quickly." Damien saw her teeth flash as she smiled. "So perhaps you best tell me why you are here, Vampire."

"Your Queen requires healing or she will die."

"I do not need you to tell me that, Blood Drinker."

She took a step closer, finally coming into the light.

Damien had never seen her like in all of his long life. She was a Lycanthrope, no doubt about it, but her coloring and her fragile figure clearly hid surprises and mysteries he could not even begin to guess at.

Then he realized who it was that confronted him.

He had first heard stories about her little more than a century past, and then nothing until recent reports of brief glimpses of an unusual Lycanthrope female had been delivered by his ambassadors who had made the odd visit to Siena's court over this most recent decade.

"You would prefer she die, Princess, and make you Queen in her stead?"

Damien heard her breath catch and saw the infrared flush of heat as her anger exploded through her chemistry.

"How dare you suggest such a thing," she hissed.

"I dare," he interrupted her quickly, "because I know nothing about you except that you are the daughter of an accomplished, albeit insane, warlord who manage to plunge these people who now shelter you and your Queen into three hundred years of war."

"Self-righteousness from the Vampire Prince who warred with the Demons himself for a historic century of his own?" she bit back sharply.

"Touché," he agreed. "But like you, I was young and foolish then. That was well over a half a millennium ago, though, not a mere fourteen years."

"I am neither young nor foolish, except perhaps in your estimation. What concern is it of yours whether the Lycanthrope Queen lives or dies?"

"That I cannot tell you. Suffice it to say, it will serve all of our interests if she does live. Including yours, if your concern is legitimate."

"And I suppose you are going to offer this magical healing, Vampire? By taking her blood, no doubt, and letting the magical aftereffects of your bite cure her? I believe she would rather die than allow anyone, friend or foe, such a liberty."

"No. That is not my intention, Princess. I am surprised you do not know that it is forbidden for my kind to attempt to feed on other Nightwalkers. A category which your species unfortunately belongs to, or I would indeed offer those services. When I heard what had occurred—"

"I should like to know how you heard such speedy gossip," Syreena interrupted coldly.

"The Nightwalker world is not so thin in Europe as it is everywhere else. Like a small village, news of such things travels quickly."

"How remarkable," she said softly, clearly unimpressed.

Damien smiled in spite of himself, his even teeth flashing in the moonlight, no sign of retracted fangs to be seen in the charming grin.

"If I may continue?"

She gave him a dark smile of her own, her eerie harlequin eyes flickering in the moonlight.

"I was going to suggest another alternative you are probably unaware of." Damien turned slightly to look at the Queen in the darkness, the heat from her blistered skin glowing a violent red in his vision. He turned back to Syreena. "There is no cure for this degree of sun sickness. She will die unless you stray from your conventional methods of healing," he assured her.

"She will not die."

The suddenness of the low voice made both the Vampire and the Lycanthrope turn sharply. Elijah's eyes glowed pale green in the single beam of moonlight that struck his face as he coalesced into solid form. Syreena moved up suddenly, bringing herself around the Prince—directly to his side, in fact, so he was not blocking her line of sight.

The warrior was still as cool as ever, that drilling gaze pinioning the couple across from him with shrewd assessment. The circle of gold and moonstones around his arm gleamed tellingly in the moonlight, giving Damien a bit of information his gossiping sources had failed to acquire. Apparently Elijah had sensed the tension between himself and the Princess and had come to protect . . . to protect his bride, of all unexpected things.

"My . . ." Syreena cleared her throat. "My lord, Anya and I will guard the Queen with our lives, I assure you—"

She stopped when Elijah suddenly moved forward, the fire of his eyes flicking over the Vampire Prince sharply.

"Damien, I welcome your concern," he said, "but like Syreena, I do not see how you can help us."

"Elijah, your mistrust is misdirected. We have fought together at the Battle of Beltane, and for no reason other than my desire to assist your people. I promise you, assistance is all I am here to give tonight as well." He took a breath, even though breathing was unnecessary for him. "Do not push me away until you have heard me out, warrior, or you will be consigning your mate to death. A terrible death. It could take weeks of extraordinary pain before she finally—"

"She will not die!" Elijah barked out. "Damn it!" His tone turned to pure venom. "I would rather be dead myself than see Siena go through this because she panicked over *my* safety! I do not need you to stand there and give me a blow by blow of how she is going to suffer for that!"

The door to the room opened suddenly, admitting Anya, who had heard Elijah's raised voice. She surveyed the room with wide eyes for a moment, shook her red head helplessly, and then retreated back behind the closed door muttering softly under her breath. "And now Vampires . . ."

Syreena suddenly lifted her head, her gray eye sparkling in the half-light as she narrowed her gaze on the Vampire, trying to connect ghosting thoughts as the two men turned back to each other.

"I cannot heal her myself, but there are those who can," Damien said to Elijah softly.

"Foreigners."

Both men looked at the Princess piercingly, one with surprise, the other with confusion.

"Yes," Damien supported her thoughtfully. "I was about to suggest—"

"Goddess, what is her name?" Syreena muttered, interrupting the Vampire as she bit her lip and she searched her memory. "A Mistral," she clarified to them, though Elijah seemed to be the only one not following her. "Siena knows a Mistral. A few days ago she mentioned a Mistral who she thought could somehow help her on another matter."

Syreena skipped over the details of that, not wanting to reveal to Elijah how desperately Siena had tried to rid herself of his influence over her before she had finally come to peace with her fate. No sense opening old wounds or exposing secrets that were Siena's to discuss with the Demon Consort.

Damien lifted one black brow, clearly impressed with Syreena's reasoning, also curious about how the very breed of Nightwalkers he had been about to suggest had suddenly popped out of the Princess's mouth.

"Unlike most healers in the Nightwalker species, Mistrals can heal universally," Damien said thoughtfully, his steady, dark eyes skimming the small female before him with blatant interest. She did not blush or look away under his bold appraisal, impressing him even more as she stood her ground and glared right back at him.

"But at a price," Elijah said knowingly, interspecies abilities being his area of expertise. His duty, in fact. "The Mistral Siren sings to heal, to soothe, and to facilitate meditative states. The price is total vulnerability. If the Siren wishes to walk up to her subject and stab her through the heart in the middle of a singing, she can do so and her victim wouldn't be able to lift a finger to defend herself. Also, anyone in earshot will be drawn into the song, so it is not as though someone can stand guard. Siena would never stand for that. Neither would I."

"Not from a stranger, perhaps, but I believe she knows this particular Mistral very well," Syreena explained.

"It does not sound like her," Elijah said, turning to look down at his bride's blistered face, his brow furrowing in sympathetic pain to see her beautiful skin marred so agonizingly.

"It was a specific Mistral. She asked for her by name. If only I could remember her name . . ."

"Windsong," Damien said suddenly, his dark eyes lighting with understanding. "Was her name Windsong?"

"Yes!" Syreena exclaimed. "From a village in France called—"

"Brise Lumineuse," Damien supplied.

"How do you know this?" Syreena demanded, looking fairly put out that the Vampire had bailed out her lacking memory.

"How do you think you survived the illness that made you what you are, Syreena?"

Syreena gasped when Siena's hoarse voice ground roughly out of her damaged throat. Heedless of the men watching her, she raised the back of her hand to her mouth and hurried to fall to her knees beside her sister's bed. She finally dropped her weaponry, reaching to take the Queen's hand. Then she seemed to think better of it when she laid eyes on the damaged skin of the distorted fingers. Instead, it was her relieved tears that touched the skin.

"Siena," she whispered, "do not talk. You must conserve your strength," she said gently.

Siena gave a brief nod and then turned to look at her husband. Just seeing his face upset her like nothing else could. She felt relief, joy, and a dozen other overwhelming emotions that bludgeoned Elijah's thoughts with crystal clarity of the heart. He reached for her, weaving his fingers into her crisp hair, the dull tendrils wrapping around his wrist immediately, grasping him weakly in the only way she could hold him.

"I'm so sorry," she said, her voice high pitched and rasping all the more.

"Shh," he soothed her, reaching to rub her faded hair against his lips. "Don't strain yourself. Listen to Syreena, kitten."

She shook her head.

Elijah . . .

Her voice was weak, but more like her own, filtering softly through Elijah's thoughts as it grew in strength.

Relax, kitten. Do as your sister says.

No. Tell her to get Windsong. Then send them both away. I need to speak with you.

"She says to get Windsong for her. Syreena, can you do this?"

"Yes. France is but a few thermals away, love," Syreena said eagerly to her sister. "Rest and I will return as soon as possible."

All eyes turned to follow the Lycanthrope that leapt with dangerous heedlessness out of the window, transforming from human to falcon halfway over the sill.

"Amazing," Damien marveled, turning to look at the Queen. "So the stories are true. It was Windsong who saved the life of your sister. I had always thought it was a myth until I started to hear reports that you were recently addressing an unusual Lycanthrope female as your sister. Now that I have seen her . . ." Damien shook his head, looking back to the window with bemusement. "She is remarkable."

"Damien, Noah is in the Great Hall. He would wish to see you."

"I had intended on it, after making my suggestions to you." The Vampire looked from one to the other with intense, dark eyes, his aristocratic features in an expression of puzzlement for a moment. "I had never thought to see such an Imprinting. This is a new era indeed. May it serve you both well. Be well, both of you."

The Vampire then used the boring convention of the door and left the couple alone. Elijah immediately turned back to his wife. Seeing and feeling her pain, his heart literally began to hurt, and it had nothing to do with his wounds.

You must let me tell you how sorry I am, she rasped into his mind quickly.

There will be time for that. Later, he insisted.

I have wasted too much time already, Elijah.

She reached for him, wincing when her injured skin pulled, splitting in tender places that had lost their elasticity as the poisonous boils had spread. Elijah reached to stop her, his palm against hers. The contact felt so relieving, so precious and good, that he could not force himself to move away again. Clearly, she felt the same, her fingers lacing with his, heedless of how it hurt her.

I have hurt you so selfishly, she sobbed, tears falling from her eyes as her emotion trebled through him.

No, he insisted, his mental voice equally choked with feeling to see her hurting in any way. *Do not worry about me, kitten. You have caused me no pain.*

Do not lie to the one who knows your heart, however stubbornly she has refused to acknowledge it.

She drew hard for breath, and he slid even closer to her, leaning over her until they were looking deeply into each other's damp eyes.

"Don't do this," he begged roughly. "Do not tell me this

because you think you are going to die. I will not let you leave me. You have tried every way to escape me and I will not let you go now that you have finally acquiesced."

He drew in an unsteady breath, trying to empower a shattering voice. He brought his hair-tangled hand to her face, cradling it as his thumb brushed her dry lips. "You will survive this day and hunt the ones responsible for this with me, by my side where you belong, now and every moment in the future. You will survive this injury and will be in my arms once again, feeling my touch and my kiss on your precious skin, the softness of which will never cease to drive me mad." Siena's tears dropped into her hair, just as Elijah's touched her parched lips. "You will survive this to tell me you love me the way that I have come to love you. In a strong voice, with light shining in your beautiful eyes and your body wrapped around me the way your soul is wrapped around my heart."

Unable to do anything else, Siena simply nodded. Once again he reached to catch her tears on his gentle fingertips.

"Don't cry, kitten. You know it kills me when you do."

Then stop making me cry these tears, Elijah. I never have done such a thing, until you joined my life.

"Then I am certainly to blame, love. Just as you are to blame for mine." He smiled against her fingers as he kissed them gently in their place woven between his. "You have reduced me to an emotional woman," he sighed.

Siena laughed, coughing harshly immediately afterward, driving the humor out of his eyes.

"Shh," he soothed insistently.

She nodded, searching his face for a long minute, as if committing it to memory. She extended her fingers, touching his mouth tenderly. Her eyes, her emotions, her thoughts were full and bursting with her feelings for him, and it made his heart pound to feel it. But as promised, she said nothing, and would say nothing, until the moment she could meet his criteria. For the moment, she exhaled, closed her eyes, and drifted into sleep, her last thoughts urgently praying to the Goddess for her sister's swift return.

The sooner she could hold him again, the better.

Gideon rose about twenty minutes after Damien had left Noah, who had returned to his sister's bedside in order to maintain her status. The medic was as yet barely well enough to walk, but like Elijah, could not be kept from the mate who needed him as soon as possible.

Noah looked up with surprise when Gideon entered the room. The medic was powerful, but Noah had never suspected he could come back from the brink of death so quickly.

"It is no miracle," Gideon said roughly as he staggered over to his wife's side, sitting down beside her still body on the mattress. He swiftly took her face between his hands as he tried to look into her physiology. "Merely my usual ability to heal."

Gideon raised a hand to silence the King's further questions or remarks, his eyes closing as he tried to concentrate on undoing his own complex work. Noah watched carefully as Gideon broke into a sweat, feeling the Ancient's energy fading quickly while Legna remained as motionless as ever.

As unobtrusively as he could, Noah reached mentally for his brother-in-law, slowly trickling energy into him. The flow expanded exponentially over the next few minutes until the grayish tone disappeared from Gideon's complexion completely. Soon he was flush with his normal tanned skin tone, energy flaring through him in abundance.

Noah stopped pushing energy onto the Ancient when he began to get feedback in the connection he had formed between them. He exhaled as he drew back, tilting his head to stretch out the muscles that had bunched around the back of his neck. He then watched with amazement as wounds across

Gideon's hands, chest, and face began to heal with impressive speed even as Legna drew her first breath in hours.

Noah made a low sound of relief when he saw her skin pinking up. She stirred, yawned widely, as if all she had been doing was sleeping. Her silver eyes opened and looked up into those mirrored in her mate. She smiled at him and reached for his mouth with hers. She kissed him with tenderness and affection, just as she did every morning when she woke. It wasn't until he broke from her mouth and dragged her into his arms almost desperately that she realized something was wrong. He was terrified, or just being released from terror, his thoughts and his heart pounding in a turmoil of fear and relief.

Slowly she realized she was in her childhood bedroom and that her brother was drawing in harsh breaths of equal relief, pushing out of his chair and moving to look out the window in an attempt at hiding the emotion coursing through him. But he could not hide it from her keen empathy, no matter where or how far he distanced himself from her.

Between the two of them, Legna was overwhelmed.

"What happened?" she asked, her throat tight with their unshed feelings.

"All is well, *Nelissuna,*" Gideon hushed her gently, burying his face in her silken hair. "You are well, the baby is well, and we are all safe now."

Noah clearly could not bear to listen a moment longer. Without a word, he turned and left the room. Magdelegna felt his pain twist in her chest like a knife, and because she felt it, Gideon did.

She pulled away to inspect her husband more carefully, momentarily discarding her worry over her brother, seeing the splotchy patterns of newly healed skin all over Gideon's face, arms, and chest.

"Gideon! What happened!" she demanded with a gasp,

her eyes misting over as everything she was feeling finally came to a head. "Why is Noah so frightened? Why are you injured?"

Gideon took in one long breath, and then began to tell her.

CHAPTER 16

The peregrine falcon fluttered into the room, landing on the back of a chair as it shook out its wings and feathers. Shortly after, a single mourning dove, its coloring a beautiful combination of tans and soft grays, flew in after it. The dove settled on the seat of the chair fearlessly, as if the falcon above it was not normally a predator to it. It mimicked the rustling of feathers the falcon made.

Moments later, Syreena was standing behind the chair and the dove had blossomed into a fragile young woman with soft, brown and gray streaked hair and large blue eyes that looked as innocent as a child's and just as wide. She wore a soft dress of white cotton, unlike the Princess, who had to retrieve the dress from where it had fallen over the windowsill when she had changed earlier.

Siena was surrounded by people by this time. Blessed darkness had been upon them for many hours by then, and with it came new strength for the Demons and the Lycanthropes. Syreena had wasted no time in guiding the Mistral back, knowing that if they did not hurry, they might have been forced to delay their travel to avoid the daylight. The female Mistral had her own adverse reactions to the Night-

walker-unfriendly sun. Luckily, the mourning dove could almost equal the fiercely fast flight of the falcon, only slowing
down the return voyage by a few miles per hour or so.

The Mistral Siren rose to her bare feet, the soft elegance
of the movement riveting to all who watched. Her fairylike
beauty and fragility were quite breathtaking to male and female alike, her motions and the flawless flow of her graceful
body a symphony of delicacy. It was said the Mistrals could
cast spells with their beauty as well as their song, and looking at this frail creature made the other Nightwalkers believe
it.

Siena was apparently the one with the most exposure to
this reclusive race, so everyone watched with interest and
fascination as the female neared them, her soft hair floating
in a cloud around her shoulders as she moved.

"Windsong," Siena greeted her with a croak. She was
looking only slightly better as the darkness comforted her.

Elijah still sat beside her, his fingers remaining laced
within hers. Only now, he was healed almost to perfection
himself, his battle wounds that had been ignored all of this
time healed because Gideon had visited him directly after he
had tendered healing and a retelling of his tale to his mate.

The Siren paused a moment when she took note of all the
people around the Queen's sickbed. She blinked, pushing
back her fears of strangers with a surprising will that drew
Legna's sensitive attention. Legna had felt the keen anxiety,
but above it she felt whatever debt of gratitude and sincere
emotion it was that Windsong felt for Siena. The Mistral felt
clear and nearly debilitating pain when she first saw the
Queen's endangered health. To Legna's experienced senses, it
was as if the creature was an empath, but a physical one
rather than perhaps a mental one. She seemed to be feeling
those injuries much in the way Legna would feel sadness or
joy from another being.

Windsong moved closer to the grouping as she placed a silencing finger on her lips while looking meaningfully at the injured Queen. The Mistral looked from Siena to Syreena, then turned back with a silent brow cocked.

Elijah sat up slightly.

"She says, 'Yes, this is the Princess you saved one hundred years ago,'" he interpreted for his mate as she spoke into his mind.

The Mistral's expression turned to surprise and speculation as she looked from the Demon warrior to the Queen, her full mouth quirking into a serene smile.

"Yes," Elijah said again, becoming Siena's only voice. "We are mated." Then he clearly spoke for himself. "Can you help her? She is in tremendous pain."

Again, in utter silence, the Siren glanced at Gideon, Legna, Syreena, and Anya. Those huge, blue porcelain eyes then flicked back to Siena.

"She wants everyone but . . . but 'the star-child' to leave," Elijah explained, sounding as puzzled as everyone looked as soon as he said it. "Who is the star-child?"

The Siren smiled again, her angelic face lighting up as she reached toward Legna and gently touched her face with elegant fingers. Then she let that gentle touch fall to Legna's belly.

"She means the baby," Gideon murmured thoughtfully. "Star-child?"

"Siena doesn't understand it either," Elijah said with a shrug.

"How is Siena communicating with her?" Anya asked, as bemused by the exchange as all of them.

"Telepathy . . . left between them because of . . ." Elijah furrowed his brow slightly. "The Spirit-singing. What is a Spirit-singing?"

The Siren moved closer to Siena, nodding as if giving permission, as she sat down gently on the bed. Elijah didn't even feel her weight shift the mattress in the slightest as she did so. He turned his attention to Siena's thoughts filling his mind with explanation.

"The Spirit-singing is an exchange between a Mistral and another where . . . a part of the one's spirit is borrowed to help heal another's. In this case, Syreena was the recipient of that shared spirit when Windsong borrowed from Siena's spirit to heal her decades ago during a childhood illness. It left Siena and Windsong with a telepathic connection that switches on whenever their spirits come close to each other."

"How come I never heard of this?" Syreena asked in wonderment, looking from her sister to the enigmatic Siren.

"Because it is an intimate, secret exchange and Siena was not allowed to speak of it until given permission." Elijah then looked up questioningly at the Mistral. "She says I need to stay. I understand that, but why does Legna?"

There was silence between the relays of the telepathic trio and finally Elijah looked at Legna.

"She says she will need me for the Spirit-singing, to borrow from my spirit to heal Siena. As her mate, I am the best candidate."

"But—" Syreena began.

"She says that you are too complex to be a part of this, that your exposure to dual spirits, yours and Siena's, was responsible for the alteration in your genetic code. She had never Spirit-sung for Lycanthropes before and it was an unexpected side effect. I am . . ." He paused for words. "I am now sharing my spirit with Siena's already, as she shares mine, so there will be less chance of ill effects."

"So this is not a foolproof method. There can be damage?" Gideon asked. "That makes me question Legna's being present for this even more."

"The danger is only to myself and Siena," Elijah continued. "She says the star-child will protect Legna and that . . ." Elijah blinked and looked at Siena for a confused moment that made it clear he was unable to understand what she was trying to tell him for a moment. When he spoke he still sounded confused. "She says she has given your son permission to listen to the singing."

Elijah laughed with disbelief. That is, until he saw Gideon's expression. Legna reached behind herself to grasp her husband's hand, her eyes growing wide as she received his startled thoughts.

"She knows it is a boy," he said aloud. The medic suddenly realized there was more power and ability to this enigmatic species then he had come to know even during his long life. "I could not help but find out just by touching my wife once I realized she was with child, and, of course, as soon as I knew, Legna knew. We had decided we would not tell anyone else, that we would let it be a surprise. But I suppose that is no longer an issue." Gideon looked at the Siren with narrowed, perplexed mercury eyes. "How can you talk to an unborn child? I may not know much about your species, but the fetus is barely six months—"

"I did not talk to the babe. The babe talked to me."

It was the first time she had used her voice, and suddenly everyone there understood why. It was musical and sweet, full of every amusement, every sadness she had ever known in her life. It was a seduction and a comfort. It was bewitching in every way a thing of pure beauty could be. Everyone was enthralled by it, the spell of it holding them rapt and silent for a long minute. Gideon was the first to draw a cleansing breath.

"My son talked to you?" he asked roughly, his hand reaching to cover Legna's on her belly. There was no explaining the sensation of wonderment and elation that rushed over the couple.

"She said . . ." Elijah paused to clear his throat. "She says your son is a powerful being and soon will be able to speak to you as well, even from the womb. She says . . ." Elijah found himself smiling in spite of himself. "She says he has his father's power and his mother's temperament."

Legna laughed, unable to help herself as delight rushed

through her. She turned to Gideon and kissed him, excitement and enthusiasm rushing over her.

"I want to stay," she said.

Once the room was cleared of all except the patient, her mate, and the fascinated mother of the so-called star-child, Windsong touched Siena's hair gently, tsking with her tongue at the lank, brittle feel of the usually brilliant curls.

She smiled, touching the couple's still joined hands and nodding once. It was clear that she wanted them to remain thusly joined, and it was a good thing because Elijah had no intention of letting go.

His heart was racing in spite of Siena's attempts to reassure him. He did not like the idea of being helpless, as he would reportedly become, but he cared more about Siena becoming well than he did about his own safety at that point. The anxiety was only natural.

The first sound to blossom out of the Mistral was a hum, a haunting vibration from its very inception. It only took a minute after that for Siena, Elijah, and Legna to fall into a deep, healing sleep.

None of them would ever know what happened after that.

None but the unborn child, who wasn't about to give any secrets away.

Legna opened her eyes slowly, taking a breath, knowing instantly that she had never felt so rested, so at peace, as she did in that moment. All of this in spite of her years of accomplished meditation, which brought her to a similar state. She looked at the pale and beautiful countenance smiling down at her. Windsong reached for Legna's belly and without speaking sent emotions of warmth, gratitude, and absolute delight to the empathic female Demon.

Legna understood, though with bemusement. The Siren

was thanking her for the privilege of being allowed to sing before her baby.

"You are welcome," Legna said softly. "Are they well?" she asked, glancing at the sleeping couple in the bed who now lay tenderly curved around one another's bodies. Elijah's large form blocked Legna from seeing Siena.

The Mistral female nodded and smiled wider.

Then she tilted her head, that cloud of airy hair shifting position with a swirl.

"I have foretold the future to your child," that chiming voice said softly. "And because he is yours, I will allow you to know it and remember it when you become aware once again." She took Legna's dazed face between her slim, cool hands, knowing the empath was already floating in that world of subawareness her speaking voice had sent her to. "Your baby will lead your people into a new era, just as the one who came before him will. Together they will change the world as you know it. They will lead the other children who will come of this time of change into a millennium of remarkable destiny and bliss. In this lies my future as well, and I am grateful to you for creating part of what will make this so. Remember my prophecy as the ages pass," she instructed softly. "May it give you the comfort it has given me."

Then, without waiting for clarity to return to the Demon mother, the Mistral turned into the mourning dove and flew out the window, reeling away on the wind as if sheer joy lifted her wings to the heavens.

Legna was smiling when she became aware once again. Forgetting everything else, she leapt from her chair, knocking it over heedlessly as she raced to find her husband and tell him everything she could remember.

Elijah woke to the sparkling sensation of a warm, lush mouth rubbing against his.

He opened his eyes, and then opened them quite a bit

more when he saw the familiar golden gaze of his mate glowing with life and mischief in her gold-and-pink splotched face.

A face healed of all blisters, only new skin that would soon fade to normal, luxurious, beautiful gold once more in what promised to be no time at all.

"You look like hell," Siena remarked, her voice muffled against his mouth, but its usual rich tone was otherwise free of defect and injury.

He felt glorious.

Elijah reached for the covers and yanked them down, tumbling her off his body as he sat up and inspected her from head to toe, his hands tracing where his eyes went, affirming her healing state with tactile, as well as visual, proof.

"Are you trying to turn me on?" she asked, arching one shiny gold brow with a distinctly lecherous humor.

The last thing he reached for was her glimmering, springy, and oh-so-lively hair, sifting the tightly sprung curls through his fingers as a huge grin spread over his face.

Siena sat up, bumping his nose with hers.

"Is that a yes?" she asked, crossing her eyes as she tried to focus on him.

"You are . . . amazing," he breathed, his hands framing her face eagerly, the rough warmth of his palms becoming so familiar, so wonderfully necessary for her happiness, that she smiled wider.

"I think I look like a leopard," she remarked, pulling back to inspect her spotted arms and legs. Then that mischievous smile blossomed over her gorgeous lips. "Want to play connect the dots?"

Elijah threw back his leonine head and laughed from deep in his belly, dragging her into his embrace so tightly she gasped for air with a laugh even as he covered her mouth with a soul tattooing kiss that made her feel light-headed and joyful.

The sound of the door opening made them jump apart,

and Elijah instinctively jerked the covers back over his wife's bare body as she wiped a guilty hand over her damp mouth. He reached under the covers to pinch her for that, making her hello to her sister and her General come out half squeaky.

"Siena! You look great!" Syreena gushed happily, rushing to hug her sister from one side while Anya rushed at her from the other. Elijah had to lean back to avoid getting crushed by the tangle of females.

"Hey! You've had this fantasy before!"

Elijah laughed and turned to look at Bella, immediately opening his arms and beckoning her to them. She jumped into his embrace with a delighted bounce, hugging him as tightly as he hugged her.

"Thank you," he murmured softly into her ear. "Thank you for what you did. But as your teacher, I should tell you to never do that again," he said with fierce scolding.

"You have a deal," she said intensely as she practically strangled him with grateful affection.

"And I thought he would be boring once he got married," Jacob remarked dryly to Gideon and Legna, who crowded the doorway with him.

"Absolutely not," Gideon said suddenly, locking his arms around his wife when she went to rush into the room with intentions of joining the love fest.

"That, I believe, is my line," Jacob said with a chuckle as he moved to retrieve Bella before her chokehold on Elijah deprived him of oxygen any longer.

Women tumbled off the bed on all sides, everyone chattering and exchanging their side of the same story at once.

Until Noah cleared his throat from the doorway and said one soft statement: "Ladies, gentlemen; I believe we have a hunt awaiting us."

CHAPTER 17

"This is where you tracked them to?" Siena asked softly, squinting her eyes so that her keen vision focused on the forest below their perch on the mountainside. "This is not one hundred miles from my castle."

"And barely twenty from where I was attacked," Elijah added.

"I don't know about you guys, but this looks like a staging ground to me," Isabella remarked, holding up her binoculars again. "Jacob, move back, you're making this thing blurry."

She reached behind herself to push him away, and the Enforcer, who needed no such devices to see at a distance, backed up as ordered. He continued to peruse the same area she did from an added distance.

"Ah, better," Isabella said, clearly pleased to be able to use the human invention.

"I think Bella is right. Magic-users so close to Siena's seat of power? Risking being so deep in 'Thrope territory?" Elijah shook his head. "What else could it be?"

"A search party."

That remark made everyone look back at Gideon, who was leaning back nonchalantly against the rock face, his feet casually crossed at the ankles.

"Look back farther, beyond the encampment," he instructed. "See the ground? It has been churned up like a farmer's field, even deeper than that in some places. You know, I once spent well over a century of my life pursuing the ancient histories and cultures of medicine. I do not claim to be an expert on excavation, but those grids of twine in the field look very much like those in an archaeological dig. It appears to me that they are looking for something and they are going about it very carefully."

"Looking for what?" Siena queried. "Goddess, just look at the size of that dig. It's enormous. It would take years to properly excavate anything of that size." She turned to look at Gideon. "Why are they in Russian territory, in *winter* no less, digging in near-frozen ground?"

"Yes. In winter. When the usual traffic in this territory is almost nil because the only beings who could present any possible danger to them are all settling down for a nice, long nap," Elijah speculated.

"Yes, of course! A third of us are already in hibernation. More than half of the remaining population probably went to the caves right after the Samhain feasts!" Syreena spoke up in a hushed voice. "Let me fly over and take a look."

"No!"

The chorus of voices and hands that stopped her from rising made her crouch back down immediately.

"There are wards all over the place. You cannot see them, but I can," Jacob told her. "They make unnatural currents in the wildlife and vegetation."

"And before you say it, they are in the air as well," Elijah added before she could point out that she intended to fly, not walk.

"Oh." Syreena felt more than a little foolish for her unthinking haste, and her skin flushed. "How is it that you see this, yet we who are of the forest, we who live here constantly, cannot?"

"Do not sell yourself short," Gideon said quietly. "We do not see them easily either. You have to be looking for them, and the signs are almost impossible to sort through without centuries of experience. Even so, Elijah no doubt tripped a few of those wards the day of his original attack. That is, after all, what brought their attention to his approach. It was also quite likely the motivation behind their attempt to murder him."

"Don't remind me," Elijah said wryly. "Some warrior I am. I walked smack into the ones on the ground."

"You could not expect to see them. The rhythms of the wildlife and the forest are not your area of expertise," Noah countered him, dismissing the warrior's self-recriminations. "On the contrary, I think you just happen to be a little too good at your job. I don't think they meant to attract you. I also do not believe they set out to trap you in specific, Elijah. Just anyone who came too close to uncovering their clandestine proceedings."

"The purposeful trap came later," Siena mused aloud. "They probably cast wards around the battle area shortly after, setting the trap for anyone who came looking for Elijah's body. Only they didn't realize that he had been rescued before they had even stopped running away from the cougar's scream."

"So close," Anya said softly, the bitter edge to her voice attracting their attention better than a shout would have. "These are my woodlands," she explained, her sleek eyes glittering with hard anger. "My territory. My responsibility is to guard and protect them exactly as I guard and protect the Queen who rules them. I should have at least set a territorial perimeter of guards after the Battle of Beltane. This is an unforgivable lapse in security."

"And I should never have taken Legna to a known territory last night when Ruth was aware that our Imprinting would leave us ... shall we say ... sufficiently distracted from concerns of safety." Gideon looked the half-breed over calmly. "I believe we can come to the consensus that we all have made some mistakes over this past year. It is to be expected when there is so much for us to think about. These women, these stained creatures, are focused on only one thing. Eradicating us. All of us. That gives them the luxury of uncommon focus."

"For them, it is a holy war," Noah added. "They have the advantage that fanaticism gives them. They do not struggle with their consciences like we do. To them, it is black and white. We are evil and we must be destroyed for it."

"This search, I guarantee you, is probably a means to that same end," Gideon speculated darkly. "Every Crusade was as much about gathering valuable relics, religious or otherwise, as it was about upholding claims to religious principles or lands."

"Ah, the good old days," Isabella quipped with a lopsided grin as she winked at Magdelegna. "Memories of a reckless youth, Gideon?"

Gideon flicked the little Druid an acidic glare that only managed to send her into a fit of giggles.

"As much as I would love to hear about Gideon and Richard the Lionheart rounding the pubs of the Byzantine Empire," Siena said seriously, although there was repressed humor in her golden eyes, "I want to get these particular crusaders off my territory."

"Well, Siena," Noah mused, "since I have a feeling you will not take kindly to a speedy, exterminating forest fire, what do you suggest we do?"

Siena bit her lip in thought for a moment, absently scratching a patch of newly healed skin beneath her ear until she heard an unexpected chuckle echoing inside of her head.

What?

You were right. You do look like a leopard.

Very funny, warrior. Do you think we could pay attention to the problem?

Elijah turned to look over his shoulder at the congregation of expectant faces. A strange sense of distance fell over him as he did so. Oh, he would always be close to these people; there was never going to be any doubt about the depth of his affection for them. Be it the one year he had known Bella, or the hundreds he had known Noah, nothing could truly separate him from the feelings he had formed for his comrades.

But in this moment, he was realizing he was about to leave a dramatically important period of his life behind him. He was clearly turning toward the new one he was entering with Siena.

That meant that these woodlands were now his, because they were hers. It required him to be aware of the fact that her interests and concerns became his, whether they involved the Demon race or not. The comfort that came from this era of change they had been clumsily breaking into was the realization that the Demon race and the Lycanthrope race would be intermingled with one another for as long as they lived their lives. Destiny had proclaimed it to be so the moment She had linked Elijah to her, and Siena to him.

Frankly, it was an impressive solution. The mating of enemies. Forcing an integration of species and making them come to understand one another more clearly. Destiny had made her mind clear to all of them. There would be no turning back to old squabbles without risking the separation of the mated couple who, under Imprinted compulsion, would rather die than allow anything to separate them.

Siena reached up to rub her hand over Elijah's where it was curled around her bare neck. It was yet another reminder, a clever, voiceless coercion, to have him focus on the issues of the moment instead of mulling over things that would take much longer than that instant to resolve. He flicked his attention to the half-breed, Anya, who had stood up and begun to pace. He knew that expression and the thoughts behind it just about as well as he knew himself.

"The problem is the way they are entrenched," Anya remarked, kneeling closer to the cliff side. "Granted, this is the high ground, but those wards are as good as the solid walls of a castle fortress. I'm willing to bet not all of them are merely part of a sensor net. I'd put money on many of them being active defenses. Half of us will get fried if we cross those barriers. Not to mention the fact that they are humans, in spite of everything else, and that gives them access to munitions."

"I doubt we will have to worry about that, Anya," Elijah countered thoughtfully. "First of all, Ruth is very likely to be in that camp. She was in the fray pretty fast when she had her little minions all over me, which tells me she was pretty close by. That means she would have had to come up with excuses to keep the area clear of things mechanical or technological in nature, else she would tip her hand about being a Demon herself. That's the advantage of making this an archaeological site. It is expected to be done by hand, rather than with machinery."

"Ruth also knows that in close combat, our chemistry will cause malfunctions to complex equipment. Those malfunctions would be far more likely to backfire onto her fighters rather than do damage to us," Jacob added.

"Their weaponry has been of the most efficient type to harm Demons. Iron bolts in crossbows, iron blades, magic."

"Yes, but they are in Lycanthrope territory," Siena mused. "The hunters in there would be unable to resist their nature to arm themselves for so real a possibility of encountering one of my people."

"That means silver," Anya added. "Silver bullets, to be exact." The half-breed rolled her eyes. "As theatrical as it may be, it's effective enough."

"Okay, wait a sec," Bella piped up, nibbling on her bottom lip as she ordered her thoughts. "They are prepared for Demons. They are prepared for Lycanthropes. Let's just take that for granted. But given your history of war together, I bet there's one thing they are *not* prepared for."

"Both!" Anya said immediately.

"Just like at the Battle of Beltane," Siena added. "I still wonder if she ever figured out that there were more than Demons there that day."

"Don't underestimate Ruth," Elijah warned "She was warrior before she was Councillor. She's a skilled tactician, and I never knew her to make the same mistake twice."

"Guys," Bella said suddenly, her head tilting as she turned her focus onto something she was sensing. "I hate to say this, but I have that funny feeling I get in my belly when there is a Transformed Demon nearby. I think they are being guarded by a lot more than magical wards." She sighed loudly, the breathy beckoning encouraging Jacob to reach out automatically. He slipped his hand beneath her hair and rubbed soothingly at her neck. "You know," the little Druid continued, "for once I wish there was such a thing as a *good* sorceress. One that was on our side. Someone who could un-ravel the wards and change Transformed Demons back to themselves again."

"Impossible," Noah said quietly, instantly quashing the naïve hybrid's fanciful desire. "To become a sorceress or a warlock, you have to pick up books of magic and spells that are, in and of themselves, innately unnatural and evil."

"I thought magic-users were born magic-users. Just like Demons are born with their abilities."

"You will find that to be true of the more powerful magic-users," Noah agreed. "But most learn to become what they are by intellect, resources, and studying alone. You could pick up a spell book, Bella, just like Ruth has, and learn that magic as easily as any one of them has. But the moment you begin to use tainted spells from tainted books, you become corrupted yourself. Unfortunately, the easy access to those powers is why there are so many of them, so suddenly. It is spreading like a cult."

"A cult lead by the powerful magic-users who are just . . . born that way?"

"I am afraid so."

"Are you telling me that being born with the natural potential for magic makes you innately evil?" Bella's body language was a matching protest to her words as she became extremely tense. "That means they never had a choice! Just like you never had a choice of what element you were going to rule, or Siena had over what forms she takes."

"They have a choice. They can choose not to pick up the black magic," Jacob retorted. "Do not try and defend them, Bella. It would be a mistake to feel sympathy for them."

"So you are telling me it's a choice between pursuing your innate power . . . or not? Jacob, that is not fair. It would be like it was when you and I first met, as you tried to fight off what you instinctively felt for me. No matter how wrong you felt it was in your moral heart, you could not resist. How many of us who are here now have come to understand how impossible that is?"

"Fine," Elijah bit out suddenly. "Forced to the choice or not, it does not change what they are. It does not change the fact that they hunt us and destroy us with impunity, save what we ourselves bring to their door in answer."

"I see. And if a wild animal attacked you because it was in its nature to do so, you would feel justified in killing it?" Syreena spoke up suddenly, her gray brow rising toward her hairline.

"An animal has motive and instincts. It kills to eat, protect itself, or in madness from some disease such as rabies. Nourishment and self-defense are the right of every living creature, and I condemn no one for having those needs. It does not even matter to me how crude or sophisticated they are in the methods they use to bring those needs to fruition.

"But I assure you," he continued, his voice one of deep

ice and impenetrable steel, "I would destroy a rabid animal in a heartbeat. An animal of that maddened ilk will infect anything it can sink its teeth into if I do not take action to stop it. I will destroy these women with the same ease," Elijah assured his sister-in-law coldly. "These women are rabid. They are spreading their disease and sacrificing hundreds of innocents in the process. Those they lure to join their task, those they steal from us, and those of us who have been brutalized during their attempts to hold authority over us."

"Syreena, you are a Monk of The Pride. Half warrior, half pacifist," Gideon said, his tone far more diplomatic than Elijah's. "We all understand your tendency to view all sides of an issue. Have faith when I tell you that these are questions we have been asking ourselves for as long as even I can remember. Our conclusions were not approached lightly when it came to these issues."

"Do not forget, Isabella," Noah added, "that your human integrity, while noble, does not always suit creatures of our kind of power. It is a different standard with high consequences if not handled with a stricter level of jurisprudence. I think you know that."

"Kill or be killed?" Bella spoke up bitterly. "I despise the idea of my daughter being raised in such times."

A moment later, she sighed softly, rising to turn toward her husband. "Don't be upset, Jacob," she said gently. "I would feel the same if it were a human war. You know that, in my heart, I prefer that she become part of a species where affection, love, and morality are such abundant standards. My upset is with our enemies, not with our society."

"Forgive me if I seem to be continuously ignorant," Syreena said quietly, "but, as Bella originally asked, is there no such thing as *good* magic?" Syreena looked at her sister pointedly. "In my lessons, I was taught these bands we three wear"—she indicated the slender link around her throat— "are enchanted. This necklace is made with natural products, but imbued with abilities and properties you cannot find in nature. That is what I would call magic," she said. "Does it follow then that because they are made of magic, they are evil? I know of no Nightwalkers who can make anything like this. So if it was not us, then who created them? Magic-users? These creatures of evil?" She extended a hand toward the distant woodland. "I refuse to believe something so intrinsically evil had a hand in this magic that is so powerfully a part of Lycanthrope traditions and our way of finding our soul mates."

"This is not an exemplary moment for philosophical discussions," Gideon said abruptly, his serious silver eyes gleaming in the moonlight as he looked at Syreena and Isabella pointedly. "Nor is it a prudent time for investigating the histories of our races. Whether there is such a thing as 'good' magic or not, innate evil or not, we are assured in our understanding of these particular enemies.

"Here and now," he continued, "these women are a threat to all of us. Here and now, those women are growing stronger and deadlier with every moment they continue to immerse themselves in their arts. And if we do not take action against them *here and now,* Ruth and Mary and every last female in that encampment will introduce themselves to us once again, and it may not be a meeting any or all of us will be so lucky as to survive this time."

"Point taken," Anya agreed firmly. "The medic is correct. We are risking ourselves with 'what if' and 'could be,' wasting this time better spent finding a realistic resolution to our immediate problem."

"Agreed." Elijah nodded sharply. The two of them could never be mistaken for anything other than the fighters that they were. From their stances to their focus on the battle to come, they were both warriors to the last.

The group, guided by their example, refocused on the matter at hand.

"I believe . . ." Siena turned to inspect the lay of the land once again. "Yes. I think I know of a way we can get past those wards." She turned to Jacob, giving him a once over and a grin. "Yes, I think I do."

Mary entered her mother's tent in the encampment to find her parent pacing the relatively luxurious accommodations she had been given due to her position of leadership. Like Demon society, the rank in this grouping of females was according to power, and none of them could top her mother. That was because there was more to Ruth than the abilities of a mere "sorceress." But, of course, the magic-using simpletons that surrounded them did not know that.

There were old, musty books stacked around the small desk the female Mind Demon had been studying at incessantly since they had encamped there a little less than a month ago. But it was clear her disturbance was keeping her from studying them further.

Ruth was a brilliant female, but she was no scholar by nature. Her abilities had always been focused on the battle. She had been a warrior before she had become a member of the Great Council. It wasn't just luck and power that gave her the ability to outstep Demons as skilled in hunt and battle as Elijah and Jacob were. Ruth had spent centuries as their ally, and as such knew everything about the way they acted, reacted, and how strong they really were.

"Mother, what troubles you?" her daughter asked, sounding as bored as she looked. The boredom occurred often when Mary was not kept amused by attacks and excursions against others. She had developed a significant taste for those things. "We have killed Gideon. You should be celebrating."

"No," Ruth said sharply. "This celebration is a waste of time and energy. We should be back in the dig site looking for our treasure. Especially now. Noah will be livid when he finds his dead family, and we should be prepared."

"Noah?" Mary snorted out a contemptuous laugh. "The great pacifist Demon King? He doesn't get angry."

"Do not be a fool!" Ruth whirled on her daughter. "What do *you* know? You know nothing about it! Since he reached adulthood, I have known Noah to lose his temper only three times." Ruth ticked them off on her fingers. "When his mother was murdered, when his father died, and the night his precious little sister was Summoned.

"When his family is threatened or damaged, Noah's rage has the force of a nuclear fury. It is nothing you ever want to see, girl. Believe me when I tell you that. Tonight we killed his sister's Imprinted mate and very likely Legna herself. And if Legna is dead, Noah's unborn niece or nephew died with her. If he ever catches up with us, our deaths will come in a conflagration to outshine the humans' ideas of hell."

"But no one knows where we are. Who would look for us here?"

"Elijah knows!" Ruth snapped at her child. "We were just lucky he did not arrive a few minutes sooner. Together, Gideon and Elijah would have destroyed us easily." Ruth took a breath as she stopped to slam a hand on the pile of books. "And now that it is confirmed that Elijah is alive, that means he has reported what happened to him to Noah. Now, despite all my work to mislead the Enforcers who tracked him, they probably will soon know exactly where we are."

"But surely they would have come here sooner—"

"Mary, who do you think walked through the wards the other day, coincidentally where Elijah's dead body was supposed to be? It had to be Jacob, or even the Warrior Captain himself retracing his own steps."

"That is twenty miles from here," Mary pointed out.

"And you do not think Noah has the wisdom to widen a search for us from there? Stop being so ignorant, girl!" Ruth turned her flaring blue eyes on her offspring. "For all we know they are already on their way."

"Then we should go," Mary said, sounding suddenly fearful.

"Yes. We should. But I am not leaving without spending every possible second searching for what we came for. I can teleport us to safety in a heartbeat. We can let these ninnies distract Noah's forces while we escape." Ruth paced some more, rubbing slim fingers over her tense forehead. "Legna is the only one who might be strong enough to interfere in one of my teleports. Even if she did not die in the fire, it was Gideon's power that was making her such a force to contend with. Without him, she will no doubt revert to her common, simpering little adult self once more."

"I will get the others back into the dig site," Mary said, her boredom gone now that she was aware of the danger stalking them.

"See to it. We need that spell book if we are to destroy Noah and all those self-righteous idiots he calls a Council."

"I will, Mother. I think we are very close. That lesser spell book that we found may mean the other is close by."

"I would count on nothing if I were you, child. I will join you shortly. We need to remain close to one another in case of an attack. If we leave before finding the Black Tome, they will know we were looking for something and no doubt continue the search themselves until they figure out what we were searching for. We will have led Noah right to it. If he finds the Tome and if he is half the scholar he is claimed to be, he will figure out what we are up to shortly after."

"Mother, you said yourself that no one knows about the Black Tome. You said no one even knows about the scroll you found that has led us to this place. If they find it, they won't know what it is for. Only magic-users can read it, you said."

"Trust me, daughter. The Warrior Captain will have no trouble coaxing a magic-using prisoner into deciphering the book for the King once Noah figures out that it is required.

In that case, our only hope will be that it takes us less time to manage alternatives than it takes him to figure things out. Now go. We are wasting time. I can feel it pressing on me."

"Even if they do come, the wards and the Transformed ones will keep them busy," Mary tried to reassure her. "We have some time still."

"Let us hope so."

CHAPTER 18

"Well, this place looks familiar," Elijah murmured against Siena's ear, making her chuckle as she nudged him gently in the ribs with her elbow.

"These caverns go for miles with dozens of outlets like this one," Siena explained, her rich voice echoing as they entered the unpopulated tunnels off the cave Jinaeri had made her winter home. "Many of them are hibernation habitats, but not all of them for Lycanthropes. If we cross paths with wildlife, let the three of us handle them." She indicated herself, Anya, and Syreena.

"You mean the four of us," Jacob said, reminding her that his abilities were on par with hers as far as charming animals was concerned.

"Conserve your energy, Enforcer," Siena reminded him in return. "There is no outlet from these caverns that empties into the encampment. We are just using these passages to pass beneath the wards undetected. We are counting on you to get us to the surface."

"I would not worry about my energy reserves," he assured her.

"I do not understand why I can not simply teleport us into the campground," Legna complained for the third time.

"Ruth would feel us coming," her husband reiterated with surprising patience. "Unfortunately, she is pretty much a match for your strength. Tactically speaking, it would not be wise to let ourselves be surrounded like that."

"Gideon, I can get us out just as quickly."

"I doubt that," Noah said, his tone meant to put an end to the argument. "Bringing us all in there, in and of itself, would be impossible for even your considerable power, Legna. Taking us out afterward? It could never happen. You are simply not that strong. Frankly, in my opinion, you should not even be with us."

"Do not even think about giving me some prissy lecture about the delicate needs of pregnant women," Legna warned her brother sharply, "or I swear I will teleport you to the North Pole, where there is nothing combustible for hundreds of miles around."

"You know, I used to think *my* people were overconfident," Siena remarked, "but I see now why my father had a hard time winning against your people. You are very stubborn."

"You have no idea," Gideon and Noah chorused.

Elijah chuckled as he leapt off a ledge to the floor about four feet below. He reached up without thinking to assist Siena with hands on her waist. He did not realize until she hesitated that she might interpret the gesture as somewhat demeaning to her undoubtedly excellent ability to take care of herself. But she reached for his shoulders a moment later, moving into his hands as he lowered her to the floor easily.

"Do not worry," she assured him softly as she linked her fingers through his and squeezed his hand. "I sometimes forget that you were born when men were gentlemen. However, I think it could grow on me."

"I am glad to hear that," he said with a grin. "However, I

am wholeheartedly willing to forgo gentlemanly manners and let the door hit you in the ass at your immediate request."

"You are too kind," she laughed.

The group continued to move through the tunnels, following Siena's sure lead. The cavern floor was often slippery, the limestone filled with water that dripped off the points of stalactites and mist from underground falls and hot springs.

"It isn't far now," Siena told them as they worked their way up a slick slope. "I wish we had a way of sensing those wards from here."

"We have Bella. She's better than any sensors."

"How?" The Queen turned to look back at Elijah curiously.

"Bella can dampen power."

"Elijah, we want to avoid that if possible," Jacob reminded him. "The side effects of it are proving to be damaging."

"But imagine how much simpler it would be to just walk through those wards once I dampen the power. We wouldn't have to go through all of this." She jerked her hand away from the touch of a particularly slimy wall. "Yuck," she said, making a face as she wiped her hand on her jeans. "And above all, Ruth and Mary can escape in a teleporting flash if I don't give them the whammy. I don't see how we can avoid it."

"You are not to have contact with Ruth no matter what," Jacob warned, this time brooking none of her stubborn refusals. "She is so tainted, and in ways no one has seen before, that we cannot even guess at the damage it might cause to any of us. Ruth would never have been able to touch Gideon six months ago. Not even Ruth and Mary and a dozen necromancers could have done so."

"She is very powerful," Gideon agreed grimly. "We must

all remember not to treat this like any ordinary battle. There is great risk involved here."

The conversation stopped when Siena suddenly halted in her steps. They watched her cock her head, and immediately nine heads turned in unison to listen.

"I have never been here before," Siena murmured. "There is something peculiar about this place. I cannot put my finger on it. Can any of you?"

It was Noah who raised his brows in surprise.

"Must. I smell must and . . ." He searched, shaking his dark head.

"Books!" Bella erupted suddenly. "I smell books. I've spent too many years in a library not to know that smell."

"But no one has been through these passages in years," Siena mused. "The stone growth, the water flow and passages are wholly unspoiled. Besides, it's too damp to make sense of storing books in here. They would ruin easily. Jinaeri has to keep hers covered even though she is in a dry area."

"I'm telling you, it's books," Bella insisted.

"I think she's right," Noah agreed.

"Look, over here." Jacob leapt onto a natural ledge, crouching down to inspect the wall nearby. "It may be unspoiled now, but someone definitely altered this rock face at one point. See these grooves? These are manmade, though trying to keep an appearance of natural occurrence. See? The water does not flow over this section here, so why is it worn into a groove so deep?"

Jacob reached to touch the fist-size indentation.

"Jacob, don't!" Bella cried out suddenly, making him freeze immediately.

She hurried over to him, grabbing his arm and trying to pull him down to her side.

"Something isn't right. I can feel it. Please come away."

"Bella, step back. I promise I will be careful." He extracted his hand from the death grip she had on it and shook off her fingers when she tried to maintain her hold.

Siena watched with narrowed eyes as the Enforcer skimmed searching fingers over and around those slight grooves, trying to search her memory for something, even though she had no clue what it was.

"Jacob, stop!"

The chorus erupted simultaneously from Elijah and Siena. In unison they had experienced a moment of clarity, Siena recollecting a snippet of a story she had heard during her childhood over one hundred years ago, and Elijah's closeness to the sudden fear that leapt up in its wake in her mind prompting him to echo her warning.

Jacob pulled away this time, listening to yet another warning from a source he could not dismiss as being over-protective. He jumped off the ledge even as Siena pushed forward toward it. She sprang up easily, feeling Elijah's hand guiding her up with absent habit.

It made her smile even as she dusted her hands across the skirt of the dress Legna had loaned her. Magdelegna had a more conservative style, so the skirt was longer and more cumbersome than the Queen would have liked, but she simply pulled it out of her way as she knelt to inspect the suspicious grooves.

"There is a legend among my people about the times before we ventured out of the caves and into the world. Like my castle, whole cities were supposedly built underground. In those times, it is said we never went into the light of day." She peered closer at the wall. "We have only found small abodes that hinted at this truth. Otherwise, our only other proof was the stories we handed down verbally and the odd scrap of written lore."

"So what does that—?"

"The legend said all the entrances to this city were disguised and trapped to keep out accidental as well as purposeful intruders. If the curious person did not know how to harmlessly bypass the trap, it was tripped and the intruder would be killed."

"You don't believe this is a city," Bella said with clear disbelief.

"No. I do not," Siena agreed. "But I do believe this could be an entrance fashioned with those same traps."

"Tell me you know how to disarm it," Jacob encouraged her.

She didn't have to. She touched both grooves simultaneously, a loud click echoing around them, making them start with surprise. Then, after a brief, studying search, she placed both hands on the wall and shifted her weight and the pressure of her touch slightly to the right. The wall dropped away so suddenly that it startled the Queen, who stepped back into Elijah's steady frame as he vaulted onto the ledge in a heartbeat to prevent her from falling off it.

"Nice reflexes," she murmured to her husband.

"Thank you," he chuckled, drawing her to his back as he peered into the pitch black of the entrance. "Noah?"

"Consider it done," the King responded. Reaching out with his refined senses, he felt the presence of tarred torches and lit them in a brilliant surge of light. Everyone winced as the rows of the torches blinded them momentarily.

"Whoa. I think I know what Ruth is looking for," Bella said with eager awe, having recovered before the others because her eyes were not as sensitive to dark and light theirs were.

Eyes cleared and a chorus of gasps came out of the group as they hurried to crowd around the entrance of the hidden room.

"Told you it was books," Bella murmured.

It was an understatement. It was actually an underground library. It was a bit worse for wear because of the years it had spent being ignored—the damage of water that had changed course over the years of erosion ran down walls that had been meant to be dry—but it had at one time definitely been a well-appointed library. It had red runners between every set of shelves in the corridor, the embroidered ruby velvet of it clearly once very rich and very fine. The torches lit up study tables as well as podiums that held singled-out tomes of enormous size.

And, of course, along both sides of the corridor were shelves and shelves of books reaching well beyond what even their keen sight could see.

"Wow," Legna said, at a loss for any other reaction. "Okay, how would Ruth, of all people, know this was here?"

"Clearly she doesn't know it's here. She thinks it's up there," Siena said, pointing above herself to the stone that would block Ruth's progress even had she suspected something beneath it.

"True. Mary does not have the power to burrow through earth and stone. That is a male Earth Demon trait," Jacob said, his eyes as wide as everyone else's as he scanned the library slowly. "Do you think it is safe to go in there?"

"I think so," Siena murmured, "but I wouldn't put money on it being completely harmless, so keep alert."

The battle they had been headed for was completely dismissed, all of them understanding that this was a more critical task. They moved into the isolated cavern, males linking hands with females, everyone wary as they prepared to take whatever forms they needed to in order to escape damage and carry those with them to safety as well.

Siena preceded them all, wide golden eyes skimming over the titles of the nearest volumes. Elijah was close behind her, so close that when she stopped, he bumped into her back and then remained there until she continued on.

"Siena, this is the Treasured Tongue," Syreena whispered, her sense of reverence coming through loud and clear as she reached to take a book in her hands, holding it as if it were a precious gem. "The historic language only the members of

The Pride now know. It would be lost to them as well if not for the fact that they spend so much time maintaining their knowledge of it."

"That means this is a Lycanthrope library?" Elijah asked.

"No."

Everyone turned to see Bella pull another book down.

"Jacob, this it the ancient language of Demonkind."

Heads turned from one woman to the other. They crossed to meet each other and inspect the books.

"They aren't the same," Bella informed them. "Let's see if there are others."

There were. Books in languages both known and unknown to those in the room.

"The language of the Vampires," Gideon said, shaking his head. "This looks like Shadowdweller print. These are those bold, picturesque characters they use."

"It's a Nightwalker library," Siena said, her whispering voice echoing off the ceilings high above them.

"A lot of them are ruined," Elijah remarked, dropping a saturated book onto a table, where it immediately disintegrated.

"Noah, have you ever heard of anything like this in your history?" Siena asked the King.

"Nothing. This . . . this is beyond anything we would ever know."

"I never heard about this from The Pride, and they have a knack for telling some pretty primordial tales," Syreena said, continuing to inspect the shelves with skimming fingers. "Is it possible this precedes even our forbearers?"

"And none of them thought to tell any of our historians about it? I find that hard to believe. Surely some kind of story or legend about it would have survived . . . some written proof or mention of it somewhere," Noah insisted.

"Oh yes," Bella said, her eyes rolling and her tone dry, "just like you were aware of that happy little prophecy I found that said we were all about to get tossed into a clothes dryer, tumbled around, and literally spit out just to see what comes out in the wash."

"Good point," Elijah chuckled.

"Jacob, look at this." Noah beckoned the Enforcer. Jacob came to peer at the book over the King's shoulder.

"Is that what I think it is?"

"What?" the others asked.

"Spells," Noah answered, his dark eyes serious and weighted with concern. "Magic-user spells."

"In a Nightwalker library?" Isabella pushed through them, inspecting the huge volume with sharp eyes. "Latin. Italian . . . this is . . . I don't even know what this is," she said shaking her head. "But there's even Egyptian hieroglyphs in here. This is, like . . . the unabridged spell compendium of the whole world! This is what Ruth and Mary are looking for. I would bet my stash of chocolate bars on it."

"I think she is right," Noah agreed, leafing through the pages gingerly, but finding them all too sturdy. "We have to destroy this."

"Absolutely not!"

"Bella," Noah warned.

"Don't even think it, Noah. There's a reason this is in a Nightwalker library, and maybe you should figure out what that reason is before you go around willy-nilly playing *Fahrenheit 451*."

"Bella, do you know how dangerous this book would be in the wrong hands?" Noah argued.

"But it isn't in the wrongs hands, Noah. It's in yours."

"Noah, I think she may be correct," Gideon spoke up, his silvery eyes suddenly flicking to the King's so the monarch understood how serious his opinion was. "We have been looking for ways to block the Summoning and Transformations for centuries . . . for millennia, even. Maybe this book or these others hold those answers."

Noah immediately appeared to take that into consideration.

"There is one thing we can all agree on." Siena spoke up suddenly, her voice deepening with grave seriousness. "We must keep Ruth and Mary as far from here as possible. That volume is probably only a scratch on the surface of what this place holds. The power that they would potentially have access to if they discovered this library is immeasurable. And I don't know about the rest of you, but I think they've had more than enough advantages since they defected."

"Agreed," Jacob said shortly. "Noah, Bella . . . I know the temptation of all this knowledge is overwhelming to you both, but we had best deal with our traitors and their compatriots before we let ourselves be distracted any further."

"Also agreed," Noah said with a sharp nod. "But I do not feel comfortable leaving all of this open like this."

"It has gone undisturbed for untold centuries, Noah," Siena reminded him gently. "I will return the seal and locks to what they were when we first arrived. Once we have dealt with Ruth, we can worry about guarding this place any further than that."

It took a long moment, but eventually Noah nodded his acquiescence. The powerful group immediately backtracked out of the library, leaping down from the entrance so the Lycanthrope Queen could reseal the tricky door. It took some effort and a little helping counterbalance from her powerful mate to reseal the ancient mechanism, but eventually they too were able to leap off the ledge and into their party of companions.

"Come on, let's kick ass," Bella offered with irreverent enthusiasm, grabbing her husband's hand and hurrying him into the deeper recesses of the caverns.

Mary was marching restlessly up and down the side of the dig site, her arms folded around her waist, chewing her bottom lip as her nervous energy radiated off her in waves. Her mother had not yet joined her, making her more than a little concerned for her safety should something suddenly go wrong. However, her mother had remarkable power, and that included the ease and speed of her teleportation abilities.

Her mother had sufficiently frightened her, mentioning the powerful men and their mates who were potentially out for their blood. Mary had been raised in perpetual awe of those names, even in spite of her mother's constant derision.

Noah. Elijah. Jacob the Enforcer.

Especially Elijah. Mary had once followed her mother to the training grounds when she had still been a warrior under the fierce Captain's command, and had seen for herself how brutally cold and powerfully calculating that Demon could be even when only practicing. When she and her mother had stood over the warrior in the Russian forest not too long ago, watching him die with a seemingly baffling simplicity, Mary had still been awed and afraid, in spite of his apparent weakness and their apparent victory. It came as almost no surprise to her when she had discovered the warrior had somehow managed to cheat a so clearly imminent demise. She had always believed him undefeatable, and that was reinforced now more than ever.

Her nervous gaze twitched over the rows of women working patiently on the hard, cold ground that supposedly concealed the Black Tome her mother was searching for so desperately. According to the scroll, it was supposed to be the centerpiece of an ancient library that had existed long before even Gideon's time. It was a concept hard for one as young as she was to wrap her mind around. That such a thing would even survive all that time seemed impossible, but her mother had already discovered a companion book, so it must still be possible for the Black Tome to have survived even all these ages.

According to her mother, that book would have the power

to destroy even the most powerful of enemies. Even Noah, the extremely potent Fire Demon who could probably destroy the entire Earth if he put himself to the task.

But Mary didn't think they needed it. They had just destroyed Gideon, the most Ancient of their kind. If they could do that, they could do anything.

"I would not rest so comfortably on that assumption if I were you."

Mary jolted out of her private thoughts with a gasp, whirling to face that low, cold statement's birthplace. She found herself staring up into fearfully cold silver eyes, the mouth beneath them twisted into a sardonic smile of cruel confidence that she would never hope to know the meaning of.

"Uh, uh, uh," asked a soft, warning voice behind her, making her about-face once more with speed and terror to face a matching set of silver eyes. "I know what you're thinking," Magdelegna warned with a cruel smile of her own. "Your mommy cannot help you now."

Mary's heart pounded with violent speed as she realized she was telling the absolute truth. The young Demon was surrounded by all those Demons whose names and legends she had so feared for all of her life.

"Jacob, Bella, concentrate on keeping this little brat under wraps. Ruth will come for her soon enough."

This order was given by the Demon King as he and the others turned at the sudden shouts of warning coming from the churned-over field full of magic-users and hunters.

"As a Druid I know once said, let's kick ass!"

After that gleeful statement, the next thing to exit the Lycanthrope Queen's mouth was the chilling scream of the cougar.

Ruth was jolted out of her study of the open book before her by the loud sound of startled, urgent voices outside of her tent. She stood up so fast that she knocked back her chair, and, grabbing protectively at the heavy, old volume before her, she reached out with her powerful mental senses.

She abruptly realized she was under enormous threat. Worse still, her daughter was being threatened. Frantically, the Demon traitor pushed back the knee-jerk fury and blind urge to react that her mothering instincts demanded. Luckily for her, her centuries of training as a warrior reminded her that fighting under duress of emotion was the surest way to lose a battle. It was, in retrospect, exactly how Gideon had managed to obtain the upper hand so unexpectedly in her attack on him. A mistake she was apparently still going to pay the price for, she realized as she sensed the Ancient's presence close by. Angry fingers wrapped around her slender throat, gripping at bruises that were no longer there except in her memory of how Gideon had made them and almost killed her in the process.

Now they sought to capture and harm her only living child—even after what they themselves had done in their arrogance to cause Mary to suffer in the first place! If not for their self-righteous laws, Mary would have been mated to a Druid male who would have loved her with incomprehensible power, doubling the girl's potential, or perhaps more. But no. They had not seen fit to save that poor Druid male from a terrible death by starvation. They had only changed the laws to suit themselves when one of their elite clique had been in need of it. The Enforcer and his bride.

And now those two same dared to hold her daughter captive, their self-righteousness radiating off them like a reeking plague. Ruth knew they were using Mary to bait her, but she would not be so easily fooled, nor her purposes so easily circumvented.

Isabella stood nearly toe to toe with the young Earth Demon, her violet eyes full of barely repressed anger toward her. Mary and her mother had ambushed her when she had been pregnant, beating her down in a specific attempt to end her child's as well as her own life. The female Enforcer would not soon forget or forgive that slight. Neither would her mate who, at present, was casting out a sensory net meant to prevent Ruth from sneaking up on them the way they had crept up on her encampment and unprotected off-spring. In the field, necromancers and hunters were being engaged and easily defeated. The hunters had no weaponry outside of the odd excavating tool, and the necromancers were heavily dependent on their concentration and no doubt a great deal of preparation before being effective in battle. Only those to whom the power came more naturally would present a true challenge. That and the fact that the infiltrators were quite outnumbered.

Isabella was unconcerned, however. Redemption was a powerful motivator. There wasn't a Demon or Lycanthrope on the field who didn't have good cause to visit redemption on this particular group.

Suddenly, Isabella felt an eddy of displaced air striking her strongly in the back, making her stumble forward. Jacob whirled to face his bride as his sensory alarms blared loud and wide. Elijah also felt the eddy even at his distance in the field and was distracted from his current adversary long enough to look in the Enforcers' direction.

The warrior knew the feeling of displaced air from a tele-port when he felt it. So did the Enforcers. The problem was, there was no one or no thing at the center of the displacement.

"Where is she?" Isabella asked frantically, instinctively backing closer to her mate.

Elijah saw their confusion, and a sick, cold trepidation crawled up his spine as he watched them flail for a target. The sensation got the attention of his bride, and he saw her turn to look at the Enforcers out of the corner of his eye. Her golden eyes slid closed and her whiskered nose lifted into that trace of a breeze. Immediately, the hackles on the back of her neck rose to full attention. The cat shifted to the Werecat with heart-stopping speed. Elijah knew her thoughts instantly. Ruth was there. Despite what their eyes were telling them, the senses of the cat could not be so easily tricked.

Jacob caught Siena's metamorphosis and the clarity of its motivation a moment too late. Isabella was suddenly yanked off her feet and sent flying in his direction. He couldn't avoid catching his wife even if he had wanted to, but even with her petite stature, the speed of her impact into his chest sent him reeling and tumbling over backward.

Elijah reacted instantly, focusing on the younger traitor Demon and demolecularizing her into nothing but a breath of air. His wife was covering land in awesome, powerful leaps, literally following her nose in order to find the other, who had somehow masked her visual presence.

Ruth materialized with a scream of frustration just when Siena was not more than two leaps away from pouncing her into the ground. The Elder traitor flung out a violent hand toward the Lycanthrope female. Siena struck a wall, midbound, and recoiled off it and into the dirt with a startled cough. Ruth had teleported a solid rock into her path at too short of a distance for her to change her direction. Stunned, Siena touched a padded paw to the rend in the fur across her forehead, coming away with bloodied fur for her effort.

Ruth then teleported herself away. Elijah braced himself, feeling quite surely that she would follow her daughter's trail at any cost. Since forcing Mary into the noncorporeal state took a great amount of effort, more so because she was fighting it tooth and nail, Elijah whipped her back into her natural form by his side before he lost the opportunity to do so. No sooner had he done this than he felt Ruth appear violently at his back.

Ruth had always been an accomplished backstabber. Literally. It was one of her favored attack strategies. Elijah had taught her how, so he was well prepared for the blade that came slicing toward his exposed flank. He didn't waste precious energy changing form, but instead ducked and rolled with remarkable agility and speed. Even so, the blade breezed past his ear, nicking the lobe.

The warrior didn't have time to note the injury. Ruth teleported again and was once more at his vulnerable back. Instinctively, Elijah blocked her stroke with his arm, sending sparks flying as the metal of her blade contacted the links of his golden armband. Without concern for the wickedly sharp blade, Elijah wrapped his bare arm around it and jerked downward, disarming Ruth neatly, although at the expense of a good bite into the flesh of his biceps and forearm. Again, the armband saved him from the worst of it.

Ruth turned to look at her child, clearly trying to focus on her to teleport them both away. But as it had been every time she had tried so far, something was preventing her from taking her daughter with her. Frustrated and enraged, Ruth teleported away, alone, before the Demon warrior gained his feet and could regroup to attack.

Elijah did get up, but he had a different target in mind. He grabbed the disoriented Mary by the throat, using the hold to jerk her back against his chest. Mary gasped, then gurgled out a restricted sound of panic as that enormous hand cut off her air supply. She was too young and inexperienced to use any of her innate abilities after being jostled around from captor to captor like she had been. All she could do was flail and grasp at the steadfast hand locked so firmly around her neck.

"Ruth! I will rip her head off right here and now, I swear it!" Elijah barked meanly into the night air. "End this! Meet your fate like the warrior you once were!"

Ruth materialized once more, this time with such violence that several of her compatriots were blown back off their feet. Elijah was instantly on edge when he realized the traitor had appeared right behind Siena. He needn't have worried. Siena had apparently been prepared for just such a tactic. She was a blur of golden fur as she whirled around with amazing speed. Ruth reacted, throwing out her arms as she tried to leap back. But Siena was faster, her reflexes honed as true as her targeting abilities. The Werecat's claws ripped through the front of Ruth's dress, scoring through chiffon and flesh.

The Elder Mind Demon screamed in pain, staggering back, her eyes wide with sudden fear as the Werecat snarled and crouched, black and gold pupils narrowing on her as if she were going to be the cat's next meal. Her senses became aware of the Enforcers approaching, that the ranks of her camp were dwindling down to nothing, and that if she stayed and fought for her daughter a moment longer, she was very likely going to be captured as well. The last thing in the world she wanted was to come under the retribution of the Enforcers and the King. If she were captured, she would no doubt die for her crimes.

In a last desperate attempt to save her child, Ruth tried to think of a way to help Mary escape a similar fate. She had only a heartbeat to come to a solution before she would find herself under the pounce of the cat and her rending claws. With desperation, Ruth stole a digging pole with a metal-tipped spike that a hunter was using some distance away as a speared projectile against Gideon. It reappeared mid-flight, heading straight for Elijah and her daughter, who protected his chest. But Mary was just small enough against the giant so that her shoulder was sitting just below the span of ribs that covered the Warrior Captain's heart.

The projectile was too unexpected and moving too fast even for Elijah to react. But Siena had already begun to fly at this Demon bitch who had caused her so much pain. Without realizing Ruth had launched a last, lethal attack at her mate, she leapt onto the Demon woman with a bone-chilling scream. Startled, Ruth fell back with fear, her full attention forced to pay focus to that horrible, animalistic war cry. It was only her centuries of reflexive training as a warrior that made her scramble in the right direction to avoid the claws aiming to disembowel her with a single stroke.

Too late, Ruth realized she had lost control of the spear she had aimed at Elijah's heart. Scrambling again to avoid Siena's deadly accurate pounce, she whirled to check if she had freed her daughter from the giant's throttling hold.

For a moment, empowering delight surged through Ruth as she saw the warrior kneeling, hunched over in the long grass. In the next second, however, he turned to face her and his mate, shock and pain written over his expression. Ruth's eyes moved down, and her entire world exploded into agony and rage. Cradled in the blond giant's arms was her daughter, speared through her heart by the weapon Ruth had intended for the Warrior Captain.

Ruth's vision went black and then red, the inconceivable picture and understanding of it echoing through her unbalanced mind with maddening persistence. With it came the calm and clarity only insanity could provide in such a moment. She turned reddened eyes of hatred onto the Werecat before her and snarled low in her throat.

"This is not over," she hissed to Siena. "You will all pay for my child with your own. You have my curse on that! All of you!"

Then Ruth teleported away with one last violent withdrawal, leaving for good now that there was no longer anything to keep her there. With the Demon traitor's chill words still ringing in her ears, Siena turned to look back at Elijah. Only then did she realize how serious a threat it was that Ruth had just made.

Mary was dead.

And Ruth had promised to see to it that they paid for it with the blood of their own children.

CHAPTER 19

The wind that swirled onto the balcony outside the library of the solitary log cabin solidified in the coming dawn into the forms of the Queen and the warrior. They were already wrapped securely around each other, almost as if supporting each other. They were worn out both mentally and physically, so they were probably doing exactly that. Elijah moved first, reaching to touch his warm, firm lips to the recently knitted cut slashing across her golden brow.

"I look forward to the time when Gideon will actually be able to assist your people in healing," he said softly against her skin, his heart clearly in the desire. He hated to see her harmed even in the slightest. It would take him a great deal of time to forget the sight of her, blistered and broken in her sickbed.

"Shh . . ." Siena soothed him on a soft breath, her mouth drifting to his throat. "I am in your mind, warrior." It was as much a scolding as it was a reminder. She was not accustomed to being worried over any more than he was. "Gideon is quite brilliant. I have no doubts that he will find his way into our chemistry. Meanwhile, this will heal rapidly enough on its own."

She lifted her head from his and looked around slowly, taking in the lightening darkness that surrounded them. The entire night was gone, though it had only been a few hours since they had risen for battle. Elijah had swept them through numerous time zones, following the curve of darkness until they had come there, where dawn was breaking.

"This is not Lycanthrope territory," she remarked, looking at the sprawling, treeless prairie and the moat of long grasses blowing in the natural breeze. Autumn was just beginning in this place. The first snows were due any moment in her home province.

"Exactly," Elijah murmured, pressing warm lips into her hair as he drew her closer. "No castle. No guards. No ambassadors, Counselors, or Generals . . ."

"No night," she pointed out dryly.

"No problem," he countered with a chuckle. "Trust me. My point is that there are no enemies, no threats, and most of all no immediate worries that cannot wait for a few hours."

"That is an impossibility to achieve with that insane creature roaming the planet," she sighed in sad response.

"Until we know exactly where she has run off to, it is momentarily out of our hands. Only Jacob and Isabella have a hope of finding out where she has gone. She has gotten too good at covering her tracks for it to be left to the skills of a warrior, no matter my power. The Enforcer was born with the innate ability to track his own. He will find her. She is cursed and blackened, mutated and poisoned, but she is still a Demon." Elijah sighed, closing his eyes as the dawn breeze brought the scent of earth and grass around them. "She will hide, will make it damn near impossible, but I have unfailing faith in Jacob. Meanwhile, kitten, we can't live our lives only to hunt and battle her. It would give her a victory the extent of which even she could not imagine."

Siena shuddered softly, reaching to wrap her slender hands around his thickly muscled biceps, her thumb stroking the band that bound him to her.

"When I think of how close you came to being killed . . ."

"Never. I am faster and stronger than her tricks, kitten. I was nothing but air by the time the weapon struck Mary. I only wish I'd had the time and strength to protect her as well, but with the wound on my arm . . ." He sighed softly as her gentle fingers traced that healing blade mark beneath her hand. "There is a part of me that will forgive Mary for what she did under the sway of her love for her parent."

"I never will," Siena insisted hotly, blinking the burn in her eyes away as she rested her cheek over his heart. "Defying your parent for what you believe is right is a hard choice, but a choice you must make if you face it. I was not much older than Mary when I made that choice. I even accepted the realization that one day my father would have to die, that he *must* die, if what was right was to ever come to fruition." She looked up when he tensed beneath her touch. "It is the cycle of life on this Earth that the young shall inherit their place upon it in the wake of their parents' deaths. Every living creature, animal or humanoid, fulfills this perpetual destiny. You know this," she insisted intensely, her voice falling to a hoarse whisper.

"I know this," he agreed quietly. "But for intelligent species, being a part of this cycle in so direct a manner does not come easy."

"It shouldn't. I would hope it never does for either of us."

Siena lifted her head and, breathing deep of the wind, took in all the alien scents of this part of North America that she had never been to.

"I have traveled so little in my lifetime," she noted, taking another deep breath, scenting everything from flora to fauna. "I am always amazed that the air itself can smell so different just by changing location."

"Yes. It is a remarkable phenomenon. Somewhat like you and I, and this bonding we are sharing. Unique, yet simplistic in its make-up."

"Mmm," she agreed. Then she stepped back from him

with a smile. "The sun is creeping up on us. Don't you think it is time you showed me your home?"

"The tour," he said with a low, mischievous chuckle, reaching to sweep her off her feet and into his arms as he kicked open the library doors and crossed the threshold with her, "can wait until later. I have other plans that will require you to become familiar with only one room of this house."

"The bedroom?"

"The bedroom," he agreed, making her laugh that sexy, robust laugh that he loved so much. He instantly felt the fire of need for her burning the surfaces of his skin, sparked by that throaty, decadent laugh.

"Did it never occur to you that, after defeating an archenemy and routing out a forest full of necromancers, I might be a little too tired for the kind of plans you have?"

"It had," he said with a silly grin as he strode across the upper landing and into the master suite, "but you are too much like me, Siena. After the heat of battle, the heat of passion is the first thing you crave. Besides, I was promised a game of connect the dots, and I intend to collect."

"I would not be much of a Queen if I began reneging on my promises," she mused agreeably.

"You don't have it in you to go back on your word, kitten," he said with a grin as he dropped her legs and let her slide down his broad body very slowly, allowing himself the well-earned luxury of the feel of her.

Siena responded instantly to the sensation of his rock-hard muscles against her own suppleness as they contacted her sliding body everywhere. Taking a deep breath, she released it in a slow purr of pleasure as she cuddled sexily against him. She burrowed a cheek into his shoulder, absorbing with every last molecule she owned the awareness of his hands rubbing over her back.

"So this is what it is like to be truly alone," she murmured contentedly.

"You are not alone," he reminded her softly.

"No, but *we* are."

"We were alone at Jinaeri's."

"Time we wasted," she retorted, lifting her head to look into his eyes.

"Black," he said.

"What?" she asked.

"You are supposed to say 'white,'" he told her in a conspiratorial whisper. "I could swear you live for the thrill of contradicting me."

Siena laughed, his humor delighting her so much that she wrapped strong arms around his neck and found his mouth with firm, insistent lips. She wooed him with silky, skillful kisses. The assertive sweep of her tongue teasing his into play captivated him completely. When she finally released him, he was breathless and warm beneath her seeking fingertips. The Queen spread eager palms over the expanse of the broad chest that was rising and falling so quickly.

"I love to feel you breathe," she whispered, closing her eyes and allowing her face to reflect her honest pleasure at the sensation, the sound, and the very essence of his life moving in and out of his body. Her passion for so simple a function stirred him all the deeper.

"Siena," he exhaled, closing his eyes as her seeking hands swept slowly over him.

"Back at the Ancient's home, when I saw Gideon and felt that he was dead, all I could think about was that if something could kill such a great being . . . what chance could you possibly have against it? I was certain I would never feel you breathe again," she said, her voice vibrating with the gentle rasp of remembered fear, the tightening touch of her hands on his moving chest clearly the only thing keeping that emotion at bay and in the past where it belonged.

"Siena . . ." he hushed gently, cradling the back of her head with both hands, interlacing his fingers through her hair as he looked into her golden eyes.

"You promised me, Elijah, that when I was well and when our enemies were defeated, I could speak aloud what I feel."

He watched her blink quickly, trying to discard the dampness in her eyes. He reached out with his thumbs to touch the soft corners of her golden lashes, making ready to catch any tear that dared to escape his vigilance. His heart tightened with her emotion and it flooded through him, radiating like sunlight and moonlight.

"Siena, before you say anything I need to ask you something."

"Yes. I know. You have been thinking hard about something you have been concerned will disturb me. I felt it the entire time we traveled here."

"I have to get used to your perception of my thoughts," he said regretfully. "Forgive me, I was not trying to be deceptive."

"I know that," she insisted. "You were doing what any wise person would. You were thinking through your thoughts before voicing them. Although I must tell you that whatever it is, I do not believe it warrants so much of your concern. I am not as unreasonable as you think I am."

"You promise to hear me out?"

"Always," she assured him.

"Very well." He began to speak, his cadence quick and clipped, the efficiency of a distasteful task but one that must be completed. "In light of today's events and all the danger I believe we are going to be facing, I must ask you to temporarily release me from my promise to resign my post with Noah. This situation is going to become much more volatile before it is resolved. As of now, there is no one I trust to replace me who will garner the respect and the power that I do with Noah's forces. Noah is a great leader, but he is more of a scholar than he is warrior. As formidable as he is in battle, it is not where his talents or his energies are best spent. He relies on me heavily to manage matters of security and defense, and I believe that if I leave, it will prove to be an advantage to this renegade we seek. I would sooner sleep in an iron coffin than give Ruth such power."

"Elijah," Siena whispered softly, reaching to frame his face with warm, long-fingered hands. "If you serve Noah, you still serve me. If you recall, I never asked you to resign your commission. You made the offer as a gesture, and I was honored by it. Just knowing that you would have made such an astounding commitment to those who don't even know or accept you yet is enough to impress on me the seriousness of your need to be a part of my life and my people's lives. That feeling will not change. Besides, you were meant to be who you are, in the position you are in, just as I am. I would no more want you to resign it than I would want you to ask me to resign as Queen.

"We will manage," she assured him. "We will muddle through with patience and as much refusal of bias and petty behaviors as we possibly can. And you are right; it is no time for extravagant changes. There will be enough adjustments as it is. Live with me, love with me. All else do as you deem necessary. Besides," she smiled, "I feel that I will be spending great amounts of time between the courts, just as I think Noah will feel compelled to do. As leaders, we must set the example for the others who will be watching us for guidance on how to discard the old scars and prejudices of the past."

"Watching longtime enemies come together in a joined effort will have an interesting impact. I believe your next overture might be best served in Damien's direction. He has been habitually solitary of other Nightwalkers for as long as I have heard of him, but of late he has come among us of his own design. He showed a singular concern for your life that I, personally, will always be grateful for."

"Elijah, I do not wish to talk about state matters all day long. Why do I have the sensation that you are avoiding what I wish to discuss with you?"

The warrior released his hold on her face, stepping back

with a telling awkwardness. He turned and studied the artistically stained glass windows that were so popular with his people, surrounding the entire bedroom in their many casements. The soft-colored light was a great pleasure to sleep under, allowing just enough lethargy to make Demons sleepy and relaxed without overwhelming them and dragging them down into a state that made it impossible for them to protect themselves in the event of an attack or emergency.

Still, he realized as he looked at Siena over his shoulder, even that soft light would be harmful to her. And if he was using it as a reason to continue to avoid his emotions of the moment, then so be it. Siena was aware of his thoughts but was also aware he was using his concerns over the sunlight like a shield, preventing himself and her from seeing what had suddenly disturbed his peace of mind. She watched him with steady, neutral thoughts, though, as he closed his eyes and stirred up scudding clouds. She smiled as the darkness of them drifted over the house.

"Are you going to maintain cloud cover the entire day?"

"No." He smiled slightly. "I am not able to continue to focus my power even in my sleep. I think maybe Gideon and Noah would be the only ones who wouldn't surprise me if they could do that."

She was about to ask what his plan was, but the cloud cover suddenly split apart, pouring out a sudden rain shower of impressive weight. He turned toward her slightly and grinned, wiggling an egotistical brow of mischief.

"I did this to Jacob once. I told him I could move the Earth just like he could, and he dared me to prove it."

"Like you knew he would."

"Yup." Elijah chuckled. "So I made it rain like hell and caused a mudslide that ran right over him."

That was when mud began to splatter against the windows, darkening the room first on one side, then the next. The rain stopped so it wouldn't wash the mud away. The wet soil had been dragged from the muddy ground in a small, wet dust devil of sorts that shook the mud against the building like a wet dog. When it dried, it would form a perfect lightproof mask.

"Very ingenious," she commended him with half a smile, crossing her arms beneath her breasts, drumming fingers on her forearm as she waited with obvious expectation for him to turn back to her and face his thoughts.

"Yes, yes," he sighed, finally facing her as her knowing curiosity penetrated his mind.

"It is not like you to avoid speaking your mind," she prompted.

"My thoughts are no mystery, really. You have been having similar ones." Elijah moved to seat himself on the bed, reaching to take her hand and guide her to him until she stood between his knees and he could wrap his hands around her waist. "We are married, kitten, and only know the basics about one another. How can we expect to take on the roles of bringing the Montague and Capulet families peacefully to the same table?"

She nodded once, briefly, her hands coming to brush soothingly over his shoulders. Which of them she was trying to soothe, she did not know immediately.

"And we have not even so much as thought about the issue of children," she added.

"Neither of our species is shy of children, but I disagree with bringing a child into a union where the parents are still strangers to one another in so many ways."

"If indeed we are even biologically compatible enough to have said children," she pointed out.

"Another consideration," he agreed gravely. "The heritage of your throne . . ."

". . . is secure in Syreena's care no matter what," she interrupted smoothly. "We have time beyond measure to work all of this out. You cannot sit here and try to solve a list of the tasks ahead of us all at once. Pardon me for saying that you are thinking rather like a human. Humans are different, Elijah, because they do not have such compelling conditions as the Imprinting. This condition has propelled us together, though we are little more than strangers, but that does not make it a disadvantage. I wish to ease your mind and tell you that I am far more interested in us discovering more about one another than I am in rushing to fulfill my duty to produce royal heirs."

"I feel the same," he said quietly.

When he looked away from her once more, Siena sighed in exasperation and dropped to her knees between his feet, her hands falling to his thighs and squeezing so as to get his unwavering attention.

"Elijah, can we get to the honest point which you are still skirting?" she asked with earnest.

"Damn," he muttered, giving her a wry half smile.

"Yes, I know. It sucks having a woman in your mind."

"That could be the understatement of the century." Elijah reached out to touch his fingertips beneath her chin. "I need to know if you are willing to keep a household that is joined in the heart and the spirit, but divided in traditions," he said at last.

"To begin with," she responded softly, "our house is already joined in the heart and spirit. You would not allow me to say so, but I will tell you now. I love you, Elijah." Her voice broke, but it was from fullness of emotion rather than any hint of uncertainty. "I do not care if it takes ten years or ten centuries to know all these minor details that so concern you at times. I have seen your spirit. I have felt it mesh with mine. I know now that we are two halves of a single creature. An honorable warrior, a fierce loyalist, a powerful leader, a tenderhearted lover. All the rest becomes minor details because these basics are all I need to know about you. It is the essence of you. These things sculpt who you are and what you do just like they do me." She picked up one of his huge hands, drawing it to her face where she pressed a kiss within the palm, her golden eyes flickering with painful intensity.

"And I beg you to forgive me for being too much of a coward to tell you so on our wedding night when you needed so much to exchange the words and feelings with me." Her rich voice was awash with hoarse agony. "When I think that I could have lost you to the next life without you knowing, I am ashamed of myself and doubt I even deserve this precious thing."

"Siena." He repeated her name on a sigh as he swept her tightly against himself. Elijah had never known such elation as he had felt when she had said her words of love. All of the rest, the recriminations and sorrow, could not penetrate that feeling. He nearly squeezed the breath out of her as he tried to pull her deeply into his body. "I would think you would realize that I am too stubborn and far too egotistical to die without the satisfaction of hearing you tell me these things."

He made her laugh, compelling her to reach around his waist, hugging herself even tighter to his chest, exactly what he needed and wanted her to do.

"I was trying to have a serious, loving moment, but I truly do not think you are capable of one," she announced with exasperation.

"I was entirely serious," he said, making sure he sounded serious. Siena only laughed again. "But I must tell you that . . ." He paused and his voice filled with infinite gentleness and tenderness. "You are so very precious to me," he whispered against her neck. "You are my heart as it beats within my chest, my soul as it moves through my mind. The breath in my body that so fascinates you is your essence pouring in and out of me in a wave that drowns me over and over again until I cannot breathe for wanting you. Needing you."

Siena tried to swallow, but her heart was stubbornly caught in her throat. He was doing it to her again, making her entire being swell with emotions beyond her capacity, her eyes burning with the overflow.

"Elijah," she whispered into the golden fall of his hair, her tears skidding down the filigree strands that fell over her cheeks as she buried her face in his neck, "I love you. I will share your traditions just as I share your heart. The Goddess brought you to me; your traditions secured you to me and mine secured me to you. If not for both of our beliefs coming together as they did, we might never have known these feelings. Might never have had this love. Of course I will respect your beliefs and traditions. They are proving to be not so different from ours."

"Mmm," he agreed, smiling into her hair as he petted the strands softly. "I am so lucky to have so wise a wife," he told her. "Although I confess I was thinking of a specific tradition."

"Tell me," she encouraged.

"I was considering the *Siddah* ceremony and my responsibilities in that role when Bella's babe reaches the proper age." He pulled back to see her expression. "It will mean fostering a child. A very powerful child with very unique abilities, if our prophecy is to complete itself. I see great opportunity for learning if she shares our lives in a court of combined cultures. But I will relinquish the role of *Siddah* if this troubles you too much. I understand it is a hard responsibility. Though, I confess, it would pain me greatly to disappoint Bella and Jacob in such a way."

"I would never think of asking you to do such a thing," Siena scolded him. "The rearing of children is one responsibility both our species take very seriously. She would be lucky to have you as her mentor. Luckier still to have *me.*"

She chuckled when he reached through her hair to pinch her for being impertinent. Siena responded by running warm, apologetic hands up over his back. She felt him sigh heavily and she knew it was because her touch relaxed him as much as her generous responses did. He did not have to worry so much about so many things all at once. Time would sort everything out. He was tired and weary from a battle that made the future a tenuous thing, so she understood his disquiet.

She also had a cure for it.

While his head buzzed with thoughts and questions, she began to whisper a soft litany into his mind in her native language. It was soft, imperceptible in the clamor of his thoughts, and she did not even know for certain if he knew the language. However, if he wanted to share traditions, this was one she was happy to provide. Normally, the words were spoken aloud to one's mate, but Siena had the advantage of telepathy to aid her, and this left her mouth available for other things.

She began to rub her soft mouth against his neck, finding the beat of his pulse, feeling it for a moment because it represented the beat of the life coursing through him. Then she parted her lips and touched her tongue to that steady throb. Elijah's focus immediately took hold of a single point of interest, discarding everything except the velvet slide of warmth and moisture slowly licking a path up the length of his carotid artery. Heat like a flash fire exploded in his mind, rippling over every inch of his skin, finally settling low and hot in his body. She was on her knees between his thighs, her incredible breasts cuddled against his chest, and her hands were reaching down to slide over his denim-covered thighs.

Elijah felt the instantaneous reaction that she always struck up in him so easily. He made a quiet sound of agony as her teeth came into play against his neck. She nipped at him and he felt a bolt of erotic lightning spear down the center of his body. It was then that he began to hear the words drifting in his head, in her native tongue, a language he had learned long ago, as any wise warrior would have. It had the rolling cadence of Russian to it, but it was far older than that, far more elegant, deeply reflective of the Lycanthropes with its sexy, guttural consonants and the roll of the tongue that made the words sound almost like soft growls.

You are for me. I am for you. My body is yours. Your body is mine. Touch me. Taste me . . .

Elijah groaned from the depths of his soul, the words a

delightful enough torture all on their own, but Siena's hands were sliding into the junction of his legs, stroking him through painfully confining denim. She pressed her fingers up along the hard heat contained just beyond his fly, her palms following. She nipped at his neck again. She shifted so the sensual weight of her breasts drifted across his chest, her nipples teasing points of excitement right through her dress.

Then, quick as a twitch, she was reaching for his tank shirt, dragging it free at the waist while she surged up to find his mouth. Elijah complied, seizing her mouth in a wild, rampant kiss. She drove him mad with her aggressive tendencies, like a sexual fantasy come to life. He felt her sliding silkily through his thoughts, picking out what he would like, what drove him out of his mind. She shucked off his shirt and immediately dragged her mouth from his in a line right down his throat, over his breastbone, straight down his belly until she was back on her knees and he was a firestorm of arousal and need.

Elijah's hands were anchored in her hair, his fingertips massaging her scalp with frantic undulations. He felt her smile against his belly, knowing he had been plunged so swiftly into her surprise trap that he could hardly think. She reached up and pushed him back onto the bed, her body and mouth following all the while. Her hands slid down his sides as she leaned forward to lick a tracing line over the definition of his abdominal muscles. His entire body clenched with need, exploded with molten heat. He twitched harshly beneath the scrape of her teeth as her lips began to shadow the golden path of hair leading to his waistband.

Her fingers fell deftly to the buttons of his fly, and he was finally released from the torturously tight fabric, bursting into her waiting hands. Siena heard his savage groan as she engulfed him with her eager fingers. He was hard and thick with need. Need for her. And there was no way in the world to describe how exciting that was. How powerful. But there were thousands of ways to feed that power, to make it grow.

She stroked him softly at first, just the pads of her finger-tips shaping the contours of velvet skin stretched over iron. She embraced him, wrapping both her hands around him and gliding up the length of him. Elijah's exclamation of pained pleasure echoed off the high ceiling above them. Before he could finish the outcry, she suddenly slid her tongue over the sensitive tip and then took him into the hot seduction of her mouth.

The warrior felt as though he had been run through. He was helpless with shocking sensation, his belly and loins a conflagration of torrid need. Her mouth was wickedly hot, a wet, skillful haven that sealed with perfect tightness around him. He felt that sinuous tongue of hers, tasting him hungrily, using his flavor to excite herself until she was breathing hard against him. Elijah knew she was going to kill him. His heart was pounding so hard he expected it to burst from his chest any second. She was relentless, too damn eager and full of an unholy curiosity that was just unbelievable. He couldn't take it another second.

Siena felt the demand of his hands in her hair, drawing her up his body, away from her delighted explorations of his body. He dragged her to his mouth and attacked her with a savage kiss that left her bruised and breathless. Then he disappeared from beneath her hands, and she felt herself disappearing as well seconds later. One moment she was there, and then she was air. When they shifted back to solid form, all of their clothes were gone and Elijah was trapping her beneath his heavy, powerful body. She laughed up at him when she saw the wild desire burning emerald fire in his eyes.

"So you like teasing?"

It was a threat, loud and clear and capped off with a male growl of intent. He devoured her mouth in endless chains of kisses even as his hands roamed with untamed compulsion all over her lushly curved body. He filled his hands with her breasts, taunting the sensitive nipples until she cried out into his mouth, arching her body up hard into his. He drank it up like a potent narcotic, feeling the burning of her golden skin, smelling the arousal pooling wetly between her legs. He reached up for both her hands and dragged them off his body. He cruelly captured them and pressed them flat onto the bed. It left him only with his mouth as a tool to torture her in return, but that was just what he had intended.

He dragged himself away from her addicting kisses and rushed a wet trail down her throat and sternum. He instantly seized her left nipple with his teeth, lips, and tongue, sucking hard and wild until she was moaning those feminine purrs of pleasure that he loved so much. She tried to free her hands instinctively, but he refused. He switched breasts and she cried out. Elijah licked the tender gold-and-rose point, laving her wetly, and Siena felt an almost malicious intent chuckling through his mind. Suddenly a breeze blew into the room. Not just any breeze, but a very cold one. A burst of nearly freezing air blasted over Siena's exposed, dampened body and she screeched with the erotic sensation of hot and cold contrast. She shuddered and shivered as the breeze died away. Her entire body was shaking with a fine vibration, and Elijah enjoyed it as he replaced cold with fire, burning a trail to her navel, then lower still. His lips slid through filigreed curls, and then his tongue reached out to taste her.

Siena gasped wildly, her hips wrenching upward, reaching for that velvet stroke of his tongue even as he repeated it. Fire. An inferno exploding up her body, starting at that center point where he created magic against her. He would not release her hands, but he did change his grip so their fingers interlaced. She was seeping heat and honey and Elijah cherished the confection of her even as he teased her into a numbing world of promised release. Her entire body was locked with the impending crash, even the leg she had blindly thrown over his shoulder to drag him closer when he wouldn't release her hands. He teased her relentlessly, loving the raw, primal sounds of feminine need that burst out of her.

"Elijah! Please!" she screamed out, begging him to have mercy.

He let go of her hands suddenly, grasping her hips, and held her to the precise position her wanted her to be in. He needed only to drag his beautiful mouth over her three more times before she ignited. She expelled a lusty shout that went on endlessly, even as he pushed her beyond a single peak of pleasure. He was relentless. He had no choice. The shocking jerks of her body, her cries, the hot spice of pleasure flowing over his taste buds was all too addicting.

The warrior broke under the pressure of her pleasure and his need. He had never felt so heavy and violent with it before. It raged like a berserk beast inside of him, crouching low and demanding satisfaction.

Elijah grabbed his pleasure-limp mate with rough need, dragging her off the bed and herding her with his steely body and fast strides that barely allowed her feet to touch the floor. He stopped only when her hands slammed against the log wall, her cheek pressing against the smooth surface as her hips were jerked back against his, the enthusiasm of it lifting her feet off the floor. His scent, rough and masculine, poured over her as he crowded her against that solid wall. She felt him, titanium hard against her bottom as he leaned to press his lips against her exposed ear.

"I have wanted this since I first laid eyes on you," he confessed hotly, his breath a burning wash over her ear and shoulder. "I saw you, so proud and so damn confident." He tilted her hips in his calloused hands and he slid against folds of wet, feminine flesh. He was hot enough to burn, and Siena gasped. "I knew right then that you were the sexiest, hottest woman I would ever lay eyes on. You made me hard, scorched me with those haughty golden eyes, and all I wanted to do was grab you, throw you up against a wall, and . . ."

He plunged into her in one violent stroke, burying himself completely in the center of fierce heat, unimaginable tightness, and sweet, slick heaven. Siena, already highly keyed to pleasure, burst into instant orgasm, crying out long and loud as his ferocity of need swept over her. Elijah felt her convulsing around him, muscles rippling like violent vises, taunting his control. Her pleasure licked at him enticingly, but he would not give up his fantasy so soon. She had unleashed this, and she would tame it. There was no other solution.

He roared inside, like a tempest, a wild hurricane that wanted to tear up everything it could get its hands on. And his hands were on her. His chest pressed to her back, his mouth falling open against the crest of her shoulder, his hands holding her hips so he could draw himself out of her and return in a thundering force of ever-hardening need and craving for depth. Siena felt it, the need, the pulse and swell of his body inside hers. Every move, every thought was erotic to him, because it was her, and it brutalized him with his own want.

"When I first saw you," she gasped as he suddenly began to search her for a rhythm, "I could not help myself from wondering. Your size and stature, your hands were so large and so calloused, and I wanted to know what it would feel like to be held between your hands, against your body, to know the feel of your powerful legs—!"

Siena released a strangled cry as Elijah found her sweet spot, the understanding in her awareness immediately flooding his thoughts, and he instantly incorporated it into the deep tempo of his thrusts. She could no longer speak or think. She couldn't even hold herself up. Elijah commanded her every movement, and he did it masterfully.

You are so tight, kitten.

Apparently he couldn't speak either, and even his thoughts were a long groan of pleasure. Siena thrust herself into his mind, into the wild haze of animal need and almost cruel dominance. This she understood. Oh, so well. It was primal. Possessive. Territorial. She was his, and he was going to make damn sure she and everyone else knew it.

That was when his teeth pierced her shoulder. It was partly to pin her in place, and also a very distinctive mark. He couldn't seem to help himself. He couldn't restrain the brutality of his body as it surged harder and harder into hers. The tempo raced faster, she was screaming with ecstasy, and he could feel the blinding force of it in her mind and body even before he felt it clutch at him, relentless and tight, her entire being shuddering around him. He kept her there, catching her thrown-back head against his shoulder, deafening him with those incredible screams, until he couldn't bear it a single second longer. He crested, exploding inside her like a violent bomb, thrusting deeply and shouting to the heavens, which answered him with a furious crash of thunder.

They both fell to the ground, a tangle of limbs, perspiration, and the unwillingness to move a single millimeter. They gasped for breath, even Elijah unable to regulate his oxygen needs in that moment. A hand rested limply against his chest, and he lifted it to kiss the palm. Instantly he saw the huge raw patch and blisters. He sat up suddenly, reaching for her other hand. It was equally damaged. As if coming out of a raging, senses-confusing storm, he looked at his mate.

"Siena!" He reached for her, gathering her against himself. What had he been thinking? She was fresh out of her sickbed, exhausted from battle. Now she lay battered, bruised, and blistered.

And bitten. Don't forget bitten if you are going for an alliteration theme.

The smart-assed thought instantly eased his impending guilt. He knew that tone well enough to know she was doing better than fine. He had half a mind to dump her out of his lap and onto her head.

Siena's eyes flew open.

"You wouldn't!"

"Don't test me!" he retorted. "Damn it, woman, you mess with my head!"

"Well, you need to learn not to worry so much. A few love bumps and bruises are all part of the game for Night-walkers." She reached to soothe him with a warm, spicy kiss. "It's nothing to the way you turn me inside out when you make love to me like that," she murmured, her golden eyes glittering with her pleasure.

Elijah suddenly felt lighthearted. He stood up and yanked her to her feet in a single smooth motion. With one more tug she was bumping into him and they were both falling onto the bed. The Warrior Captain rolled his bride beneath himself, pinning her to the mattress with his significant weight. He leaned to catch her mouth, kissed her until her pretty cheeks were flushed a rosy red.

"Before the sun comes up, I am determined to get back to the part about my powerful legs," he said silkily against her damp, smiling lips.

CHAPTER 20

"Child of the night, walking in the night, beloved of the night . . . We name you."

Elijah stepped forward as he reached toward Isabella, letting her daughter take tight hold of one of his fingers. Legna stepped forward and did the same.

"We name you Jacina," Isabella said strongly. "This is your name of power, known only to the four of us. It will be used to care for you, discipline you, and mold you into a proud reflection of the newest generation of our people."

"I name you Leah," Jacob said, touching his babe gently on her dusky forehead. "This is your call name, my daughter, which many will use to become your friend, your teachers, and, one day, to write your existence into histories where you will distinguish yourself with greatness."

"We are *Siddah*," Legna and Elijah intoned in unison. "We will foster you, Jacina. We will temper you with love and shape you with respect and guidance according to the ways of our peoples. We will always love you as our own, Leah."

"Blessed be by Destiny," Elijah said, grinning suddenly from ear to ear.

"She is the first child of a new era for so many of us." Legna sighed with satisfaction, reaching to hug the proud parents warmly.

"And never the last," Isabella agreed, touching Legna's belly with a smile.

"Come. My bride has laid a feast in our tradition for us," Elijah said, herding the group away from the altar deep in the Russian woodlands. It had snowed earlier and it was far too chilly for the baby to be out much longer, even though she was tucked warmly against her mother's breast.

"A Lycanthrope throwing a Demon feast," Jacob chuckled. "I never thought I would see the day."

"You never thought Elijah would be married," Isabella teased, nudging the warrior with an elbow.

"Give me my fosterling before you lollygaggers freeze her to death."

Elijah snatched Leah from her mother and disappeared into the brisk winds.

"Elijah!" Bella shouted after him. "I'm going to kick your ass!"

"He is going to spoil her rotten," Legna predicted.

"*Now* you tell me," Bella said wryly.

Elijah materialized before his wife with the babe cradled in the crook of his banded arm. Siena was dressed in formal attire, literally glowing gold between the short silken dress she wore, her glowing eyes, and her luminescent skin.

"Our fosterling, I presume." She greeted him warmly, rising from her throne, her collar winking in the gaslight as she moved to touch the child her husband held. She lifted her mouth to his, letting him kiss her with the gentleness she knew never ceased to amaze the court that was still getting used to seeing their former enemy by their Queen's side.

"My Lady Queen, may I introduce Leah, daughter to the Enforcers."

"Hello, Leah," she said softly, her eyes twinkling with

sudden mischief as she looked up at Elijah. "You look frighteningly natural holding a child, my husband."

"Don't get any ideas, kitten," he warned with a chuckle.

"No. I won't," she assured him. Then she touched soft,
delicate fingers over the baby's lightly furred scalp. "At least
. . . not for a few months yet."

Elijah's breath froze in his chest and she felt the chill of
shock that rushed through him. She threw back her head and
laughed so hard that the entire room turned to look at her.

"Did I say months? I meant years," she corrected, laughing so hard she brought tears to her eyes.

"That was not funny," he growled at her.

She ignored him, stepping past him to greet her recently
arrived Demon guests with a combination of hugs and a few
formal kisses on their cheeks.

"Come, and be welcome. My people and I warmly greet
you all," she announced loudly, expansively opening her
arms towards the enormously festive banquet. "Let us celebrate the naming of this beautiful child. And let us celebrate
all of our futures, for as sure as this child's name will never
change, our futures will never again be the same."

As Elijah watched her move forward, the regal hostess
from head to toe, he closed his eyes and slipped warmly into
her mind, making sure she knew without a doubt that he
would grow to love her even more than he did in that moment.

Siena turned to look at him as his pale green eyes flicked
open. She reached to touch her collar absently, smiling at
him as she did so.

I love you as well, warrior, she whispered into his
thoughts. *Perhaps more than either of us will ever know.*

I will know, he corrected her. *I will always know.*